HALL OF SHADOWS

HALL OF SHADOWS

MARIAH STILLBROOK

ALSO BY MARIAH STILLBROOK

In The Pines

The Lost Erwain

For SBM. Thanks for the inspiration and for putting up with all my shadows.

PART ONE

CHAPTER ONE

The thing about being a smudge of darkness against a black backdrop is that no one ever sees you. That is until there's smoke. I've always been a creature of the night. Not like a vamp—although that would be kind of badass. I wouldn't ever want to be like the sparkly ones, but I wouldn't have an aversion to the cult classic: razor sharp fangs with no morals kind. Like They Thirst or Salem's Lot, but maybe with a little more humanity left inside the creatures. I could totally rock alongside The Lost Boys.

I've always clung to the shadows. It's safe there. You know, like the night sky, or the stars. The twinkle of just that small bit of light breaking through this world. It knows me, unlike this place. This place is crawling with filters that no one else seems to notice—colored lenses that sharpen the edges of what most people, if given the chance, wouldn't want to see. My Grandma Reanin used to say the same things. I guess that's why I make so many people uncomfortable. I look for the details most people find cringy. Imagine if they knew the truth about me.

"Tess? Are you listening?"

Nope.

Okay, redo. Insanity is nothing more than repeating our mistakes . . . right? And that's what I was victim to. An endless cycle of finding myself in these kinds of places. The top of the juvenile learning services food chain. In this case, I was in Mr. Greene's office.

Mr. Greene was Ignatius Academy's headmaster—that's what the ritzy upper-class people loved to call their principals. Headmaster, like he was the Master of Child Rearing Ceremonies. Gag. Anyway, how was I supposed to pay attention when there was an actual storm raging inside me. Not like a cute little relaxing thunderstorm that people try to mimic from apps on their phones. No, like a hurricane unleashed from Hades and set to take the earth whole in one valiant swallow. The storm made it hard to concentrate; it made it near impossible to end this cycle.

"Tess?" he questioned again.

My gaze slowly lifted from the small speck of white on his stylish button up. The shirt was peach, patterned by red dots; the fabric looked like it had Chicken Pox. He'd spent at least fifty bucks on it. Of that, I was sure. I might've been sewn into this disaster of a three-piece uniform, just another version of the same set of clothes I'd been wearing most of my fifteen years of existence, but still, I knew fashion. And I knew that particular shirt came from the likes of Boutique Loren, a posh haven for every hipster within a thirty-mile radius. It also just happened to be right around the corner from Ignatius Academy. Gawd, what a name for a school (heavy eye roll).

In accordance with his taste in clothing, Mr. Greene had staged himself across from me in a blue microfiber chair that didn't match the orange leather chair in which I'd been corralled.

Between us lived a silver coffee table with a goldfish

floating in a round bowl; it was not a pet but a decoration. Trendy, Headmaster Greene. Kudos.

His frustration and complete uncertainty about what to do with me wasn't just brewing, it was boiling over the sides of his cauldron.

"Yes, Mr. Greene. I heard you."

I was here because the two girls I'd been paired with in chemistry class (because, as usual, no one had volunteered to be my partner) had insisted that it had been me who had set their hair on fire. (Excuse me while the corners of my lips turn upwards).

"You may not believe me, Tess, but I don't think you meant to actually harm those girls."

Harm none, bitches. Isn't that the correct phrase?

I caught myself staring at the white flake on his shirt once more. "Raymond Wells."

He frowned. "Excuse me?"

"Your shirt," I said matter-of-factly. How else would I reply? "It's a Raymond Wells. $67.80, if I had to guess." It was. I'd seen it with my own beady little eyes. Okay, they weren't beady, but they were different colors and that freaked most people out.

Mr. Greene's eyebrows did a little jig, as did the corners of his mouth.

"Am I right?"

"Well . . . yes, actually." His frown deepened and my attention was drawn to his naked ankle, dangling next to his right leg. The lack of socks screamed that he was making a statement about how he was cool enough to pull off red loafers without sweat protection. "And as much as I appreciate your attention to detail, we are here because—"

"And your shoes, they are Burgan Teek. $152.99."

Again, with the dance of uncertain facial expressions. I knew it made people uncomfortable when I communed with them like this, but I continued to do so because for one —it was just who I was. And two, it amused me. I'd grown bored after doing the nice-nice thing with everybody for so much of my life, not to mention, it hadn't worked out. People shied away from me whether I was being 'proper' or unruly.

"And you don't have to beat around the bush. I know why I'm here."

Mr. Greene's mouth opened part way as he took in an audible inhale. "Well," he said, attempting to sound like an authority figure. "This is very good. You understand that what you did was wrong."

False.

I scoffed at his assumption, at his dirtied attempt at playing the character of the job he'd taken to appease the pressure society put over his shoulders. I slumped down into the orange chair, crossing my arms over one another just like the ceramic logs inside the fireplace beside me. I could sense the ashes left behind underneath the gas replacement, and I could still smell the embers from the last real fire this room had experienced.

"I know for a fact nobody saw me do anything wrong."

"Tess."

My stomach soured from his tone. As if the garbage hadn't already hit the fan—it had only been three months since I'd lost my grandmother and mother to just another NYC crime.

Add on the loner badge I was forced to wear and the burning secret I'd had cooped up inside my chest since I was seven years old—I didn't have time for this.

"I could have just been in the wrong place at the wrong time, but you haven't even bothered to run that scenario through your brain."

"Tess," he repeated my name in the same disparaging way

that made me want to set his hair on fire. "Everyone in the class, apart from three people, saw you do it."

Again . . . false.

The three undesirables—not creepy like me, but the three other unwanted peers in our class—these were the kids who I had to assume didn't see me hold a torch to the long, bleached hair and extensions of Darcy Gruber and Holly Sharp. And wouldn't it have been a little obvious if I'd used such a tool? Seriously.

"The three kids who didn't see me do it are the only kids in that class who don't hate me for having the ability to breathe." Not that they were my friends. I didn't have any of those—at least not my age.

Mr. Greene steepled his hands and rested his chin over the tips of his fingers. "From the sounds of things, you have other abilities as well."

Oh! For the love of—

I couldn't help it, my emotion leapt from the autistic stare I commonly used as a shield. I stared bullets at him as I refrained from replying, from giving him the satisfaction of getting myself into even more trouble.

No one—at least not in this institution—was ever going to understand what I was capable of. They called me a witch because I was quiet in class, and because in the right light my eyes changed color like a flame dancing between orange, red, and blue. I wasn't like them, so they had to give me a label. I just hadn't expected a supposed grown man to come at me with the same accusation.

Headmaster Hipster wrinkled his nose and nodded his head. "Don't you think it would just be easier to admit that you set their hair on fire?"

Invisible sparks of fury exited my nostrils. "I refuse to take the blame for what the boys sitting behind us did." Because that was totally plausible. "I'd tell you to check their pockets for a lighter, but stupid as they are, I would think they still had enough brains to ditch the evidence."

"Now you're trying to switch the blame to the boys sitting behind you. I don't think—"

"I'm not trying to. I'm stating the obvious."

Mr. Greene released his hands down into his lap. "Okay Tess, I can see that we aren't going to get anywhere here."

"No, we aren't. Because you're conditioned to believe in the actions of the 'cool' kids, the beautiful people—the chosen. You haven't even considered the observations of the three unpopular kids who said I didn't have anything to do with the hair burning incident."

"Ms. Moreau, we are all aware that you've taken quite a hit with the loss of your mother and grandmother as of late" –oh no he didn't– "but making accusations is a nasty habit."

I did my best impression of a brick wall, letting my gaze fall back down to the speck of white on his shirt. "I wouldn't say what I was doing was a nasty habit, as I wasn't assuming but just stating the truth. Smoking, on the other hand, is a nasty habit." I raised my eyes to meet his, just as the corners of his mouth ticked and fell. "Who even smokes anymore? I mean, it's just gross."

He was swimming in befuddlement . . . and I was loving it. "Ms. Moreau—"

"Oh no," I said, as perky as one of the dumb blondes now walking around with fizzled extensions. "I wasn't done. Now then, let me save you the time of making something up." I stood and parted ways with the orange chair, crossing over to where Mr. Greene had begun to turn the corner from apprehensive into slight terror. I stuck my finger onto the fleck of leftover ash and held it up to the natural light coming through the eighteenth-century windows. "It's the same old story. People don't like what's different, what they don't understand. They begin to fear what stands apart from everyone else, because what if this different person is more powerful than them? What if she can make everyone see how miniscule they actually are? So, what do they do to that person? They turn them into a freak, and sometimes, they even chain them to a stake and light a match under their feet." I studied the speck balancing over my fingertip, my skin a magnet for creation.

My gaze grazed the face of the man seated just below; he was wearing Old Spice deodorant and it had just gotten way more potent. Without looking away from his quivering lips I allowed the speck of ash to return to that from which it came —a smoking Camel cigarette. A spark of amusement filled my chest as I watched his eyes widen to the size of disco balls. Unable to stop myself, I brought the cigarette close to my lips, as though I was going to take a drag, but just as quickly pulled it away and held it out to him. He gawked at the thing held between my fingers before raising a shaky hand up to grasp the habit he probably thought was his own dirty little secret. As soon as it was between his fingers I stepped away. "It really is a nasty habit, Mr. Greene."

"I only have one a day," he said so quietly I could barely hear him.

"Not that. Well—yes, that too. But what I was really alluding to, was the habit of granting dominance to the 'cool' kids, even when they might be guilty of acts of cruelty." I bent down and placed my hands over my knees, looking my 'superior' directly in his eyes. "Change has to start somewhere, Mr. Greene. But don't worry, I know you don't have the guts to be that person." A genuine smile graced my face. "Hey, at least you've got great taste in décor."

That was enough. I'd had my fun. I stood and marched towards the thick wooden door surrounded by dark wallpaper and took my leave. But not before taking just a moment for the sake of glory. I glanced back once more before stepping out the door, just in time to find Mr. Greene staring out the window with terror still in his eyes, the reincarnated cig coming up to his lips so that he could steal a drag.

I guess today you will have two cigarettes, I thought with a snicker as I left his office and stormed out of Ignatius Academy. As I flew out of the double doors and down the stone steps towards the New York City sidewalk, I knew very well that I would not be returning.

CHAPTER TWO

Jamae Carpenter was, like, my sole reason to keep existing these days. She was twenty-seven, a pagan, and had what she referred to as an interminable debt. She had pale skin, an odd tattoo on the back of her neck, dyed black hair with blue highlights, and an endearing affinity for cinnamon chewing gum. She also owned a metaphysical shop called Hexed—it had become my favorite after-school hangout. I'd been frequenting the magical place ever since I'd come across a flyer for it in my grandmother's building (before she bit it, obviously).

Hexed was seriously more than a hangout; it was my coping mechanism. My place of refuge. Even before two-thirds of my family was wiped out, I'd been consumed by the ever-present loneliness that hung around my shoulders like a lacy black shawl—the kind that could've been swiped from a mannequin in a dusty, vintage shop.

I mean, sure, being an only child had its perks, like extra cash from the tooth fairy and all the toys in the world. As I got older books replaced the toys, and recently my pink bicycle was elevated to a brand new flashy red Lexus SUV. Except that one was a little different. The vehicle—still with a ridiculously huge bow on the hood—waiting for me to turn sixteen in a few months, wasn't as much an only child perk as much as an 'I'm sorry your mom and grandma are dead, and this is the only thing your dear old dad could come up with to make it better' gift. I'm pretty sure the SUV was also some sort of bribing tactic to encourage me to make friends. Unlike my mom, who only showed signs she was aware of my existence when she yelled at me for messing up, my dad had always had this thing with flinging me into the throes of society—like he thought if I could configure the underlying psychology of humanity, I might be able to act a little more 'normal', or something. *Heavy scoff.* Whether or not that was his big plan, I didn't care. I was good at being a recluse and I liked books more than people. Books didn't need me to impress them with a shiny new car.

However, riding solo most definitely had its cons. Constant solitude wasn't all that bad, but I would be lying if I said it *never* bothered me. Even when I'd had two living parents, each of them had been hounded with demanding careers. If it hadn't been for my grandmother—my one true love, my only legit string of pearls—I would have been just another NYC rich kid who had more of a bond with the housekeeper of the month than my parents.

More than any other reason, there was an obvious disadvantage to being an only lonely: I had no one else to compare my gift to. My magic.

Maybe if I'd had a little brother or sister, they might have displayed some unusual abilities as well. I might have been a little less inclined to think of myself as the only one in the world who could read ashes like tea leaves—who could manipulate them back to life.

Jamae came into my world a year ago, bringing with her more than the sisterly relationship I'd come to crave. Her existence gave me someone to confide in. And when I was handed the news of my mother and grandmother on a dusty serving tray, void (mind you) of any cocktails to lessen the blow, Jamae brought me into the back of her shop with a box of old china and told me it was all mine to break. Yeah, you could say she was my best friend.

The second my heels had hit the concrete just outside the Ignatius Academy, I knew there was nowhere else to go. It was Tuesday, so both Jamae and Ethan would be at Hexed—Ethan was the boyfriend. Also a self-proclaimed witch. Both Ethan and Jamae practiced witchcraft, but they'd never exhibited *real* magic—at least nothing like I was capable of. The extent of their skills seemed to be lighting candles with matchsticks and chanting with crystals strewn around their necks.

As I trekked across the New York City sidewalk, the midwinter air bringing with it just the smallest gift of freshness— as it fought the smog and filth of the city—I silenced my phone before returning it to my pocket. Usually when I got sent home from school, I could expect an irritated and hasty phone call from at least one of my parents. My mother had often been more concerned with her precious life being interrupted, whereas my father nearly always had the sentiment of an exhausted parent who couldn't be made to understand his child's motivation. This time was different. Not only had the plural of parents become singular, but this time I'd let my freak flag fly. I hadn't the faintest clue how Mr. Greene was going to handle that nonsense. For all I knew he was curled up in his blue microfiber chair smoking the rest of his Camels. Either way, I wasn't ready to deal. All I cared about was the welcoming scent of Frankincense, sage, and the invitation of clean energy from hundreds of crystal allies.

The shop's bell jingled over my head as I entered Hexed. I was immediately greeted with a seismic grin from Jamae. I noted, as I stalked towards her, that there was something different about her. It wasn't until a freshly manicured hand unabashedly pulled at the strand of white hanging next to a blue highlight, that I could put my finger directly on it.

I stepped up to the counter. "This is cool," I said, pointing to the white in her hair. "When did you do that?"

A fresh burst of sandalwood slapped my face. Recently, both Jamae and Ethan had been bathing themselves in it. Jamae's eyes darted to the albino strip. "Yesterday. I was in a mood." She smirked, then quickly diverted her expression into a sly one. "What the hell are you doing here anyway. It's like eleven in the morning. Aren't you supposed to be in school?"

I gripped the counter as if the floor was moving. "I'm pretty sure I got canned. Again." I let one of my elbows sink to the surface just so I could rest my chin in it. "I'm so not in the mood to listen to my dad's lame attempts at parenting so I'm escaping. The only way he knows how to make anything better is to buy me more crap anyway."

I regretted the words the second they fell from my lips. Jamae had never said a single thing about it, but it was super apparent from the moment I met her that she'd never known privilege. I grew up in a Brownstone on the upper east side, and Jamae—not so much. She'd relayed to me early on in our relationship that she'd driven to New York in a beat-up Beetle she'd bought off her cousin before fleeing the broken home she'd come from in Missouri. Everything her and Ethan worked for, they put right back into their shop. It's what kept me up at night sometimes. I was terrified that the only friends I had in this lonesome world would come to see me as just another *Gossip Girl*.

Even though she'd squashed all my anxieties with a tight fist as if they'd been nothing more than a juicy cockroach, I still fixated on them. The shiniest jewel in my treasure chest had been stolen—my Grandma Reanin—which meant that Jamae (and Ethan . . . and my dad) were all I had left. My weak, blackened little heart would never be able to keep beating if I lost any of them.

Sidenote: why wasn't my mother included in that little box of shiny things you ask? In that little corner of my soul where I'd always kept my grandmother? Simple. She'd never asked to be. Yes, there was more to that, but even in her death, I wasn't sure what to do with it. Let's leave it there for the time being. (Sore spot, remember).

If Jamae had reacted to my admission of pampered guilt, she internalized it. Instead of judging me like the rest of the world, she simply asked in the sincerest way possible, "Wanna talk about it?"

"Not really," I answered honestly. "I acted impulsively and now I have no other option but to hang out and see what happens next. What's done is done."

"That sounds ominous. Did you happen to do anything *strange* today, Tess?"

My tongue slipped between my lips. I didn't want to talk about it yet. "No. So hey, what's this you're reading?"

She looked down at the opened book as if she'd forgotten its existence, then sighed audibly. "Oh, it's just a bit of light reading, really."

Without permission, I pulled at the weathered book until it was facing me, then slipped my hand between the pages to save her place before flipping to the cover. "*Confronting Your Shadows.*" I raised my brows. "Interesting."

"Yeah. It's kind of groovy."

A subtle frown seeped onto my face as I perused the Table of Contents. "What's it about?"

"Shadow work," she retorted.

I glanced at her. "What's that?"

"You know, facing your demons and all that. Like, instead of trying to bury the things about yourself you don't find all that savory, you face them. You talk to them. You have tea with your dark side."

"Hm. That's kinda cool," I noted as I skimmed the page she'd been reading. Immediately intrigued, I started reading it out loud. "'Be aware that facing your shadows may result in opening literal worlds that you never knew existed. It is up to you whether you enter but be wary if you do. There is no darkness without light, and there is no light without darkness, but know that if you leave the ground you've always stood on for a different realm, you will no longer be protected by what is familiar, and you *will* be hunted.' Shit." I looked up at my friend. "This is heavy. Who wrote this thing anyway?"

I started flipping back to the cover to see who the author was, but I never got that far. Instead, I became distracted by a name scrawled on the top right corner of the first page. My mouth unhinged, but before I could draw attention to the familiar handwriting, Jamae retrieved the book into her rightful hands and started flipping through the chapters— taking my breath right along with it.

"Juanita's wife, Maggie."

Juanita was the head priestess of Jamae and Ethan's coven. I'd never been invited to their meetings, or circles, or whatever they called them. I'd also never asked to go.

"Wh—What?" It was all I could manage.

"You asked who wrote it. Maggie did—like over forty years ago. This thing's so old."

"Oh . . ." I muttered. I could've cared less about when it was written. What I was concerned with was the name I'd just seen scribbled inside the cover.

Completely oblivious to the fact that I'd mentally wandered off, Jamae continued to rattle on. "There's a lunar eclipse happening soon, and Juanita said that it's the perfect time to address our chaos. She handed out these little lost treasures at our most recent gathering and told us to begin accessing our shadows." She paused, then read aloud the section I'd just recited. When she was finished, she added, "You know, this could have a double meaning, this part here. '—know that if you leave the ground you've always stood on for a different realm, you will no longer be protected by what is familiar—and you *will* be hunted.' That could mean that you might be hunted by something other than what's in the shadows."

I temporarily set aside the shock of what I'd just seen scribed into that first page and returned to the conversation. "Like what?"

"I mean—I don't know. Like, who is to say what's truly wrong with the world and what's supposed to be right? Who defines who belongs to darkness and who to light? You know?"

"I guess," I ventured.

"There are screwed up people out there. Trained or motivated to end someone's life simply because of what they don't and won't understand. They never stop to examine the intention of who or what they are after; they just exterminate what they've been taught to get rid of."

Jamae was a person who was passionate about her opinions.

"Heavy."

She ticked her head to the side. "I guess I just read this passage with that in mind."

One of my fingernails found itself between my teeth as I balanced between the image of that name scribbled in that book and whatever it was Jamae had tried to infer. I was still balancing over that tight rope existing in my mind when Ethan poked his head out from the purple curtain that separated the reading room from the rest of the shop. Within seconds, he was at Jamae's side, his energy brimming with assumptions.

"Whatcha all talking about?" His eyes were hungry.

Jamae set the book down over the counter and patted the top of it. She answered him with a spooky voice and a little shoulder jig. "Shadows."

"Righteous." He bobbed his head up and down. "Have you gotten to the part about opening portals yet? Cause that shit is straight up wicked."

Had he just said *portals*?

"Oh yeah," Jamae said, retracting the book back into her hands. She flipped to a dog-eared page, set it back down on the counter so it was facing me, and pointed to an underlined passage. "Check this out."

I bent down and read over the paragraph. *Once in a new dimension, the shadows may draw energy from you, but you—overseeing your own darkness—may draw as much power from them.*

I lifted my eyes to the two pagans. "Are you guys messing with me?"

Ethan shook his head as he leaned in, his sour breath close to my neck. "No, this is legit. Look here." He pointed at the paragraph I'd just read. "Maggie became so enlightened after years of shadow work that she began to see past the veils humanity slipped in front of her eyes. She quickly figured out how to distinguish where otherworldly dimensions begin and end."

"She what?" I asked.

Ethan continued without a hitch. "She figured out how to access other worlds, literally. After years of exploring, she eventually learned how to lock the doors to many of the worlds that she found wicked. She closed portals all the time back in the day. Like permanently."

"Uh . . . okay," I said. "What exactly made these *worlds* so wicked?"

"What do you think?" he quipped, his eyes grinning. He backed off so his shoulders were in line with Jamae's.

I looked from him to her then back to him. "I—I don't know. Because there are scary things in the dark . . ." Gawd, I sounded so lame.

Jamae turned and looked up at Ethan, who returned her stare, before they broke out in high-pitched squeals.

"Something like that, kid," Ethan smarted.

I cringed. Whenever I was hit with a childish moniker, I began to detach.

Oblivious that he'd offended me, Ethan reached for the book and began flipping through it. "Portals exist all over the place. Maggie, here, just had and still has, I'm sure, a natural talent at uncovering them." His eyes fell over me with a thump. "She can reach into spaces and manipulate the elements in a way that most can only dream of being able to do." He casually let the book slip from his hand back to the counter. It was right there, ready to be plucked, and I had a burning desire to snag it. I just wanted to look at that name once more, to see if this time it might speak back and tell me what it was doing there. Unaware that I'd drifted quietly away, Ethan continued. "Apparently Maggie got all freaked out sometime after writing this book. She doesn't dance with her shadows anymore. In fact, I think she made sure her writings went out of print. Guessing Juanita had to scrounge to come up with these copies."

"That's cutting her some slack," Jamae smarted. "Maggie doesn't do much of anything anymore other than selling the occasional crystal ball."

My gaze was still fixated on the book, memorizing the author's name. Maggie O'Brien.

"If she's Juanita's wife," I said, sounding very much like I was coming out of a trance, "then isn't she part of your coven?" Wouldn't she be pissed they were reading her book?

Jamae shook her head. "She's a solitary witch—always has been. Juanita used to be, but she started craving group work shortly after this was written. She started the coven we're in back in the eighties. *And* even though Juanita still calls Maggie her wife, they don't live together anymore. They never officially split up, but I think this whole business" –she gestured to the book— "caused a rift between the two of them that they just couldn't ever fully repair. They still talk, but only for the sake of their cat."

My eyebrows shot up. Hadn't they just said that the couple had separated after the book was written? If the book was written over forty years ago, then . . . "How old is their cat?"

Jamae smirked. "A witch's familiar can live for a very long time."

"Interesting," I mused. My fingertips were hinged over the edge of the counter. The book was right there, within reach. That name inside the cover—it belonged to my heart. "Do you think that, like, if someone accessed one of these portals, or I don't know, like dug so far deep into their shadow work, that they could like . . ." My words drifted out into the ether. I wasn't sure how to ask this.

Jamae's gaze inched closer to mine. "What are you trying to say?"

My chest rose and just as quickly fell, my question escaping via the whisps of my breath. "Could someone take magic from the other side of things, and like, harness it?"

Oh my gawd. That sounded so stupid.

But if she thought so, Jamae didn't show it. She leaned in, laying both of her hands flat against the book's cover. "Anything's possible. Like, the world tells you *that* when you're a little kid, then when you get to be your age, they start to take parts of those promises away. And when you become an adult, they ensure you understand that everything in this place comes with limitations. That everything has a price tag attached to it. Even your paycheck." Her brows reached for the ceiling as she said that last part. "But that's what's so groovy about witchcraft—there are no limitations. Humanity can do its worst to take it away, but magic surrounds us always. Both ends of it. All Maggie did was uncover the truth."

"And you know what," Ethan said, pointing at the book. "This stuff is pretty advanced, even for someone like you, Tess. Come on." He gestured for me to follow him into the room on the other side of the purple curtain. "Let's get back to it. You'll never get a job here reading for people unless you practice."

I tried not to be obvious as I gave the book one final last desperate look as Jamae shooed me off in Ethan's direction.

"He's right. Go read some cards. And quit cheating by looking up all the meanings! Use your noggin!"

I hesitated for only a second before nodding my head. "Right."

My shoulders fell though, as I walked away from what felt like the last prize at the carnival. It was dusty, and most other kids wouldn't give it a second glance, but I saw the potential in it. That book was something that I could play with. Something that could perhaps help me open other worlds and maybe even grant me some answers.

As I followed Ethan past the purple curtain, I knew—I had to get my hands on that prize. It was a must.

CHAPTER THREE

Ethan's reading room was nothing more than a table and a set of tarot cards. The centerpiece was a crystal ball covered by a lady's scarf—he'd confessed the first time he'd led me into the space that the ball was primarily for show. He said something about it being a locked door, but I never cared enough to ask what he'd meant by that.

The first time I laid eyes over a set of tarot cards, I felt wild. Kind of like the first time you see a Ouija board in person. Like maybe this was something I wasn't supposed to play around with, and *that alone* made me want to touch them. However, now that I'd shuffled more than one deck in my hands, and since I'd been educated on what they stood for and the respect they should receive, tarot no longer held that spectacular rebellious vibe. Now I saw the cards as a way to create independence for myself. Because once I became a good little witch like Ethan and Jamae were training me to become, I could read cards for the public (and perhaps even more than that). I could have an identity of my own. Fifteen and already half an orphan wasn't what I was striving for. Neither was spoiled city girl. Maybe I really didn't know who I was, and doing readings may not fix that, but it was a start.

Ethan used a few different decks in his readings, but we'd been practicing with the same old cards that most everyone has seen at some point in their lives. These were the cards that were waiting for me on the small round table in the reading room.

"You know what to do," Ethan said after I had a seat across from him.

I pulled the deck into my hands and began to shuffle, an action that was quickly becoming familiar and more comfortable. "When do you think I'll be ready—to you know, like, read cards for actual people?"

Ethan smirked. "*Actual* people?"

I didn't have to fake the deadpan stare I sent his way. "What else are there in this world?"

Again, he just grinned. After another moment or two, he fidgeted in his chair, crossing one leg over another. "Jamae thinks you should be a little older, but I don't really think that matters. What I want to see is you unloading your burdens. I mean, you can't really help others until you've cleaned house, if you know what I mean."

I swiveled my head, so my chin was sticking out and to the side. "No. I don't think I do know what you mean."

"Just, you know. Let it out, girl. You've got some serious shadows in there. You've had a rough go at life. Bullies, and all that. Two-thirds of your family departing too early hasn't helped either. You gotta let it rain sometimes, you know."

I swallowed a ball of thorns before nodding my head, careful to hide the shame trying to lift from my shoulders. I wasn't above admitting my weaknesses, even though Ethan and Jamae were the only two pairs of eyes I'd willingly peered into and confessed my experiences of being shoved repeatedly in the school hallway.

"Other than that," Ethan said, "if you can pull off decent divination without pausing to reflect upon what others have written" —he picked up the booklet that explained the meaning of each tarot card then threw it back down— "then I'd say you're good to go whenever. And really, you could start reading ashes anytime, we all know you've got that in the bag. Plus, no one else can do that. Once you get going on that we'd have a hard time keeping the doors closed, that's for sure." He winked at me in that all knowing way, then started to add, "But again—"

"*She* thinks I'm too young."

He scrunched up his nose and nodded.

I sighed. "And she *is* the boss."

"That she is," Ethan echoed.

It was super hindering, but it was what it was. Ethan and Jamae were cool as hell, but they still had a thin layer of adult on them. Jamae wanted to talk to my dad in person before agreeing to let me work at Hexed.

Ethan had been right about something, though. I could do what no one else I'd ever met could. All I needed were the ashes of someone's hair, or the ashes of someone's person (hair just seemed to be less gruesome). Once I had that and was able to sift it through my fingertips, I could read someone's past, present, and future like a storybook.

Interestingly enough, I hadn't been aware of that little skillset until I met these two weirdos. I mean, I knew I could return ashes to what they'd been before they'd been burned, but I didn't realize how much a pile of dust could tell me about a person.

In the beginning, I'd been slow to trust Ethan and Jamae. At least enough to allow them in—to let them see the freak I really was. Sure, they called themselves witches, but they had only ever demonstrated as much magical ability as my brick of a dad. It wasn't until my grandmother and mother were taken, and I was at my weakest, that I confided in them. It was shortly after that that Jamae had suggested we mess around with what I was capable of. What better way to take my mind off my losses, she'd said. It was her idea to see if I could read ashes like tea leaves. Before I knew it, she'd snagged a gray hair from the green wool coat of one of her customer's and put it in my palm. "Go to town," was all she'd said, handing me a lighter.

We'd learned many things about the woman in the green coat that day. Her name was Shelly Roads, she was a hereditary witch, a content individual who lived alone, and would die peacefully in her sleep on a Thursday night. Thirty years from the day of the reading to be exact. It was such positive feedback that I didn't feel at all bad about intruding on her life.

The results had been legendary; I had a gift. But still Jamae was a roadblock.

I'd heard her and Ethan arguing in the back once, about letting me work there—they hadn't known I was eavesdropping. Jamae had said that my skills could attract the wrong sort and Ethan had shot back with, "It's inevitable so why not just rush through all this and get it over with." He'd also said something about how they couldn't keep this up forever, and how it had always been me who had come to save them. . . Yeah, that was weird. Either way, Jamae had held firm and stayed rooted to her initial statement that I wasn't ready.

There was no way I was going to admit that I'd heard them. If nothing else, all any of that meant was the shop wasn't doing all that well, and Ethan knew my rare gift could help bring in new customers as well as a new clientele. But who was I to get between them and their business? They were all I had and if I started taking sides, I could lose them both. It was best to keep my mouth shut.

"Whatever," I finally retorted, shoving the conversation under the rug. "Who am I reading for today?"

Ethan had told me when he first took me under his wing that it was taboo to do too many readings for yourself, therefore he'd had me read primarily for other people. Namely celebrities. He and Jamae never allowed me to read for them; their excuse being that the cards couldn't tell them anything that they didn't already know. They had a 'been there, done that' sort of attitude about the whole thing. I'd yet to read for anyone who was in the same room as me, but Ethan had told me time and again that the person didn't have to be with you to have their cards read.

"You."

The cards slipped between my fingers. "Huh?"

"Yeah," he said casually. "I think it's time."

Another thorny ball materialized in my throat. "I—I don't know . . ."

It wasn't that I didn't want to read my own fortune, or have it told to me—I was fifteen, teetering on the edge of sixteen, I was more than curious about what the years before me were going to bring. But it was all a little scary, especially considering that I'd never met anyone else like me in the world. Ever. What might these cards say about my magic?

"What if it says I'm like one of those portals in Maggie's book? What if it says I'm cursed? That I should be closed."

Ethan rested his back against his chair. "Come on, you know better than that." He pointed to the cards in my hand. "They can't tell you anything you don't already know."

"That's exactly the problem," I whispered. "I *really* don't know what my heart has to say."

The room was quiet for a moment as I continued to move the cards around in my hands. Finally, I placed them over the table and cut them into thirds, before collecting them back into one pile. When I was ready, I rolled my shoulders back and looked up at Ethan.

"Now what?"

He didn't move a muscle as he said, "It's a good day for single card draw."

I raised a brow. "Just one?"

"Yeah. It's good practice. It goes well with daily meditation, to pull a single card every day. It's like facing your shadows," he added with a gentle smile.

"O*kay*," I said, hesitant. I slowly pulled my right hand out from where I'd tucked it under my lap.

"Just like always," Ethan said. "Do so with an open heart."

I slipped my fingers around the top card, and though it should've weighed nearly the same as a feather plucked from the ground, it felt like I was turning over a boulder. My eyes grew as soon as I set it down next to the pile of cards. I gulped as I looked up at my tarot teacher.

"Three of Swords."

He showed no emotion at all. "What's it mean?"

"I—I can't—"

"The illustration, Tess. What does it say to you? If you were writing a story based on what you're looking at—how would it go?"

I returned my attention to the card. It was a red heart, punctured by three swords; in the background there were clouds and rain.

"A storm is coming. The clouds make me think—"

Ethan was shaking his head. "Don't say things like, 'this makes me think.' Just say it."

"Right," I agreed. It was so hard to keep all the notes about how I was supposed to do this in order, but if I ever wanted to work at Hexed and find my identity then I was going to have to get good at this. I needed to sound believable.

I readjusted my posture and tried again. "A storm is coming, and it's heavy. There's going to be heartache."

"And why is that?"

I pointed at the swords. "They've punctured the heart. And the way they are set makes me think—I mean, the way they are crossing each other at the bottom—there is— betrayal." I sat on the word for a moment. "There's betrayal in my future." I sat back as the realization sunk in. "Shit."

Ethan chuckled. "Very good. But don't get all bent out of shape, the card could be communicating any or all those things. Considering your recent losses, this card is most definitely signifying your heart break over your mother and grandmother."

My gaze settled over his. Sure, that sounded about right, especially since they'd been found with punctured hearts, but my gut was struck with that storm in the background. The heaviness of it. It was more than a little foreboding.

"Here," he said, plucking the card from the table and lighting the end of it with the white candle burning between the two of us. He held it in his hand until it got too hot, then let it fall to the table, not caring about the burn marks it would leave as it turned to ash. "Does that make you feel better?"

I sighed. "Not really." I touched the ashes and reanimated the card. "There is no such thing as out of sight out of mind when you can do what I can. Can I read one for Miley Cyrus now?"

Ethan's light snicker turned into a full-on laugh. "Yeah, Lil Tess. Go on."

"Cool." I picked up the cards and started shuffling again. As I did, I couldn't help but scrunch up my nose. "No offense, Ethan, but what did you eat for lunch? It smells like rotten garlic in here."

His pale cheeks colored a very light red as he brought a hand up to his mouth and smelled his breath. Then, without missing a beat, he reached into his pocket and pulled out some mints, popping a couple into his mouth. "Sorry. Philly steak is my downfall."

I smirked, then let my expression soften. "So, I turned an ash that was sitting on my headmaster's shirt into a cigarette about an hour ago."

I didn't look up, but I could feel Ethan's astonishment permeating my energy.

"In front of him?"

"Uh huh." I pictured Miley's face as I sorted through the deck.

"Is that why you're not in school right now?"

"Yep."

"Maybe you should, like, tell your dad—you know—about what you can do." I grimaced. "You never know, his reaction might surprise you."

I set the deck over the table and cut it into thirds for the second time that day. It wasn't the first time Ethan or Jamae had urged me to speak to my dad. And it wasn't the first time I'd had to say what I said next. "He really wouldn't understand. He's got enough on his plate right now as it is; he doesn't need to find out that his only kid is a freak."

"Whoa." Ethan leaned over the table and placed his hand over mine. My heartbeat softened. "Tess, you're anything but a freak. What you have is an incredible gift, one that you should be proud of." He seemed to waver back and forth before stating his next thought. "Maybe if you'd told your grandmother about what you could do before she died things would have been different."

I glanced at his hand over mine before pulling mine away. The comment stung—twice. Not only was my Grandma Reanin's name imprinted in my mind at the moment, but his lack of concern for what my mother would have had to say about all this while she'd been alive was an interesting hypothesis. Then again, both him and Jamae knew the relationship I'd had with my mother had been non-existent. That the only two people I'd ever really loved had been my dad and grandma. My mother never wanted to get to know me. She never said that, but she hadn't needed to. I only ever wondered why my father stuck around; she'd treated him the same way. Maybe he stayed for me. Who knew?

"Whatever. Let's see what fortunes are looming before Hannah Montana."

Ethan once more leaned back in his chair. "Fine. Begin."

We worked on readings for about an hour before Jamae stuck her head between the curtains and announced there was a regular in the waiting.

"Who is it?" Ethan asked.

Jamae rolled her eyes. "Miss Connie."

As soon as the name left the tip of Jamae's tongue, Ethan's head fell backwards as he whimpered, "God dammit."

"Not one of your favorites?" I questioned, gathering the cards together and placing them in the center of the table.

Ethan's head remained tilted back as he answered, "She's not here for herself. She has the cards read for Miss Pretty."

I couldn't help but giggle as I asked, "And who is Miss Pretty?"

Both Jamae and Ethan answered together. "Her cat."

I bit my lip as I walked back out into the store and an older woman with blue gray hair bowed past me while clutching her purse to her stomach on her way through the curtains. Jamae leaned in and air kissed my cheek, her phone clutched in her hand, pasted against her ear—I was struck with another cloud of sandalwood.

"Catch ya later, lady," she mouthed. "Sorry, I'm kinda in the middle of this."

"No problem," I whispered. "See you soon."

She nodded before strutting to the backroom.

I started for the door, but just as I was about to reach out and pull it towards me, I glanced back at the cash register where Jamae had been perched when I'd first walked in. Sure enough, there it was. The book.

I bit down over my lip again as I thought about what I should or shouldn't do. I hadn't ever made a habit of stealing from friends, but I didn't really have a lot of friends . . . and this wasn't really stealing. I'd return the thing in a day or two. Jamae would understand.

Without a second thought, I sprinted to the register and yanked the book into my coat before running for the door. It wasn't until I was about a block away that I got up the courage to pull it back out and reopen the cover to where that name was printed in blue ink.

Reanin Wells. My grandmother. Sure, it could have been a coincidence, but I knew it wasn't. That was my grandma's signature, I was positive. Not to mention this exact signature was inscribed on the inside cover of every single book my Grandma Reanin owned. What I couldn't be sure of and was one hundred percent curious about, was what my *Good Housekeeping*, women's poker club playing, clad only in tan slacks and satin blouses, *grandmother* would have been doing with a book about shadow work.

It was a long shot, but all I could think, as I dodged the passersby coming at me from the opposing direction of the sidewalk, was what if my grandmother had indeed worked with her shadows? What if my magic wasn't an accident at all, but had something to do with my grandma going too deep? Had she wandered into a dark passageway that hadn't been meant to be found?

I flipped through the book until I found the passage I'd seen earlier. "*The shadows may draw energy from you, but you —being in charge of your own darkness—may draw just as much power from them.*"

Was it possible that my magic was the effect of my grandmother venturing into another dimension? I let the book close in my hands as I came to a halt in front of a busy crosswalk. Jamae had just said, that when it came to magic, anything was possible.

CHAPTER FOUR

Even after all my juvenile shenanigans in Mr. Greene's office, I hadn't heard a peep from my dad all day. Nothing good *or* bad. When he got home that night, at almost nine, all he did was stick his head in my room and ask if I'd had a good day at school. It was . . . bizarre. I was left with only one explanation—the Ignatius Academy must not have called.

"School was fine," I lied.

"Good. What did you have for dinner?"

He was only asking to make conversation. Most of his meals were had out with clients; when he was home, he didn't have much of an appetite.

"Mary Joe wrapped up some chicken and vegetables—there's some left." He made a face. It was warranted; our current housekeeper hadn't been hired for her culinary wiles. She'd been with us for six months. Our previous one, Hilda, had been old and set in her ways but her cooking had excused her behavior, as well as her sideways comments about how my mom and dad weren't home enough. At least she was forgiven by me and my palette; neither my mom nor dad had ever really fully tasted her food. That's what you get when both your parents are high-end real-estate agents in NYC. "I think there's still a frozen pizza or two in the freezer if you don't want to soldier through the chicken."

He nodded. "Cool. So hey, I need to talk to you about something." *Ugh, here we go.* "Someone else inquired about Grandma Reanin's apartment today."

What? That wasn't what I'd been expecting.

Bricks fell from the ceiling. And dust. So much of it. Okay, maybe not literally, but it might as well have. I set down my laptop and rested it over my bed's comforter. My screen was filled with searches on portals and other dimensions. I'd been researching shadow work and its effects. So far, no one else had mentioned anything about discovering other worlds after accessing their shadows.

Redirecting my energy to my father, I chirped out a somewhat innocent and non-judgmental, "Oh?"

This was the second time he'd come to me with this topic. The first time someone hit him up with an offer, he immediately slapped it away. As he should have. Truth: my grandmother's apartment was like a New York City hot cake —as soon as it hit the market, it wasn't going to sit there for long. Still, I'd been dreading this moment for a *while*. My grandmother's apartment was all I had left of the woman who had practically raised me. Who had let me eat mac n cheese for every meal and sit on her lap until I was too big as she read to me her favorite book. *The Last Unicorn.* It had become my favorite book too. I'd read it five times since she'd gone.

"It can't sit there like that forever, Tess," my dad said. "She didn't leave it to you so it could just collect dust."

And there it was. I rolled my eyes until they met the wall. Yes, she'd left her apartment to me. No, it didn't matter. I was too young to do anything with it, so it was in my dad's hands.

Thoughts scampered around my head like rabid mice as I

refused to meet my father's gaze. Most of my warped musings were in the form of 'why?' Like, why was the world so cruel? Why did this even have to be an issue? Why had she been taken from me?

I mean, it *was* New York . . . muggings happened. It's just one of those things you grow up thinking won't ever happen to you or anyone you love. There were no witnesses, but it was obvious what occurred. As the headline read: *Reanin Wells and daughter, Janine Moreau-Wells, were found stabbed to death in an alley.* It was just behind my mother's favorite restaurant. They'd been meeting for lunch. It was tradition. It had been my mother's birthday.

It was a busboy who found them that night. The first autumn chill had been in the air. My initial reaction, after I heard the news, was that they must've been cold . . . lying there like that all day and into the night. It's funny the way our brains work when devastation finds us. The second thing I thought about was how it might not have been as heartbreaking if my grandmother hadn't been there.

Like, who even thinks like that? I'd been in a mental battle with my thoughts ever since that day. Going back and forth in anger towards my mother for having a birthday at all—for taking them to their deaths. Then shaming myself for not finding the right hallway to enter, the one that would lead me to where my grief sat on a pedestal. You know, the grief I should have had for my mother passing away.

Yeah, it was morbid. But no matter how icy it was, the fact remained—I only missed my grandma. I couldn't change the way I felt. Maybe if Janine had done more than just run through the actions of being a mother—like telling me stories as she put me to bed for instance or laying a hand over my forehead just because; but she'd never done those things. Instead, she seemed to move through a mental checklist of things mothers *should* do. I was enrolled in swimming lessons by age four and sent to the finest scholarly institutions money could buy. Both my parents had been workaholics ever since I could remember, but at least my dad made me his first stop every night he came home, and those nights that he got home very late, he snuck into my room and laid his hand over mine. I knew he loved me. I'd heard him whisper it many times when he thought I was asleep.

"You are so special," he'd even said one night not that long ago. I'd almost opened my eyes, so he would know I'd heard him. But I didn't.

Conflicted. That was how I felt about losing my mom, but I was sore all over from my grandma's death. And now we had to talk about her apartment like it was in the way, when it was the last little bit of her that I had left.

Without catching sight of my father's eyes, his sunken demeanor, I replied to his comment. "Whatever. Sell it if you must."

"Tess . . . I didn't say I was going—"

"No, I get it." My words were so sharp it was as if they'd been clipped at the ends. But in reality, I didn't get it. When the will had been read and her wishes laid out for all to hear— that I was to inherit her home and all her belongings, my dad hadn't put up even the slightest argument. He'd been really chill, but when days and weeks passed and I refused to go check on the place, he started getting on me about it. I still couldn't understand why he was so adamant about me checking in; her building had strict security and those neighbors of hers were always lurking.

When I didn't say anything more, he added, "Tess, it's just sitting there. You said you'd go and check in on it every now and then, but you never do."

"It's an apartment, not a dog," I whispered heatedly.

"Look, I know it's been difficult, but she left that place to you for a reason."

Oh my gawd, I couldn't listen to this overdone sermon one more time. So, I did the only thing I *could* do. I looked him in the eyes and stated firmly, "I got suspended."

The man visibly deflated. I tried to look away, but I couldn't. He wiped a hand down his face and nodded. "We're running out of schools to send you to, Tess."

"Nobody likes me, what else can I say?"

A line appeared between his brows. "How come I didn't get a call from the school?"

I shrugged. "I don't know."

"You didn't do anything *strange*, did you?"

"Like what?" I asked defensively.

He stared bullets into me for a moment before relaxing his gait. "Whatever." He started to pull away from the doorframe. "We'll talk about this tomorrow."

"Fine," I retorted.

I kept my sneer in place as I pulled my laptop back up onto my lap, pretending to read about portals. He was gone, but my thoughts were still racing. Of course I did something strange, but what would he know about any of that? I'd never exhibited any of my special skills to any other school; today was a first. Gawd, he was acting just as weird as I was. And why *now*? We'd already lost so much. Why did he have to add my grandma's apartment to that list?

I wasn't sure if I'd ever be fully ready to part with it, but I one hundred percent wasn't ready right now. And it wasn't just because it was all I had left of her; it was because of what I knew had to be in there somewhere. Secrets. Deep down in my twisted guts I knew that's what I was really upset about. My dad couldn't sell that bit of property just yet, because somewhere in between the city views and mirrored reflections —under all the clean lines and light-colored walls—I had always known them to be there. The explanations for why my grandmother seemed to be an enigma.

I'd whispered as much during the will reading, loud enough, evidently, for my father to hear.

"What did you say?" he'd asked, discreetly looking down at me.

"She left me her place so I could finally get to know her," was all I'd said in return.

He'd reached for my hand and squeezed it. "I think you're right, Tess."

That's what was really bogging me down about his little retort concerning the sale of my grandmother's place. He might not have known that I always suspected something was off about my grandma, but he knew how much that apartment meant to me. The more I thought about it, the more I began to wonder . . . Was he actually alluding to a possible sale, or was he trying to encourage me to do something I hadn't been ready to do as of yet?

If the latter *was* the case, what was his motivation? Unless . . . maybe he'd seen it too. Maybe my grandma wasn't just a mystery to me. On the surface, she was nothing more than another wealthy New York woman wrapped in silk—but behind her eyes, something was lurking. A piece of the puzzle was missing.

No one ever mentioned my grandfather. From an early age, I'd learned not to talk about it around my mom; the subject irritated her. Reversely, my dad coached me to hold onto the question for when I was older. For when I was wiser. So that was weird.

I'd asked my grandma about my grandpa only once. What she'd said had confused me.

"He's locked into the ocean waves. Just like all the other unicorns."

I knew the book she was referencing; I knew the part she spoke about—but I still couldn't make out what she was trying to say.

"One day, Tess," she'd said. "One day you'll understand."

Maggie O'Brien's book was just the topper on a whole sundae filled with oddities when it came to Reanin Wells. Because none of it—none of the parts of her life that she'd so carefully glued to her like sequins on a sweater—none of it fit. For years I'd tried to pinpoint what it was that was so off about my grandmother, but it wasn't until I'd seen her name etched into that book that it came to me. The woman had, buried underneath the blue of her eyes and hidden by the fancy clothes that didn't seem quite right on her, shadows.

My stomach couldn't stop tying itself into knots, because even if my grandma had buried her shadows or hidden them away, I just knew that they were there. In her apartment. They had to be. I just didn't know where to look or where to even begin.

I picked up the stolen copy of *Confronting Your Shadows* and opened the front flap. I stared down at my grandmother's signature; then, with a heavy sigh, I allowed the pages to open to the first chapter and began to read.

If I couldn't ask my grandma why she hid her shadows away, then maybe I could find the answer the same way she had. Through experience.

Extinguishing the Flame

The room is dark, save for the light of a single candle. Mirrors are set in a circle around you. If one were to enter the space, you would appear alone, but you know in your heart that you aren't. For there are many entities with you, reflecting at you and dancing along the shadows of your face. Up until this very point, you've been taught to bury your demons as far deep as you can— into the cells of your skin and bones. You've been taught to soak in the candlelight and find the burn, for that is where you will feel enlightenment.

But what would happen if you acknowledged your shadows? If you wet the tips of your fingers and killed the flame? If you found a bit of light reflecting at you from inside the darkness . . . inside the reflections? Here's the thing, readers, if you don't try, you'll never know. What if you're missing a whole other part of your existence because you've been trained to see the world only during the day? Imagine what you could see if you allowed the darkness to dance with you instead of away from you.

CHAPTER FIVE

The next morning, I came down for breakfast wearing my school uniform. My eyes were a train wreck—bloodshot and full of luggage. I'd slept two hours, tops, since I'd dedicated most of the night and early morning to reading Maggie O'Brien's book from cover to cover. The mania I'd built up from the new neural pathways paved into my brain completely overshadowed any and all exhaustion.

Page twenty-three of *Confronting Your Shadows* spoke so directly into my soul that goosebumps covered every inch of my skin: *Make a list of all the characteristics you've been taught to reject about yourself. Has the world told you that you shouldn't lust for your true desires—that you should be content with what you have? Have you been shoved down and told to simply stand back up and forgive the hand that threw you? Do you find yourself burying hatred you feel towards certain people or aspects of your career? I want you to address all these things, then I want you to look yourself in the eyes and tell yourself what YOU want. Because bringing these things to the surface is just the first step. You need to shake hands with these parts of yourself that either you or society has told you aren't acceptable. It is time for you to introduce yourself to the feelings you have hidden in the shadows. It is time to walk with the storm.*

Being of the young and privileged variety, power and greed were two things I didn't have any use for, but from the moment my parents had sent me into the 'wild,' (privately owned schooling institutions) I'd been ridiculed and treated like a misfit. By the age of five, I was already internalizing hatred and frustration, and not long after that I began burying so much more—my magic, and my true self.

This book—this was *it*. It contained exactly everything I needed to hear. Screw all the bullshit every headmaster or mistress had ever fed me; those bitches didn't have shadows—their energy didn't go deep enough for that. This sort of work was specialized for those who weren't afraid to step out of, as my Grandma Reanin had said more than once while she'd been alive, the simulation most humans called life.

As soon as I'd read that paragraph, I set down the book and went directly to my vanity, sitting on the small circular stool that faced the mirror. I'd meditated before; I knew the drill. Close my eyes, find the peace within. Glow, shine, fucking float.

This was not that.

I looked at the girl in the mirror. She was sort of austere, apart from her eyes. They'd been described as *interesting* on more than one occasion. I held the stare, and instead of finding peace like I'd been trained to do, I began to search for all the things I'd buried.

The first picture that surfaced in my mind was one of Vanessa Bridges. It was my first day in kindergarten, and Vanessa, a miniature version of a British Karen, walked right up to me and pulled on my flat, mousy colored hair. "You're quite plain, aren't you?" she'd said. The comment from the aristocratic offspring infuriated me. At that age, I hadn't yet figured out what I was capable of, but I knew I was different.

I'd hissed at the girl. The action had resulted in my very first 'appointment' with a headmaster.

"We expect manners in this institution, Tess," the suited man had said. "I encourage you to upgrade your social skills."

He'd *actually* said that. It hadn't mattered that Vanessa was the little twirp who started it. Everyone could already sense that I was different, even when I was a little girl, and they didn't like it. The world, especially the posh and trendy city dwellers I grew up around, had been taught to feel comfortable only around bright and shiny things.

The memory had resurfaced, and I'd addressed it for the first time since my little five-year-old kicks had struck dirt over it. I let the memory come full circle, my skin prickling as I experienced it all again. My mother, seemingly ignorant of how the rest of the world was destined to treat me, and my father always whispering in my ear that I ought to at least try to fit in. How Vanessa Bridges was put on a pedestal by our peers and teachers, with her blonde hair and emerald eyes. Her pale skin. It was maddening, as were all the other Vanessas I'd had to come face to face with over the years, the Mr. Greenes. I'd internalized it all, even though I was smart enough to realize it wasn't a healthy practice. Things had a habit of boiling over.

Ultimately, as the feelings I'd collected over the years began to seep from my pores, my fury literally began to choke me— like it was lodged somewhere in the back of my throat. The only way I could get it out was to let it out. So, I turned from my vanity's mirror, grabbed for a pillow, and screamed into its fluff more times than I knew to count. When I had nothing left, I dropped the pillow to the ground and faced the mirror once more.

My eyes weren't changing from blue to green like a groovy lava lamp—they were black. In their reflection I saw the two girls from chemistry class, and a wicked grin lined my face as their long blonde hair went up in flames all over again. Yes, this was the vexed version of myself, the one I'd been holding hostage. This was the piece of me that would have loved to add Vanessa Bridges to that table of blonde ash. My reflection wailed in delight, incensed by the joyful rage coursing through my veins as I allowed myself to return to the scene where the young socialites screeched and hollered as their bleached hair was scorched.

The longer I let it go on, the stronger I felt. This was hatred, and I'd given myself permission to enjoy it.

I'd been taught that this was wrong. Society feared those of us who had been shoved down hard by our peers. We were taught to exchange our animosity for forgiveness. I'd even been told by some Joe Somebody that I should erase the anger in my heart that seeped in after my family was murdered in an alley to make room for mercy. I mean, really?

Society worried that if kids like me addressed our hatred instead of talking to paid professionals about our pain that we might just throw on a black trench coat and get violent. But maybe they had it wrong. Facing my shadows felt *good*, and as I continued to peruse my reflection—my hatred—my eyes began to return to shifting golds and greens. My shoulders relaxed. I saw myself floating above those three unimportant girls, and I noted that as soon as I allowed myself to hate them, they became powerless. I was suddenly struck with the realization that it was petty to grant them any amount of my feelings at all—good or bad. They weren't worth it.

I let go of them—of what they'd each done to me, and as soon as I did, something released from somewhere within my core. The hatred disintegrated. I was clean.

I couldn't be sure if there were shadows all around me or if I'd just unleashed some sort of demon like I was in a stereotypical horror flick, but I did know one thing. I felt loads better. I was also struck with a demanding thought: all these years I'd been asking myself why my peers were treating me this way, when what I should have been asking myself was why I'd been letting them.

I didn't feel like lashing out at them or tearing at their beautifully exfoliated flesh—I honestly didn't care about them one way or the other. They weren't as happy as they put on, because if they were, they wouldn't be looking for ways to make themselves taller. That was their problem, not mine.

And that was just one exercise in a book full of them.

The latter part of the book dealt with dimensions. As intriguing as it had been, it hadn't been as in depth as I'd been hoping for. Maggie O'Brien didn't offer a tutorial on how to open such places. She simply stated that the more open one is —the more enlightened—the higher the chances become of removing the blindfold society has placed over the eyes of its inhabitants. That is when one may unknowingly stumble into a whole other world by simply stepping into a rain puddle. Or open the door to a watering hole and find yourself face to face with a mythical creature.

I wasn't sure what I thought about that.

I may not have found the answers I'd set out to collect about why my grandma had owned this book, but I was glad to have it for myself. Plus, I'd already decided—my grandma's apartment wasn't sold yet—I was going to head over there as soon as possible and do some snooping. I'd waited long enough, and there had to be something in that vast space of slick white counters and crystal vases filled with marbles and silk flowers that could lend a hand to wherever my grandmother kept *her* shadows.

My dad didn't even look up from his coffee and tablet when I sat in the seat next to his with a plate full of eggs and toast.

"Why are you wearing that?" he asked of my uniform. "I thought you were expelled . . . or suspended."

"And I thought we were friends, but friends don't sell other friend's property. I don't care if it's your job."

He rolled his eyes. "I never said I was going to sell it, Tess."

I paused with my fork just below my mouth. Okay, so maybe he *was* just pushing me to get off my ass and go find what I couldn't while my grandmother had been living. Either way, I decided to pull back my attitude by an inch or so. "I don't know if I got sacked or not. I left Mr. Greene's stupid hipster office before he got the chance to tell me whether I was welcome back."

He set down his mug full of coffee that served as his breakfast and stared at me as if I'd just told him I took a crap in his sock drawer. "Why do you do this?"

I set down my fork and added a little hot sauce to my eggs. "Why do I do what?"

"Make everything so hard."

"Dad . . . I didn't mean to—"

But he was already standing. "I'm going to be late for work. Just finish your breakfast and go to school. Or don't. I obviously can't control what you do."

"Don't you even want to know what I did to *maybe* get sacked?"

"It doesn't matter. The outcome is always the same." He paused from where he was starting to walk away and without turning to face me, said, "You have one role, Tess, and you can't help anyone in this world if you don't know how to help yourself."

What? "Huh?"

But he didn't offer an explanation. I watched his back as he left the dining room and my heart dropped as the front door shut. I was left in an empty room with a nagging feeling.

Maggie wouldn't say she was sorry, I thought. She would tell her pain to get bent and ask her anger to have a seat at the empty place setting that my father just made available.

But all I'd done so far was learn to scream into a pillow. My troubles had roots, and those didn't live in the shadows. They lived underground.

"Good lord," I muttered as I pushed away my plate. "I'm gonna need a shovel."

I'd only made it as far as staring up at the double wooden doors to the Ignatius Academy. The fact that the administration hadn't called my dad led me to believe that I wasn't kicked out; at least not yet.

Could it be that Headmaster Greene was actually afraid of me? A small, or perhaps a considerable, piece of me hoped he was.

I'd dove into Maggie's investigations while reading through her book. She spoke of the existence of witches . . . like true witches. I fit the mold. And even though I still needed much of what she'd written to be explained to me, I was brutally aware that maybe people like Mr. Greene *should* fear me. I may not have understood the origins of my magic, but I was pretty sure that it had the potential to turn me from the insignificant person these people thought me to be into something much more powerful.

While diving into her shadows, Maggie O'Brien had figured out how to walk between worlds, and she'd investigated some really (for lack of a better word) frightening realms—home to creatures who looked like us and others that didn't. Places where magic was as accessible to those who lived there as air is to humans. "Doorways to the wicked and hungry," was just one description the author had used.

What if I was like these otherworlders? Wicked . . .

Maggie had insinuated that she'd met entities who were desperate to find a way into our dimension because they desired something they couldn't have where they were currently residing: a body.

"They call to us," she had written. "The gifted who open these doorways, they do so because they believe they've found something undiscovered, when in reality the evil lurking on the other side of the wall has been sending them messages in their dreams or whispering into their ears when they aren't aware, asking them to open the door. I have visited some of these places, and I can tell you firsthand, it is not a destination worth risking your life for.

"You have to be strong, and you have to be able to swim without air for longer than seems possible. They will not just try to steal your wits, *they will*.

"Now then, listen carefully, for this is a true warning. I've spoken of many different portals in many different worlds. All of them I found lurking where darkness swallows the light. I personally found no friends in the shadows; even the few allies you might find will have agendas. Why then, you might ask, would one even venture into these places? To this I would say: why do people swim with sharks? Own lions, tigers, or bears as pets? For the experience, perhaps, or for the love of it. Really, it's a question only you can answer. But remember this, you don't walk out of a lion's den unscathed unless you've learned to offer your predator the respect they or *it* deserves.

"Now for the opposite of all that. Though mostly all the dimensions I have found are dark, they aren't all bad. Just like the shadows that belong to us, some of them are simply misunderstood. Wisdom is needed to tell the difference. The intuition."

I couldn't help but wonder yet again as I looked up at my school—*had my grandma found the darkness?* And if she had, had she brought something into herself that had been handed down to me? My mom had never exhibited a single characteristic that could have lent itself towards being magical. Neither had my grandma, though.

All I wanted was to talk to Reanin and find out if her past life had had something to do with the fact that when I was seven, I discovered that when I cupped the ashes from our fireplace in my hand, I could bring back the logs . . . and upon further investigation, I could bring back the seed that made the tree that made the logs.

It had taken several years for me to understand what I was dealing with, and I still wasn't sure about the limitations of my magic. All I knew was that I could tell a story from what everyone else considered a dead end.

Whatever the case, I was sick and tired of playing the part of the weirdo, and if I walked into that school there was no way *in hell* that I was going to give the 'cool' kids the satisfaction of allowing them to believe they ranked higher than the other kids in the school, just because they'd decided for themselves that they were better. All I had to do was show them what I was made of. They'd been calling me a witch, practically since I began at that blasted school, and now after reading about how to confront my shadows, I felt like I had the tools I needed to possibly get through life, and I was prepared to own the accusation.

For a fleeting second, I thought about what Ethan had said the day before—*should* I tell my father about my secret skill? I'd have to show him, of course, and then what? He'd stare wildly at me? Drop his jaw? No, it was a dumb idea. The look on his face that morning just reaffirmed that fact; he was overloaded as it was and telling him would do nothing more than add to his stress.

My phone pinged and I sighed in relief, thankful for the distraction. It was Jamae.

J: You going to school today?

I typed back three words.

T: I don't know.

J: Grounded?

T: I don't know.

I stared down at the screen, waiting for the bubbles. Finally, she wrote back.

J: Not looking to get you into more trouble but there's a metaphysical fair today. Ethan and I are going if you want to tag along.

I glanced back up at the Ignatius Academy. I might not have been suspended or kicked out yet, but I had a feeling I wasn't welcome. I didn't have to see through the walls; I could sense Headmaster Greene staring down at me from his window up above, willing me to walk in any other direction than towards those two wooden doors.

T: I'm there.

J: Cool. Meet us at the store and we'll go together.

I sent a thumbs up and immediately turned away from the school, heading in the direction of acceptance rather than discrimination. Not to mention, there was no other place in the world to find out more information about shadow work and a possible connection that good old grandma might have had with it than at a place crawling with supposed witches.

CHAPTER SIX

J amae and Ethan were in the back of the shop when I got to Hexed, so I discreetly pulled the copy of *Confronting Your Shadows* from my bag and snuck it just under the register, on the ground. That way maybe Jamae would come across it and believe it fell when she wasn't looking.

Once I was on the other side of the counter, however, I quietly cursed myself. This was exactly the kind of nonsense Maggie would have told me to pitch. I was in the middle of shaking my head at myself when Jamae resurfaced.

"What's wrong, babe?" she asked, reaching behind the counter for her purse.

My hand had found my forehead and was working on smoothing out the wrinkles. Without overthinking it, I pulled down my hand and pointed at the cash register. "I—uh—I brought your book back. I think it fell from where I stuck it. I'm sorry I didn't tell you I wanted to borrow it. It was super lame of me just to take it."

Jamae slunk behind the counter and looked around for a minute before snagging it. "No kidding? I didn't know you wanted to read it. You should've just said." She smiled. "Did you like it?"

I dragged my teeth over my bottom lip. The heaviness that had set in over my chest several minutes ago lifted. "Yeah, actually. It was kinda cool."

She flipped through the book before tossing it back on the counter. "Did you read the whole thing?"

"Yeah." It was always embarrassing to reveal how fast I could consume a book, especially when I was already an outcast. But that had always been our thing, my grandma and me. Used bookstores, coffee on a rainy day, sitting in her overly bright apartment and scouring through novels like they were chocolate chip cookies. I pulled at my hair as I toyed with the idea of telling my confidant why I'd been so interested in that book in the first place. But in the end, I chose to hang on to the mystery alone for just a little longer. "I didn't really have any homework, so . . ."

"Right," Jamae said with a wink. "Well, I've got loads of inventory to do this week, so you and Ethan might just have to give me the cliff notes."

I still had a grip over the same strand of hair, something to hold onto, to ground me from falling too far south. "You said Juanita handed those books out, right?"

"Uh huh," she answered, while digging through her purse and eventually pulling out a stick of pink gum. The scent of cinnamon joined the sandalwood already heavy in the air.

"Do you think she just had them lying around? I mean, the copy you have looks pretty used."

"Naw. Maggie got rid of most of the copies years ago. I'm guessing Juanita picked that one up at a used bookstore or something. Why do you ask?"

I dropped my hand down and immediately became fidgety. Grappling my fingers together, I shrugged a single shoulder. "I don't know—I was just curious."

For a second, I thought I was busted as a playful grin began to form over Jamae's face, but whatever she was thinking she kept to herself. Instead, she walked up and punched my shoulder playfully. "Hey, don't feel like you can't borrow stuff. Let us be your library. We're here for you—always have been."

A slow breath left my lips, and I rolled my eyes. "I know. I've got some things to work on."

"What's that?" Ethan asked, pulling on a puffer coat as he walked into the store from the backroom, dragging in the scent of even more essential oils. Did they, like, bathe in it?

"Nothing," Jamae answered for me. "Tess was just talking about how she wasn't sure whether she's going to head back to school after this."

I mouthed a 'thank you' to her when Ethan wasn't looking. It wasn't a big deal, but I was happy to know that only one of them had to witness me acting like a juvenile.

"Back to school, huh. Like today, or ever?" he asked as he walked past us and turned off the lights before reaching for the door.

"Ever," I answered.

He shrugged his shoulders. "Whatever. You've got skills you can't learn in school. You've got bigger and better things in your future anyway, kid."

Jamae sighed as she leaned towards the door and flipped the open sign to closed. "Mattie would have your head on a sword for that one—filling his kid's head with the idea that she should drop out. He wants her to experience real life."

"Who cares," I started to say, but just as quickly redirected my gaze from the thin blue carpet back up to Jamae. "How'd you know his name?" I was pretty sure I'd only ever referred to my parents as mom and dad. Or absent and mostly absent. And what the frick was that last part about?

Jamae just looked back at me for a moment, then shrugged her shoulder. "You've said it before."

"I have?"

Truly, I don't think I ever did.

Ethan dug around his coat pocket before pulling out some mints. "You call him that all the time." He popped a mint into his mouth, then rearranged his face to look like a teenager during a rant. "Oh my gawd, you guys. Like, Mattie is all up in my shit. All he does is nag!"

My tough girl persona was betrayed as a smirk fell over my lips. "I don't do that."

"Oh whatever," Ethan retaliated. "You complain about him all the time! And hey, while we're on the subject, didn't you say once upon a time that you would've given your right hand to have your mom mad at you just once, cause that would mean that she was paying attention to you? Mattie sounds like a good guy to me. He nags because he cares, you know."

I hated when grown-ups were right.

"Yeah, well, whatever." I still didn't quite buy that I'd ever used my dad's name . . . but I must have. It *could've* slipped out, I guess. Either way, it wasn't important. What *was* important was me gaining control of myself. Of confronting my shadows. "You know what, Ethan—you're so right. I do have bigger and better things in my future. Screw that headmaster and all those stupid kids at the Ignatius Academy for underestimating what Tess Moreau may one day be."

More sandalwood flew into my nostrils as Jamae threw an arm around my shoulder, giving me a strong side squeeze. "That's what I'm talking about, sister! Embrace yourself!"

I tried to dull the smirk over my face as we walked out of the shop inside a cloud of essential oils and cinnamon gum. I could feel it, somewhere behind the beating of my heart, a shadow was beginning to unfurl.

CHAPTER SEVEN

I didn't know what to expect when we got to the metaphysical fair; this was my first one. Essentially, it was just as if Hexed had blown up to accommodate more merchandise and more people.

There were massive amounts of tables set up—crystals for days, tarot cards, books, swords, and broomsticks. I had to backtrack for a moment . . . swords? Interesting. Magical tools were laid out over every other table—athames, wands, pendulums. Reiki healers and fortune tellers were lined up against the walls. People were selling tapestries, incense—which was heavy in the air—statues of every goddess and god, as well as various dragons and fey. It was seriously magical.

I'd found my first portal (at least that's what it felt like), and I didn't care whether it was dark or light, because here—I just knew—I was accepted.

"Oh my god, oh my god, oh my god—they're *here*!" Ethan chirped. He was squirming in his pants like a little kid.

"Who's here?" I asked as I stared around at the endless crowd, wondering if anyone in this place had magic that matched mine.

"The authors of *Spells for the Cauldron: It's Getting Hot in Here*, that's who."

"Oh my god, they *are* here," Jamae echoed, her hands cupping the sides of her face. "We have to go get a signed copy before they sell out. There's already a line. Come on."

"Hang on, guys," I said. Both Ethan and Jamae turned part way around from where they were already five steps towards their destination. "You mind if I hang back, maybe look around a little."

"Whatever, just don't take off without us, okay?" Jamae said.

"Sure." I nodded. They were out of my sight within the next ten seconds.

I stood idle for a little bit longer, casing out the joint before deciding where to start. I ended up sashaying through the aisles, browsing table after table—picking up a stray crystal here or an interesting looking book of spells there. No one really said a word to me, not until I found myself surrounded by shelves of tarot cards.

"Hello, dear. May I help you?"

I looked up to find a strikingly beautiful middle-aged Latina woman staring down at me; she had long black hair and green cat-eyes. She totally fit the new age stereotype in her ankle length tie-dye skirt. I for sure hadn't seen this outfit at Boutique Loren.

With my hands cupped around a deck called *Awaken the Goddess*, I returned my gaze to the back of the box and skimmed the details. "Um, I don't think so. I mean, I just started reading cards, so this is all kind of new to me. I've only read the traditional tarot; I've never looked at any other decks before."

"Ah," said the woman as she raised a brow. "As you might already know, choosing a deck of cards is much like choosing a crystal or a pendulum—any magical tool. You must trust your intuition. Find what calls to you."

I placed the box of cards back on its shelf and squared my shoulders with the lady. "Are they all the same?" The card I'd pulled just yesterday flashed through my mind. "Is there a Three of Swords in all of these decks? A lady? A devil? Or do they all translate to different fortunes?"

The woman's thick pink lips widened and smoothed out. "Some are what you've called traditional tarot and just have different artwork—fairies, witches, elves." She pointed to the one I'd just returned to the shelf. "Goddesses. While others are completely different." She turned her attention to the various boxes of cards before plucking a green deck from where it had been contentedly seated. "If you want to get specific, these decks are often categorized as oracle cards. This one, in particular, has about thirty cards and is made up of characters, like vampires and werewolves; the cards are based off of fictional characters in a popular fantasy novel. But if you were doing a reading with the cards you're used to and this one, you could expect to get the same message."

I reached out and took the oracle cards from the woman, inspecting the deck. "Only thirty cards?" There were seventy-eight in the deck Ethan and I primarily used.

"Yes," she admitted. "In fact, one of my favorite decks has only twenty-three cards." I was overcome with the scent of flowers as she leaned in. "It fits in my pocket."

"Huh," I mused.

"Are you sure you want to leave those there?" The woman asked as her eyes flitted to the goddess cards.

I teetered back and forth. With a sparkle in her eye, she retrieved them and replaced them with the deck that was currently in my hand. Almost immediately the goddesses grew heavy in my palm. Like a treasure. "Actually yeah, I'd like to buy these."

The woman grinned as I pulled out the cash and handed it to her. "Good choice," she said with a wink, accepting the money. "Well then, I'll let you look around. Let me know if you have any other inquiries."

"Thanks," I replied. I pocketed the deck into my bag then stood in place, wavering between asking the question burning a hole in my head and simply turning my back to the woman. Clearly, though, the tarot lady could see right through me.

"Is there something else on your mind?"

I centered my gaze over hers. She was sincere. Kind. Somehow, I knew—I could trust her.

"I'm sorry if this is super straight forward—but are you a witch? Like, a real one?" I felt like such a nitwit the second I asked the question, but thankfully the woman didn't jump on me for being inappropriately nosy.

Her gentle eyes relaxed, and she smiled as she clasped her hands together. "Yes, actually."

My head hinged forward a little as I awkwardly tried to find a reply. "Oh." My eyes flitted down to my feet. "So, are you part of a coven then?"

Jamae had said once that the witch community within New York City was pretty tight. I couldn't help but wonder if anyone here had heard of my Grandma Reanin.

The lady tucked her chin as I slowly raised my gaze to meet hers. "I'm a solitary witch, which means I prefer to practice alone, but there are plenty of covens in the city. Are you curious about joining one?"

My tongue moved around in my mouth like I was searching for a popcorn kernel stuck in my teeth. "Maybe. I kind of just found out that my grandma used to be a witch . . . I think." I wasn't sure if reading a book by a witch made you one, but if she *had* been one, it would have made sense. I don't know why, but it just would've. "I was hoping to connect with someone who might've known her back in her witchy days."

The woman's head fell to the side. "Of course you'd be curious about that." She stepped back and scanned the people in attendance. "How old would your grandmother be today?"

I stared down at my fingers that I'd tangled together before my stomach. "She just died a few months ago. She was sixty-eight, I think. But she looked a lot younger than that." My Grandma Reanin looked like she was thirty. It used to drive my mother mad. People always thought they were sisters. My mother looked really young, too, even though her features were the dark to my grandma's light. I guess one could argue that the sharp characteristics belonging to my mother made her look a little older.

Finally, the tarot woman pointed a light brown finger towards a table full of crystal balls. "If I were you, I would go speak with Maggie." My ears perked up at the familiar name. "She's been on the scene for a long time."

"Maggie," I whispered. My gaze followed the woman's pointed finger to where an older woman stood before her merchandise. There was no way that this Maggie was the same Maggie whose book I'd been bound to last night. No way. Even if it was, I wouldn't have known. Maggie O'Brien hadn't put a picture of herself on the back cover like so many other authors did, so there was no way for me to know what my new favorite witch looked like.

"Yes. She owns Mystical Maggie's, an online divination shop. She hardly ever comes out of hibernation anymore except for these events. She used to be quite involved though —she's your woman if anyone is."

Oh god (or goddess, or whatever), please let her be my woman! I thought, as I shot the tarot lady one last final look. "Thanks!"

"You're welcome," she said to my back. I was already off in the direction of optimistic discoveries. "I hope you find what you're seeking!"

"Me too," I huffed.

Within seconds I was standing before a table covered in a dark blue cloth, the color of the night sky just before the moon fully rises. Laid across the table and accompanying shelves were many balls. Some were crystal or rose quartz—obsidian. Some with inclusions, some with cracks, and some as clear as a crystal lake.

"Hello," the older lady named Maggie said as she came to stand opposite me, across the table of orbs.

"Hey," I said back. I tried with all my might not to be creepy, but I couldn't help but look as deep into her eyes as I could.

"Are you interested in scrying, young lady?"

I peeled my gaze from hers and dropped it down to a beautiful, oversized crystal ball. For a moment something materialized . . . an extremely bright ball of light exploding and then coming back together in a black, glittery mass. The vision disappeared as quickly as I'd seen it, leaving me stunned.

"Are you all right, dear? Did you catch a glimpse of something?"

I slowly unglued my eyes from the ball. "No—I mean . . . I don't know." I looked up at her. I didn't have time for whatever *that* had been. I had an agenda to keep. "Um, this might sound kinda weird, but I was hoping you might be able to help me. My name is Tess Moreau, and I was wondering if you've ever heard of a woman named Reanin Wells?"

My breath caught in the back of my throat, for as soon as my grandmother's name fell from my mouth the woman's eyes grew to the size of her merchandise.

"Where did you hear that name?" she whispered gravely.

A cluster of moths freed themselves from my chest as I stared at her. "You're *her*, aren't you? Maggie O'Brien."

She pressed her lips together, then answered. "You've read my book." It wasn't a question, and she didn't sound pleased.

"Yes." I paused for a beat. I wasn't sure what to do or say; I hadn't actually thought that I would meet this person, at least not so quickly.

Maggie lifted her chin as she chirped out her next words. "Disregard anything you think you've learned. Writing that book was a mistake, and you can tell Reanin just that." She then lowered her gaze to where her fingertips had formed into tents over the table.

"I'm afraid I can't do that," I said slowly, waiting for Maggie to look back up at me. "Reanin, my grandmother, was mugged and left for dead three months ago, along with my mother." The woman gave me her full attention. "And just yesterday, I found a copy of your book. Even though I found it more than a little interesting, that's not why I'm here. What I really want to know is why my grandma, whose wardrobe consisted of different shades of creamy whites, wrote her name on the inside cover of a book written by a *witch* who for three hundred pages described how one can confront the shadows in his or her heart."

I was starting to think she wasn't going to answer me, that was until she very gingerly pulled a dark stick from the baggie pocket in her skirt. My jaw unhinged and I was just about to ask her what the hell that thing was, but I didn't get that far. A second later, the sounds of the fair muffled into sudden silence and the lights began to fade until all that was left was a halo around Maggie and me. I stared out into the darkness before returning my attention to the witch.

"What just happened?" When she didn't answer right away, I gazed down at the stick in her hand. "Is that what I think it is?"

"I think it's best if you leave well enough alone," she said in a tone that matched our new surroundings.

My mind fell blank. Leave well enough alone? Did she

understand that she was talking to a teenager right now? I was nothing if not *more* than curious.

I looked back into the darkness, catching a bit of glitter floating around inside it—kind of like what I'd just seen in the crystal ball. "H—How are you doing this?"

But Maggie just repeated herself. "Let it be. Disregard anything you've read of mine and stop worrying about why your grandmother had my book."

"You don't understand—I *have* to know. No one in my family is like me. If she was reading your book, then there is a chance that she was a—"

"What do you mean, nobody in your family is like you?"

I didn't think twice about answering honestly. "I—I can do things. Like magic, I guess." I gazed out at the void she'd conjured. "Though I don't know how to do *that*."

Maggie's stare didn't soften, and she seemed to be looking into me instead of at me. "It is not safe to speak like this—not here. Especially for you."

I narrowed my eyes at her. "What's that supposed to mean?"

She studied my unusual eyes; they were probably turning all sorts of different colors right now. "I'm not even sure," she admitted. "Your safety depends on whether or not *they* know you exist."

"What—who?"

But she simply shook her head, causing everything inside of me to clamp up. "This isn't the time or place."

My skin was starting to feel like it was on fire. I couldn't let this woman out of my grip, not yet. Not today. "Would you at least be open to talking to me later? Wherever you feel like it is safe?"

A muscle twitched in her jaw.

"*Please*," I pleaded. I didn't care about looking weak or

pathetic. I would have groveled at this witch's feet if necessary. "There's no one else who can help me."

Another excruciating moment passed us by in the halo of our enchantment before Maggie replied. "You may come to my studio tonight. At eight." A sigh of relief released from where it was being held captive in my chest. "But I cannot promise to have the answers for what you're seeking. I knew very little about your grandmother. She came to me years ago and I helped her. That is all."

She was lying. I didn't know how I knew that, but I just did. She knew more about my grandmother than she was letting on.

I blinked several times before asking, "What did you help her with?"

But she was done.

The darkness lifted and the fair came back to life. The orange lighting shone down and *so* many voices filtered back into the shuffle. I looked down to find that in my palm was a card: Mystical Maggie's. On it, an address belonging to lower Manhattan.

"I'll see you tonight," Maggie said, before facing a customer who was scoping out a small obsidian ball on a black stand made to look like a raven.

I nodded her way before turning from her table. Not that she saw me or was willing to acknowledge the gesture. But I didn't even care. I had in my hot little hand an address.

"I don't care where this place is," I muttered to myself as I walked off towards the edge of the fair. "I'd head straight into the ninth circle of hell if it meant finding out the truth."

"That's an interesting thing to say."

I nearly jumped out of my skin at the sound of the man's voice.

"Gawd," I hissed, covering my heart with my hand. I hadn't been watching where I was walking, and I'd accidentally stalked right into the land of fortune tellers. "Uh —sorry. I didn't mean to—"

The man who was looking up at me with his undivided attention seemed to glow as he disregarded my apology. "Care to have your fortune told? It sounds like you're carrying around something kind of heavy."

I paused, quickly trying to decide what I should do. I looked up and scanned the crowd for any familiar faces, but I couldn't find any trace of Ethan or Jamae.

"Come on," the guy pushed. "Have a seat."

I stared down at his name tag. All the fortune tellers seemed to have them on. Nick. He looked like a Nick, with his blond hair and glass blue eyes. I didn't find him attractive or anything, but then again, I didn't find many people (whatever their gender) attractive. That was another thing I got bullied for. The kids at school called me—

"Asexual."

I blinked.

He smirked. "I'm legit. Don't let the gold tablecloth fool you."

Had he just read my mind? Like, really? And should I be surprised about that after the theatrics I'd just been through with Maggie? I looked from him to his crystal ball, then to the deck of gold-plated tarot cards he had with him.

"It's nothing to be ashamed of. It's who you are."

"How did you—"

"I told you. I'm the real deal." He patted the table. "Have a seat, Tess."

A puff of air left my chest. "I didn't tell you my—" This time I stopped myself. It was time to realize that I wasn't the only one in this place with actual magic at my disposal. "Okay," I said. "If you're the real deal then why isn't anyone in your line?"

Every other fortune teller had at least five people waiting to hear what they had to say.

His head ticked to the side. "It's the guy thing. But I've got skills that none of them do, plus I've got Lucille."

I raised a brow. "Lucille?"

He glanced at the ball.

"Lucille ball?" I asked hesitantly.

"Um hm."

"Dang," I cursed quietly under my breath as I had a seat. "I have to give you a shot now."

His icy eyes twinkled as his smile widened.

CHAPTER EIGHT

"What's your pleasure?" Nick asked.

I couldn't stop staring at Lucille. Even though I was wildly interested in having my fortune told from the crystal ball, I was more curious about what might happen if he read my cards. Ever since I'd pulled the Three of Swords I'd been walking around with unsteady heartbeats. Sure, Ethan had tried to settle the rhythm by connecting the card to the heartache I could be experiencing from my losses, but I still couldn't shake the feeling that there was more to it than that.

Betrayal . . . that ugly little word kept cycling through my head, and with everything that happened in just the last day and a half, I was more than a little curious about Nick's translation.

I was just about to voice my opinion on the matter, to choose the tarot, when Nick shot me an interesting look. "You seem genuinely interested in Lucille," he said while laying a hand over her as if she was an old friend. "You look at her as I do."

"And how's that?" I asked suspiciously.

"Like you see past the reflection and into her heart."

I didn't flinch as I asked the question. "Does she really have one?" It was a comment that would have earned me a black eye in a dark corner at the Ignatius Academy.

"Of course she does," he replied easily. "Just not in the same way as you or I do."

I hesitated for a second or two before switching gears. "All right, I'll bite. What's she have to say?"

He held my stare for a little longer than what would be classified as 'normal' before pulling the ball from her stand and holding her. As he did, he closed his eyes.

I frowned.

"Don't worry," he said, as if he could still see me. "This is how we communicate."

I remained quiet while he dove into concentration. At first, his expression was neutral, but the longer his eyes were closed, the tighter they became.

Finally, and without opening his eyes, he said, "You're—" His brows furrowed. "You can do things other people can't."

When I didn't say anything, he opened his eyes.

I didn't move an inch in my seat. "Maybe."

He held onto Lucille for what felt like forever more, when in reality, it was maybe two minutes. If that. When he was done, he set her back on her gold pedestal and grappled his hands together over the table.

"You're different." It was all I could do not to scoff—we'd established this already. But then he took it one step further. "Do you know why?"

I shook my head very slowly.

Nick's chest filled then emptied in about a ten second beat. "Let me try and figure out how to word this."

I waited in agony.

"You are special, Tess. In fact, you're probably the most gifted entity in this place, and that's saying something." I bit the side of my cheek as he leaned over the table. "You've got shadows in your blood."

A metaphorical sack of bricks fell on either side of me. I was pretty sure he heard them.

"This isn't new information for you?" he asked.

I gulped. "I—no. I mean, yes. I—I didn't know they were in my blood." *What the hell?* I'd only just started experimenting with shadow work.

Nick kept his gaze uncomfortably steady over mine. "I have a message for you."

"Okay." By this point I was as hinged forward in my chair as he was. When he didn't answer fast enough, I urged him on. "What is it, then?"

"Be careful."

Black. The room became painted in black.

And then it was gold again.

"What?" I asked, my voice mouse-like.

"What do you think of when you think of shadows, Tess?"

Maggie. And then just as quickly my thoughts jumped from her to, *how do you really know my name?*

"I don't know," I answered. "Darkness maybe. Or maybe not." This was starting to feel like an interview. I quickly revised my answer. "Power."

At that, he closed his eyes and took a deep inhale. When he looked at me again, I thought I saw pity radiating from all parts of him. "It is up to you how much of yourself you sacrifice. Giving to the shadows may grant you power, but at what cost?" He paused as if for effect. "Promise me that you'll not let anyone tell you differently."

"I'm not in the habit of making promises to people when I'm not sure of the terms." It was the honest truth.

Nick spread his hands apart. "You are more than a smart girl. I'm only communicating what I know: you are venturing down a path that you may not yet have the footing for. My guess is that you will be pushed to hatch before you learn how to fly."

A slow and disbelieving, "Yeah," fell from my lips. "So, anyway—"

"Just remember this conversation, Tess."

Something like cement filled my guts and I cocked my head to the side, readying to push my feet against the ground and stand. "*Okay.* Look, I appreciate what you're trying to do —I think . . . But there are other things I need to focus on right now, and—"

His eyes flitted to the golden tarot cards. "Why don't we do what you really came here for then."

My next words stilled in the back of my throat. He had me. I desperately wanted to know what those cards had to say. My knees relaxed just a little and my spine curved. "Fine."

"Good," he said, retrieving the tarot and shuffling them in his hands as though they were made of the same material as he was.

I didn't say anything, and neither did he. We stared at one another in a way I couldn't seem to define. It was like he knew me, but I didn't know him. Then again, he was a very talented fortune teller. Legit didn't cover it.

"Would you mind just pulling a single card? I don't want the full reading."

He didn't hesitate. "Of course."

He finished sorting the cards and placed them on top of the table, a golden crystal ball illustrated over the top card. He brought a single hand over the pile and let it levitate over it and without saying a word, used his eyes to communicate—to ask if I was ready. I flicked my head up and down in a quick nod.

And then it reappeared. The Three of Swords. Just as foreboding as it had been the first time.

"Betrayal . . ." The word left my lips before I knew it was

coming. I looked up at Nick; everything I already needed to know was written on his face.

"I believe you're right. And this isn't the first time you've seen this card."

"No."

He waited a few breaths before collecting the card, along with all the others, back into his hands. "Do I need to clarify what lies before you?"

Again, I stated simply, "No."

He laid the cards back down then gave me his full attention. "Look, I'm going to be completely honest with you. You've got swords pointed at you from every direction. You have allies, but you also have enemies. There is no way of telling who is with you and who is using you, but it is in your best interest to look at everyone with a discerning eye. Do you understand me?"

I gulped. "Yes." His warning caused me to feel dizzy. "And when you say that there are people who are *using* me—"

"For your abilities, and for what swims in your blood."

"You're talking about the shadows?"

He pressed his lips together and nodded.

Were these shadows something I'd conjured the other night when I'd been messing around with Maggie's instructions? Had this happened when I'd introduced myself to my actual hatred?

"Are these shadows—are they a bad thing?" Because just last night I had thought they were everything.

"All you need to know is this." He placed his hands over the table, lacing them together. *"Eligere lux."*

My tongue poked my left cheek as my chest rose and fell. "What?"

"Choose the light."

My eyelids lowered part way over my eyes. "As opposed to what?"

"I think that much is obvious."

Was it though? Perhaps it should have been as simple as black and white, but I couldn't help but feel like I was drowning in the shades of gray—then again, that's what shadows were made from.

"Let me ask you this, Nick, since you claim to know so much." He made no move to react. "These shadows in my blood—are they a part of me or have I caused them to find me?"

"I believe you were born this way."

"Then how do I choose the light, as you have predicted I should, if I was born between the worlds of light and dark? If what I am *made of* is the in between?"

The sound of the fair seemed to fizzle as a thick silence filled the space between him and me. The blood around my heart froze from Nick's icy stare, and though he glowed, I felt anything but warm in his presence.

I inhaled a ragged breath and stood, pulling a couple twenties from the pocket of my school uniform, and tossing them on the table. "I should go. Thanks for the perspective." No wonder Ethan and Jamae never wanted me to read for them; this was a bust. Sometimes it's better not to know.

Nick looked at the bills spread out over the table. "I don't want your money, Tess."

"Yeah well," –I pressed the pads of my fingers down over each bill and scooted them closer to him— "I don't want you to know my name, but some things are apparently out of our control. Take the money. Give it to charity if you must."

And then, before he could say another unwanted word that would just further knot my guts together, I turned and strutted away. His gaze never left my back, that much I could be sure of, not until I meandered further enough into the crowd that he lost track of me—and man, did I want that guy to lose track of me. It took a good five to ten minutes for my heartbeats to regulate to their normal rhythm.

Once I was nothing more than just another follower in the crowd of witches and whatever else these people considered themselves, I tried to pretend that I hadn't been warned (twice now) that I might be in danger. Instead, I focused on browsing the merchandise flowing before me like ocean tides —nothing but magical paraphernalia for as far as the setting sun.

Unable to locate Jamae or Ethan right away, I made three passes around and through the fair, carefully keeping my distance from the land of fortune tellers. I'd kept the tarot booth lady's wisdom close to my heart as I perused through the crystals; she'd mentioned that these sorts of things often choose us, other than the other way around. Jamae and Ethan both swore by the healing and protective properties of crystals. I was thinking it wouldn't be a bad idea to snag one or two, or a few, if any of them called to me. If there was a time for a guard dog in the form of a rock, I'd say now was that time.

I was just beginning to think that I had no emotional connection to any of these crystals when a table I hadn't seen the first time down this aisle grabbed my attention. The guy manning it leaned in over his merch as I lingered in place over a very interesting necklace.

As I picked it up, connecting to the heaviness of the three crystals fused together, he said to me in a fateful, far-out voice, "They choose you, you know."

I looked up at him with only my eyes. "I've been told." My gaze suffered back and forth between the man and the stones in my hand. The seller was older and gruff looking, his skin greenish, his teeth yellow, and he smelled like he'd never heard of a shower. "Is this one crystal or three that have somehow grown together?"

"They were born in the handle of the same foil who took

their hearts." He nodded his head like a stoner in deep revelation. "You called to them. They heard. They've been waiting."

"Right," I said after a second or two. Looking back down at them, I pulled at the leather string that served as the necklace. There wasn't a price tag. "How much?"

He shook his head and held out a discolored hand. "They belong to you."

I opened my mouth to reply but nothing came out. After a small round of indecision, I finally decided to just go with it. Letting my palm close around them, I said to the odd man before me, "Uh, thanks."

He nodded back, his mouth parted enough that I could see his tongue glistening inside his purplish mouth. I started to turn away but decided Jamae might want to have his info for her shop. She was always on the hunt for a good crystal dealer.

"Hey, do you have a card or some—" But as I spun around, I realized he was gone. I was staring at a lonesome space between a table of books and a woman selling faery and dragon statues, and as I attempted to gain my balance and sanity (because *what?*) I bumped into a wisp of a girl who was holding a light blue dragon to her chest.

"Oh—sorry," I muttered.

The girl, who looked to be about my age, lifted her gaze to meet mine. The second our eyes met, my breath stilled in my chest, then froze before slowly evaporating. Her irises, which had been blue, flashed purple, then back to the color of the sky. The lightness of her eyes against her darker skin made her look majestic.

"Hi," was all she said. Flirty . . . her tone had totally been flirty.

I hesitated before taking a step back. Only because it felt like there were magnets between this girl's chest and mine; like there was an unseen force pulling us together.

"Hi," I retorted—my lips twitching. *Don't grin, you fool. Stay cool.* "Um, cool dragon." *Gawd, you sound like a moron!*

The girl grinned, and for a second, I thought I spied her ears poking out from her short pixie cut (and they were razor sharp), but in the same second they'd caught my attention, the tips faded (like they hadn't wanted to be seen). The girl held up the dragon as she said, "Thanks. He reminds me of my familiar."

I realized I'd been holding my shoulders up to my ears and slowly let them fall. "Your what?" I knew what a familiar was. *Why was I stuttering so much?*

"My pet," she said, her bouncy expression unrelenting.

Before I knew it, she had laid a hand over my shoulder. "There's something recognizable about you."

My mind was completely blank. I'd never come face to face with someone who had caused the blood in my veins to dance before. I had a feeling that my eyes were shifting colors like crazy. But just as I was sorting through lame retorts to offer this beautiful stranger, her eyes grew, and panic seemed to overtake her. I followed her gaze through the crowd to find a strikingly built woman with short light pink hair and dark skin; she was staring bullets at us.

"Gotta go—catch ya later," she said.

A second later she was gone, and after searching through the crowd of new age faces, so was the pink-haired lady.

I stood in place for a few seconds, letting my heartbeat regulate. When it appeared that the brief encounter was only that—brief—I reopened my now sweaty palm and hung my new necklace around my neck.

"Well then," said the lady manning the table of statues, "your friend took off without payment. Don't suppose you want to pick up her tab?"

"Oh, I don't know her. I literally just bumped into—" The woman had her arms crossed over her chest. I was just another punk kid to her. "You know what, whatever. How much was the dragon?"

"Sixty bucks."

I rolled my eyes, then pulled out the cash. I'd just gotten a free necklace, so I could stand to pick up the dough for a runaway hottie. My hand got stuck in my bag as the words I'd just thought returned to flutter around my head. *Hottie* . . . it was the first time I'd ever found anyone, regardless of their gender, attractive.

"Well?" asked the woman with firm brows, "you got it or not?"

"Uh—yeah," I retorted, pulling out a wad of cash and handing her three crumpled twenties.

"Thanks," she said. She was pretty unappreciative, seeing as I'd just paid off someone else's debt. But I didn't hang around long enough to respond. All I wanted to do was kick dirt and get the hell out of this place (especially since it appeared *my* unicorn had just disappeared).

I found my friends shortly after that. Ethan had an arm full of books and both him and Jamae were both scouring a table littered with athames.

"Yo, where have you been," Ethan asked.

"I—uh," I stopped short. All I could think as I looked at the two of them staring back at me, was *were these my allies or my enemies?* Collecting myself, I tucked a stray piece of hair behind my ear. "I was going to have my palm read but the lines are super long, and I got sick of waiting. I've just been walking around."

"We've probably been stalking each other without even knowing it," Jamae started, but just as quickly did a one-eighty. "Whoa!" She lunged forward, drawing her eyes directly across from my new necklace. "Where'd you get that thing?"

My gaze floated over the heads and tents of all the vendors. I gestured out into the vastness of it all with my chin.

"Somewhere over there." I didn't want to say out loud that I'd gotten it from a ghost tent. It already sounded too stupid in my head.

Meanwhile, Jamae was practically drooling as she listed off what I hadn't yet ventured to guess at. "Black tourmaline, labradorite, and blue kyanite."

For the first time I noticed that Ethan's stance had cracked a little. When he spoke, he sounded a little shook. "That's just surface though."

"Yeah," Jamae said, standing up straight, her gaze still locked over the three fused stones. "It's got one hell of a protection charm. There's quartz in there too." She took a step back so both her and Ethan's elbows touched, then raised her eyes to meet mine. "Magnifies its power."

I flicked a finger over the nearest stone. "Protection charm?"

"For themselves," Ethan muttered.

"Okay," I stated calmly, but irritation was beginning to seep slowly in. "What's going on?"

"It's just a protection charm," Jamae said, blinking a few times too many. "A wicked cool one at that." She turned and shoved her boyfriend, rattling a few of the books in his grip. "Right Ethan?"

He clasped a falling hardcover then hugged the literature tighter. "Uh—yeah. Just haven't seen anything like that in a while."

Ignoring their strange behavior, I looked down at the stone Jamae had called blue kyanite. I hadn't heard of that one before. "What's this one do?"

"It keeps people from messing with you," Ethan answered quickly.

"It also aids in concentration," Jamae added. "Helps you keep your wits when you're under pressure." She nodded as she added, "That, right there, is heavy." She glanced at Ethan.

"And you thought this place was going to be a waste of time."

His bloodshot eyes bugged out as he shrugged his shoulders. Gawd, his eyes really were red—they hurt to look at. Both him and Jamae had started to look a little like they were falling apart lately; the way grown-ups often did when they were super stressed out. I couldn't help but worry that this was about the same thing it always was—keeping the shop open. The color of their skin even seemed off today.

Seemingly trying to offset the mood, Jamae perused my arms for any additional baggage. "What else did you get?"

"Uh, just some oracle cards," I answered, casually bottling up the truth as my thoughts ran about an octave above their usual tenor. *And a ton of heavy ass information.*

"Cool," Ethan said. "So what do you guys say? Wanna get out of here and hit a movie?"

I nodded a little too quickly. I loved frequenting the dollar theatre with my adult friends on any day, but that was exactly the distraction I needed right now. I was anxious to meet Maggie, but eight o'clock was a long time from now, and it wasn't going to get here any faster if I went home and stared at the walls.

"It's my treat, though," I said as we started for the double doors that would take us to the street. Jamae started to argue but I immediately shut her down. "You guys bought my ticket. It's only fair." I was thankful that they didn't put up a fight. Out of the three of us, I was the last one who needed to save her coin.

As we were leaving the fair, the sensation of a curtain being pulled behind us—like a shadow flitting from one corner to the other—caused invisible fingers to tickle the back of my neck. I paused, the three of us just outside the double doors that we'd used to lead us to the city sidewalk.

"Sup?" Jamae asked, looking confused.

I stared back at the door, watching it as it closed, then followed the brick walls that made up the building on either side of it. If I stretched my eyes, I could've sworn I saw the bricks wiggle, as if an invisible creature was sliding against its surface.

"Nothing," I muttered. "Just my eyes playing tricks on me, I guess."

Jamae and Ethan shared a look, then Jamae wrapped a sisterly arm around my shoulder and pulled me along. "We've been educating you on far too many things lately. Let's go catch a sappy rom com and leave the night terrors for another day."

I nodded. "Right." I did want to leave them for another day, but something deep inside was shouting that this was a luxury, that for once, I would not be able to afford.

CHAPTER NINE

Eight o'clock took *forever* to roll around. As soon as it was close enough to the marked hour, I ordered an Uber and headed straight to Maggie's studio. A residence (because I had to assume the witch lived there) that was nothing more than a simple purple door with the numbers 420 on it. It was sandwiched between a dispensary and an insurance office. My age surfaced for a second and I giggled at the thought that this address really should have been given to the dispensary instead.

Gathering myself, I double checked the address one more time and looked over my shoulders—I'd felt stalked all day because of all the unnerving warnings. But just as I was about to knock on the door, it opened from the other side.

Maggie didn't even say hello before hammering out, "Did anyone follow you here?"

I stared back at the whites of her eyes as they reflected off the dim streetlight looming like a reaper on the corner of the avenue. "I don't know. I don't think so."

She looked back and forth before stating in a tone just as unwelcoming as the first, "I'm positive you were."

My brows sank. "Why would you have invited me here then?"

She didn't answer. "Did you tell anyone you were coming?"

"No." I hadn't even told Ethan and Jamae, even though I was burning up inside with the desire to divulge *all* the details from my bizarre morning. When Maggie didn't soften her expression, but hardened it, I added, "No one knows I'm here. I promise." A promise I was starting to second guess. Like what if Maggie wasn't my ally? What if she was one of the one's holding a sword to my back? I mean, I didn't really know a thing about her apart from what she'd written. Then again, she wasn't trying very hard to get me to trust her. If anything, she was doing me a favor and she wasn't very excited about it.

Suddenly her gaze of discontent fell to the crystals hanging around my neck. "Those are new. *Old*, but new."

I raised my hand to the necklace but didn't touch it. "You like it? I got it from the fair today."

"It's carrying an interesting vibe," she said, sounding very much like the old hippie she appeared to be. "I suspect there's a story there."

"What *kind* of story?"

"I don't know . . . Its lips are sealed."

"That's an odd thing to say," I related truthfully.

Her gaze shot back up to mine. "Yes, well . . ." Her lips pursed together as she swung open the door, just enough for me to squeeze through. "Come in—quickly."

I let her usher me into a stairway that led to nothing more than three bare walls.

"What the actual—"

The door shut and locked behind us as Maggie shoved her way between my shoulders and the narrow opening to the staircase. "Hang on." Standing before me, she glanced back over her shoulder—in her hand, the same stick from earlier. "I sell online only these days, other than trade shows and fairs that is. I do my bidding here, but it is also where I call home. Safety is key."

My mouth moved around the words that I refused to say out loud—*your bidding?*

I followed reluctantly as she began walking up the stairs. When we reached the top, she tapped the stick against the doorless wall until a keyhole appeared. She stuck the end, of what I could no longer deny was a magic wand, into the hole and turned it; a knob and the outline of a door appeared. She opened it. As she stepped into the hidden space, she turned and faced me. "Well, come on then."

My eyes had to be the size of planets. "How?" It was all I could manage. My brain was already full from the day I'd had, and I had an inkling that it was about to struggle with keeping the contents (of whatever else was coming) within its containment.

Maggie's patience was so obviously already at the end of its rope as she waved me in a second time. "Just come in, would you?"

I hesitantly lifted one foot and set it on the other side of the threshold. When it didn't automatically burst into flames, I continued with the other. As soon as I was inside, Maggie swished her wand at the door, closing it.

"What's happening?" I asked in a sing-song voice.

She began moving around, pulling together a couple of chairs around a small table. "You said you read my book, yes?"

"Yeah."

"There are other places one can access in and out of the world you're accustomed to, and not all of them are in the shadows. This was just a blank spot." She groaned as she pushed one of the chairs closer to the table. "I've been using it for years. Of course, because of recent news" –she turned towards me and raised her brows— "I may be in need of finding a new situation. Not that I want to. It's quiet here, there are no solicitors, and it really cuts down on thievery."

I took a moment to absorb my new surroundings. Maggie's studio looked a lot like any other shitty one room apartment in the city. It was on the smaller side and had no windows. There was a full-sized bed off in a nook that served as a bedroom and the rest of the place was lined in shelves, brimming with crystal balls.

"Why would you need to move?" I questioned, still taking it all in.

Maggie went to the area that must've served as her kitchen and tapped her wand against a ceramic blue teapot, before reaching for two mugs and bringing them over to the small table. "Reanin is dead, and who knows if they've caught *your* scent. Hunters will be on the move, that is if they haven't already started sniffing around. I've been out of the shadow opening and closing business for years, but they don't believe me." She set the mugs down and filled each one with steaming tea. "I knew I should have trusted my gut and stayed away from that fair." She shook her head. "'Tis the reason I hardly leave. Though everyone needs some fresh air from time to time, and an exchange of energy." She took a breath. "I never should have written that blasted book. Ruined everything."

My ears were *more* than tingling as I had a seat opposite the old woman. "Hunters?"

"We'll get to that in a bit." She shifted to the side of the seat she was in and pulled a candle from her baggy pocket like it wasn't an unusual thing to do, then proceeded to set it over the table where it balanced perfectly without a stand and lit it. The flame became the color of my ever-changing eyes.

"That's groovy," I said, stealing a line from Jamae.

"Yes, well," Maggie said, taking a sip from her tea then sitting back in her chair. "It is needed."

Without asking what *that* meant, only because I needed all the other details way more, I asked wistfully, "How do you do it? The magic, I mean. It's like, *real* for you."

She laid her wand across her lap. "I wouldn't think this is all that unusual since you've mentioned you have abilities."

"Not like this," I admitted.

She sighed. "It's *real* for you too. In fact, it's real for everyone. It's just a matter of whether they can be taught to access the parts of their DNA that have either been lost or covered up. I come from a lineage whose DNA was altered long ago—making it easy for me to access the elements freely."

"You mean to say that you come from a line of *actual* witches?"

She shrugged her left shoulder forwards in what I construed to be agreement.

"Far out."

She made a face. "You don't speak like most kids your age." She paused. "You don't radiate the same energy as them either. Your vibrations are quite high."

"I'm not on the spectrum if that's what you're insinuating. I've been tested, like, five thousand times." No one could ever understand why I was so weird.

"That's not what I meant," Maggie said. The flame grew a little and she shook her head. "We must proceed. I cannot be sure how much time we have."

"Okay," I said, twisting my hands together in my lap (wishing that I, too, had a magical wand to hold). "You said my grandmother came to *you*."

"She did."

"When?"

"October of 1977. It was a Thursday." She crossed her

ankles under the chair and licked her lips before continuing. "Reanin came to me because she found my book. She believed that because of what I'd written, I could help her. And I did, though in the end, I don't believe she would have said the same." She looked down into her hands before returning her attention to me. "The grandmother you think you knew wasn't real. Whatever scene she painted for you was only ever held together to placate her situation, which for clarification purposes, was dire."

Heavy.

"Are you saying she came to you because she read your book, or that she read your book and came to you because of something else?"

"The last one," Maggie replied easily. "Reanin didn't need to confront her shadows for they were already a part of her—they were in her blood."

My ears more than burned. In a raspy voice, I asked, "What's that mean?"

She inhaled a deep breath and lifted her chin. "She was married to the shadows. The only reason she came out from them at all was because she and her mate ran into a bit of a snag, and the world they'd created was in jeopardy."

I had forgotten how to blink at this point. "The—The world they created?" *Her mate?*

I could've sworn the old lady was taking pleasure in my astonishment. "You heard me correctly." Then, readjusting her hips, she leaned to one side of her chair, continuing to rest her hands over the wand in her lap. "Tess, your grandmother was the reason I stopped doing shadow work. Not because what she and Kage created was the darkest dimension I'd ever seen, but because it was the cleverest. In the wrong hands, the magic that has been rumored to exist within the confines of The Hall —well, it could be world ending at its worst."

"Wait a second—" There were so many things she'd just said that required explanations. "Who's Kage?"

Once more, she took a deep breath, except this time she breathed in through her mouth and waited until her ribcage was lifted and her thin lips were closed before letting the air sift through her nose. "Well then, I suspect he would be your grandfather, now, wouldn't he?"

The walls seemed to shrink around us. "I don't have a grandfather," I whispered.

The woman raised her brows. "Everyone has a grandfather, Tess." Her gaze rolled down over my shoulders until it met the floor. "And I suspect he's rather annoyed right now. He'll be more so when he learns that your grandmother has been murdered."

"Whoa," I said, holding up a hand. "She was mugged, not murdered." Was there a difference? It felt like there was.

"You said she was left for dead. Therefore, I was left to assume that there was a body." Then she muttered so softly I could barely hear her, "A body, I'm sure, that was missing its lifeline."

Ignoring whatever *that* meant, I said, "There were two bodies."

She half smirked, half sneered as she jumped on the line, "But you only cared about one of them."

I wiggled my brows before settling on a decent frown.

"Sorry," she said unconvincingly. "You're wearing your truths on your sleeve and I'm inherently intuitive." She let her comment settle for a moment before moving on. "May I assume that your mother and your grandmother were stabbed through the heart?"

"How did you know that?"

She sighed as if this was getting rigorous. "The only way to kill the sort of magic that flowed through your grandmother's veins, and I suspect your mother's—and perhaps yours—is by piercing the heart."

"Like a vampire?" I said in disbelief, my eyebrow reaching for the ceiling of the enchanted space.

"I suppose," Maggie answered coolly. "Though it wasn't blood Reanin lived from—at least when I knew her. While she was living in The Hall, she was not in need of anything to keep her veins filled and substance circulating. However, when she was forced to close the entrances and exits of her and Kage's world, she began to crave more than just air to survive on. It's odd for a human to transform as she did, but stranger things have happened. Then again, she started out about as human as me."

My breath was being held hostage as I hinged forward in my seat. Was it safe to let my head explode now? What the hell was *The Hall*? But more importantly— "What did my grandmother need to survive?"

A look of unsettled satisfaction settled in over the witch's face. And if there was one thing I was absolutely positive of, it was that Maggie was a full-fledged witch. In every sense of the word. "Souls." She waited for the shock of the semi-truck she'd just rammed into my tiny little hand-me-down sedan to wear off (which was ever so polite of her) before going on. "In The Hall, they refer to them as sirens. Humans are very attracted to these creatures, and it was this attraction that reminded Reanin of the old tales she'd read once upon a time. She named them, and then she became one of them."

"What . . . the . . . fuck?"

Maggie seemed to be enjoying the show from her end; watching me wiggle around like a worm who had been spliced through with the end of a gory and gut drenched hook. But I didn't care about all that. What I cared about was finding out more.

"Look," she finally said, "like I told you, I only dealt with your grandmother on a personal level for a small bit of time. After I learned about The Hall—"

"*What is that?* You keep repeating 'The Hall' like I should know what it is."

Her hands danced over and under one another—still clasped protectively over her wand. "It's where she met Kage. The Hall of Shadows is an underworld accessed via a portal, or a series of portals—just like many of the ones I used to open and close. As I was saying, Reanin came to me because her world was in trouble. So was she and so was Kage. I showed her how to close portals and where I hid the doors once I was sure they were locked. The problem was, The Hall didn't just have one door, one entrance—but many. And something like that was much too strong to stay silent." Maggie's expression tightened. "Kage has a brother, and for the sake of shortening this tale into something you can easily digest, let's just say this: the two of them didn't just grow apart. A bridge grew between them. A bridge that only those who aren't afraid to face their shadows may cross. Still, across that plank—where darkness meets light and reflects something truly different—there is something quite valuable. Something so desirable that even Kage's brother—an individual who considers himself one with the light—would create a world full of madness to get to."

I crossed my brows. "I'm not sure I'm following you."

Maggie lifted her chin. "If your grandmother was truly murdered, which I believe she was, then it would have been by his hand. Kage's brother. Either that, or one of his followers."

"Followers?"

"Yes. Ever since he caught a whiff of the raw power tucked inside his brother's world, he's had a line of drool coming from the side of his mouth." She turned her head to the side, thinking out loud. "It's always the ones who shout to all four corners how strong they are that are really the weakest." I was in the middle of trying to piece together a response to all this nonsense when Maggie pinched her pointer finger between her teeth. Before long she returned her attention to me. "I've no doubt to believe that he is our culprit, but how he found your grandmother is very puzzling. Reanin wasn't cut out to make mistakes. She hid quite well for plenty of years. If he found her, it was because she wanted him to—or—"

"Or what?" I asked when she was taking too long.

"Unless . . . I wonder, Tess—what was your mother like?"

The flame between us grew a hair taller, but Maggie was so invested in my reaction that she didn't seem to notice. "Why the hell does it matter what my mother was like? What it sounds like to me, is that you're insinuating that my grandmother was some sort of evil succubus, and that my family tree has roots in hell."

Maggie dropped her hand back into her lap. "There is no such place as hell. It's siren, not succubus, and evil isn't a word I really care for . . . even considering the subject of our conversation."

I was starting to get carsick from all this weaving back and forth. "*You walked away from your work with the shadows.* You got shook. How can you say what you discovered, with or without my grandma, wasn't evil?"

Maggie recentered her gaze over mine. "I didn't care for the way they were doing things. It was almost like a corporation down there. I'd already pitched in too much, helping to create an appealing entrance for any curious soul to enter . . . It wasn't and isn't for me. I prefer to stand on neutral ground these days, that's all."

That's all? I'd spent the previous night reading all about how this very woman had walked into places the human mind would have more than a little trouble deciphering. And her home— "We are living and breathing inside a portal that you opened, *here and now*. You're still at it. How can you judge one portal from the next?"

"This is the last one I ever opened, and unless I am forced to move, there will be no more. At least not from my wand. This space isn't made from light or dark matter—it's a pocket."

"A pocket?"

She nodded.

"Right," I said, unconvinced. I turned and looked at the door. "And if I wanted out, could I just turn the knob and expect to leave? Or is that simply a glamour to make me feel like I haven't been lured into a strange dimension?"

She all but rolled her eyes. "If anyone was doing the luring, it wasn't me. And yes, it's a door. If you can see it, you can open it."

"Fine," I replied shortly. Then backtracking, I said, "You showed my grandma where to hide the doors to the portal she came from. So, where is it? The entrance to this Hall of Shadows."

Maggie narrowed her eyes. "Believe it or not, I didn't agree to meet with you so that I could hand over a broken entrance to a world that I never wanted anything to do with in the first place."

"Then why did you agree to this meeting?"

She stilled for a minute. "I was curious . . ." There was more; I could tell that there was so much more. But just as Maggie prepared to answer me, the flame between us began to move erratically. Seconds later there were footsteps on the opposite side of the door.

My eyes widened. "Who else knows about this place?"

"My wife—" She shot me a sideways glance. "And whoever else you led into this den."

"I didn't lead anyone—"

"Shhh." Maggie put a finger over her lips, shushing me.

She listened for another moment before adding, "Damn it all. Come." She reached for my shoulder and pulled me up, dragging me towards one of the shelves closest to us. Pointing her wand at one of the crystal balls, she whispered something haughtily under her breath, and when the orb began to ripple from the very center of the thing, she literally pushed me towards it. "Hide," was all I heard as I opened my mouth to scream.

CHAPTER TEN

What happened next was a blur of swirling clouds and rippling tides that left my skin as dry as the desert. Maggie hadn't pushed me aggressively into a shelf of glass balls—she'd shoved me *into one of them*. The orb swallowed me whole, and all at once, the world turned gray and silent. It was cold . . . but not entirely uncomfortable.

I marched forward over the dirty sand of whatever hellish world she'd tossed me into like I was nothing more than a sack of garbage. Immediately, I was encompassed by a swirling fog that fuzzed out one of my five senses, and the wind carried some sort of debris that tore at my cheeks. I carefully held out my hands. As I scrunched my fingers into my palms then fanned them back out, my thoughts began to race. *What was this place? Why had Maggie thrown me into it?*

Still blinded by the fog, I jumped to the side as something scampered on the ground not terribly far from where I stood. I was just about to hunch down, curl into a ball for protection, when the mist and wind dissipated—my feet back on solid ground.

I found myself back in Maggie's eyes. They were as hard and cold as the place she'd just sucked me back out of.

"What . . . was . . . that?" I asked, my chest heaving.

The witch remained stiff as a board as she grabbed my shoulder with unnecessary roughness and began ushering me towards the exit. "You must go."

"What?" I all but squealed, snagging my arm away and facing her, my teeth bared. "You can't just open a can of worms like the *Hall of Shadows* and expect me to gather them all back up without knowing how. And what the hell was *that* about?" I gestured back to the shelves she'd just pulled me from and stuck a finger out in the direction of the glass ball I'd literally just been inside of.

Maggie heaved a sigh, her arms by her sides, along with her wand. She used her chin to gesture to where we'd been sitting just moments ago. I followed her gaze to find that the candle she'd lit was no longer burning. "The flame went out, which means our time is up. You need to go, and I advise you to watch your back. You will most likely be followed."

Yeah, okay. No.

"What does any of that even mean?"

She offered no advice as she continued to stand there, watching me like an angry statue.

My eyes flitted from hers to a shelf full of crystal balls then back to hers. I had to keep the conversation going—I couldn't get thrown out. Not yet.

"Who came to the door?"

"It was my wife." She gestured to an orange Tabby sitting on the kitchen counter as if it was his priority to guard it. "We share custody of the cat."

Juanita . . . I didn't want to announce that I knew more about her situation than I should. At least not yet.

Playing dumb, I questioned, "She doesn't live here with you?"

"No. We're separated. It's complicated." She kept her stone-cold stare over mine. "Look, that was a false alarm, but while she was here the flame went out. We must be cautious."

I shook my head in confusion. "Wouldn't that mean that she was the one we need to be wary of?"

"Not exactly. It means danger is *coming*." She pursed her lips together before going on. "Tess, you are connected to one of the largest underworlds there is in this universe, and not only that but your blood is thick with shadows."

"It doesn't make sense . . . My mother never once exhibited any clue that she was anything other than human. And if she had magic at her disposal, she was super good at hiding it. The same goes for my grandma."

Maggie blinked slowly and methodically. "Your grandmother was in hiding, and your mother could easily have hidden her abilities from you and everyone else. Reversely, your mother could've been ordinary; it is not uncommon for hereditary magic—that which swims in the blood—to skip a generation. You have already declared that you can do things—"

"I can more than do things." This was my way to keep her invested. No witch could turn from the intrigue I held at my fingertips. I was sure of it. "I can bring things back. I—I can return ashes to what they were before they were burned. I can—"

She'd become extremely rigid. "You can do what?"

I lowered my chin just a smidge. "I can read ashes like tea leaves, but I can also manipulate them."

Without warning, the old woman lunged forward and hastily gripped my face with her hands. Ice cubes ran up and down my spine as she glued her eyes into mine, and for a second, I saw something reflected from her pupils. A vision of myself . . . older. Red eyes, a wicked smile, and no—that wasn't right. It couldn't have been me.

A dark shadow seemed to fall over the old woman's shoulders as she backed away. "Oh, dear child." My heart fell as she walked around me and reached for the doorknob. "It is time for you to leave."

My entire *everything* sunk. "What—no. Why?"

"I've told you," she said, without looking me in the eye.

"What did you just see in me?" I stammered out.

She refused to meet my eyes as she muttered, "This world is not safe."

"From what?" I exploded.

Her breath was shaky as she continued to stare down at her feet.

"Look lady, you can't just tell me there are hunters out there, and maybe even some kind of army out to get me. You just went on and on about a whole load of fantastical crap and now—"

Her gaze shot up. "None of what I said was a lie, and it most definitely wasn't fantastical crap." The blacks of her eyes were near burning as she slowly removed her hand from the doorknob. "Kage's brother has started something that can't be undone, something that may never cease to be. For more years than you can count, he has gathered covens from all over the country, and most likely the world, and convinced them to follow his instruction. He has lured witches from his gossip about the great power that can be found in The Hall. These covens are now cults. The witches who have been gathered are nothing more than blinded followers. All he has to do is stick a scent to your hide and you are as good as captured."

I waited a second before I asked, "What kind of great power are they after, and does it truly exist in the Hall of Shadows?"

"All I feel comfortable saying is that there is magic in the shadows unlike anything anyone may ever find on the surface."

"What kind of magic?"

She more than sighed. "I am unsure. I never allowed myself to get close enough to see it."

I squinted at her. "You're lying." She wasn't the only one who was good at reading souls.

She narrowed her eyes, and when she spoke, she did so in a shaky, apprehensive voice. "Even if I told you what the hunters are after, it wouldn't matter. The entrances to The Hall are permanently closed."

My head might as well have been shoved through a wall. I couldn't understand this witch. Not for the life of me. Why even agree to see me at all if this was how it was going to end?

"What happened to you, Maggie? Why do you live like this now?"

"It wasn't what happened to *me*," she shot back.

"Then what was it?"

She raised her gaze to fit securely into mine, then spit out two words. "My wife."

I bit the inside of my cheek. Her wife, also known as the high priestess of Ethan and Jamae's coven.

Swords. I had swords at my back.

"I made the mistake of allowing her to be there the night I met with Reanin. The night we completed the spell to close the doors to The Hall." Her eyelashes fluttered as she looked away. "I wrote it myself in that book that led you to me. When it comes to the dimensions that can be found in the shadows, trust no one. I should have known better." She heaved a sigh. "I agreed to help your grandmother, and that's what I did. The Hall of Shadows is huge. To close its doors—it required a lot of energy. That's why I allowed Juanita, my wife, to be there. Three was better than two. I thought I could trust her. But once we'd finished, she asked to hold the cards in her hands . . . As soon as they were in her grasp, she could *feel* the magic I had spoken about. I knew as soon as I saw that look wash over her that she wanted nothing more than to fully experience that hidden magic, and she wasn't going to stop until she had it. I had no choice—I had to destroy those things. If I didn't, she would've moved mountains to get to them, and she knew enough about portals from living with me that she could've succeeded in finding them."

I leaned in closer to Maggie. "Cards?"

Her mouth turned to the side. "In order to close a portal, you have to make the entrance physical. It is only then that you can hide it in a pocket."

Her explanation spun around in my head on an endless reel. And then my gaze shifted to the shelves and shelves of crystal balls. This wasn't just her inventory . . . The fingers from my right hand felt for my mouth as I muttered the blaring truth. "They are in there, *in here* . . . all the portals you've ever closed."

Were the supposed cards in here too?

As if reading my mind, she looked at me with a face full of war paint and said, "Don't even bother searching for them. I destroyed the Hall of Shadows, Tess, and then I told your grandmother what I am going to tell you right now. Leave. Don't come back. I am finished with this work." She reached for the doorknob again, but this time she pulled it open. "Isn't it bad enough that my marriage was destroyed? My wife has never been able to get over that shot of heroin she felt from just a hint of what that hidden magic could offer."

I was dedicated to my current lane. "You destroyed them. But did you keep them?"

Nothing.

Were these cards the reason my grandmother left her apartment to me?

Maggie refused to answer.

I hung my head and shook it. "All I wanted from you, Maggie, was an explanation. I'm not a threat. I'm just a girl."

"No," she said gravely, "you're not."

My gaze shot back up to find that her eyes were hardened and full of distrust. I wanted to wring her neck; not because I despised her, but because she had all the tools to help me, and she wouldn't. "Are you sure you didn't gain your abilities from one of the darker worlds you traveled through? Because all you are to me right now is straight wicked."

"My magic was passed down to me just like yours, Tess. But mine didn't come from the shadows. Not that there aren't those who have traded part of themselves to the place between dark and light. But no, I am not one of those *things*. Now, please go."

She was adamant, so I left—the door nearly slamming shut over my heels. I knew there was no going back, but still, I might as well have been moving my feet through hardening concrete with each step I took towards that purple door. I'd peered back over my shoulders only once, and it was to find that 'the pocket' had already gone. I wasn't welcome back. Which was way more than just infuriating. That woman had an endless disposal of information, and I could benefit from all of it.

But it was of no use. Mystical Maggie had been turned off from the shadows because my family had created an underworld corporation of sorts (whatever that all meant). I mean, *wow*. And then the woman had taken it upon herself to demolish what she'd helped my grandmother create. But how? I mean, there was only one reasonable explanation and that was—

"Oh my god," I said, my soles back on the cold New York City sidewalk. "She said she destroyed the cards . . ." It hadn't rung any bells before, but now the alarms wouldn't stop ringing.

Up until the point Maggie met me, she thought the key to unlocking the doors to the Hall of Shadows had been tossed and thrown away. But then I'd gone and admitted what I could do. Maggie didn't just see me as Reanin's granddaughter, heir to an entire underworld. No, I was also the key to unlocking it. I could return ash to its original form and that terrified the witch, because Maggie had *burned* my grandmother's world to the ground.

CHAPTER ELEVEN

The television was blaring from the center of the house when I arrived back home, which meant only one thing, my dad was docked. I checked my phone —it *was* after nine-thirty. It was odd getting in after him.

It wasn't unusual for my dad to eat supper at this late hour, or simply be sitting before a plate of cold, uneaten food. He often claimed that he was too exhausted to eat by the time he was able to break away from his heavy clientele, but I knew the real truth: he drank his dinner. I mean, it didn't show; I don't think I'd ever even seen him drunk. But he was always meeting his high-end clients at ritzy Manhattan bars.

I moved around the house like a serpent until I found him sitting at the same dining room table where he'd upped and left me that morning. Just as I suspected, he was watching the news. His dinner companions, a plate of untouched lasagna and a nearly empty bottle of red. *How long had he been sitting there?*

"Sorry I'm late," I said, sulking down into the chair opposite him where there was a second cold helping of pasta.

He pushed aside his uneaten portion and downed what

was left of his wine before pulling up a white napkin and wiping at his mouth—traces of red dotting the paper. We'd stopped using the cloth ones after my mom died. Dad and I weren't as concerned with outward appearances as much as she'd been. His gaze fell over the necklace I'd scored from the fair and stayed on each stone for a beat too long, before he asked, "Where were you all day?"

I folded my napkin over my lap before looking back up at him. "Out."

He rolled his eyes towards the flatscreen mounted on the wall and allowed his head to follow.

I pulled at the lasagna with my fork but didn't load any of the noodles or homemade pasta sauce onto the utensil. Mary Joe put carrots in her sauce . . . I was partial to the act. My appetite had been crap lately, but that was normal considering the string of unfortunate events that had been occurring in my life.

"Look Dad, I'm sorry I've been kind of an ass lately. There are things I want to tell you, but I don't think you'd understand. It makes it hard to blend in at school, and even though I try, I still stick out." I looked down and away. "And not in a good way."

When I dared to return my gaze to his, he was staring directly *into* me. "The school called. They think it would be best if we parted ways."

My chest lifted then quickly fell. "Shit."

His hand was curled over a napkin on top of the table, and he was pulling it under his fingers in a slow, torturous manner. "I don't believe any of this is your fault, Tess."

I blinked, studying him across from the uneaten lasagnas as if he'd just admitted to finding a chest full of precious stones. "You don't?"

He shook his head then redirected his attention to the television. "I can't for the life of me gauge why you don't think I'd understand what's making you feel so different, but I know you are, and believe it or not I know how hard it is to be different when you're a kid. In fact, it's not always that easy to be different when you're a grown-up either." His gaze was still stuck on the news guy who was in the middle of declaring that the stock markets had taken a dip. "I'm not as blind as you think. I mean, come on, Tess—you can't even cry."

I gulped.

Not once, in all my almost sixteen years, had this subject ever been brought up. Not ever. It was one thing to hold in a whopper of a secret, like being able to manipulate ashes back to life, but it was quite another to pretend like it wasn't weird that I hadn't shed a single tear, *ever*.

My dad used to joke about it. "You were such a good baby," he would say. "You were so quiet; we had to check on you all the time because you never let us know when you were mad or upset." Then there was the time, when I was six, that he and my mom took me to see the 'nice lady with a room full of special toys.' It was the first of the evaluations, but not the last. The prestigious primary school I'd been attending had insisted that I get evaluated to see if I was on the spectrum. Apparently though, I didn't fit into any of the special needs boxes the school was hoping I might, and I wasn't completely without emotion. I was just a creep who couldn't or wouldn't cry.

Yeah, I was one hundred percent aware that it wasn't normal. The thing was, I didn't even know *how* to cry. I mean, it wasn't like I hadn't ever tried. At least when I was smallish, my parents (mostly my dad) encouraged me to 'let it out.' He took me to the river and showed me how to throw rocks in the water. Essentially, even though I know he wasn't aiming for this, he showed me how to access my violence to better deal with emotions.

As I got older, we all just sort of stopped talking about it.

Whenever I got red in the face, they just left it—or my dad would take me back to the river. My grandma was the only one who ever tried anything else. She used to wait until it was raining then take me outside. "Stand in it, Tess," she used to say. "Stand in your tears." It's weird . . . because it seemed to work.

When my dad said nothing more, I stated quietly, "It's not my fault. I wish I could cry sometimes . . . but that's not why they all think I'm a freak."

The newsman had moved on to whatever it was the liberals and conservatives were all angry about now; I was near positive that Mattie wasn't listening to it even though he hadn't moved his attention from the screen. "You don't even try to make friends, Tess," he said sharply under his tongue.

I heaved a breath in and out of my nose. "That's not true."

His head moved in my direction like a slow rolling boulder. "I'm not talking about those freaks at that store you're always at. They're almost thirty."

"Gawd Dad!" I exploded. "What are you doing? *Trying* to make me cry!" I pushed away from the table and my cold plate of wilting food and stood up. "I thought maybe we could have, like, a normal conversation for once, but I see now that's not going to happen." A noise eerily similar to a predator's growl left my lips as I started to walk away and head up to my room, but I stopped just short of exiting the dining room. "And *those freaks*, they know who I am inside and out, and they don't care. They are the only ones, apart from Grandma Reanin, who I have ever trusted." I watched as sadness fell over his firm expression and softened out the rough edges. "You don't even know me, Dad. You don't know what I can do— what—what I'm capable of. I'm not the normal little girl you wish you had and I'm never gonna be." I stared him down for two more heavy breaths before storming off for my room.

After I slammed the door, I pulled out *Awaken the*

Goddess from where it had been taking up room in my bag and fell into my bed. I mindlessly unwrapped the cards, keeping them together before letting them fall into my hands. The house was quiet as I shuffled. The muffled sound of the television blaring up the stairs had even cut off after I'd shut my door.

My fury festered in my guts as I cut the deck into thirds then brought them back together, plucking a card from the top of the pile. "Whatchu got for me now?" I chirped at the card as I pulled it over. "There aren't any swords in this pile." But as I pulled the card away, one that had been stuck to it fell into my lap. Ignoring the one I'd meant to pull, I picked up the other. "The Goddess of the Witches. Interesting . . ."

Considering the day I'd had, that seemed like a sign. I studied the woman on the card—her eyes very similar to what I saw every time I looked in the mirror. Her skin was pale, her lips were full, and she wore a black cloak.

"Got anything to say to me, Goddess?" I asked in a snarky voice. As soon as the words left my mouth the card grew hot, and I cursed as it fell to the comforter. "What the—" I started but was immediately drawn away from one odd occurrence to another. For it was then that I really looked at the card I'd meant to pull. The one looking up at me from my lap.

"What is this?" I muttered.

The card wasn't blank; in fact, it had a depth to it that I would have felt foolish describing to someone. It was foggy almost, and if I squinted hard enough, I could almost see movement in the background. Like whoever was in there, was coming to life.

I was still in the middle of trying to sort out what was going on with the goddess card when there was a knock on my door. I quickly threw the cards together and tossed them under my pillow. I cleared my throat and smarted an angsty,

"What?" I barely acknowledged my dad when the door opened, and he appeared in the doorway.

"Hey," was all he said. His shoulder found the door frame as he crossed his arms over his chest. "I'm sorry. I didn't mean what I said—about Ethan and Jamae. I know they're good to you. I just wish you would try it on is all, you know, being a kid. Having friends your own age. The whole package. Because—" He lingered in place for a moment before going on. "It'll all be over in a flash."

"Being a kid sucks. All I want is for it to blow over quickly."

He shook his head. "Don't say that."

"It's true," I muttered.

"Look." He wiped a hand across his forehead. "I'll make a deal with you." I perked up only a little. "You've been pleading with us to do online school for years. If you promise to try and act like a little human for a little longer—to make some freaking friends—then I'll allow it." He'd barely finished his sentence before I'd hinged forward. He immediately jumped on my preemptive excitement. "I mean it, though, Tess. I need you to make at least one friend—semi close to your own age. It's important for you to grow some empathy."

I nodded enthusiastically. "I'll try my best."

"No," he stated firmly. "You won't try. You'll do it." He paused, studying me. "Jamae called me; she said you want to work there. At that Hexed place."

My organs froze. She *called* him. What? How did she even get his number?

"I'm thinking about letting you, but—"

Again, I started bobbing my head up and down. "I'll make a friend, I promise."

He continued to hold my stare for a while longer before dipping his forehead and staring at his socks. "It's settled then. We can get you set up next week for online classes. For now, why don't you just take what's left of this one and do whatever it is you do."

"Okay." I closed my mouth around the other words that didn't come and waited for him to say more. But he didn't. At least not right away.

When he did, it wasn't what I expected.

"You know, I do understand."

"Understand what?"

"What it is to be different."

I furrowed my brows as I waited for more, but this time he really was done. He gave a curt nod, said good night, then backed away—closing my door as he took his leave.

I fell back against my pillows, cupping my new necklace in my hand. I'd been slowly realizing this truth throughout the day: there was a palpable magic in these stones, an energy paralleled to emotion.

"All right, rocks," I said as I cradled them into my fingers. "If you're the real thing, then guide me. Tell me where I'm supposed to go next—or whatever it is I'm supposed to do."

There was no initial change. No direct answers. The demands of the day had finally caught up with me, along with the lack of sleep I'd been dealing with for months. I gathered the cards from *Awaken the Goddess* back together (noting that the card I'd pulled was still unidentifiable) and tucked them into my desk. I'd deal with them later—I already had too many supernatural mysteries to deal with. Shortly after that, I turned off the lights and closed my eyes.

When I woke up the next morning, all I could think about was heading over to my grandmother's apartment. And I knew more than ever that this was something I ought not to put off for any longer.

CHAPTER TWELVE

My grandma's apartment was only one block away from Central Park. She'd bought the place in the seventies; that was something I couldn't help but fixate on now that I'd heard Maggie say that my grandma had found her in 1977. Reanin probably didn't give a lick about the fact that the thirteen hundred square foot apartment, complete with vaulted ceilings and a whole second level (a mere mansion to the present-day city dwellers) would end up being a gold mine. A place like that might as well have had gold buried in the walls. That wasn't why my dad was pressing me to go check on her place, though. I had this feeling that I couldn't shake, ever since our last convo, that he knew as well as I did that it wasn't what the apartment was worth that made it so valuable. It was what was buried in those walls. And I doubted very much that it was gold.

I'd been thinking about it a lot, ever since I'd learned more about my grandma . . . Could she have known that I had natural abilities? Did she want to make sure that nothing of extreme value to her—like an entire *other* or *underworld*—get lost once she was gone, and out of familiar hands?

If Maggie had been telling the truth, then it brought a whole different light to what my grandma had said about my grandfather once upon a time. She'd said he was locked away into a spell, just like the unicorns in her favorite book. I'd just assumed she'd been speaking metaphorically, but in hindsight, she'd been completely literal. My grandfather, whoever the hell he was, was locked inside the Hall of Shadows.

I slipped my key into the lock of my grandmother's apartment door and turned it to the side; when the mechanism unbolted my heart skipped a beat. I crammed my eyes shut and held my breath. I hadn't been back since the day of the funeral. I'd walked in and walked out in the same heartbeat that day, because it was too painful to be there without her. But this wasn't just about me anymore, this was about the possibility of so much more—so many more people or souls who could be locked away in a world that had the potential of making sense to me. So, I pushed through my hindrance, opened my eyes, and let the door hang open.

My feet stayed rooted in the hallway as the natural light bled into the soft colors my grandmother had used for the synthetic living space. I walked a few paces into the apartment, letting the door close behind me. Dropping the keys on the edge of the couch, I wandered over to the windows I'd spent so much time staring out of as a child. My thoughts were reeling around a cycle of insanity. Magic, locked doors, shadows . . . soul sucking grandma. I was still having a lot of trouble with that last one. I mean, I'd seen her eat food plenty of times. Mostly salads and stuff—the occasional bloody steak, but that often caused her to get sick. Was that weird? I'd always attributed it to her veggie diet—like her body wasn't used to that kind of food.

I flipped around and stuck a finger in my cheek, as I took strides towards the kitchen. If she was such a succubus, then would she have had any food? I stood before the pantry, throwing open the door and inspecting its contents. mac n cheese, cookies, chips, canned green beans—all *my* favorite foods. Okay, well, maybe there was more stuff in the fridge. But when I opened it there was nothing. Perhaps Mary Joe had come over and cleaned everything out so it wouldn't rot. I hadn't heard mention of that, but it wouldn't have been unheard of.

Suddenly, in the mood to ravage, I moved back to the cabinets and began to ransack every available nook and cranny, but other than a few pots and pans (that looked like they'd been used only a handful of times) there wasn't anything in there. Sure, this wasn't completely bizarre, not for a New Yorker. Our people were used to eating out; ovens had a tendency to store purses. Still, the only food in this kitchen was meant to serve me. There were no other snacks, no Perrier —there was nothing, save for the empty bottle of bourbon I came across with a note tied around its neck. I didn't recognize the handwriting, and the scribbles didn't make an ounce of sense: *For when his wings are singed. –Melody*

I'd never heard of anyone by that name, granted I had never formally met any of my grandmother's supposed card shark friends. I only knew she had a card game group at all because our old housekeeper had brought me over to her apartment once after picking me up from school unexpectedly. After another 'incident.' She hadn't been able to get a hold of my parents and she couldn't watch me (I was like seven and she didn't want to leave me alone). Anyway, we'd showed up to my grandma's apartment and when Reanin answered, her place was full of people—most of which I recognized as tenants from the building. My grandma had said they were getting ready to play cards . . . even though I hadn't seen a single deck in any of their hands.

Maybe Melody had been mixed in with that crowd.

Or maybe she was from The Hall.

Whichever . . . *whatever* the case, I didn't have the luxury of pondering over the what ifs. I'd come here in search of a lost portal, and I couldn't leave without a thorough investigation.

Leaving the empty bourbon bottle where I'd found it, I began to search through the kitchen a second time—pounding on the back of the cabinets and seeking out false walls wherever I could. Because that's where things of this nature existed, right? Behind secret passageways. When there was nothing to find in the kitchen, I moved on to the living room, which proved ordinary. Nothing but clean, definite lines; shiny surfaces that you could see yourself looking back in. Her walls were lined with mirrors and paintings. I'd never been interested in the artwork even though my grandma had often liked to impress upon me that all the paintings had been done by a famous artist.

"Never just stare at a painting, Tess," she'd said to me more than once, while admiring her collection. "Artists hide their truths in their work. Sometimes, we feel drawn to a piece because we feel a connection to those hidden gems."

Her descriptions were super weird. But as I laid a hand against the portrait of a woman, too busy with her own distraction to look my way, I couldn't figure out if my grandmother had been hinting at something with her odd speech, or if she'd simply been daydreaming.

There wasn't time for evaluation.

I heaved up cushions and looked under chairs, I pulled books from the shelves—realizing as I did, they had never been anything other than props. Reanin had a bunch of famous authors, the kind you often see next to the checkout registers at the grocery store: Danielle Steel, Mary Higgins Clark, James Patterson, and John Grisham. She'd written her name on the inside of every single one, but the only one out of her entire collection that didn't gasp for its first breath of fresh air (the way a book always does when it's opened for the first time) was her very well-worn copy of *The Last Unicorn*.

I was puzzled. Why have a collection of books that you would never read? It was almost like she'd set me up to find that copy of *Confronting Your Shadows*—to know that it was her by her reading signature.

Eventually I left the bookcases and moved on, but I wasn't successful. By the end of my time in the apartment, I'd ransacked every corner, every cabinet, drawer, and pill bottle. If it could be opened, turned over, or shaken, I'd done it. But there was nothing.

I couldn't make sense of any of it. Maggie had hidden portals in crystal balls. She'd shown my grandmother how she could do the same with the Hall of Shadows. But there were no crystal balls in this place . . . no pile of ashes that I could see or smell. And yet, I one hundred percent believed that my Grandma Reanin was a party to an otherworld of some sort, because what other explanations were there for *me*. For my abilities.

You have shadows in your blood.

I couldn't get that fortune teller's voice out of my head.

Choose the light.

A shiver ran down my spine.

There wasn't anything here and I couldn't be in that apartment any longer. My chest was heavy with superstition, loss, and something foreboding that I couldn't explain. There was only one place I could think to go—Hexed.

I didn't know yet who to trust. Whether Ethan and Jamae were standing with me or against me. The card had been pulled twice now—*betrayal*. And there was that awful thing that Maggie had insinuated, that there were hunters out there willing to give part of themselves away to access The Hall to retrieve whatever it was that was so valuable. But what did they give to the shadows? Goosebumps raised the hairs of my arm.

I didn't want to believe that Ethan and Jamae were only pretending to like me to get to my grandmother's magic. Call me shallow, but I refused to. Innocent until proven guilty.

I was out of my grandma's hood and into my comfort zone in a heartbeat.

"Hey, there's trouble," Ethan said, sounding super lame, as the door to their shop chimed over my head.

"Hey!" Jamae echoed, popping her head out from a display of mini cauldrons. "Are you ever going back to school?"

"Actually," I said with a raise of my left brow, "no." Average human learning seemed kind of inane when reflecting on the idea that I may partially belong to another world. "My old man finally caved. I'm starting online, like, next week."

"No shit," Jamae said, leaning an arm on the table next to her. "That's groovy."

"Yeah, it is," Ethan said. "And you'll have tons of extra time to work here if you want—"

"Ethan," Jamae said, stitching in a stern look.

I usually didn't butt in between the two of them, but this time, I couldn't help it. "The cat's out of the bag, Jamae. I know your secret."

Jamae's expression stilled, as did Ethan's.

"Oh?" was all she said.

I rolled my eyes. "My dad said you called. And he's cool with me working here."

They each seemed to let out just a little bit of air.

Looking from one of them to the other, I said, "What?" Gawd, it was like the world had tilted on its side.

"Nothing," Jamae said, almost defensively. "I just—I'm just happy."

"For real?" I asked.

She returned to her merch. "Yeah. We'll talk. Next week though. I've got too much shit to do right now."

The air around my head was buzzing. Yes! Finally, things were starting to turn around. I could do online school and work here—except, I was getting way too ahead of myself. I needed to halt the celebrations until I could sort out who was looking to stab me with their sword and who was on my side.

Reeling in my enthusiasm, I tucked a hand into my coat pocket and bobbed my head. "Cool . . . Sounds good." Then, trying to sound as if I wasn't leading an investigation, I walked over towards the register and leaned in against the counter. "So hey, I keep meaning to ask. What's the name of your guys' coven again?"

"The Witches of the Shadowed Heart," Ethan replied as he thumbed through some paperwork.

My eyes widened and I had to make a conscious effort to calm them back down. "That's right," I said softly. "Why 'the Shadowed Heart?' What's that mean?" *And was it a cult?*

"I don't know," Jamae answered with a shrug as she continued to stack mini cauldrons on different platforms. "Juanita named it, and she does like her shadow work." Her eyes darted to mine. "Why?"

I shook my head a little too quickly. "I was just asking." I waited for her to return to unpacking her merchandise. "Does Juanita, like, ever talk about searching for dimensions? You know, like in Maggie's book?"

"Now and again," Ethan said. He recentered his gaze over mine and squinted. "Are you trying to access that shit? Cause that's pretty hardcore."

"No," I replied a little too quickly. "I was just curious."

He reached for a clipboard and pen and handed it to Jamae before returning his attention to me. "If you are planning on messing around with that sort of work, *please* tell us. We can help you."

I bet you can, I thought presumptuously, then just as quickly smacked my own hand at the thought. I shouldn't judge. Not yet.

"I just haven't been able to get it all out of my head, you know, since I read that book." Jamae stood from the box she'd been digging through and looked at me. My gaze drifted away from hers as I said, "The worlds Maggie found and locked away—they were intriguing. I just think it would be difficult to be married to someone who had lived and breathed so much of something so extraordinary, and just not care to find out more about it."

Jamae's head fell to the side. "It is a difficult thing, and I'm sure that's part of why they aren't living together anymore. Also, I can't say for sure that Juanita's head is always in the right place . . . no one's is one hundred percent of the time."

I unconsciously pulled at the crystals around my neck. "Right," I began, but just as quickly lost my voice. My vision faded and I was no longer standing in Hexed, but instead in Maggie's hidden pocket studio. I was in the corner looking at a circle of runes scribbled on the floor and in the center was Maggie, bleeding to death. The frightening image faded nearly as soon as it came to me. My hand dropped away from the stones, and I was once again in Jamae and Ethan's store.

"What the hell?" I muttered.

"What's up?" Jamae asked.

I barely took the time to look around in confusion as I headed straight for the door, "I—I have to go."

"Whoa!" Ethan hollered at my back. "Where's the fire?"

"I—I don't know. I mean . . ." I raced through my mind for possible excuses. I didn't want to say anything about Maggie just in case these two weren't the allies I so hoped they were. "I just realized I left my curling iron on."

"You don't curl your hair," Jamae said suspiciously.

I glanced back at the two of them before opening the

door. They were peering at me like I was trying to steal off with something of theirs. "I was bored—thought I'd try something I saw on YouTube. But I, uh, forgot all about it until now." I stepped a foot out onto the cold sidewalk, then added, "I'll catch you guys later."

Without waiting for a response, I ran to the nearest curb and flagged down a cab. I didn't have a single second to waste. If what I saw was real, then Mystical Maggie was either dead or close to it, and I had the wickedest intuition that it had everything to do with me.

CHAPTER THIRTEEN

Every inch of my skin was tingling. As for the buzz of the city, all I could hear was my own blood as it pumped past my ears. The air didn't just have the familiar sting that winter sometimes is known to deliver—it was metallic.

After ravaging my way through that blur of a sidewalk and the faces I'd had to swim through to get to my destination, I was finally facing the same purple door as I had the night before. Maggie's card hadn't offered a phone number, otherwise I would've already tried calling her like a thousand times. I shook away the apprehension crawling up my spine like an oversized spider and tried the door's handle. When it opened, I froze.

The stairway was dimly lit, but unlike the first time I'd come to this place, the door to Maggie's 'pocket' was visible.

"Maggie?" I called out.

I stretched my ears for any sort of commotion, but the city was to my back, and it was nearly impossible to hear anything. Cautiously, I let the door close—muffling the noise of honking and chatter—and started walking up the stairs.

"Maggie? It's me—Tess. Are you in there?"

Still, there was nothing.

"Shit," I cursed, the toes of my black combat boots edging their way up to the door at the top of the stairs.

I placed my hand gingerly over the brass doorknob. When I finally got up the nerve to turn it (finding it unlocked), I started to whisper Maggie's name as I pushed open the door; all that I got out, however, was the first syllable before my hand fell away from the knob and my legs froze as if they'd suddenly been filled with lead.

Lying on the floor, just like the vision I'd seen back at Hexed—blood trickling from her eyes, nose, mouth, and ears —was Maggie. Her gaze fell from the ceiling to where I was standing, and I gasped. I'd no sooner begun to lunge towards her when her bloodied eyes widened, and her mouth opened in a silent scream as she attempted to raise an arm.

I halted before a circle of drawings that had been etched onto the floor. Runes had been drawn in blood in a circle around Maggie. Ever so slowly, I lifted my gaze and glanced around the rest of the space. Nearly all the crystal balls the witch owned had been thrown from their shelves—most of them shattered. Entire worlds now forever lost.

"Oh my god, Maggie," I whimpered. "What happened here? Who did this to you?"

Her lips trembled as she tried to speak. "I've wronged you."

Every line belonging to my face deepened. "What?"

"I—I was wrong. Again." A breath wrought with barbed wire threatened to puncture her lungs. "I'm afraid I've made . . . a mistake. You've got to protect the magic. Keep it . . . from them. They won't stop till they have it . . . or till they're dead."

I shook my head, terror edging its way further into every crevice of my being. "What are you talking about?"

"I'm so sorry, Tess."

"Sorry about what?"

"I couldn't imagine someone like you—" She swallowed and blinked hard. "I have forgotten my own words." A bloody tear ran down her cheek as she mouthed a line I'd read only a day ago. *We are conditioned to trust the light, but deceit so often hides in the sun. The real truth can always be found in the darker materials, however frightening they might appear.*

The weight of the world came crashing down over me. All my life I'd kept the truth about my abilities locked up. I'd kept them safely hidden, because I was so afraid that if anyone found out about what I could do that it would wind up biting me in the ass. As I listened to her script replay in my mind, I knew—I was the darker material. She'd feared me.

"Maggie, what did you do?"

Her tears were now mixing with the blood. "I feared that you would . . . reopen it. And what that . . . would mean . . . for this world. I—I told them you were the only one who could . . . reopen the doors."

This time my tone was fierce. "*Who* did you tell that to?"

"You're being stalked."

The weight over my chest sunk further down upon my sternum.

"They have shadows in their eyes. Not—not in their blood."

I wanted so badly to reach through the circle and grab her hand—to shake her shoulders. My gums *actually itched* as I yelled, "Who did this to you, Maggie!"

Her lips came together as she swallowed what was left of her confession. "There's no time." She tried to pound her fist onto the ground, but it was so obvious that her strength (as well as what was left of her life) was waning. "You must find Kage," she said in a near whisper. "W—Warn him. Get into the Hall of—" Her speech was interrupted as she choked on her own blood.

I fell to my knees, getting as close to the old woman as I safely could. I nodded as I chirped back, "The Hall of Shadows—of course! Just tell me how!"

She closed her eyes and swallowed more blood. "I burned the cards."

"I know."

The look she gave me as her head rolled to the side was everything.

"Maggie," I said, urging her to finish what she was saying before this curse finished eating her alive. "I can't get to my grandfather unless I find those ashes, and you're the only one who can tell me where they are."

She pressed her bloodied lips together and lifted her chin in as much of a nod as she could fathom. "Warn him—but also—keep the magic safe. You do that—you can save more than one world." She coughed and blood sputtered from her lips. When next she spoke, it sounded like gravel was coming up from her lungs. "Psyche Opening the Golden Box." Two lines of blood were coming from each side of her mouth as she dragged out the last of her speech. "Reanin used the shadows in her blood . . . You must . . . do the same." She coughed and red droplets erupted from her mouth like confetti. "Do you understand?"

I nodded too quickly. I had no choice but to understand. There wasn't time for a lesson on witchcraft and I could trust no one to help me.

Her lips sputtered again as she tried with all her might to keep speaking. "Kage's br—brother—"

Her eyes were dimming.

I leaned in. "What about him?"

"He's . . ."

"He's stalking me," I answered for her. It seemed that much was obvious by now.

She both nodded and shook her head. "He is but . . . he can't do anything until . . ."

"Until what?" I asked impatiently.

"He needs you to open the portal."

"He can't do it himself?"

She did her best to shake her head. "He can . . . but he won't. He'll be waiting . . . at the end." Her eyes closed as the last of her words fell from her mouth. "Tell Kage that the waifs have her heart."

And then, before I could question a single thing, Maggie froze, and any breath she had left, evaporated. She was gone.

"No," I whispered. Then, pounding the floor with a fist, I yelled out, "No, no, no, no, NO, NO!" I just sat there for a moment, rocking back and forth on my heels. "Shit!" I cursed, jumping up and back from the dead body.

My gaze quickly began darting to all the corners of the room. Kage's brother was on my trail—was he here now? I didn't see anyone, but what did that even mean? In this new world that I was just learning about, who knew if someone had the potential to turn invisible?

I exhaled a curse as I backed away towards the door.

I didn't have a clue as to whether this portal or pocket, or whatever the hell it was, would remain open after its owner had died. I sure as hell didn't want to get stuck in it, that was for damn sure. Not to mention that if Kage's brother wasn't already here, hunting me, he would be soon enough. I whispered a sage good-bye to Maggie and pressed my lips to my fingers, sending a wish that wherever she was off to next would be better than this, and in the seconds that followed I was out the door and sprinting down those steps.

I was back on the sidewalk and walking in any direction that would take me as far away from that supernatural hobbit hole as fast as possible; as I strutted along, I pulled the hood of my jacket over my head. I was still trying to separate my racing thoughts and sort them into folders that made sense as I pulled out my phone and rapidly typed in what Maggie had said. Psyche Opening the Golden Box. As soon as the image popped up, I came to an immediate halt. I didn't notice or feel as the people on the crowded walkway bumped into me, curses bouncing off my shoulders like spitfire. I paid no mind to the fact that I was a boulder dividing what had been a swift moving river. I didn't care.

The world might as well have shut off as I looked up from my phone—the winter air seizing to chill my bones. My grandmother had hidden the ashes of the world she'd helped build and she'd done a very good job of it. It wasn't in a crystal ball or even anything remotely close to that. No, Reanin had been thoughtful. She'd hid it in a box . . . in a painting, that up until that moment, I had found rather old-fashioned and dull. A painting I'd just had my hand up against only an hour or so ago.

CHAPTER FOURTEEN

I was back at my Grandma Reanin's apartment building. Except . . . something was different this time. Adrenaline was pumping so profusely through my veins that I was surprised I noticed them at all, the residents. How they were lingering in the lobby as if waiting for a voice to come over a hidden speaker somewhere in the corner of the ceiling. As I walked towards the elevators, I couldn't *not* pay attention to all the pairs of eyes glued to me—like I was on my way up to board a rocket on an earth-saving mission.

I tried not to stare back at any of them for longer than was necessary as I boarded the lift and rode up to my grandmother's floor. It didn't get any less strange when the doors opened.

"What's going on?" I asked, the gold-plated doors closing behind my back as I looked down my grandmother's hallway to find two women and three men standing outside their apartment doors. They ranged in age from mid-twenties to, oh I don't know, eighty something.

Mrs. Rathjen, an older woman who I'd baked cookies for

when I was younger, spoke first. "We're here for *you*, Tess. Just like we were here for her."

An itchy sensation crawled up my spine. This was a little too much *Rosemary's Baby* for me.

"What?" I questioned, looking from one neighbor to the other, before a heavy realization hit me right in the gut. "Oh my gawd . . . You're all from The Hall, aren't you?" I didn't know how it was possible, but I just knew it had to be so. When not even one of them answered, I asked plainly, "So, are you guys, like—what?" *What were they?*

"We're here for you," Mr. Delaney said in the exact same way Mrs. Rathjen just had.

"*Okay*. How did you know I'd be coming right now?"

"We have our ways," said Mrs. Shupe from 334.

"Go now, child," said Mrs. Rathjen. "Follow your destiny."

I remained frozen in my tracks; my gaze stuck on each of their faces as I tried to sort out how none of this had been real —ever. This apartment was as fake as the card games and books on my grandmother's shelves. These people, (were they people?) who lived in this building, may have been nothing more than part of the set design Reanin created.

"Did—Did you guys know Maggie?"

No one said anything for almost a minute. Then the younger guy, I think his name was Dave—and come to think of it, he'd had that same young face forever (actually, none of them had aged)—anyway, it was he who finally said, "Go on, Tess. Open the doors."

"Right," I whispered, before sweeping past them and unlocking my grandma's apartment for the second time that day. I let the door close as I stepped over the threshold, but I could still feel all their eyes on me.

I headed straight to the spot between the white bookshelf and the ivory bench and stared straight into the essence of the painting in question. The piece was simple. A woman in nature, draped in a pale pink (or peach) robe, or dress, and she was peeking inside of a golden box. Thus, Psyche Opening the Golden Box.

Maggie's last words ran through my head—that my grandma had used her shadows to hide the ashes. That I needed to do the same to get them back.

You have shadows in your blood.

I knew what I needed to do. In a flash I was away from the painting and running into the kitchen. When I had what I needed, I returned. I stared at the painting for only a few moments more before the knife I'd swiped from my grandmother's unused collection grew itchy in my hand.

I sucked in a quick breath, closed my eyes, then laid the blade into my palm. I tried not to think about the pain as I jabbed it into my flesh. Still, I cried out as soon as the wound was inflicted—the knife dropping to the floor along with a ribbon of my blood laced over its shiny blade. Then, before the act could be all for nothing, I pasted my bleeding hand against the woman in the painting.

I panted, my palm throbbing. My thoughts running around a hamster wheel. *What if I was supposed to do something else? What if this was all for nothing?* But just before my doubts began to completely overshadow my beliefs, the painting began to *drink* from my hand.

"Holy cow," I muttered. If I had been able to cry, tears would have been streaming down my face.

I closed my eyes and tried to breathe through the agony of magic feeding upon magic. When I reopened them, the woman in the painting was looking down at me, holding out a hand. I didn't hesitate, instead I took it and let her pull me up into her world. Into the painting.

Once inside, Reanin's apartment ceased to exist. It was just the woman from the painting and I and the nature the woman clung to. She looked at me speculatively as she released my hand from her own. "You're not Reanin." Her voice was rich; it made me think of thick caramel and chocolate ribbons.

"No." I shook my head. "I'm her granddaughter."

"Ah." The woman moved her gaze to the box she'd set down while helping me up. She reached for it and lifted it in her hands, then looked back at me. "You share her blood, so this is for you as much as it is for her."

I realized suddenly that I'd been holding my breath; I jerked as air entered my lungs. I held out a hand, accepting the box. I smiled as soon as I lifted the top. Ashes.

"Reanin was a little less thrilled with its contents," said the woman.

I reached inside and let my fingers dance around the ash. "That's because, for whatever reason, she was unable to do this." And with that, I lifted a set of divination cards from the box as if they'd been there all along.

Psyche, if that was her name, gasped. "No, I don't believe she had the skill for that."

I studied my new prize. They were the size of typical playing cards. "What now?" I asked.

She shrugged. "I've done my part. Good-bye, granddaughter of Reanin."

I didn't even blink before realizing I was back in my grandmother's apartment, the painting looming before me just as it had been right before I'd bled into it. The blood was gone, my wound was healed, and the woman in the art was back to peeking in her box. I wondered only for a moment what *she* saw when she looked in there.

My chest rose then slowly fell as I looked down at the cards and slowly began to count them. I wasn't surprised to find that there were thirteen—my grandma always said it was a lucky number.

The oracle deck was anything but conventional; in fact,

each of the cards was blank. As I slowly came down to my knees, I inspected each card—every one of them so crisp and new. The face of every single one of them was blank. Kind of like that rare goddess card I'd pulled recently. However, the title was clear. Each card was decorated in an elegant script amongst a black background, Hall of Shadows printed in white and silver.

I was trying to sort out how to move forward with this whole thing—was I just supposed to pull a card or what? When all of a sudden the cards lifted from my hands and landed directly before me on the floor, taking on an astrological spread, or one that ran clockwise. I was so grateful just then that Ethan had been so frustratingly thorough. I knew from what he'd taught me that in this sort of spread, with the twelfth card on top and the thirteenth in the middle, that the first card I was to flip over was just to the right of the twelfth.

If this was truly a portal, then there was only one way in that I was aware of.

My hand was shaking as it hovered over that first card. "Screw it," I finally said, and before I could talk myself out of it, I reached down and flipped it over.

At first, nothing happened.

I sat back on my haunches, holding my breath. But just as my heart beat began to still in fear that too much time had passed—that maybe portals had some sort of expiration date on them—the card that had been empty when I'd turned it over began to run with color, a picture forming of a desk cluttered with books. I was so entranced by it that I didn't notice that the room I was in had begun to transform as well. It wasn't until I heard a chair screech behind me, like wood on wood, that I turned around and figured out I was sitting in a different place all together.

Very slowly, I came to standing. I faced a young woman,

maybe about the same age as Jamae . . . but there was something not quite right about her. Her skin was somewhat gray, and her dull blonde hair was streaked with chunks of white. She reminded me of the man who had given me the crystal necklace.

"Welcome to The Library," she said. She sounded relieved.

As she stood apart from the table where she'd been seated, I realized why she looked so eerie. It was because she was dead.

PART TWO

CHAPTER FIFTEEN

My heart was pounding so hard it was deafening. As I took methodical steps backwards, I peered over the dead woman's shoulders into the vast space surrounding us. There were rows of books for as far as the eyes could see.

"The library," I repeated, drawing on the fraying ropes of strength I held against my fear.

The woman hadn't moved an inch since she stood, and, as I backed away, she made no move to follow. She wrinkled her forehead as she spoke. "Yeah, that's what I said. Pretty obvious I would think." She seemed to let down her guard a little as she said the next part. "Goddamn though, it's really bangin' to finally have these doors unlocked. It was only supposed to be like five years—tops."

Bangin'? Who was this chick? Not to mention, she was wearing an orange two-piece suit that did nothing for the putrid color of her skin. I tried not to scowl (and failed) as I asked, "What are you . . . exactly?"

She rested a hand over the top of her chair. It was then I

noticed how golden her irises were. "You can call me Rachel. And I'm a waif."

Right away, I was reminded of Maggie's last words. *Tell Kage that the waifs have her heart.*

"Are there more of you?" I asked.

Her expression lightened. "Uh, yeah."

"Oh . . . okay. So, um, do you know anything about a heart?"

She looked at me like I'd lost a few marbles. "You're going to have to be more specific than that, doll."

I bit my lip. "That's all I know."

Rachel looked down at her feet and as she did, I caught sight of the top of her head. I didn't mean to gasp as loud as I did, but I couldn't help it—her hair was thinning, and through the white and honey strands that were left, her gray scalp was showing.

When she looked back up, she seemed to find my stricken expression amusing. "Don't worry," she said. "I won't bite."

My eyes grew. "I wasn't worried you would."

"Yeah you were," she said, kicking a foot out restlessly. "Don't worry, I'll look better in a few hours, thanks to you unlocking those damn doors. I gotta say, it's been a real bummer being locked in here." She readjusted her stance and studied my face. "Where's Reanin? Did she get rid of him? Is it over?"

I literally didn't know what to say. Suddenly, she looked at me differently—like maybe I shouldn't be there. "Actually, who the hell are you anyway?"

I gulped. "I'm um—so Reanin isn't coming—"

"Oh my god . . ." Rachel said, seemingly taking in what I was wearing for the first time. It wasn't much—black jeggings and a gray top. My standard boots. Still, I'm sure my fashion didn't match what she was used to. "How many years has it been?"

1977. That was the year my grandmother found Maggie.

"I—it's, um, it's been *a while*, I think."

"Like, how long is a while?"

"It's January . . . of 2022."

Everything about the waif standing before me wilted, and that was saying a lot seeing as she was already decomposing. "No shit," she whispered. Then, raising her eyes to meet mine, she asked, "Where is she? Where's Reanin?"

I could tell by her tone that any hope she had been clinging to was quickly evaporating. Still, I chewed over the words for a minute before depositing them, my chest falling in as Rachel slumped down into her chair. "She was, um—"

"Hunted."

I nodded, as Rachel trained her gaze to rest on the floor. "She was found dead with my mom, like three months ago. I —I just found out about all of this."

Her gaze shot back up to mine. "That's impossible. Reanin was a beast. If that asshole found her it could only mean—wait. Who *are* you? You said she was found with your mother."

"Oh. I'm—um—"

"Oh my god," she whispered. "You're her grandbrat."

I peered into her golden irises. I didn't have to answer, she already knew everything. More than I could wish to know, that was for sure.

I was just about to try and summon something to say back when she jumped up from her seat and started strutting down an aisle between two rows of shelves. I didn't hesitate to run after her.

"Wait! Where are you going?"

"Where else?" she replied without turning around. "To talk to the boss."

For a dead chick, she sure was fast. My breath hitched in

my lungs as I tried to keep up. "The boss? Kage? That's great! Take me with you! I came here to find him."

Rachel came to a halt, turning to face me with a hand on her hip. "You know I can't do that."

A slow humming erupted from all four corners of my mind, my eyes flitting from side to side. "Why not?"

"You arrived with the cards, right?" When I didn't say anything, she pointed past me to where the oracle cards were still right where I'd left them. "You have to finish the reading before you can do anything."

The word fell from my tongue like a blade. "What?"

"Didn't she tell you?"

"*My grandma* didn't tell me anything."

The waif hesitated. "Then how'd you get here?"

My shoulders fell. "It's a long story."

Rachel started backing away, then turned around and started back in the direction she was initially headed. "Sorry, babe—I don't have time for a long story."

"What—wait," I muttered in disbelief, before running after her. I caught up just in time to see her take the spine of a book in her hand and pull it towards her. As soon as she did, the shelf opened like a door. Into what, I couldn't tell.

"Look kid, I'd love to help you out, but the cards were designed a certain way. You wouldn't be able to follow me through here even if you tried."

"So, I'm supposed to just what—flip through each card?"

"Well, it's a little more complicated than that. Each card belongs to a shadow. You must go through each one, and each one may ask a little more of you. But hey, if what you've said is correct then consider this a gift from Reanin. You're about to find out more about her than she ever could have possibly told you."

She started to stick a foot through the door, but I stopped her again. "Wait! There are thirteen cards—this could take forever! There are hunters out there and the doors are open! Kage's brother is one of them and he's after some sort of crazy magic that you all have down here. I need to warn my grandfather."

She didn't look at all fazed. "There are very few things Kage doesn't already know. And I promise you, the magic they are all after—they aren't going to find it. Not any time soon. Don't worry about Kage's brother or any of the others, worry about yourself. The shadows have been on lock down. They are hungry, sailor. They'll need to be fed before you can move forward."

And then, without any further explanation, she was gone.

I wavered in place for no longer than ten seconds before lunging for the same book she'd yanked towards her body to get that door to appear. But the book didn't budge, not even a little. Not for me.

"Great," I muttered. Now I was stuck there with nothing but her confusing directions to figure out. I would need to feed the shadows to move forward . . . Feed the shadows. *With what?*

A shiver ran down my spine and I shook it off before reaching into my back pocket for my phone. It was dead, nothing more than a hunk of useless technology. Big surprise. Returning it to my pocket, I stood very still and listened for signs of movement. Was there anyone else in this place? It *was* a library after all.

I walked on a few more paces, keeping my ears peeled. Finally, I heard it. The sound of a page turning.

Careful not to lose track of which direction I'd come from (because this book labyrinth could become very confusing very quickly), I began to jog down the aisle until I came to a small clearing with about six tables inside of it. Sitting at one of them were more dead people. Or waifs. Whatever *those* were. Two women and a man—all different stages of rotting.

The man, wearing a fitted green vest and a brown bowler hat, was the first to look up from his book. As soon as his eyes met mine, they grew.

"You're new."

And you're super old, I thought.

The two women looked up as soon as the man spoke, and as all three of them gave me their full attention, the blood in my veins began to curdle. I couldn't help but feel like they were *very* hungry.

"Who are you?" one of the women waifs asked in a British accent, her tongue finding the corner of her deeply green lips. "And how did you get in here?"

"I—I'm Tess. Reanin's granddaughter."

The other dead woman stood, leaving her knuckles on the table. "The doors are unlocked?" She had a heavy Jersey accent.

I gulped, then nodded.

"He's dead then?" the same woman asked, her excitement a bit palpable. I could feel it rising in my own chest.

"Who?" I asked.

"That twat of a rishi. Nisroc," the British one said. "Who else?"

Rishi?

I shook my head. "I don't know who that is." Or what that is.

The Jersey waif looked at me like I was dumb. "Kage's brotha." She cocked her head to the side. "Where's your grandma, honey?"

A dam broke in my mind. Kage's brother had a name.

"I think we're scaring her," the man said, closing his book. "She's from the other side, probably hasn't ever seen one of us having a bad day before. If this is Reanin's granddaughter then we've been stuck in here for a lot longer than we thought."

Redirecting his gaze back to me, he said, "How'd you get in here? Did Reanin come with you?"

I shook my head again.

"How long have the doors been closed?" the British one asked me.

I looked up at the ceiling as I did the math. "Forty years . . . ish."

I backed up a few steps as the three of them exploded in hysterics. When they finally started to come down, the man muttered, "Well then, I suppose that's why we stink."

The fingertips of my right hand nervously came up and touched the crystals around my neck. As soon as I touched them, I felt more at ease. I was able to configure my thoughts enough to ask, "What are you guys? I mean, I know you're waifs, but I don't know what that means."

"Didn't Reanin tell you?" asked the British one.

It was the man who answered for me. "I think it's safe to say that Reanin didn't tell her anything. Look at her, she's as pale as a ghost." He leaned in over the chair he was now using as a kickstand. "Reanin's not comin', is she?"

"No."

All three of their heads seemed to lower.

"How'd you get in here, sweetie?" asked Jersey.

"The shadows in my blood brought me here." It was the most honest answer I could summon.

The three of them looked at one another, then the man looked at me. "We're waifs, darlin'. We work here *and* we call this place home. Our service keeps this place going."

I pushed my tongue between my top and bottom teeth in an effort to be polite, but I couldn't help myself. I had to ask. "Why do you look like that?"

"We've traded part of ourselves for the sparkle that can be found in the shadows," the British one answered. "We don't always look like this." She tossed a layer of half long black locks saturated by blocks of white and gray over her shoulder. "If we don't keep up our end of the bargain then the magic we've inherited begins to eat away at us." Her eyes reached for the ceiling. "Forty years, you say. We've been down here a significant amount of time. We're lucky we haven't hit the point of no return."

"Yeah well," said Jersey, "the doors are unlocked now, ain't they? Now that we can travel, we'll be back to normal in no time."

"What's your end of the bargain?" I couldn't help but ask.

All three of them looked at me gravely.

"What happened to your grandma, hon?" asked Jersey.

I shook my head super slowly. "I'm starting to think that I don't really know."

"Ish," said the British one. "I like that word."

"Well, we best be off," said the man to the other two. They nodded as he looked at me. "Good luck. Grandma's got one hell of a show for you."

"What's that supposed to mean?" I whispered.

But none of them seemed to hear me. One by one, they began to make their way from the table they'd been huddled around for a very long time, gathering as many books as they could into their arms.

"Good luck, hon," said Jersey (her breath so very foul). She laid a hand over my shoulder as they prepared to walk by on their way out.

"Hang on," I said. The three of them turned around in unison. "I know I can't follow you. I came via the cards, and I've already been told that I have to play the game—"

"It's not a game," said the British one. "Those cards that Maggie helped Reanin create will be a real game changer, you just wait and see."

My ears perked up. "You guys knew Maggie?"

"No," said the same waif. "But before the doors were sealed, Reanin mentioned her."

"She did? So then do you guys know anything about a heart?"

All three of their heads started moving back and forth, and they were in such bad shape I was a little worried their heads would just fall right off.

"What has ya askin'?" asked Jersey.

I tipped my head to the side. "I don't even really know, if I'm being honest."

"Reanin didn't make it, did she?" the same one asked.

I couldn't bring myself to tell these people or whatever they were that their head mistress was dead. So instead, I just stated what I knew to be true. "It's not over and Nisroc isn't dead. Maybe if she'd known about my magic, I could've opened these doors a few years ago. Maybe I'd have better news to share with you all. But I didn't tell her about my magic and now the only thing I can do is try and finish what my grandma started."

Not one of them said a thing as I walked through them, back to where I'd left my spread. They didn't follow me, and moments later I heard a door open and shut.

I knew better than to think that I had time to waste. I didn't bother pulling any of the books from the shelves, although one had to wonder what sort of books could be found in an underworld library. I returned to the oracle spread and stared down at the second card. Rachel had said I would need to feed the shadows. I had no idea how I was supposed to do that, but I had to assume they didn't want my light.

I picked up the card where I was currently situated—The Library. "Well . . . what do you want from me?"

A squeaking wheel caused me to look up from where I was crouched over the cards, and I caught sight of an old book cart coming my way. It was moving on its own.

It came to a halt about a foot away from me. As soon as it stopped, I came up to my knees and inspected its shelves. There was only one book. A hardcover which matched the artwork on the oracle cards. Very carefully, I picked it up and flipped it open. As I did, an old-fashioned feather pen appeared over the page.

"What's this for?" I questioned as I picked it up.

As soon as it was in my hand, the slip of paper attached to the book like an old-fashioned sign-out card, twinkled with script. The message grew smaller the further down I read, so I had to squint to read it; even at that, it was barely legible.

Welcome to Hall of Shadows
Adventure awaits.
Please sign to enter.
No entrance without signature.
Not responsible for any bites or scratches.
Participant takes this journey at their own risk.
Cannot be accountable for client's refusal to accept his, her or their shadow work.
Disregarding one's shadows may result in getting locked in.
Please don't feed the tigers.

"Uh—okay . . ." I said as if the book could hear me.

My eyes flitted to the feathered pen in my hand. No inkwell had appeared, so with no other option I simply set the tip of the naked pen to the paper and began to sign. But I got no further than the first two letters.

Te

I doubled over, barely able to keep the pen and book in my hand.

"What the actual—"

The pain was so excruciating that I could barely talk. I looked down at the two letters I'd managed to scribble. They were written in black, and as I continued to study them, I noted how the ink (I don't think it was ink) twinkled. It sparkled like—

"Shadows." I pressed my lips and eyes together and took a deep breath, swallowing before standing up straight. "You're making me sign with my shadows."

It was hard to believe I was all alone in this great big place, but if there were any other creatures in the library, they didn't make themselves known. I fidgeted, trying to figure out what to do. Unfortunately, there weren't a lot of other options. If I didn't sign, would I get kicked out? It was either that or stay permanently in this giant library run by stinky waifs. And it wasn't like getting sacked was a viable option. I was here for a reason.

"Fine," I said, as I set the tip of the pen back down to the paper. And then, like a little kid readying to jump into an ice-cold lake, I took a deep breath, and ripped off the bandage.

My hand didn't shake as I wrote out my full name. There wasn't enough time for that. In fact, I'd never signed my name faster.

Tess Moreau

As soon as the deed was done—my first shadow checked in—the pen disappeared, and the book closed then flew back onto the cart, which wasted no time wheeling itself away. The pain had only lasted as long as it had taken me to sign my name. However, I did feel like I'd given something away.

I wasn't sure what I'd just done. But what was the point of being young and the granddaughter of a dude named Kage if I couldn't be reckless?

Unsure if that was all I needed to do before blowing this joint, I knelt back down and tugged at the second card. It flipped over easily.

"Guess that was the first feeding," I said, just as the room fell cold and the dim light turned black.

CHAPTER SIXTEEN

The card shimmered as it colored into the portrait of a mirror, the label under the illustration saying just as much. I froze, hunched over the spread, waiting for the dim lighting from the library to brighten as I entered this new dimension, but it did the opposite of that. It wasn't just darker. It was pitch black.

I cautiously began to turn on my heels, only to discover a small bit of white light shining into a gray spot filled by an empty chair. I'd just gotten to my feet and was about to near it when I heard a voice calling out from the light.

"Constance? Is that you? The mirror is finally rippling!"

My ears perked up, and I began to take delicate, thoughtful steps towards the light.

When I got close enough, I saw the face of a woman (maybe in her fifties) staring back at me. As soon as she saw me, she fell back, but not so much that I completely lost sight of her.

"Hello?" I called out.

The woman's eyes narrowed as she peeked back in through

her side of what was very clearly a portal. She slowly inched her shoulders back into the frame.

"Where's Constance?"

I shook my head. "I don't know who that is. I've only just turned up here."

As soon as the words were out of my mouth, the quiet creak of a door opening sounded from somewhere in the vast void that made up this shadow. The door shut and footsteps rounded their way up next to where I was standing, until another woman—eerily similar looking to the one staring back at us through the portal, appeared.

Hardly paying me a second glance, the woman sat in the chair and looked up into the portal. "The Hall has been reopened. How long has it been?"

"Forty-five years," said the other one in a deep, throaty voice. "Where did you go?"

"To The Forest. I was warned before the doors closed that I may want to switch positions." The seated woman rolled her eyes. "I suppose it was a good thing I did—forty-five years! My goddess, you'd think the mistress would've at least poked her head in now and again for an update." The woman, Constance I had to presume, finally turned to me. She had very bright eyes, like a cat, and her nose was pinched and long. Her mouth was set in a pucker. "Did Reanin send you?"

"No," I answered a little too quickly. Then added, "Maybe. I don't really know."

Constance didn't move a muscle. "Well then, come out with it! Who the hell are you?"

"Goodness Constance," said the other one. "Why must you always be so blunt? The girl looks as confused as we do."

Still, the seated woman didn't budge. "Well?"

"I'm Reanin's granddaughter," I answered. Constance's eyes turned into small slits. "She left me the remnants of the doors to this place."

Again, she looked at me questionably. This time, her twin copied her expression.

"You know—the ashes."

"Ashes?" Constance chirped.

"Yeah, because the oracle cards she created—" She frowned even harder. "I—I just assumed you knew about them because the others did—" I started to point back towards the library as if I knew where it was in this twisted labyrinth. "You know, the cards that served as the entrance to The Hall—"

"I know about the damn cards," Constance snipped. "What is this other nonsense you're spewing on about?"

"Okay," I said, wrapping my hands tightly together in front of my stomach. "The cards ended up getting set on fire. That's why the doors were locked for so long. But as soon as I found out about them, I was able to manipulate them back into cards. It's kind of my thing . . . doing that." I sounded as awkward as I felt and the way the two of them were staring at me just reaffirmed that.

The woman on the other end of the portal was the first to speak up. "The gray witch burned the cards." She was shaking her head. "I knew Reanin was treading over choppy waters with that one."

"Never trust an Irish witch," Constance added.

They continued to chatter, and as they did, my neck started to get tweaky from chasing one likeness to the next. "Look," I finally said, interrupting their commentary. "My— Reanin—she didn't make it." Silence. Eerie, thick, heavy silence. "I didn't know about any of this until after she was already gone," I waved my arms around to denote the shadow world. "She left the cards, or the ashes, to me. I've come here to meet Kage and deliver a message, but apparently, I have to flip over each of these cards before I can do that."

Before I could deliver more on the urgency of my

situation, the one in the light spoke. "So Reanin is gone." After a short pause, she asked her twin, "Did you know Reanin and Kage had a child?"

Constance shook herself back from wherever she'd temporarily gone to get away from what I'd announced. "There were rumors before she left that she had created life, but those assumptions stayed mostly between the waifs . . . that is all I know."

"This girl can bring life back from death, Constance."

"*'Tis* interesting," Constance echoed.

Though I couldn't hear it, I knew there was a clock ticking somewhere. I needed to move quicker through these shadows. As I tried to figure out my next move, strategize what this shadow might want from me, I realized for the first time what the woman on the other side of the portal was looking through.

"This is a mirror," I said airily, pointing up at the face of the woman.

When neither of them confirmed nor denied my realization, I reached my fingers further towards the light. Once they were close enough, the air turned wet and rippled, but I was unable to push any further into it or through it than just that. When I retrieved my hand, it was dry.

"It's a reflection actually," Constance hammered out. "Cordelia has the mirror on her end. This was one of the first ones to be used in The Hall."

"Cordelia," I muttered. It was the first time either of them had mentioned the other one's name. "Are you twins?"

"No," snapped Constance.

"We were once one witch with two sides," Cordelia explained, her tone containing all the chirping birds and rainbow ends that Constance lacked. "We were one of the most powerful gray witches to walk the earth. We believed in the light just as much as the dark. It was Kage who discovered us; he communicated to us that his world could benefit greatly from our services, but to aid in the growth of his shadows we would need to divide ourselves. Constance is our dark half, and I am our light. I cannot walk the shadows as I am, so we devised a way to keep in touch."

I exhaled my reaction in one simple word, compliments of Jamae's vocabulary. "Rad."

Cordelia continued. "The Mirror is here to demonstrate to those who need it, how to distinguish between their own dark and light. It is a teaching tool, one we helped Kage reform and create. But furthermore, our dark side—Constance—provides a very important addition to The Hall. As long as she is a resident, she can sense a breech."

"I'm like a feline," Constance said as her lids dimmed over her bright green eyes.

"A security system," I observed.

"Yes," Constance answered simply.

"Cordelia stared down from her vantage point and locked her gaze with mine. "Do you know the name Nisroc, child?"

"I do now," I said with regret.

"It is a cursed one," muttered Constance.

Cordelia neither agreed nor disagreed with her other half's assessment. "He is the reason your grandmother left this place. He threatened to take down The Hall so Kage swiped something very important of his—something he needed to remain a threat. But somehow, the object was returned to Nisroc."

"A traitor in the midst," Constance whispered in a crackled voice.

"Perhaps," Cordelia answered carefully.

"It was," snipped Constance. "If anyone else had broken in I would have known. I knew the second this little prat fell into The Library."

"True, but the idea that there is a traitor in the shadows is not something we can be sure of. If it was a resident, then I am sure they have only themselves to contend with now."

"Chipper nag," Constance griped.

I bit my lip as Cordelia grinned. "Always so half empty, Constance." Before her dark half could snag yet another insult, Cordelia returned her attention to me and continued to glue together some of the stray pieces I'd been collecting. "Nisroc, as he is, cannot enter this world without sacrifice. It is one he wasn't, and I'm sure still isn't, ready to make."

"What kind of sacrifice?" I asked, a heaviness settling in over my heart.

"It doesn't matter," Constance said, mockingly. "Ignorance has stained his soul. His shadows are thick, yet he claims he has none. He will never face himself; he will only build more armies and convince them to do what he cannot. To claim what he has no right to claim."

I recalled what Maggie and I had spoken about before the witch was so brutally killed. "He's after some sort of magic that can only be found down here, right?"

Constance's cat-like eyes rested over my shoulder before she heaved a great sigh. "He seeks what so many unworthy traitors seek. The Stones of Gehenna."

I scrunched up my nose. "What?"

Cordelia jumped in. "Kage was the first to set foot inside this world. His peers tried to stop him, even after he'd warned them to leave him be. He knew the outside world wasn't for him, that he had been bred for something else. The possibility of what the Hall of Shadows could be was what got his heart beating. Still, his friends and colleagues, like Nisroc, thought they knew what was best for him. They held up their swords against him and tried to keep him from falling into the shadows. He warned them; he gave them every opportunity to remove themselves from his path. But they were stubborn."

"So he murdered the prats," Constance announced.

"Don't be so brash, Constance," Cordelia scolded. Then returning her attention to me, clarified, "He didn't *murder* them, he defended his choice. In the end, they were turned into stones. Stones that contain an unknown amount of magic. Many have felt their power, in and out of The Hall."

A slow breath fell from my lips. "And these stones are what Nisroc and his followers are after."

"Yes," said Cordelia.

"And the stones are rumored to be here—in the shadows."

Cordelia nodded.

"Kage isn't some novice," Constance growled. "The stones are under supreme protection."

My grandfather murdered three of his kind and they turned into stones . . . I couldn't help but reach for what rested against my chest.

No, that was impossible.

I loosed a ragged breath then looked back up at the nice half of the gray witch. "Have you ever seen them? The Stones of Gehenna?"

"I have not," she replied.

"They used to be on display in one of the shadows," Constance offered. "They were safe there, for the only hand that had the ability to grace them was the one who created them."

"Kage," I said.

Constance dipped her chin. "However, they are not where they used to be."

Cordelia frowned. "They were moved?"

Constance remained quite still in her chair as she answered. "Yes. Just before the doors were locked.

My jaw unhinged, but anything I had to say was stuck in the back of my throat. Yes, it was glaringly obvious that I was wearing a necklace made from three stones that had been delivered to me in a more than mysterious way. Probably by a waif. But no—there was no way I was wearing the remains of three dead—whatevers.

I returned my attention to the two witches. "What exactly is my grandfather? What is Nisroc?"

The waif in the library had said something about a rishi, but I had no idea what that was.

Constance, her arms crossed, looked up at me. "They're angels."

Before my eyes could finish rolling out of their sockets, Cordelia barked at her other half. "That's such a broad term, Constance. You must remember where this girl—what's your name child?" I answered her. "You must remember where Tess has come from." She redirected her gaze to fall through the reflection and land over my shoulders. "Your blood has been formed from what a lot of people call angels, but *please* do not associate this term with what you think you might know about them. They are guardians—messengers—meant to protect whichever planet they've been assigned to. They were given free will just like all of us, but just like humans, there are many guardians who have forgotten that simple fact. Kage never felt comfortable in his wings, so he traded them to get inside a portal that offered him a new beginning. That is the truth."

I'd heard about four words out of all of that. "He traded his wings?"

"Magic is nothing if not irrational," grumbled Constance.

My shoulders slowly began to fall. My grandfather had traded his wings for shadows. "Kage is a fallen angel."

Cordelia straightened out on the other end of the connection and looked directly at me.

"The Hall of Shadows is an underworld, child. How does this make you feel? And before you answer, this is not the place to slough off verbs and adjectives that leave you feeling uncomfortable. This is the place to let the infection grow. To satiate all that discomfort—for to feel is to live. Numbing yourself is purgatory."

"I—I don't know how it makes me feel."

"Lies," Constance barked. "What did she just say, Tess?" She pointed up to Cordelia.

I swallowed, hard. "That this is not the place to hide." I stared from one pair of eyes to the other. "Okay . . . I've never thought much about underworlds or anything, but I guess the first thing that comes to mind is that this is some sort of hell." My chest lifted as I looked for any sort of reaction (mostly from Cordelia). But they were both straight-faced. "From all that you've said, though, I can only assume that this is not that. And I've never believed in the devil, so there's that."

"There *is* a hell," Constance spat out. "Each and every human has experienced it. It's called their lives."

I hesitated, waiting for Cordelia to snap at her for being brash, but she never did. Apparently, they agreed on that one.

Finally, Cordelia elaborated. "An underworld is where someone goes between lives. It is where your soul is enlightened and brought around to remember all the lives it has ever lived—all the lessons it has gained or failed to address. If you had other lives to speak of before this one, you would take Constance's seat and I would show you in this mirror who you've been and who you have the possibility of being. As it is, you are—different."

"What's that mean?" I asked.

"'Tis your first life," answered Constance gruffly. "Your only."

I grimaced. "What?"

"She speaks the truth," Cordelia said. "Don't fret, Granddaughter of Kage and Reanin. It's also why you're here, is it not? To find out about yourself. About why you have creation at your fingertips."

"Yes," I whispered.

"Good," Cordelia said with a slight dip of her forehead. "We should let you get on with it then. But let me leave you with this: When Kage found this place, he knew it could be momentous. Somewhere for those like him to gather. To go into the darkness and grapple with the parts of themselves that weren't ever going to be pretty. It was and is the gritty that most of us find enlightening; it is in the shadows that we find our inner truths. Just because we've found it before bodily death doesn't make it bad or evil. At least we don't think so."

I didn't give the next words to leave my mouth permission to do so, but still they did. "Then why are you on the other side of the reflection?"

She didn't skip a beat. "Because I am the light in the gray. Darkness can handle only so much light at a time. Though I am too much of one thing to stand where you are, there *is* some light inside The Hall. If there wasn't, how would you explain the shadows?"

Just then, Constance cleared her throat and stood before cracking her back in a standing backbend, then she proceeded to climb through the reflection like a spider. Only a second later, she stood neck and neck with the other half of herself.

I couldn't help it, my jaw dropped. "How in the world did you do that?" I asked, craning my neck to try and follow the awkward angle she'd just achieved to get herself from one end of the portal to the other.

Constance shrugged. "You opened the doors, didn't you? We can all come and go as we please now." She turned to Cordelia. "Nice to see you. Forty-five years—ha!" And then she stalked off.

I stared at Cordelia in astonishment. "What if the portal closes again?"

"I expect it won't," she said with a wink.

I pointed to where Constance had just been standing next to her. "But she's the security system. What if someone, or someone's *army* tries to break in now that the doors are open?"

"She won't go far, and she won't be long."

I continued to stumble over my words. "Wh—Well—How many other doors are there in this place, exactly?"

Cordelia lowered her chin. "Many." She paused before adding, "It was very nice meeting you, Tess. You have a bit of a journey in front of you, therefore I shall need to be letting you get to it. As for me, I need to be with my other half now; we work better separately after we've spent some time together and we have much catching up to do." She began to step away but returned just as quickly. "Oh, and a word of advice, child—just because you have no other lives to compare to this one, that doesn't mean The Mirror won't expect to be fed."

I nodded unenthusiastically. "I assumed."

Cordelia smiled in a way that encouraged others to truly see that there is always a hint of darkness even in the pureness of light. "I realize you are on a mission, but please do not disregard that this is *a gift* your grandmother left to you. You are, in fact, working through the reading of a lifetime."

Then she was gone, for real this time. And I was left all alone in a dark room with only the light from the mirror's reflection to lead me back to where my spread was waiting.

I knelt against the ground where the oracle cards had materialized. The floor was like a lake of black marble. With my hands over my knees, I looked up from the cards and out into the void. A piece of me was curious as to whether there was anything else in this room—it just seemed like so much space to remain empty. Then again, Maggie's book had mentioned that the depths of the shadows ranged from person to person. Entity to entity. Perhaps the extra room was needed for some.

Unsure of what to do next, I drew up my hand and

reached out to turn over the next card, but try as I might, it wouldn't budge.

"Great," I muttered, and was just about to throw my head back in exasperation when the mirror Cordelia had been looking through began to tilt.

I sat back on my heels, the mirror beginning to spin before it moved from its place. Like a helium balloon, it began to drift over to where I was sitting, turning counterclockwise. Eventually, when it was close enough—levitating directly above the cards—it stopped spinning and remained in place.

"Groovy," I whispered, another vocabulary hand-me-down from my witchy adult friend.

The reflection had changed; it was no longer discernible what I was looking at. Finally, it started rippling, appearing much like the surface of a dark lake. When it stopped, it wasn't myself I saw staring back. Instead, a recording from the past played before my eyes.

I was looking at a white armoire against an ivory wall; it took me only a few seconds to place it as the same one I had in my bedroom.

"Mommy! Mommy, come find me!" came the small, young voice of a child.

Then nothing, for maybe a full five minutes.

There were a few more cries and pleas, but when no one came, the left door swung open and a pint size me jumped out from the closet. Already I could see it in the ever-changing colors of my eyes—sadness. I was let down because the one person who was supposed to love me the most in the world didn't even try to play with me. Not ever.

"Mommy," the tiny me said again.

This time my mother appeared in the memory.

"Tess, I've told you time and again that I don't have time for games." She shoved a school uniform into my doll-sized arms. "Put this on then come downstairs. I have places to be, and this is your first day at this school. We don't want to be late." And then she left.

She was always leaving. Always handing me things to put on (new and different uniforms seeing as I couldn't seem to stay at one school for very long).

The miniature me looked up at the real me as if she could see me. "She never hugged us. Not once. She never said 'I love you.'"

I shook my head, burdened by my inability to produce even one little hot tear. "It's not our fault."

"You don't believe that. You hate her because she's made you hate yourself."

A bowling ball might as well have socked me right in the gut. It was one thing to hear those words, but quite another to hear it from your past self.

"I don't hat—"

Suddenly the vision of my bedroom and all the light that went with it faded to black along with the little girl that had once been me. The Mirror was nothing more than a mirror, a reflection of myself. Except it wasn't necessarily my exact likeness, for *my* jaw was slightly unhinged, and the girl who I was staring at had closed lips.

"This is not the place to hide," she said.

"Who are you?"

"I am the one you thought you pulled out the other night. When you screamed into a pillow. You only just woke me, but here—here you can't push me away. Not unless you want to stay inside this shadow forever." Her eyes flitted over my shoulders as if she was looking at something. "You're not alone. When the crone came back into this place, she let something in. Something that has been studying you from the darkness. It doesn't seem to want to nibble on your skin yet . . . but it's well past its prime, and I suspect it might get hungry sooner than later."

My head ticked back in the direction she'd been gazing, but I saw nothing but blackness. "What are you talking about?" I asked, slowly returning my gaze to fit inside the mirror. "There's nothing in here."

"Nothing that *you* can see," she returned with a sneer.

My breathing returned to choppy. "Okay—whatever. Either way, I want to move forward. How do I get out of here?"

"All you have to do, Tess, is admit it."

"Admit what?"

"What we've already discussed. That your hatred for the one you called Mom for so very long happened because she neglected to love you, thus causing you to hate yourself." She waited for me to answer. When I didn't, she reiterated, "You're not going anywhere until you do this."

I heaved a sigh and rolled my eyes. "I don't hate myself."

"*Quit* lying."

"I don't!"

At that, she sat up straighter. Her eyes darkened and her neck seemed to grow longer. When next she spoke, her jaw elongated, and I could almost see down her throat.

"*I* am your hatred! *I* exist because of that woman. Your mother. Because she didn't provide even a morsel of love for her own daughter! I cannot be terminated, and I *refuse* to be ignored!"

My heart was thumping so hard that I worried the vibrations would rattle the mirror and send it toppling over and into pieces . . . though that probably wasn't a possibility. This wasn't an ordinary piece of looking glass.

When I dared to speak, I did so softly. "I never meant to ignore you."

Her entire body seemed to lower, her features relaxing into a less terrifying reflection.

"What do you want me to say? Because, sure, I can tell you

that everything you've said is true, but if I don't feel it to be, then it won't matter. The card still won't turn for me."

"Who cares about the card?" she spat out. "You're here to confront your shadows—to meet me."

"I'm only fifteen. This kind of stuff is sort of above my pay grade."

"More lies. You are raw, teetering between shedding the layers of humanity you've come to know and replacing it with coming into your power. Accepting the dirty details of your life is the only way to walk up those stairs."

I hesitated, unsure of what to say to that; but she didn't make me search anymore. Instead, she slipped a hand from the reflection and held it out for me to take. I stared at it for maybe a little too long. It was my own, but the skin was different. Grayish, made from shadows. Finally, I reached for it, and as soon as our skin made contact, everything shifted.

My head was under the ocean. The waves were livid—shaking me back and forth like a doll in the hands of an angry child. The undercurrent was taking blows at my guts like I'd officially offended it. There was only a faint glow around my body, but it was enough to shed light over what was happening to me.

If I was sure of anything it was that I was *not* going to drown in the dark.

Her voice rang through my ears. "If you refuse to fight, then you must slowly die over and over again."

I opened my mouth to scream, but all that happened was an accumulation of air bubbles and the rankest water I could've ever imagined as it forced its way down my throat. Still, it didn't drown me.

Her words rang through my head. "Why do you hate?"

I started to think to myself that I wasn't ever going to pass this test. And then I saw her . . . not my hatred, but my mother.

She was floating across from me in this unruly tide. Her face was as it always was, neutral. She never smiled at me the way I'd seen other mothers do for their children. I never once thought, 'this woman would die for me.' If anything, she would feel lighter if I'd been taken from her side.

"Why didn't you love me?" I shouted at her. This time, the water didn't flow into my mouth. This time, I felt a little air in my lungs.

When she didn't answer, a bit of flame lit up inside my chest.

"I know you didn't care!" I shouted. "You didn't love me or Dad! It was always about *you*, and whoever you really were!" As soon as the words left my bluish lips, I knew they were true. "Why did you even stay? We would have been better without you—Dad and I would have been just fine! But you continued to live next to us, breathe beside us, and never once did you make us feel like we were a family." I shook my head, noting as I did that the water was starting to slip away. It continued to evaporate until I was facing my mother over a patch of black sand, nothing but darkness hugging our shoulders. "Even now . . ." My chest caved in. "If I told you I hated you, would you even hear me say it?"

Hatred appeared beside her. A vision of myself painted in shadows.

"I honestly don't know if she *can* hear you," she stated. "But does it matter?"

"Yes," I said as clear as day, the rhythm of my heart so very irregular. "Why does any of this matter if I can't speak directly to her—to tell her how she destroyed me while she was living?"

"It's not about her, Tess."

I started to talk back. . . but quickly stopped myself. Letting Hatred's words sink in, I finally heard her. I finally understood.

A slow drizzle began to fall around us and in the silence that followed, our clothes and hair began to dampen. I held out my palm and accepted the light rain. I don't know why, but as it touched my skin—as it ran down my wrist—a heaviness lifted from my ribcage and a shudder of breath entered my lungs.

I matched my gaze with my hatred. "Okay."

Still standing just next to the image of my mother, she tilted her head to the side. "Okay?"

"I understand. You exist because of her . . . because of her disinterest in me. If it wasn't for her, I would have had no reason to hate myself. To think that there was ever anything wrong with me." I let my next thought roll around my tongue before I let it out. "I may have even thought to tell my grandma, or even my dad, about my abilities. I might not have thought I was such a freak."

The rain continued to drizzle around us for a few more beats and then it was gone. And then the hologram of Janine Moreau-Wells was gone . . . and then it was just me sitting before my oracle cards.

The mirror was back in place, over the solo chair, and in it, Hatred smiled.

"See, was that so hard?" She didn't let me answer. "Go on then, Tess. Get out of here—before that thing behind you gets too interested. Too hungry."

The hairs on the back of my neck rose as I peered into every corner. Still, I saw nothing. When I returned my gaze to the mirror, Hatred was gone. At least from sight.

As I placed my hand over the next card, the third one in the reading, I said to her, wherever she was, "Thanks."

I thought, as I flipped over that next card, that I felt a hot breath over my shoulder, but I was gone and into the next shadow before I could find out what it was. If, even, it had been anything at all.

CHAPTER SEVENTEEN

The Pendulum materialized onto its card as a golden chain with a smoky colored stone hanging from the end. I'd seen pendulums before; they hung like necklaces from a thin wooden bar inside Hexed. I'd reached out a few times to see if any of them reached back, and even though the same one always did, I'd never got up the guts to actually take it into my hand.

Jamae insisted that the one interested in me was very special. It hung from a delicate silver chain and was made of amethyst and a vial of charged moon water. She'd tried to give it to me, but I'd refused it. I don't really know why . . . I reacted that way sometimes when I wasn't sure about something. Like, since I didn't know exactly what to do with it, I didn't want to try it yet. But now, as I turned and faced one of the biggest pendulums I'd ever seen, I kinda wished I'd taken Jamae up on her offer. I would've at least gotten a little practice in. There was no doubt about it, I wasn't getting out of this shadow without that monster swinging one way or the other.

I stood, taking in the enormous magical tool hanging from

what was clearly a stage. This place was brighter than the last two rooms, if you could call it that. A room was just a generic term for these spaces inside The Hall. What they really were was a network of dimensions, and I was beginning to value the difference in each one.

The Mirror had felt small yet endless; it was blanketed in darkness, save for the reflection of Cordelia's mirror. The Library had been vast, and again, endless. And this, well, this was an old, dusty auditorium. *Very* old, from what I could gather. It wasn't quite as small as a high school auditorium, but it wasn't as large as the play hall my parents dragged me to a few years ago to see some symphony I didn't care about. Here, there were maybe two hundred seats, tops.

The giant pendulum hung from a black bar directly over the worn wooden stage. It had large golden hoops for a string, and one hell of a large crystal hanging from its end; the stone was one I'd seen before, but I couldn't remember the name of it. It matched the pendulum on the card perfectly.

My attention traveled to the curtains hanging around the stage. I was sure that at one point they'd been blood red, but now they were faded. Hints of fuchsia and orange broke through the thick fabric. I also noted that the stage was littered with old flyers, much like a school hallway would appear if the lockers threw up all the bits of notebook paper hibernating inside them. But that wasn't all that was contained inside this shadow. Out in the audience, where rows of wooden chairs did their best to remain intact, was a waif.

My heart started at the sight of him. He was older than the other ones I'd seen, but not ancient. Maybe in his late fifties. He was dressed in all leather: chaps, vest, and a Brando hat with a chain across the visor. All that was missing was his motorcycle. His skin was a rare tint of green and his fingernails were black. As soon as I laid eyes on him, he spoke.

"You that one they all talking about? Kage and Reanin's

kin?" He didn't have an accent, but his speech offered a slow drawl.

I neared center stage, all the while keeping my gaze on his, and stood just in front of the hanging pendulum. Cupping my hands together in front of my stomach, I answered. "Yeah. Who are you?"

"They call me Frank."

My attention lifted and roamed around the rest of the abandoned auditorium. "You know anything about a heart, Frank?"

"No, I don't believe I do, and that's a strange question."

"That it is," I agreed, but it was one I would need an answer for at some point. My eyes still roaming, I added, "This place looks like it was well used at one point." It still smelt of the blood, sweat, and tears of so many performers.

I bent down and picked up one of the flyers. The title, *Cinderella,* was printed over an illustration of ten ballet dancers and an old-fashioned carriage. *September 18th*, it read. *Starring Reanin Wellington. Directed by John Wellington.*

I blinked with purpose as I reread the yellowed piece of paper at least three more times.

"Reanin Wellington," I whispered. ". . . John."

"Figured that might catch yer fancy," said Frank. "She barely changed her name when she left that life."

My gaze lifted then fell over the waif. I raised the odd find up in the air as if I'd just plucked a winning lottery ticket from the ground. "What the hell is this?"

The waif remained seated as he pulled up a hand and rested his chin in it. Then, waving around his other hand to the rest of our surroundings, he said, "It happened occasionally when they started creating these places. Reanin's shadows filled in quite literally."

A snippy, "What?" fell from my lips.

"Well, ya know," he said, sounding very much like any old timer I'd ever heard say that line. "Kage and Reanin built this whole thing together, but then, you know, Reanin's heart bled out a little more. Her shadows are responsible for much of the décor." He clicked his tongue. "I reckon the performance she did here really did a number on her."

"How well did you know my grandmother, exactly?"

"Oh." He raised his brows. "I knew her quite well. This place was a staple in her hometown—that's why the stage is so small. The town was just big enough for a place like this. By the time she graced this stage, she was used to dancing in much bigger venues. John made her come back here—said it was good for her reputation to bring her back to her roots. I think that sadistic pig just wanted to watch her squirm."

I let my attention flutter down to where all the flyers were scattered, forgotten. "My grandmother was a ballerina?"

When he didn't answer right away, I looked out to where he was seated. He had a finger against his dark brown lip, and he seemed to be studying me. "You really didn't know her, did ya?"

I shook my head. "I guess not."

As I said it, I searched through my memories, trying to piece together any clues that would lead me to believe that the woman I'd known had ever graced a stage. She *could* have had the body of a dancer; she'd been average height, thin. Her limbs were usually covered by some sort of expensive designer fabric. The few times I'd seen her legs, they were sculpted—so were her arms. But I would've guessed yogi over ballerina. My grandma didn't seem to have a dancer's temperament. Then again, what did I know about any of that? I was a recluse teenager whose best friends were, like, thirty.

"She was big," Frank said. "First debut was back in 1896. She was all over the New York stages by 1901."

"1896 . . ."

I'd just come to find out that my grandma had been connected to one of the biggest underworlds ever created by two pairs of hands. I'd also been informed that my grandma, maybe, wasn't even quite human when she was killed. But I'd had yet to assume that she'd come from a different era. That her life had been extended.

I mean, I guess it wasn't super far out to admit she could've stopped aging at some point. Everywhere we went, she was accused of having a young face—but who balked at that? We lived in New York City; it was almost expected for a woman of Reanin's status to have work done. Except she never had, and I knew that.

Good genes, potatoes, and little to no sun—that's what good old granny had always preached. That was the secret. But it wasn't. The secret was magic.

I lifted my chin while keeping my stare geared over Frank. "Who was John?"

"Who do you think?" When I didn't say anything, he jiggled his jaw back and forth then added, "At his best, he was a wisenheimer. The rest of the time he was a raging bull. His ballet had to be perfect, and if one toe was out of place, the whole production felt his wrath."

"If he was such a dick then why did my grandmother marry him? I mean, I assume that was the situation, seeing as they shared the same last name."

Frank cleared his throat. "Same old story. He lured her in with promises of fame and fortune. He told her that her talents were unmatched by anyone else on earth, and he didn't show his truest colors until after the ring was on her finger. Also, you should know that your grandma came from nothing. She didn't even have the luxury of coming from a poor situation. She was raised by a sickly aunt who expected her to continuously grovel for rescuing her from a mother who would have sunk her under the river water the second no one was looking. When she was old enough, Reanin snuck into the wagon of a traveling carnival and pretended to be part of a minstrel act.

"Performing came natural to her, ya see, and it wasn't long before her long legs and graceful movements were discovered. Pete Ginsberg was the first to take her under his wing and bring her from the circus to the stage. She was put under rigorous studies, but it paid off. Within years, the biggest ballet company in the country got a hold of her, and that is, of course, how she met John."

I couldn't believe what I was hearing.

I set down the flyer and walked to the edge of the stage, swinging my feet around as I had a seat. "You knew her back then, didn't you? You weren't just some fan who decided to give part of himself away to her vision."

He neither nodded nor shook his head. "I was a stagehand for the ballet. I saw everything. Every deep breath she took to center herself before the curtain rose, every bruise she hid with thick make-up that was destined to sweat off. I saw every time she fixed her face like stone and bit down over her tongue so she wouldn't snap at the man who had a habit of taking her chin in his hand as he yelled in her face." Frank's bottom lip reached out above the top one for a second before he ranted on. "I offered her my gun once. Told her there was no one I needed to fear enough to keep it while she was waking up next to the devil every day."

"Did she take it?"

"Naw. She said killing him wouldn't fix a thing. He was only one part of a life that she despised."

Just then, one of the auditorium doors swung open and a very tall man with pearl-like skin and a chiseled jaw appeared. He was wearing a slick pair of pants and a fitted black shirt.

This was no waif, but I was positive that he wasn't human either.

"Frank," he stated firmly, causing the waif to turn and see who was personally addressing him. Without acknowledging me, he said, "We need you at the surface."

Frank remained seated as he asked, "What's the plan?"

"Time to hunt the hunters."

Frank nodded. "Where we startin'?"

"Got the skinny on one of the newest cults. We'll start there."

I didn't have to ask to know what they were talking about.

"That sounds fine," Frank retorted. He turned around and set his attention squarely over my shoulders, while finishing up his last thought with the other guy. "Give me just a few."

The man by the doors nodded, then turned as if to make his getaway, but I couldn't resist.

"Hey!" I shouted to him. His firm gaze settled over the ever-changing color of my irises. A chill ran down my spine from his icy blue eyes; they reminded me of someone. "The cult you're all hunting—what's its name?"

"I think you already know the answer to that, Ms. Moreau." Then, before I could utter a response, he bowed his head in my direction before dipping back into what was most likely a very long hallway.

I gulped as the door shut. I didn't want it to be Jamae and Ethan's coven, but theirs was the only one I knew of.

"You got friends in low places, or something?" Frank asked.

"I don't know." It was the most honest thing I could think to say. Then, changing gears, I asked, "Who was that?"

"Garett."

"And what *sort* is Garett?"

Frank smirked. "A siren."

A ragged breath found its way up my lungs. "So, he used to be a—"

"Guardian."

Right. They had many names.

"Do they all look like that?" I asked. "I mean, with those crazy blue eyes?"

"Not all of them. I don't know if you've already heard this, but you have—"

"I have my grandfather's eyes. Yeah, I've been told."

We shared a moment of silence, my thoughts churning, and then the waif stood. He cracked his back then said, "I better be off." He gestured to the pendulum hanging behind me. "That there was Reanin's idea. You'll have fun with that." Then he started to walk away.

I froze. *Foreboding much?* "Wait! What's that supposed to mean?"

He turned only his cheek in my direction as he kept walking towards the doors. "Ask it somethin'. That's all you have to do."

Then he left, just like they all did before I was getting ready to move shadows. Except something in the back of my brain whispered that I was nowhere near sliding into the next oracle card.

I clicked my tongue a few times, delaying the inevitable. Finally, I flipped my legs around so they were back on the stage. I reached for one of the flyers, studying the illustration. How had I not seen her before? Reanin Wellington . . . she was right there. And even though she was gone, I had a feeling that she was right here, too. No way could she have designed something like this and not left pieces of herself everywhere.

I stalled in that spot, hunkered before the pendulum, for a long time—maybe even an hour. At some point I got up, walked around, searched for pieces of old popcorn and candy under the fraying fabric of the seats. Eventually I had to come to terms with the monster waiting for me.

I'd finally remembered the name of the crystal hanging from the pendulum. As I stared at it, rooted directly across from the massive tool, I heard Jamae's voice echoing in my head as she described the stone hanging from her necklace.

Black moonstone. It grounds me.

As her voice faded away, my hand came up to the stones around my neck and clutched them. As I did a whisper filled my head. *It also grants a connection with the dark goddess.*

My grip fell away from the necklace, and I jumped, completely caught off guard.

I stared down at the stones, then at the hand that had touched them.

"No way," I whispered. But still, I placed my fingers over the stones one more time. "Hello?"

We are here for you, Tess Moreau.

Once more, I yanked my hand away from the stones. As my gaze traveled rapidly from what hung around my neck and what hung from the rafters just feet in front of me, I did my best to keep my breathing level. If anyone was to pick up a haunted necklace, it would have to be me. But was that what this really was? I couldn't stop thinking about what I'd learned from those twisted witches in The Mirror. The magic that lived in The Hall had come from the immortalized hearts of three guardians, slayed for the sake of the shadows. The stones had been moved . . .

I shook my head. *That* was all just a little too heavy and I was already carrying too great a load. "One thing at a time," I muttered.

I took a few more calming breaths, in through my nose and out through my mouth, then shook my hands out by my sides and turned my attention wholly to the pendulum.

"Okay . . ." I whispered. "You can do this. It's simple."

From what I knew of pendulums, they worked like any other magical tool. Witches were known to use them to find answers to all sorts of things. From lost possessions to how many children they might have. Jamae had shown me a little about how they worked only once. She was very adamant that before I use it, I ask it to show me 'yes,' then show me 'no.' More often than not a circle meant yes and a straight line meant no, but she said it was important to clarify because the energy on the other end of the line could be a trickster, and they enjoyed playing with our wits.

"Show me yes," I stated clearly. Almost immediately the black moonstone began to move around in a circle. The circumference was so large that I had to take several steps back and to the side. When it slowed down enough to come to a halt, I said, "Show me no." This time the golden chains moved the stone towards the front of the stage and back, in a straight line.

Cool, now all I had to do was ask this thing a question, although I had an inkling there would be more to it than that. After all, this place was darker than light. Lucky for me, I'd had a very bold question brewing inside ever since I'd spoken with Maggie. Realistically, I'd been pondering over it ever since I'd learned about my unusual abilities.

"Am I human?"

I waited for the black moonstone to move either front to back or in a circle, but as I waited for it to make its move, it did neither. Instead, it began to vacillate around in no particular design. Almost like a child holding a yo-yo and shaking the string instead of letting it perform as it should. Then, as if Frank was backstage manipulating the lights as he had done once upon a time, the stage dimmed to black, and a spotlight shone over just one seat in the fifth row from the stage.

I gasped as the figure of a hooded person appeared under the light.

"Tess Moreau," said a female voice as smooth as silk and as deep as the ocean.

My voice croaked in the back of my throat. "Yes."

The woman's head lifted, and she pulled away her hood. As our eyes met, I nearly fainted.

It was the goddess from my new oracle deck. The Goddess of the Witches.

CHAPTER EIGHTEEN

I was met with the most beautiful eyes I'd ever seen— apart from my own (not to brag). They were very much like mine: green, golden, hints of blue . . . hints of darkness.

I couldn't explain it, but as soon as I saw her, I had the feeling that I would never again be alone. Like, I'd finally received a hand to guide me.

"I wasn't asking," the woman stated. "I know your name. I always have."

The woman didn't seem to breathe or blink as she faced me, and as I took one hesitant step and then another towards the front of the stage, it became clear that this entity wasn't going to budge an inch.

"Who are you?" I asked.

"You already know that." In fact, I did. She held out a long, pale hand before her and inspected her nails. "I am the goddess of the witches, and I would assume that if someone summoned me, they very well might understand who they were calling on." She lifted her eyes to match my somewhat terrified gaze. "However, this is a unique transaction."

Transaction?

The goddess's attention shifted to the part of the stage occupying the oracle cards. "You're on a journey."

My voice cracked as I replied, "I think I am."

"You are." She leaned down into a chair, then folded her hands together and sat them over her lap. "I am here to answer your question; in exchange, I have been given permission to take whatever I want from you."

I inhaled sharply.

The goddess seemed to be speculating over my entire existence. "You have the eyes of someone kissed by the ghost of a recently deceased star."

What?

She smiled, but not in the way adults usually smile at kids my age. This was more of a sneer laced with enough sugar to coax her prey into believing she could be trusted.

My spine was rigid—I could tell she was about to pounce, to give me an answer then suck the marrow from my bones as payment. "Wait!" She tilted her head to the side, and I slowly came down from where I'd been balancing over the tips of my toes. "What exactly are you going to require of me after this?"

"I'm afraid I don't offer previews."

I thought back on what others in this place had become after trading part of themselves in. "You're not going to turn me into a waif, are you?"

She scoffed. "That's not really my style. I appreciate Kage's work, but you must admit, it lacks a feminine touch." She paused, watching me watch her. And then her eyes narrowed. "Enough banter. Let's get on with it."

I cringed. I didn't want to trade anything for my question. The only thing I could think of that she was about to take from me, as unoriginal as it sounded, was my soul.

"The pendulum had trouble deciphering an answer for you.

Did you notice?" My eyes flitted from corner to corner as I tried to make speech happen, but apparently, I wasn't quick enough for the goddess. "It wouldn't have mattered anyway. The device is nothing more than a pager Reanin fashioned so that I would know when someone was calling. As for your curiosity, you would like to know if you are human." My ribs seemed to hug my heart tighter. "The reason the pendulum couldn't recall whether you have human DNA is because the humanity you have is on loan. You, Tess, are something else entirely."

My mouth parted and I tried to sort through the commotion in my head to find a simple retort. "What?"

"Your grandfather was a guardian."

Her short, snippy retorts were somewhat infuriating. "So what? Does that make me some sort of hybrid?"

"No and yes," she replied with a partial shrug. "What Kage is now—what he was when your grandmother became pregnant—it is something *different*. That has lent a hand towards your DNA composition, but only just. There are so many other ingredients . . . you are one unique dish."

"*Okay* . . . So, what is the rest of me made from?"

She winked. "You're not ready for that yet."

Unsure of whether it was advisable to glare at a goddess, I still found myself doing it. "But I asked a question, and you only partially answered it."

"Fine. You have in your possession some humanity, but it will not last."

My jaw deviated to the side. "I need more information than that."

"It'll cost you."

"I don't care."

She raised her brow. "Fine. Ask away."

"Was my mother human? Was she like me?"

She grinned like a villain on the brink of shutting the

lights off around the entire globe. "Janine," she sighed. "She was something, wasn't she?"

"You're being sarcastic."

"Very." She grinned. "Let us look at the facts before I answer you. She was a horrible mother. Her hugs were staged and cold. Her absence was felt for so long over her presence that you became more comfortable with her being gone."

"What you're describing is somewhat typical in the city where I grew up."

"Sure. However, I think we both know that Janine was anything but typical. Your mother was a monster, Tess."

My shoulders fell from where they'd been hanging by my ears. "Clarify."

"She was born a siren."

Um . . . what?

"No way."

She studied her cuticles. "I know what you're thinking—that it is an impossible thing. But I assure you, surviving from souls is quite an easy affliction to hide. Sirens don't have to drain the human to get what they need. They can take small enough amounts from the soul of the person they are feeding from, only enough to cause the human to experience a mild headache, if anything. That's how your grandmother taught her daughter to feed. But as you might've guessed, Janine had her own way of doing things."

I shook my head. "I wouldn't have thought for a second that my mother was—one of those—sirens."

"Really?" Heat began to build up through my jaw, and my gums felt sticky. "It's all there, Tess. Your mother habitually worked long hours, but if you had checked up on her you would've found that she was quite often somewhere other than where she said she was. She was born with a hunger she could never seem to satisfy—and it wasn't about the souls. She didn't just crave the essence of humans; she took pleasure in draining them of their lives. It was from that which she truly fed."

My head had started spinning. "I think I'm going to be sick."

"It does not aid in your journey to throw punches at the truth, child. Stop denying; it doesn't suit you. Replay your lives. Return to your mother's habits. Let me guess, Janine wasn't one for cooking shows." She paused as if waiting for me to answer, an opportunity I let pass me by. "Sirens do not need to eat as humans do, but as long as they've fed on enough souls to keep them strong, they can handle small amounts of bland food. I would wager that your mother often got takeout or had meals prepared for her family by someone else's hands. Am I right?" I let the stiffness of my jaw be my answer. "And I would assume she claimed to be a vegetarian."

I bit my lip.

"That's what I thought," the goddess answered coyly to my nonverbal affirmation. "Your grandmother's DNA changed when she became pregnant—it's so interesting how these bodies react to things." The comment was like an afterthought; her gaze lifted to the ceiling for the brief count of three. Returning her attention to me, she continued. "As your mother's seed began to grow within her, Reanin began to crave souls, just like the guardians who had forsaken their wings to follow Kage.

"Your grandmother figured out Janine was born a siren from very early on. She taught her to survive in the same manner as she had taught herself—without taking lives. But she was highly intuitive, as most witches are, and she quickly realized that your mother did not share in the 'harm none' philosophy."

"Reanin was a witch?"

The goddess simply dimmed her eyes over mine. "As I said, you are an interesting mix of genes."

Sooooo, I guess I was supposed to take that as a yes?

She didn't answer. Instead, she just kept talking. "Reanin did all she could to curb your mother's urges, but in the end, she knew as deeply as she had come to know her own shadows, that there was no redirecting Janine's behavior. Her only option was to keep a close watch over her daughter, which meant not only bringing in more help, but losing time that could've been spent hunting the hunter."

"Who helped her?"

"Oh child, do you really think your grandmother came out of this hall, pregnant and alone? She was a tough cookie, but she wasn't stupid. Not to mention, Kage wouldn't have allowed it."

"Kay, so what you're telling me is that because of my mother, my grandmother couldn't focus on searching out Nisroc, which was the main reason for closing these doors and returning to the surface."

The goddess nodded. "Janine didn't have even a single spark of light in her. Reanin had to keep the origins and knowledge of the world she and Kage had created secret, for if Janine had ever discovered it—"

"It would have been disastrous," I finished for her. I was reminded of Maggie's speech, that in the wrong hands, the magic from the Hall of Shadows could be world ending.

"This place," the goddess said, regarding The Hall, "would have been nothing more than a charging station for your mother. She craved power and she cared not about her shadows. She didn't have any. One must have at least a little light to manifest their grievances."

"My grandma wouldn't have been able to reopen the doors even if the cards hadn't been burned," I whispered.

"Not with Janine's heart still pounding. There is magic in these walls." She narrowed her eyes. "Even without the stones in its heart, this place is worthy of hunting."

"The Stones of Gehenna . . ."

She smirked.

A wave of nausea overtook me. It always came back to those stones.

My head was spinning—questions and answers were popping up like kernels forming into popcorn—but I needed to stay on track. My gaze rose from where it had been dragging along the ground. "How come I didn't turn out like her? Like my mother?"

"You've always been more like your grandfather."

"That doesn't help me. I don't understand—"

The goddess steepled her fingers together. "That's why you're here. To find out." She stared at me for what felt like an entire song, then she stood and lifted her hood all the way from over her head. She was beauty incarnate. "The time has come, darling, for the curtains to fall. Your card is waiting, and I would appreciate my payment now."

No. No, not yet. I had to stall—I had to figure out some way to— "Wait!"

She continued to gaze back at me like *I* was a crystal ball.

"I need to know something else, and yes, I'm aware it won't be for free."

Her head jostled lightly from side to side. "Very well."

The heat from my breath danced over my chin. "If it *was* Nisroc who murdered my grandmother and mother, then how did he find them?"

The goddess raised her brows. "That's simple. Your mother got sloppy."

"Wh—What?"

"'Tis easy to digest if you just think about it. And now, *we are done here*—" I started to argue, but she simply raised a heavily jeweled hand into the air. "We are done, Tess," she repeated sternly.

Still, I couldn't help it, and no—I didn't find her answer

easy to digest at all. I stumbled forward and began to reach out my hand, pleading. But seriously, what did I expect? What was a girl like me supposed to do against an actual *goddess*? Even if I wasn't totally human, the odds were against me.

The deity extended the same arm she'd already raised into the air—aiming it at my chest. As she did, her head fell back, and she began to mutter something that sounded eerily like an incantation. Shortly after that began, a sharp pain manifested in my chest, one that gradually moved down into my arms and legs. I couldn't help but scream in agony as what felt like burning lead filled every cell in my body. My veins became charged with fire, and an underlying feeling of fury settled somewhere in the back of my throat. My teeth *hurt*. Eventually, the heat solidified into ice, and then simply melted away.

The pain took its time wearing off, but still, I knew—it was over.

The goddess stood still as stone. As if she was handing me a receipt, she added, "The burn may have been a bit more excruciating than usual. You did ask more than one question."

Holding my right arm as if it was broken, I choked out, "What was that? Why did it hurt so bad?"

"My dearest child, it hurts anytime we let go of a piece of ourselves."

I tried to straighten myself out from where I'd been doubled over. "What did you take?" It had hurt a hell of a lot more than when I'd signed part of my shadows over in the library.

I didn't expect her to answer, but she surprised me with one last smirk. "A portion of your humanity. 'Tis food for me, and you'll not need it for much longer." A sputtering of lost words erupted in the back of my throat, but none made it out. "It was *very* nice to meet you, Tess. We will be seeing one another again. Good-bye."

She left as quickly as she'd appeared. The spotlight that had been over her body dimmed and darkness swooped in once more.

My feet stumbled into circles as I attempted to move from where I'd been planted over the stage. The oracle cards were sparkling. They were ready. The next dimension, waiting.

As I knelt before the spread, I held out my hands before me. They looked the same. The goddess had used a melon baller to scrape out parts of my humanity . . . but I didn't feel any less human. If anything, I was more grounded.

Curiosities were welling up around me like smoke. I'd finally learned the truth about my mother. Was it supposed to make me feel better? That she was an actual monster—that it wasn't just me she didn't care about.

Because it didn't.

A traveling shimmer ran over the cards as if they were impatient.

"Okay, okay," I muttered down to them as if they could hear me. And maybe they could. "I don't know what could possibly be waiting for me after that."

I began to lower my hand down to the fourth card, but just before I flipped it over, I took one last glance into my grandmother's old world. When this had first started, the thought had crept into my mind: why couldn't things just be normal for me? Why couldn't my mother have been warm? Why was my father always trying to love me for them both instead of just taking me away from that terrible woman? And why couldn't Reanin have just made cookies and spoiled me with horrible hard candy like all the other grandmas?

As I sat there, on the same stage my grandmother had danced over, Ethan's voice echoed in the back of my head and a realization came to me. *A tarot reading is just like a person's lifetime. It can't tell you anything you don't already know or haven't signed up for. All it does is lift the blindfold for a little bit. It's a reminder, that's all.*

"Right," I said, as if I was talking back to him.

Maybe it wouldn't make sense to a lot of people, but as I gripped that fourth card and began to turn it over, it made perfect sense to me. I wouldn't have been happy with that sort of normalcy because whatever I was intended to become, wasn't necessarily of this earth. As I accepted that truth, somewhere, deep inside, past the beating of my heart—I felt a little better.

CHAPTER NINETEEN

The card materialized as The Forest. At first, I imagined a world of greens and browns. Pine needles and twigs. Birds. But as a moonless, starless midnight sky fell over my shoulders, I remembered where I was. There were no forests as I knew them here in the shadows, and as I stood apart from the cards, now spread out over a slick black surface, I realized the forest was somewhere overhead. The night sky I thought I was seeing was nothing more than the earth.

I walked a few paces from the oracle spread and reached up to touch what I thought was an upside-down tree, completely void of its leaves. Upon second glance, though, it was clear that these were roots.

My lungs filled with wool as I turned and took in my vast surroundings. This dimension was on a whole other level. It was giant, like The Library, and I suspected it went on for miles (and miles). But unlike any of the other portals I'd been through thus far, this one was accompanied by something other than waifs.

They floated around in the darkness like ghosts . . . their

forms could have at one point been human, or something like human. But that wasn't the case now. They were the color of smoke, though there was no odor, and they fluttered around as if pushed by the wind—but there was no wind. I reached out to touch one, but it swooped out of reach. I began to grasp for another but was interrupted as a man came walking through the roots . . . or something like a man. His hands were clasped before his stomach; he wore a fitted suit, his skin was pale, and his chin was as long as his ears were tall.

"As above," he stated in a voice that reminded me of crystal waters, "so below. Welcome to The Forest. We've been awaiting your arrival. Word of your identity is traveling quickly through the Hall of Shadows."

Rumors were nothing new; for as long as I'd been around others, there had been talk.

"Hello," I answered as delicately as possible. When silence nipped at my ankles, I directed my gaze from the newcomer to the ghosts. "Are these shadows?"

"They are something like that," he replied, then turned the conversation in another direction. "My name is Legolas, and this" —he gestured to his side just as a sliver of light appeared, quickly transitioning into the vision of a small girl dressed in a white gown— "is Annie."

The little girl looked up at me. "Proceed wisely: novels, obscurities, monsters. Please refrain: reliance, transfer, smoke."

I frowned as the odd speech ran against roadblocks in my brain.

"Annie speaks in fortunes," stated Legolas. "You will get used to it."

I gradually lifted my attention to rest over his lengthened features. "What are you?"

"Hails from: Gray lineage, shadows, Feyland."

I looked down toward the small child before returning my gaze to Legolas. My lips had formed into a thin, straight line.

"An elf," he answered.

I dipped my forehead and let my features soften. "Of course." Out of the corner of my eyes, I thought I spied a dark figure fluttering from one root segment to the next. Whether it was real, I couldn't be sure. A place like this could do a number on your sanity.

"How has your journey treated you thus far, Tess Moreau?"

"It's been . . . interesting." I glanced up at the ceiling, or the earth's floor, and listened for any noise that could lend a hand as to what I was in for this time. "It's oddly quiet here."

"Yes."

"Is this a *real* forest?"

Was that a *stupid* question?

If it was, he didn't say so.

"If one were to pass through the mushrooms that gather in a circle amid any forest or splash of unfrequented land, this is where they may end up. Especially if they have been blessed with the sight or have made a deal with an otherworldly creature."

Foreboding? You bet your ass. "Otherworldly creature . . . like you?"

"Truth," said Annie.

The elf named Legolas laced his long pale fingers together. Even though his speech was clear and crisp, there was a depth to the tone of his voice that caused the hairs on the back of my neck to stand straight up. "It is unwise to move through a faery circle, especially out of disrespect. We do, however, welcome those in search of answers they have been unable to find elsewhere . . . for a price. On behalf of the others, I must say that we are honored to have *partnered* with the Hall of Shadows. Though there will always be those who aren't fond of change. It is wise, while in The Forest, to keep that in mind."

"Are you saying that if one was to step through a faery circle, or those mushrooms, that they would end up in the Hall of Shadows?"

"Yes. As I've said, we've partnered together."

So, my grandfather (and grandmother) invited this darkness into their world.

"Once someone is in, can they leave through the same faery circle? Or do they have to run through all the shadows like I'm having to do?"

"That is an interesting question, Tess Moreau," Legolas stated with a long face. "Before the cards were drawn up, any entrance or exit could be used at any time. The cards now present an added challenge to our guests; I believe most of us are in favor of the second option. Facing each dimension is all part of the learning process after all." He paused. "We will simply have to see how it goes. The Hall has a habit of running itself."

Words fell from my lips like raindrops. "You speak about this place like it's alive."

"Who is to say that it is not," was his only reply.

I looked back down at the little sprite. "She's not an elf," I noted.

"No. Annie is a changeling."

I gasped. I'd heard of such things from the books I'd read —the fantasy novels I drowned myself in to escape the crap hand I'd been dealt. A changeling was a baby from the human world who was taken and replaced by a baby from the otherworld. I would never, in a thousand years, have believed they were real.

Legolas continued as if I hadn't just grown three times paler. "Her mother made a deal with a faery over a hundred years ago. She knew there would be payment but was too afraid to ask what she would owe. The woman pretended not to notice when the baby she'd given birth to suddenly had brown hair, rather than the sparse golden locks that had been struggling to grow. When it was time for her soul to pass from her body, her one regret—that she had lost her true child because she'd meddled in things she ought not have—would not allow her to move forward. She found us, and, in doing so, she found Annie."

My eyes widened. "She came here? Her spirit, or whatever?"

"Yes. She stays here, by Annie's side. Always." The elf turned to the side and gestured to the same place I'd seen a dark figure flutter. As I looked deeper into the shadows, a formless dark smudge moved out from behind one of the tree's roots. "This is what Lydia has become," Legolas stated without emotion.

As I stared at what was left of a once human soul, my face contorted into an expression of disgust. "How did that happen?"

Annie repeated her wisdom. "One cannot come into the shadows and refuse to acknowledge their darkness, for it is food they will become."

I had to clean my hands of what she'd just said for a few beats before shaking my head back into the present. Trying to look away from Lydia, who was nothing more than a smudge of black on spilt oil, I gestured to Annie. "Why is she like this?" I don't know if damaged was the appropriate word, but she was *something*.

"Humans react differently to the fey realm. Annie has been with us for many years; she is content, but this is how she has chosen to communicate. This is also the age she has chosen to remain. One day she may choose another way."

It didn't matter which way you looked at it, magic was limitless. There was darkness here, arguably too much of it.

And these figures floating around—I could see them clearly now—I couldn't pretend that they weren't empty souls. Looking away from the truth had turned Annie's mother into a smudge and that wasn't a fate I was willing to follow. Here, or in the human world.

"This world is unapologetic," I whispered.

Legolas tipped his chin up. "Do you appreciate that, or do you sway in the other direction?"

"I—I don't know." I really didn't. "I guess I admire your raw ability to be who you are." Even if it was a little malicious . . . or a lot.

Annie fixed her stare over me. "She begins to submit to the shadows she's always feared. They are not plagues, but victories."

"I don't know if I'd go that far," I muttered. Legolas prepared the closest thing to a grin he could make. Returning to the subject of Annie's mother, I asked, "Why does Lydia still follow her child when it seems she is nothing more than regret?"

He answered promptly. "Lydia has but one drive now—Annie. She stalks behind us wherever we go. Too afraid to get too close. Too afraid to lose her again."

"And why is Annie with *you*?"

Legolas looked down at the fair-haired fortune-teller. "Because she has chosen to be."

Right. I mean, he was probably telling the truth, but my gut said to tread lightly around him, or any other creatures I might meet in this dimension. I didn't want to make a deal with *anyone* here, that was for sure.

Legolas proceeded to answer my next question before I even got a chance to ask it. "Kage desired our services because he thought it pertinent that those who inherit his worldly outlook be well-rounded. Our magic—fey magic—is unique. Alas, for *anyone* to exit our space, there must be payment. The only caveat being a showcase of original magic."

There it is! I thought. This elf was all inviting, but lest not forget his true nature. 'Come in, have a cookie, then hand over part of your soul.'

I'd begun wringing the end of my shirt, trying to sort out how my grandmother could ever send me into a place like this, knowing full well what could happen. I knew she loved me—she wouldn't want me to become one of these floating things, or a smudge. But then I remembered. "I do have an original magic." I rolled up onto my toes as if the realization was enough to actually lift me up. I could've sworn he frowned. "I can bring life back from death—return ashes to what they were before they were burned."

Legolas's stony expression didn't waver. "That *is* unique. However, how will you display a talent like that in this place? We've no ashes, nor fire."

Of course you don't, I thought. The fey were notorious for deception.

I was screwed.

My eyelids fluttered as I replied, "Then I don't have any original magic."

"Be wary of speaking too soon," Annie warned.

Legolas dipped his chin and laid his gaze squarely over Annie's shoulders. Was he flustered by her insistence? "I shall give you time to decide on which it will be, Tess Moreau. For now, we shall be on our way."

Legolas and Annie turned around and began to take their leave; their feet followed the pattern of a trail on the slick black surface. He'd been so quick to be off after Annie said that . . . was there something I could do that I didn't even know about? Either that, or I suspected that there was a way to perform my magic in this place after all.

Only seconds after the two had taken their leave, the

smudge that was Annie's birth mother peeled away from her hiding spot and followed them, flitting back and forth between the shadows.

I couldn't help but wonder what Lydia had asked the fey for. *And where is the faery she raised as her own?*

If there was one thing I *was* sure of, it was that I would never know the answers to those questions—and really, it didn't matter. I had my own fateful decisions to make.

Strategy. That's what was needed here. My thoughts rolled over major obstacles as I wandered. As I got further from where my cards had materialized the darkness began to lift under one area, coloring it in shades of brown and gray. Dirt, that's what I was looking at. And rocks.

"Oh," I whispered. Then reaching my gaze up at the little brown specks breaking through the dirt, and realizing they formed a circle, I muttered, "A faery circle." I'd found an entrance.

I stayed there for a while, contemplating how many humans had dropped down from that portal. Wondering if they ever got out. I wasn't so thick that I tried to get up there and pass through. First, there was no way up without a ladder, or wings, and I didn't have either. Two, it wasn't going to let me through. I was in this game now, whether I liked it or not.

I was just about to decide on turning back around or skimming past this circle and seeing what else was down this way, when a thin female *something* fell from the mushroom circle and landed as softly as a feather. Right away I took to her creamy brown skin and dark violet hair, fashioned into a pixie cut. Definitely not human; her ears were too long for that.

She'd landed with her back to me and hadn't wasted a second moving in the opposite way that I'd come from. But as soon as I said, "Hey," she turned around and faced me with a pair of glowing purple eyes. And then— "Oh my god." My gaze flitted down to the small blue dragon in her hand. "You're the girl from the fair." *My unicorn.*

"Huh?" She held herself somewhat guarded until recognition washed over her. "Oh yeah," she said, stalking a few feet towards me. The way she moved reminded me of a panther. "I remember you."

The sound of her voice caused the blood in my veins to dance again.

"What are you doing down here?" she asked.

"I—it's a long story."

She was close enough that I could have touched her . . . that she could've touched me. She looked me up and down. I found myself doing the same. She was dressed very similar to me; skinny jeans, fitted top—black boots.

A chuckle seemed to hide behind her tongue as she said with squinted eyes, "I knew you weren't human."

"I'm—" Not sure how to answer that. "I'm Tess. Kage's granddaughter."

"No shit," she said, her eyes growing wider. "I guess that's why you looked so familiar." She boldly stepped in closer to where my chest was reaching for hers. "Do you have anything to do with this nonsense being back open?" She pointed up to the faery circle.

My speech was breathier than I'd intended it to be as I said, "Long story short, I followed the breadcrumbs that led me to a cursed deck of oracle cards that reopened all the doors."

She shot me an inquisitive look. "Interesting."

"Yeah." I bit my lip. "A little party trick my grandma stirred up to try and protect this place." I shifted my bodyweight from one foot to the other as I took in her reaction. If I wasn't mistaken, she had no idea what I was talking about. Still, she was so obviously part of this world; her purple eyes and pointy ears were now out in the open. "How long have you been gone?"

"From The Forest?" she asked.

"From The Hall?"

"Shit, I don't go into the other places. I mean, I know who Reanin and Kage are, but—so wait, you're like an heir to The Hall, then?"

"I—I don't know about that. Right now, I'm just trying to get through the dimensions so I can meet my grandfather."

She held her gaze over mine. "You've never met Kage?"

I shook my head. "I just, sort of, found out about him."

"Oh . . . that's cool." Then, changing subjects like she was simply moving traffic lanes, she said, "Well, I have a duty to check in here every once and a while—otherwise I'd stay shacked up in The Hilton." She winked. "It's so close to Radio City."

My eyes nearly rolled out of my head. "You live in a hotel —in New York?"

"Of course, where else would I stay?" she asked, as if it was a stupid question. She rolled her purple eyes. "Lot more fun up there, which is why I didn't really care when I got locked out."

I was grinning like an idiot, but I didn't care. "How old are you?"

Her tongue came out and traced the corner of her top lip; for the first time since I'd been alive, I had an urge to do the same—to her lip. She stepped in closer so that we were but a foot apart. Instead of answering, she shot the question back at me. "How old are you?"

"Fifteen."

"Nuh uh." Her eyes were twinkling.

I shook my head. "I'm totally serious. I may not be totally human but that's how old I am. I have a car waiting for me when I turn sixteen and everything."

That got her attention. "A car?" I nodded. "What color is it?"

"Red." I couldn't stop grinning. Was this what it was like to feel something for someone else?

She placed a hand over my shoulder. "Tell me it's a convertible." The way she said it, it was like she wouldn't be able to breathe if I said it wasn't. I almost wanted to lie.

"It's an SUV." *Please don't remove your hand.*

"Moonroof?"

"Of course."

She remained planted in place for a few more beats, then started nodding her head. "That'll do. I love red."

And then we talked . . . for a while. We sat on the ground and crossed our legs and spoke like a couple of teenagers. It was the first time I felt accepted by someone my own age. And yes, she was older than me (by 83 years), but that was practically a teenager for a faery. She explained that not all fey donned wings (because how could I not ask about that), but she *did* have them. She said that if she needed them, they grew. She'd only used them twice in her life so far.

Her name was Liz. She grew up in The Forest. That lady who'd been chasing her at the fair was a Spotter (whatever that meant). Her parents had hired her to find Liz years ago.

The faery realm was way bigger than I could ever imagine. It was its own world. If I kept going down the tunnel that she was aimed at when she first 'dropped in,' I would have eventually come to a four way that would've led to four different cities. More roads and cities diverging from those four.

She was born in one of the first fey cities that had been founded—it was located down the tunnel. It was called Valia. She was an only child and her parents worked long hours. I knew her story so well because her story was mine. She'd gotten in a fight with her dad the night before she ran off. He called her a drifter, a juvenile. He said she had no work ethic.

I guess even faeries dabble in family drama.

She set off for the surface and planned to stay like a year or two—long enough to piss off her father before returning. However, when she tried to get back in, the doors were sealed. Because this world had partnered with The Hall, all the entrances and exits they commonly used were locked.

From there, I told her my story, all of it. And when I was finished, she reached for my hand and squeezed it. "We're so similar. You're like, the shadow princess, and I'm the princess of Valia."

I raised my brows. "What?" She hadn't mentioned *that*.

"Uh, yeah," her hand slipped away, and I immediately missed it. "My family is sort of—" she bounced her head from shoulder to shoulder— " like, you know, fey royalty."

My lips quivered into a grin. "No shit."

She smiled. "Now you sound like me, shadow girl." Her eyes danced in mine for a long minute, but it didn't feel weird; and then they fell to the stones hanging from my neck. "Dang," she said, starting to reach her hand towards them, as if she meant to touch them, but just as Jamae had when she'd first seen them, she pulled back. "I tell you what, you hand over those pretty little numbers and I'll find a way to get you out of this card reading you're stuck in. Take you directly to the head guy."

I grasped the stones. As soon as I did, a voice whispered into my ears. *It would be a mistake.* This time my heart didn't overly pound at the odd occurrence. So far, the creepy whispers had only led me in the right direction.

"I don't think so."

Liz winked. "Smart girl." She started to stand up and I followed suit. "So, look, I gotta get going. My parents have got to be, like, livid. I gotta show face for at least a week or two, but let's get together again." She tucked a piece of hair behind her ear that didn't really need tucking. "You're cool to talk to, Tess. And my god, you're going to have some stories when you're finished with this whole ordeal."

I wiped my hands on my pants. "I'd love to see you again, but—what if I don't get out of this? I'm, like, not so sure I'm even going to get out of this forest in one piece."

She looked genuinely confused. "Didn't they tell you that all you have to do is use an original magic? From what you've just told me, your grandmother wouldn't have sent you down here if she thought you were going to get stripped down by Legolas. Just, you know, do your thang, girl."

"It's not that easy. Legolas already said my magic wouldn't work down here."

"Ah," she said, her lips curving back into a smile. "You know what." She pointed at my necklace while backing away. "I bet if you ask that little ditty, it might just tell you how to get around this."

"Are you offering me advice? I've heard it's bad luck to take advice from the fey."

She chuckled. "You owe me nothing." Her eyes rolled to the ceiling as she backtracked. "Actually, you do. Once we're both free, you owe me a ride in that red SUV."

I bit the corner of my lip before replying. "Deal."

She nodded. "Cool. See ya around, shadow girl." Her words bounced off the tunnel as her back became covered in darkness.

And then she was gone. And I was alone again. Alone, but empowered. Had that one little interaction seriously filled me with the will to get through this? I would do anything to take a car ride with those mad, purple eyes. Maybe I wasn't as asexual as I thought.

Regardless, I still had to get out of here. At least I'd been given a hint.

I had already started to make my way back to where my cards were waiting for me, and as I did, I cupped the crystals hanging from my neck and asked, "What other magic do I have that is unique to me?"

Return that which has burned away to its original state.

I sighed. "I already know that. That can't help me here."

It does not always pertain to physical matter.

I dropped the stones and they fell back against my chest. For sure, I had just heard two different voices whispering to me; and I could've sworn that the last time I'd heard them, they'd been from someone else apart from these last two. If my fate hadn't been balancing over getting out of this forest unscathed, I would have been way more curious about that. I was positive that these stones weren't just black tourmaline, labradorite, and blue kyanite.

I checked my cards. They were still spread out on that black sheet of reflective ground. And just as there had been when I'd first entered this dimension, there were dozens, if not hundreds, of those bizarre wispy ghost-like figures. But they weren't just floating. They were stamped to the ground I walked on, as well to the earth above, and any other surface available to them.

Legolas's first words ran through my head. *As above, so below.*

"Is this the payment?" I questioned to no one. "A person's actual shadow. A piece of their soul."

No way was I about to let part of myself end up with these things . . . or worse, become one of them completely. As I continued to pour over my options, one of the ghost-like shadows pulled away from the ceiling and began floating away. And then it hit me: these things weren't just floating around. They were all traveling in the same direction.

I began following the one I'd just seen pull away from

where it had been hibernating. I scampered behind it, observing as more and more of them detached from the floor, the ceiling, and a few from surfaces that were too dark to even notice, until the smoky figures floated away from them. Soon, I was nearly a half mile away from where I'd first seen Legolas and Annie. I was surrounded by the moving ghosts; I was on a conveyor belt with nothing but black cloaks shuffling around me.

I kept moving until I'd easily conquered over a mile. They began thinning out, and through the pitch black, I could narrowly make out as the shadows began to vanish as soon as they passed over a specific spot.

I slowed my pace from the jog I'd taken, keeping just behind the line of smoky ghosts. Finally, my feet came to a halt, just a few steps before what appeared to be a very large black hole. It wasn't a black hole, though. I may have been a novice, but even I knew that much. It was a mechanism *run* by these shadows.

I grasped the crystals around my neck. "What is this?"

Fuel. Said one voice.

It doesn't have to be physical matter. Spoke another.

I released the stones, cutting off the whispers. Was that it? Could my escape from this wicked place be as simple as releasing these ghosts from the hypnosis they were under?

There was only one way to find out.

A shadow began to creep past me, towards the lake of darkness. There wasn't anything to reach out for, but still, I didn't hesitate. I held out my hand as if to grasp the shoulder of whoever had belonged with this smokey soul. As soon as I made contact, the shadow froze.

I left my hand there for a little longer than I normally would have, then retrieved it as if things had just gotten awkward. I didn't know what to expect. Would someone materialize from this thing? Probably not. Even though it was the fey realm, I wasn't exactly in the kind of place where fairy tales were made.

I didn't have to wait much longer. The shadow began to sparkle; first like black sand against moonlight, then very fine white sparks began to twinkle throughout the thing, until the dark smudge was no longer black, but white. The sparkle diminished around the edges until all that was left was a shining orb. Whatever it was, didn't hesitate. Once it was light again, it darted off, I'm assuming, in search of an exit.

So that was it; my original magic *did* work in this place. With that knowledge, I didn't waver; I reached for as many of the shadow figures as I could—each one pausing in its tracks and transforming into a ball of light. I moved away from the dark pool and reached my hands through the cloaks as if they were on a moving coat rack; orbs snapping into place then scurrying away from The Forest as fast as they could. I'd completed my task, I knew I had, but still, I didn't stop. I wanted to free as many of these things as I could. That was until—

"Tess Moreau."

I turned to find Legolas with Annie by his side. I couldn't help but take satisfaction in the hitch I'd been sure I'd heard in the back of his throat as he said my name.

"She has heard the voices of the sparks once taken; she has invoked guidance. It has proved worthy," said Annie in her familiar monotone voice.

"Yes," Legolas replied. His gaze unfaltering from my own, he added, "You have proven yourself worthy and now we ask that you leave."

I should have been ecstatic, jumping from the giddiness of getting out of this hell hole, but there was more to this place now than I could ever have imagined. What had Kage been thinking? Pairing The Forest with his world.

I motioned to the shadows dissolving into the lake of lost

souls. "This isn't right."

"Perhaps not where you are from. But take away the fear you feel when you think about what these shadows represent, then tell me again that it isn't right. Forget your conditioning, Tess Moreau. Everyone makes sacrifices. Who is to say which sacrifice is appropriate?"

My voice, and probably my confidence, cracked as I started to retort. "I—"

But it was of no use. I wasn't being asked to leave, I was being escorted out. In the blink of an eye, the three of us were standing before my oracle cards.

Annie spoke. "Proceed with caution, intellect, and charm."

"Good-bye, Tess Moreau," Legolas added with a firm brow, just before the two of them turned and headed back on their invisible path.

A shiver ran down my spine as the smudge of Annie's birth mother scampered behind them like a rabbit. Slowly, I knelt before the spread, my gaze planted over the fifth card. It was getting stickier with every new room, or dimension, I entered. Still, to get out—and to meet my grandfather—I had to search through every corner and narrow opening in this maze.

I looked towards the path I'd taken that had led me to where I'd met Liz. Somehow, after everything I'd just witnessed and experienced, I smiled just at the thought of the faery. I wondered what she looked like when her wings were full.

"All right," I whispered. "I gotta get on with it so we can take that car ride."

I took a deep breath of stale air and flipped over the next card. It was a good thing I'd filled my lungs before doing so, for a second later my surroundings were filled with water and whatever light had been with me in the forest went out.

CHAPTER TWENTY

I was drowning.

I must have angered the fey more than I thought. They hadn't let me go, instead they'd thrown me in the lake of lost souls and now I was going to die with the hopeless.

My lungs began to burn along with my eyes, and as the water surrounding me turned from black to blue to green, then back to black, I decided to say to hell with it. I gave in to death, because why fight what was so clearly out of my control? If anything, I'd met someone who had finally caused my heart to beat to a different rhythm. That was worth it, right? But as soon as I accepted the end, a new beginning began to unfold.

I dropped from the water onto another cold, black surface; I landed on all fours—dry as a fresh towel. And I wasn't alone. My cards were spread out in front of me.

My head rose like a wolf howling at the moon and I filled my lungs with air. I quickly began coughing and couldn't stop. I could still taste it—The Lake. According to the latest card, that's where I was. Except this was like no other lake I'd ever visited. It was definitely less relaxing, that was for sure.

Once I'd gotten myself back together, I cranked my head up to see the dancing water. If I never saw magic at work ever again, I would be just fine, because this was intense. The room was lit only from the light reflecting in the water—just like the shark exhibit at the aquarium. Except there were no sharks, at least not the kind I knew of. And there was no aquarium; no barrier between that water and where I existed under it.

I began to stand, a fist clenched over my chest as if it could help recuperate my struggling breath. The opening of the lake overhead was in the shape of a square, about ten feet on each side. I'd tilted my head, straining to get a better look at it, when a caramelized voice ran down my spine like a set of fingers.

"You've done it. The shadow has now been fed. You are transforming quickly, Tess."

My gaze shot into the darkness, just in time to find the face belonging to the voice. Whoever *this* was, she was strikingly beautiful. Her skin was a twinkling brown, and as she grew nearer, I gasped. Her eyes were the color of blood.

"It's an intense lesson, isn't it? Facing death. You accepted it quickly. You didn't even fight. Your humanity *must* be withering."

The woman's figure fully materialized in the little light we were afforded. She was dressed in aged leather pants with a matching black jacket. Her hair was the color of fire. "Who are you?"

She grinned. "You may call me Cai."

Maybe my humanity was wavering, but still, when next I spoke, my voice sounded shredded. "Are you a waif?"

She didn't react, like at all. At least not on the surface. But as we stood there, facing one another—like game pieces—a rift began to tear through my heart. I didn't know how to explain it, but I could *feel* her heartbreak. It was like the pain defined her.

"We have the ability to push our empathy onto and into others. Sometimes it happens whether I want it to or not." Without waiting for me to figure out a reply, she pointed up to the water. "I was the one who discovered this place. It's one of the deepest lakes in the world. A collapsed volcano filled in by the sky's tears. It has all the elements needed for just the right recipe: earth, air, fire, and water." She began to lower to the ground, sitting cross-legged. She let one arm dig into the ground, balancing her weight, as she kept her gaze overhead. "I often wonder if I'd never found the reflection—if any of this would exist. Furthermore, would Kage have found it on his own? If he hadn't taken that first plunge—would someone else have?"

I knew I was standing before some sort of majestic creature, but what breed she was, I couldn't be sure. So I simply stated the same question I had just a few breaths ago. "Who *are* you?"

Her attention wafted down and landed on me with a thump. "I was the first one to follow Kage."

My eyes grew. "You're a guardian."

"Was," she corrected. Her gaze drifted again. "I am so far from what I used to be now."

"You're a siren, then."

Her red irises lingered over my moody eyes. "No. Though again, I *was* one." She sighed then parted her lips, licking the tip of a very sharp incisor. My lungs tingled as a chilled breath entered their domain. "Let me give you a piece of advice, Tess. Don't ever fall in love with a narcissist." Her tongue moved out to her bottom lip and ran its course. And then she stood, signifying with a few steps back towards the way she'd just entered, that she was readying to leave. "This isn't my room— not officially. I just wanted to come say hey. I mean, like everyone else, I've been dying to meet you." She winked. "Like

I said before, you're free to move on. Once you've laughed death in the face, there's nothing more to see here."

I hinged forward, preparing to follow her if need be. "Maybe there's nothing more to see, but I'm willing to bet what's left of my soul that there's one hell of a story here."

Cai's lips curved into a smile, and though she didn't really make me feel the way I had when I'd been around Liz, I still felt inclined to touch mine to hers.

"Physical attraction. Another unavoidable trait." Her grin slowly faded, and she lifted her chin. "It's not your soul the shadows are feeding on."

"Then what *is* happening to me, exactly?"

"To experience The Hall at all is a gift most will never know. It's not ciphering bits of your soul away, Tess. It's aiding you in discovering who you truly are."

I knew it wasn't true, but still . . . "This place—I just can't swing the idea that it *is* hell."

A slighter version of the same smirk she'd already shown off returned. "Hell is a story spun to create havoc. Even if it were real—that place humans speak of—hell and The Hall are not remotely the same." Her gaze rose to meet the lake. "This was the first entrance, the very spot Kage fell through. It is, at its core, a reflection. Souls don't come here to hide from themselves. It's not that kind of venue."

"But there's so much darkness here," I whispered. The Forest was still heavy in my mind.

"Tess." She waited until I lifted my gaze to meet hers. "Nothing is one hundred percent beautiful. Those who preach nothing but love and light are teaching others to silence something very powerful. I for one, would rather walk with the storm than have it inside me. That's something I'll never apologize for, even if it's made me into this."

Even though I didn't know (for sure) what she was, I said,

"That's the thing. You've been *made* into something because you came here. Doesn't that make you angry?"

Cai's head rattled with the finest of shakes. "Don't ever assume, Tess. There is poison in that."

My chest filled with lead. "I didn't mean to assume. It's the last thing I would want to—"

"It's important for you to understand that it wasn't giving up a piece of ourselves that turned us into sirens. It wasn't Kage who did this—and it wasn't Kage who took my curse and tweaked it with the snap of his fingers. That, for your information, came from a source who claims to stand in the light."

"Who did this to you, then?"

She hummed, her head tilting back. "Someone who knows only vengeance. Someone who believes that those of us who have discovered our true selves in the shadows are worthy of nothing but being punished. We've never done anything malicious, but some fear what we might one day do with the magic we find in the shadows . . . It all comes down to fear and power. And let's face it, jealousy. For those who judge do so only because they can't face what they see in their own reflection."

"And this magic people speak of—the kind that can only be found in here—"

She waved a finger at me. "Don't get ahead of yourself. You must deal with *you*, first. Then you can deal with that." She paused, and I tried to make sense of what she'd just said. "Here's the thing. We have no need for power because we've found the strength we could never find in the light."

It was quiet in The Lake room for long enough that my curiosities stewed.

"Who broke your heart? Who made you feel so broken inside? Please don't tell me it was Kage."

The stiffness she'd been demonstrating lifted, and she

began to chuckle. "No. Oh, god no." She started to shake her head as if I'd asked if she'd ever entertained kissing her brother. "He wasn't the one. Then again, neither was the other." Her gaze fell to where my cards were waiting for me behind where I stood. "Go ahead, Tess. Flip over your next card. You're right, there's more stories here, but they will have to wait their turn. I'll see you soon."

She left, leaving me alone with the reflection above, the cards below, and a hunger for more. More of her story, more of an explanation of everything—more of the darkness that seemed to embody her like it was her lover. Still, I'm sure she was right. I wasn't even halfway through the oracle spread. There were plenty of dimensions to creep through, and ample time to feed my curiosities. Discovering what Cai was, was now near the top of that list; even though I was pretty sure I already knew. I guess nothing was impossible anymore.

As I crept back towards the cards and knelt before them, my thoughts began to run amuck. I never spoke about the night terrors that had always woken me when the moon was at its highest. About how I could see the shadows creeping along my bedside. How I would pretend to sleep as they sniffed at my hair. My dad, though so often absent, was hard to hide anything from. He'd told me once that nothing could hurt me; that it was as simple as setting aside my fear. But what about the man who stole along my bedroom door when everyone should have been asleep? The figure of a person who found the crack made between the door and its frame. This dark figure with a long pale face who I knew watched me when I slept. He was no night terror; he was real.

I'd mentioned him to my dad only once.

This is what he told me. "You will for the rest of your life attract energy. Some might even appear to be what society has termed nightmares. Don't be afraid of them, Tess. Instead, accept them. They don't know they're scary."

Only now could I make sense of what he'd been saying. What if I stopped calling them night terrors? What if I stopped thinking of them as intrusions and instead saw them as messages? Because really, if you thought about it, they were like snakes. Slimy, slithery; they weaseled themselves around your ankles even. But if we stopped fearing them and just left them alone, they would glimpse at us then simply return to their lives, which when it came down to it was a necessary role in the earth's ecosystem. What if the figure of the man who watched me while I slept was just curious, and the only time he could observe me was when the sun went down?

Or were these just mangled thoughts birthed from the darkness? I think I'd already decided that if this place was evil (and maybe parts of it were), that I was also wicked. Other than The Forest, I hadn't felt deceived.

I took one final look up at the waters that had helped me accept the reality of death, before turning over the next card.

"The Muse," I said. "You're not going to try and drown me again, are you, Grandma?" Though it took a minute for everything to come into focus as I jumped from one dimension to another, I was pretty sure I wouldn't need to hold my breath. There was no water threatening to fill my lungs, just the sound of piano music and glasses clinking.

CHAPTER TWENTY-ONE

The bar patrons were waifs, and the fashions worn by the various degrees of rotting bodies were a sundry sort. The place was kind of a dive. It reminded me of a—what were those places called? Speakeasy.

I came to a small square table with four wooden seats surrounding it; my cards that I now carried with me like a tortoise shell, took up nearly all the space on top of the table. A couple waifs turned and acknowledged my arrival. One even raised his glass of amber hops in what appeared to be a salute. It was pretty clear that by now, most, if not all, of the inhabitants of The Hall, knew who I was.

I sat back in my chair and followed the gaze of most everyone else in the bar to where a beautiful, older woman was playing the piano. A waif with yellowish skin, wearing a brown leather skirt and a beaded top (an outfit I'd only seen in the window of a dusty old thrift shop) meandered over and asked if I wanted a drink. It was the first time since I'd been in the shadows that I even thought about how dry my throat was, even after my near drowning incident.

"Do you have Coke?" I asked quietly, trying not to draw any more attention my way.

The waitress snapped her gum. "Sure, hon. You want a little somethin' in there, or just the cola?"

They obviously didn't card in the shadows. "Just the Coke. I should probably keep a level head." I pointed to the cards.

She pulled a smoking cigarette out from behind her back and took a long drag, letting the smoke exit her nostrils as she used the same hand to gesture towards the cards. "How's it goin' so far? You know you're the first one to read the cards all at once, right?"

"Yeah . . . I kinda figured." I studied the waif. "I guess it's —well, it's been interesting."

"Groovy," she said, taking another drag. She blew it out then started chomping on her pink gum. "And thanks, by the way."

"For what?"

"For unlocking those damn doors. I was really starting to worry about my decomposition. Not a thing we could do about it while we were stuck in here."

"Right . . ." I clasped my hands under my chin and leaned over them. "Do you mind if I ask you something? It's personal."

"You can ask me anything, sugar."

"You like traded part of yourself for magic, right?"

She nodded.

"What's the rest of the story?"

Her expression didn't change much as she held up a finger, sucked on the end of her cig, then walked over to the bar. After she'd filled a clear glass with brown liquid from the tap, she returned to my table and had a seat in the chair next to mine. She set down a napkin with a spinning wheel printed over it, then placed my drink on top of it.

"Figured you were pretty thirsty," she said, crossing her legs and leaning back into the chair. "You just came from The Lake, right?"

"Yeah," I said, taking a greedy sip from the soda. Gawd, it tasted so good.

She twirled her smoking cigarette in the air as she spoke. "Kinda surprised you don't know more about us, but from what I hear, Reanin kept our secret hidden real well. So anyway, here goes: It wasn't Kage who initially came up with our pact in case that's what you think. I mean, yeah, it was his idea, but it wasn't until Frankie followed Reanin into the shadows that he got a spark of inspiration."

"Frank," I said, clinging to the name. "I've met him."

Her eyes widened as she took another drag. She blew the smoke out of the side of her mouth before exclaiming, "You did! Oh, my gawd, he's such a doll, right?"

"Sure," I said, my brows furrowing. He was nice enough, but I wasn't so sure that was how I would classify the guy with the porky tummy and green skin.

"I just love that guy," she continued to coo. Then, returning to the subject matter, she said, "Anyway, so Frankie had already seen the mirrors ripple—ya know, how they do?" I nodded, even though I wasn't really sure what she was talking about. "When Reanin initially went missing, he returned to the place where he'd seen her practice her dance routines in front of the rippling reflection, and, sure enough, it let him in." She paused and her eyes darted to the ceiling. "I should probably clarify that by this time Kage and Reanin had realized that with every new soul who pledged themselves to the shadows, that the hallway between the rooms that already existed, grew. It didn't take them long to figure out that this would allow them to add more dimensions."

"Wait," I interrupted. "If Frank was the first human to enter The Hall, then how did they know that?"

She pointed her cancer stick at me. "Don't forget, hon, Kage had plenty of followers of his own kind, even before Reanin walked this hall."

"Oh . . . right." The non-angel angels. The waitress was about to pick up where she left off when something she'd just said got caught on the side of my brain like a hangnail. "Wait —the more souls that enter The Hall, the bigger it gets?" She nodded. "So, like, eventually, if this place keeps growing, there *could* be more cards added to this deck."

"Bingo, Tessy pie. But here's the hitch: for the hallway to grow, the souls that decide to pledge themselves need to call this place home. That's why there's a disclaimer, and it started with Frankie. Kage told Frankie that he was welcome to stay but that it was his new job to recruit more humans to be part of the experiment he and Reanin had started. In exchange, he would be offered eternal necromancy. But Kage warned him that if he ever decided he was through with it, that the alchemy and immortality would fade away."

"And that he would begin to rot," I added.

She shook her head. "No way, Kage never would've done that to us. It was his brother who twisted Kage's magic with the end of his stupid sword."

I frowned. "His brother? Nisroc did this to you guys?"

"Yeah. Nisroc," his name came out in a scoff. "What a fella."

"Yeah." I nibbled on my lip. "I've heard some things."

"It was that dirtbag who decided that instead of our gifts just fading away and letting us return to humans, that if we ever stopped working for Kage, our bodies would rot. It was pretty stupid on Nisroc's part. If he'd just left well enough alone, then those of us who felt fulfilled and decided to stop working in The Hall could just return to our humanity and eventually die."

"But now . . ."

"But now if we don't bring in enough, let's say currency, then our bodies rot and our magic festers into a hunger for the skin we no longer have." I couldn't help the look of horror on my face. I mean, in my defense, she looked like she was seconds away from full on zombie, as did most of these other waifs. "Don't worry," she said, as if reading my thoughts. "It takes a *very* long time to turn into a flesh eater."

The hairs on the back of my neck were still sticking straight up. "Like, how long?"

The waif shrugged. "Eh. A couple more years locked in here and the majority of us would've started nibbling at the others probably."

"So, like, all these years that you were all stuck in here, nobody turned? Not a single waif?"

It was her turn to widen her eyes. "Oh yeah, no—tons turned. But don't worry, they're all in quarantine."

"Quarantine? So, does that mean they'll get better now that the doors are open?"

"Nope. Once the change happens, it's over. It's the waifs who've turned that you need to steer clear of—and the infected, you know, those who have been bitten. They all start to look alike, waif or not." She shivered, as did I, then sat up in her chair and tapped some of the excess ash into a tray sitting over the table. "Most of us only look like this right now because we haven't been able to get to the surface. *This place* is packed cause everyone's waiting for the lines to calm down. There's about ten waifs standing before every reflection right now—might as well be freaking Disney World, ya know."

I gulped and nodded. But really, I didn't know.

She acknowledged a waif holding up an empty glass then turned back to me. As she stood, she said, "I gotta get back to it, kid. The sooner I finish my shift the sooner I can get back to work on the surface. Showers don't help when you're just a hunk of rot."

"And by work, you mean . . ."

Her tongue slipped out and rested over her purplish bottom lip as she waited for me to finish what I was saying. Thankfully, she read my hesitance. Placing a single palm down over the table, she leaned in. "We don't bring anyone down here who doesn't already belong. We seek out those who have been looking for us."

"And how do you know they've been looking?"

"It's amazing what humans are capable of. How even when they are taught to follow the path set before them by society, pieces of them still reach out for what they intuitively know will actually guide them. No one comes into their body without knowing exactly what they are there to learn. And you're no different, Tess. Even though your path is a little wider than most, you knew something else was lingering before you. Something great . . . something that lived in the shadows."

Again, I bit my lip.

She smiled at me like I would imagine an older sister would. "You're going to be okay, Tess. We all are. Just keep your head up and take it all in." She tapped the table then started backing away. "Melody will be over in a minute."

"Melody?" I questioned.

The waitress gestured towards the piano. "Yeah. She's why you're here after all. One of Reanin's favorites." She shot me a final grin then took off towards the bar.

Melody. All I could see was that empty bourbon bottle I'd found in my grandma's apartment. What had that note attached to it said? Something about how it was for when *his wings were singed* . . . Nisroc. That's who the note had to have been referring to. The bourbon was meant to be consumed after his demise. A toast to their enemy's death. But the bottle had been empty and Nisroc was still alive. Did that mean that

Reanin had given up and drank it out of disappointment? Or was there more to the story?

Either way, I didn't have much time to think over it. The music ended and Melody stood from her seat at the piano. She took a bow, and when she stood back up, her gaze landed stiffly over mine.

Before I knew it, the woman was sauntering towards my table. She wore an interesting grin, one composed of a motley crew of judgements. When the same waif who I'd been conversing with met her with a glass tumbler full of amber-colored liquid, her smile transformed from mischievous to genuine. She brought the drink over to my table, had a seat, then took a very long drink from the glass. Once she was satisfied, she set it down—on another spinning wheel napkin —and gave me her full attention.

"So, you're the infamous granddaughter of the recently deceased. It's wonderful to meet you, though I am saddened to hear about Reanin."

My words were barely loud enough to hear. "You knew her well, didn't you." It wasn't a question.

Her fingers tapped anxiously over the wooden surface as she moved her gaze to the stage. "Her and I used to drink plenty of bourbon together, right here, at this very table. The loss of my friend is one of those hapless events that makes it less desirable to find beauty in the moon. Still, the show must go on." She returned her haunted stare to rest over my shoulders. "Well then, let's see what we're dealing with, shall we?" She reached an arm over the table and held out her hand.

I just stared at it. "What's that for?"

"My hand?"

I nodded.

"For you to put yours in." When I didn't automatically dare to jump, she sighed, then lowered her hand, letting it sweep over the cards. None of them were disturbed by her touch. "I was under the impression that you were intelligent." I tried not to scoff. "And I don't offer this compliment solely because you are a descendant of Reanin and Kage. I said that because of how quickly you are moving through your grandmother's spread." She pocketed her hands into her lap then leaned her chest in. "Please don't disappoint me. I haven't the time. I'm a hit with the kids, and the doors are unlocked."

I'd almost forgotten why I was here. "You're the muse."

As she pressed her lips together and reached for her drink, I thought back to something I'd read back at Hexed. "The muse is supposed to help the seeker dig out their aspirations," I said as if in a trance.

I pulled my attention away from the table and looked around the bar as if I was searching a tarot card for its meaning. There was a waif on stage playing a saxophone next to another pulling strings on a guitar, while a siren was seated at the piano. I could hear Ethan in my head, telling me to go deeper.

"But this isn't an ordinary reading . . ." I looked back at the muse. "It's not my aspirations you're supposed to help me with. It's my magic."

Melody sipped at what was left of her drink, then held it up. "That a girl," she said to me as the waif waitress hurried over and filled it back up.

CHAPTER TWENTY-TWO

Okay, I knew why I was here. But this was the thing: before Melody and I dove into my magical objectives, I wanted to know a few things. And to be fair, if the shadows could pluck humanity from me like feathers from a chicken, then I had every right to feed a little from *their* veins.

Melody's gaze was centered over mine. She was waiting.

"I know you and my grandmother were good friends. Tell me how you met."

She didn't argue with my lane change, instead she readjusted her hips and went with it. "We were. I met her long before she met Kage. I was drawn to her; at first, I thought it was because of her dancing. She was elegant, fluid. She was the kind of dancer who made it look easy. However, as I began to see more of her, I understood why I'd truly been sent to her."

"And why was that?"

"She was disturbed."

I casually leaned forward and took a sip from my Coke. When I leaned back, I said, "Guess it runs in the family."

Her grin resurfaced. "Reanin wasn't my typical job.

Usually I'm called upon by those who, as you have already stated, are trying to 'find their aspirations.' To any audience member, Reanin had found her calling. What else could she possibly be any better at than ballet?"

"But you saw through her," I said. "Because that's what you do."

She winked. "When I first met Reanin in person, when she was without her stage make-up, she looked very much like these decomposing bodies that surround us. Dark circles took up permanent residence under her eyes, her cheeks were gaunt because John starved her nearly to death, and her will to exist any longer had been long diminished." She paused, staring out into nothing . . . or maybe it was the other way around. Perhaps she was staring at the endless abyss of *everything*. "Looking back on it, I'm unsure of how I ever coerced her to come to this place with me."

"This bar?"

"Yes. It's always been mine. Now it's both mine and The Hall's," she said with a sigh. Her gaze lingered over nothing in particular for a moment before sharpening again. "Back to the point, John was frustratingly always two steps in front or behind Reanin. Still, somehow, I managed to get her alone, and it was then that I asked if she'd be willing to have a drink with a strange woman.

"She'd seen me before, she'd said. Just before she agreed to come with me. One of the first things she admitted to, once we each had a bourbon in our hands, was that she'd started making a habit of looking for my face in her audience." Melody shook her head as she chuckled. "I'll never forget how she said it . . . 'When you're on the stage, it's the brightness that tries to blind you from seeing into the field of life spread out before you, but I've always had a knack for seeing straight into the space where light falls into dark. And that's where I saw you. That's where I see you.'"

The back of my throat tightened. "She said that? My grandma?" A tickle ran down my cheek as a phantom tear caressed my skin.

I missed the rain.

"Her heart was never meant to beat on the surface." Melody sipped her bourbon. "Gal pals, that's what we quickly became. A relationship unworthy of romance, for what we had went far deeper than that." She lowered her chin and raised her eyes at me. "One of the surest ways to open your heart to the shadows, is to have your shackles removed long enough to breathe the finest air—to know what it's like to have your heart beat to its own natural rhythm. Not just one that someone else informed you it must beat to. And then, after you've been given hope, have it ripped away as the chains are placed back around your ankles. Around your wrists . . . your neck. I suppose being with me was like sipping on fresh air after being locked in a mildewed cellar for so long. Reanin couldn't fathom going back into her cell, and that, I believe, is what led her into her dance studio with only her reflection and a piece of glass."

I gasped. I was just about to jump on the muse's last statement when footsteps came down an unseen staircase followed immediately by a pair of men in their mid-twenties. As they walked out of one shadow and into the next, they came to a halt. The music stopped just long enough for the waifs and sirens to stare questionably at the two new additions.

Someone in the back cleared their throat, and for a moment, I thought the men were going to turn right around and run back up those stairs as fast as humanly possible. But then, the same waif who I'd been talking to earlier, called out. "Hey fellas, come on in and have a seat. You're just in time for happy hour!"

The two men seemed more than hesitant, and who could

blame them? The place was filled with zombies and sirens. Wings or not, the sirens were so obviously not of the human variety.

"Maybe we should go," one of them whispered to the other.

"Nonsense!" Melody hollered as she raised her drink in the air. "Have a seat, gentlemen. You wouldn't have found us if you weren't meant to. And never mind my friends; they've had a rough go of things for some time now, but they'll all look much more pleasant very soon." When neither man even dared to move or breathe, Melody repeated herself. "Come in! First round's on me!"

And that was all it took. They shot one another pensive looks for only a second before shrugging their shoulders and wandering over to the nearest available table. The bartender/waitress skittered over with a freshly lit cigarette between her fingers and flirted as she said, "What's your pleasure, boys?"

The room came back to life, and I redirected my attention to Melody. "They *had* to have come from the surface."

"*And?*"

"How'd they get in here?"

She set her drink on the table and lifted her shoulder up to her ear. "*You* opened the doors."

"You mean there's like a legit door that leads into this place? Like—like it's a *real* bar."

She almost looked offended. "It is a real bar. I've owned this joint so long I feel like a fixture. Course, the front door has moved around a bit."

My left brow fell. "Where is it now?"

She grinned. "I believe in the city you call home."

"New York? Shit . . . You must get a *bunch* of people wandering in."

She chuckled. "We get a few."

My eyes dimmed and I let her words settle. Glancing at the two men, I asked, "What's going to happen to them?" Were they going to have to go into that forest?

A bored look seemed to wash over Melody. "Whatever their heart's desire. Now, where were we?" She started to lift her arm up and reach for my hand as she first had, but I wasn't ready.

"You and my grandmother—you were telling me how you met."

She slowly lowered her hand into her lap, but she didn't argue. "Of course. I asked her to meet me for a drink. She agreed, and then we met here. Right here."

"Did you tell her who you were?"

She blinked as she nodded. "I did. The idea of the supernatural didn't even make her flinch or blink twice. Then again, one might argue that she already knew about magic."

"She was a witch, wasn't she? Before she met Kage."

"It's quite possible," Melody answered. "All she did after I told her who I really was, was take a sip from her drink. She let it burn as it trickled down her throat, then asked me what I saw in her. Darkness was my answer."

My knuckles were white from gripping the table. "How did she react?"

"She didn't—not at first. Then" –a chuckle left her bourbon-soaked lips— "she proceeded to tell me that she'd hoped I hadn't quit my day job." Melody dipped her chin, and an almost translucent hand met her mouth as she paused. I had a feeling she was taking pleasure in the memory. "She had a sense of humor, your grandmother. Still, I assured her that I was never wrong. That there was something inside of her ravaging its way out, and whatever it was, it could only be found in the shadows. *That*, I told her, was why we'd met." She leaned in as she said the next part. "I never collaborate with a client. That was until I met Reanin. I knew the second I started talking to her that *this* was to be true: we were to create something that others like her could venture towards. Because all everyone ever seems to know is how to find themselves by closing their eyes in the light. They never think to go into a dark corner and open their eyes."

"What did she say to that?" I asked.

"She answered with a statement. She said she was positive she was the last of her kind. She didn't know what she was, but she knew she was different." My mind flashed to my grandmother's copy of *The Last Unicorn*. Interestingly, though, it hadn't been written yet when her and Melody first met. "I assured Reanin that she was not alone, that there was more of her than she could ever imagine. I told her to visualize a place where people like her could find one another. Somewhere someone could go to be with others who had been born into a world where they didn't fit in."

Melody licked her lips and let her attention veer over to where the two human men were now taking shots of tequila. She winked at them, then returned her gaze to mine. "Now then, I've given you what you've asked for. I've told you how Reanin and I met. After Reanin and Kage found one another and decided to build this circus, she insisted that I and my bar be a part of it. She said that without my musings this world would never be complete. I accepted. And now that I've completed my part of the bargain—shall we?" She held out her palm for the third time.

I stared at her hand—she was right. She'd fulfilled her end of the bargain. It was my turn. So, I set my hand reluctantly in hers. Face up. As soon as our skin touched, a glow began to radiate around our palms.

I raised my brows. "Interesting."

Melody didn't seem fazed. "It's normal; especially for those with profound destinies."

My teeth found my bottom lip and I waited as the muse

searched through the crisscrosses of my skin. She exuded a few 'hmms' and 'hahs,' before she suddenly let go of my paw and sat back in her chair. There was no more glow between the two of us as she crossed her arms over her chest.

"This is simple. It's all about what you can achieve with who you're capable of becoming."

I waited for more because there *had* to be more. When there wasn't, I started to argue. "Um—okay. I don't think I under—"

"You've already been told you're not quite human."

"Yes."

"Well, you never really were human at all to begin with. You, Tess, knew that to grow into who you would one day become meant stirring up some human emotions. You created any and all humanity that exists between your skin and bones."

Huh?

"What?"

She turned her cheek to me. "I'm not really sure I've ever met someone like you, to be honest. Still, the humanity you created for yourself exists, at least for now. Of course, you've given quite a bit of it away while you've been here, but no matter what, it is up to you how much humanity you choose to hang onto before you leave. At some point, however, what you are destined to become will find you whether you accept the challenge or not. Your borrowed humanity will completely fade away."

Okay. That was heavy. And confusing. The goddess in The Pendulum had said I wasn't ready to know about my future. I'd already had a problem with that. Now, it seemed I was getting a version of the same speech.

My voice cracked as I said, "And what am I destined to become, exactly?"

Melody chuckled, then looked down at her hands before

raising her gaze back up to mine. "It isn't my job to tell you; it *is* my role to guide you. This will not be our last meeting."

The waif who'd been playing the saxophone on stage when I'd first entered, hollered at Melody—interrupting my time with the muse. "Hey Mel—you guys are up!"

"Sure thing," she replied, as she raised her hand in the air and waved it like a flag blowing in the wind. "Guess that's us."

I held her stare for a second before looking around, checking to see who she was talking to. Because there was no way she meant for me to join her *up there*. So far, I'd been through five cursed oracle cards. I'd had a portion of my humanity siphoned from me by a dark goddess. I'd nearly drowned. But whatever Melody seemed to be insinuating, absolutely terrified me right down to my bitter core.

I shook my head. "You're not suggesting that I get up on that stage with you. Are you?"

Melody stood. "That's exactly what I'm saying. That mic has your name written all over it, Tess."

I swallowed the word as I spoke it. "Mic?"

"Yes ma'am. Time to give back." She smirked in a way that evil always does when taking pleasure in someone's discomfort. "*Tout suite*, Madame Moreau. We both got places to be after this."

The blood circulating in my body froze. My eyes lifted to the orange-lit stage, to all the waifs, and the two humans who were still completely ignorant of where they were. They were all waiting to hear my talents fizzle. I was going to be sick.

"I—I can't do that."

Melody hung an arm on her hip. "I hate to inform you, tootz, but you don't have a choice. That is unless you want to stay here forever. And I don't think you want to do that; your tab can't be paid with money, and you'll eventually grow hungry. The only cooks I got are a few faeries I snagged from The

Forest." Her gaze rose to the ceiling and lingered. "I'm pretty sure they spike the hot wings with some kind of magical pepper from their land. The chicken tends to cause my patrons to tick."

My breath was stuck in my throat. All I'd heard was that I was expected to sing. "This—that—performing is what I have to do to get to the next card?"

"Um-hm," Melody replied with a twinkle in her eye.

I swallowed a mouthful of sand, then looked down at the seventh card. That sucker wasn't going to budge until I did this.

"Come on," Melody said, waving me along as she started for the piano. "They don't call me the muse for nothing. You'll be fine."

I stayed put for a minute or two—looking out to the bar. She just said they had food, so really, I could just live here. Magical ticking peppers and all. There would be no need to move forward. Maybe I could even send word for Liz to meet me here.

But none of that was an option, and I knew it. Finally, I stood, but I made no rush of it. The waitress who I'd been speaking with earlier winked at me as I slowly let go of the bar table that I'd been using as a blanket.

"This sucks," I whispered, as I hobbled through the many tables to get to the stage. I didn't even sing in the shower. I was that bad.

"You'll be alright," said a male waif, standing to pat my back as I padded by. He lifted his drink in the air. "Everyone in here has had to do it."

I nodded back as best I could, pretending to have absorbed some encouragement, trying to push past the lead in my legs as I climbed onto the stage and took my spot behind the old-fashioned mic.

Melody was seated and waiting. As soon as I'd hit my

mark, she called out over the small black baby grand, "You know *Over the Rainbow*?"

Oh gawd. Marbles were swimming in my guts. "I—uh—"

"Sure ya do!" yelled one of the waifs. "You've seen the wizard before, right? Everyone knows that freaking song!"

No actually, I wanted to say. I hadn't seen the wizard. That's why I was here, to meet my grandpa. But I refrained.

One of the dudes who had just wandered in lifted his free beer into the air. "Yeah, get it, girl! You got this!"

I would've rolled my eyes if I wasn't shaking from head to toe. Returning my gaze to Melody, I nodded. "I can manage."

She grinned, then started moving her hands over the keyboard, as she did, she leaned into her mic and said directly to me, "Put your shadows in it. Oh, and make it jazzy."

I gulped. My throat was even drier than it had been before if that was possible. I stalled by making a visor with my hand and looking out into the audience . . . and that was when I felt it. The first connection I'd ever really had with my grandmother.

Yes, we'd been close. I loved her more than anything . . . but I was starting to understand that, until now, I hadn't ever really known her. I didn't know the woman who danced for a living or who was married to the devil. The woman who knew how to look out into the audience and see past the brightness for the shadows.

I couldn't see her, but I *could* see her children. These waifs and other followers, these inhabitants of The Hall—they wouldn't have been here if it hadn't been for her. She lived on in these souls, in these dimensions.

"Okay," I whispered, pumping my hands out by my sides. "I can do this. I can do this for you, Reanin."

My eyes closed and I reached for the mic. Taking a few more deep breaths, in through my nose and out through my mouth, I felt for the woman who had read to me about a magical creature. A creature who was so positive they were alone, when the reality was that they were fated to rescue all the other magical creatures. The ice in my veins began to melt and my blood started pumping again.

Melody had already passed the part where the song began, but there were no rules when it came to jazz. Even I knew that.

For a second, my hand touched the necklace hanging from my neck, and from there it was all . . . easy. My head bobbed. (This wasn't me, *or was it?*). My fingers snapped and my foot found a beat I hadn't ever known before. Before I knew it, a song was threading out of me like silk from a spider. It became a dance between me and the piano. My voice weaved between the sporadic chords Melody played and my body became more alive than ever. For a second, I even thought I saw her—Reanin—sparkling like an ice sculpture in the back of the bar.

It was over before I knew it. The room exploded in applause as I backed away from the mic and casually made my way back down to where the muse was waiting.

She grinned. "Told ya you'd be fine. And now you know, these shadows, they're not all corners. These worlds are all about untangling the mess of yarn humanity has thrown upon you. Once you learn how to pull your jagged lumps of wool into string you can manipulate things the way you want."

I thought over her words as she continued to pluck at piano keys like she shared a language with the instrument.

"Did you help me sing up there?"

"Normally, the answer is yes. But Miss Tess, that was all you." Her gaze fell upon the stones guarding my neck. "I don't think *they* even really played a part to be honest."

I followed her gaze and looked upon the stones. "They?" A twinkle flashed through her eyes, but she said nothing. "Do you know something about these?"

Her grin widened. I hadn't thought that was possible. "Oh honey, you're going to leave here such a different person."

My tongue traced the back of my teeth. "Okay. Thanks . . . I think." I started to turn back towards my table, but as I did, I saw again the many faces of all the waifs. It triggered a message that I'd nearly forgotten about. I turned back around to Melody and whispered something in her ear. She nodded, before putting her lips near her mic.

"Any of you near goners know anything about a heart?"

The room quieted before the waifs began to look to at one another and shake their heads.

"Sorry hon, looks like they don't have a clue. What has ya askin'?"

My chest lifted as I set my sights over the table holding my oracle spread. "I don't even really know."

I thanked the muse, said 'good luck' to the two guys who were probably about to find out they were sharing drinks with a bunch of waifs in a supernatural dimension, and prepared to enter room seven.

CHAPTER TWENTY-THREE

Bile rose from my throat and penetrated every part of my tongue. Was this some sort of sick joke? *The Three of Swords?*

I crouched over the slick black surface. It was the kind of floor one expected to be wet but was only cold when touched. This dimension was just as dark as The Mirror, save for the lights shining down over the objects levitating around the room. They reminded me of trophies until I realized what they were. The description on the card was quite literal.

I took careful, methodical steps towards what had to have been the main attraction. Three magnificent swords that hung in the middle of all the others, which were hanging sporadically around the rest of the room. There were upwards of forty or more swords suspended by nothing, every one of them identical. Save for one.

The odd one out was hanging between the three swords that happened to be more on display. It was different from the others in that it had an interesting tint to it. Whereas the rest of them were golden with a depth that one could almost peer into, this one was dull. As if it had once glowed but had since been turned off. As I inspected the weapon, I was drawn to the handle, where three small craters—about the size of quarters —seemed to give the impression that jewels used to grace its majesty.

I was still looking up at each of them, admiring how impressive they were, when a set of footsteps distracted me.

"You've made it halfway, Tess." It was a man's voice.

I waited to respond until I saw his full form. As soon as his face hit the light, I knew he was a siren. He was tall, built; his skin was the color of a pearl, and just as smooth. His hair was almost white and his eyes a deep blue. He was the vision of an angel without wings if there ever was one. It was difficult to imagine that he could be a monster, but his burden rested in the need for human souls.

"Yes," I answered. "I suppose I have. Who are you?"

"My name is Raegan. It's a pleasure to meet you." He averted his gaze to rest over the hilt of the sword in the middle. "In case you're wondering about the card's validity, there was a time when this room held only these three swords. The name stuck."

I couldn't stop looking at the swords; they were hypnotizing. "These are more than just forged steel . . . there is magic in these blades. Except for maybe this one." I pointed to the dull one in the middle.

"The magic is . . . cosmic," he said.

I moved my attention back to the siren. "These swords belonged to your kind, didn't they? Back when you were guardians."

He didn't answer at first, instead he laid a hand against the blade nearest him. His eyes closed and a pained expression colored over his face. "This one is mine. The middle one belongs to Kage, and the one on the other side belongs to Cai."

My ears perked up. "Cai?"

He looked at me. "You've met?"

"In The Lake."

"Ah, of course. She spends a lot of time in there . . . reflecting." He paused, drifting for a small amount of time. When he returned, he placed his attention back over my shoulders. "Have you heard our story, Tess?"

I'd heard a lot of stories since I'd been in the shadows. "You mean the siren's tale?"

"Yes."

"Sort of. The lines have yet to be colored in."

His chin lifted. "Allow me to enlighten you. Cai and I were the first to join Kage after he agreed to let go of his wings—as he knew them—and experience the other side of the reflection."

"His wings *as he knew them* . . ."

"Yes," was all he said before returning to his speech. "By now, you must've heard about the hiccup Kage experienced against the three guardians who tried to stop him when he first ventured towards the shadows."

I licked my lips. "If you're talking about how the Stones of Gehenna were created, then yes."

Raegan narrowed his eyes. "It was an unfortunate event, but one that was unavoidable. After the killings, no one dared to stop him—other than his brother. But the threat of just one guardian wasn't one that was going to stop Cai and me; we'd already decided that we were joining Kage in his journey. That we were going to sacrifice our wings."

I cleared my throat. "I don't get it. Aren't your wings *attached*?" Or were they like fey wings? Like Liz's wings.

"It isn't as literal as you may think. Our wings are tied to our emotions; they appear when needed." *Ah, so they were.* "Just as one buries certain emotions, we have every right to bury our wings. To pass through the reflection in the lake you experienced, we had to lay our feathers behind the beating of our hearts."

"Why?"

"Our race was created from some of the brightest energy in the universe; our wings reflect the same star we came from. It is too bright for this place." He took a moment to stare into the shadows. "Instead of internalizing our darkness, as many people on Earth tend to do, we had to tuck in our light."

"Wait—that's it? That's the sacrifice? That's where your wings are buried?"

"Yes."

I shook my head. "Then they aren't really gone. How can the rest of the guardians, and Nisroc believe that this is such a bad thing?"

"It's considered a disgrace to internalize our wings, to neglect the gift our race was given. It is much like the burning of a flag. To internalize who we are is like turning our back on our kind. Though no one dared stop us—in fear of becoming stones themselves—there was much backlash that erupted when more of us began experimenting and following Kage. The guardians began taking sides, and leading the front against us shadow plungers was Nisroc.

"Now, here's the siren's tale you've been anxiously waiting for: Kage's brother, vengeful, took the beating of our hearts and locked them into our swords. It was an act that ensured two things. One, that we would be forced to find a way to get our hearts beating again, thus the need for souls, and two, that finding our wings would be near impossible. You see, each individual heartbeat is unique; a melody created for us to follow when we are lost—when we must find something we've buried."

I gasped. "He took away your free will."

"Not entirely, but he did make things extremely difficult."

He held out his hand and I slowly offered him my own. Without a word, he placed my palm against Cai's sword. My eyes shot wide open as a pain comparable to a searing hot knife cut right through me—then continued to gut me repeatedly. Rage began to seep in from around the tears in my body as broken beats of a lost heart echoed in my ears. As soon as he pulled my hand away from the blade, I lunged forward and filled my lungs with air.

As I gasped and heaved, he stated in a choppy voice, "That is Cai's heart. This" –he grabbed my hand from over my chest and dragged it over to my grandfather's sword— "is Kage's weapon."

I braced myself for more torture, but I didn't need to. There was no horrific reaction. The blade felt only cold against my flesh.

"And this is mine." He pulled my limb gently his way then placed my hand against his sword.

Once more, my ears were filled with heartbeats, but instead of wrath coursing through my veins, I was showered with a cocktail of melancholy and vexation.

Finally, he dropped his hand from mine. As I retained my balance and relished in the silence the room offered, I did my best to center my gaze over his. "You and Cai have broken hearts."

Honesty colored in around the lines of his face that he hadn't yet filled. "We are in the shadows. One doesn't usually come here unless they've run out of room to store what they've buried."

"Right," I muttered softly. Then, slowly returning my attention to Kage's sword, I stated in observance, "His heartbeats aren't in his sword."

"No," Raegan agreed. "Kage made a great sacrifice when he slayed three of our kind, but he also became untouchable."

I gave the siren a searching look. I needed more details.

Raegan inhaled deeply through his nose. "Burying our wings is frowned upon but killing each other is forbidden. If one of our swords pierces the heart of one of our kind, the celestial magic that resides within it ceases to be."

My chest fell in on itself. "If that's so, then what happens to your wings . . ."

"They do remain, buried or not, but they are never the same. It is more than a sacrifice to kill one of our own; it is a decision to become someone else entirely."

"But *you* are someone else entirely. I mean, aren't you? You crave the souls who you were once meant to protect . . . so, what's the difference?"

"I *am* different. But here's the thing, Nisroc cursed us. He wielded his magic so the burden would fall heavy over our shoulders, which is completely ironic considering he makes a point to adamantly declare that he works only for the light. You see, to spin through the elements in the manner he did— to create both the siren and the waif curse—he would have had to access the darker end of the spectrum." He paused, letting the information sink in. "My curse, the siren's curse, is reversible. That is the main difference between what I have given into and what Kage has done. You see, if sirens take back our swords and dig out our heartbeats from the enchantments Nisroc swirled through our materials, we may rediscover our wings. However, the second we attempt to trade our wings for the shadows again, the curse, or the hunger, will return. And there are no second chances. Kage, on the other hand, will never be a guardian again."

"Okay . . . So, what if Nisroc is taken out? You know, like murdered. Would these curses cease to exist?"

Raegan's glow dimmed. "There is some magic that is rooted too deeply to ever be reversed. This, I'm afraid, is one of those kinds. However, it isn't as bad as it sounds. While in the shadows, we may still crave human souls, but we can survive for years before transitioning further. Just as the waifs' decomposition delays while in this world."

I hinged forward on my toes. "Hang on—what do you mean, *before transitioning further*?" What could be worse than depending on human souls for nourishment?

His expression hardened. "If we stop feeding from souls our hearts will eventually stop. If we allow them to stop for long enough, they need something other than souls to get started again. And from that point we are no longer sirens, but something else entirely."

I thought over the one person I'd met whose identity remained a mystery. "Cai is different than you, than the other sirens."

"Yes," was all he said.

"Can she still retrieve her wings—her heartbeat? I mean —" I pointed up to her weapon. "Her sword is still as radiant as all the others. It's not 'turned off' like my grandfather's."

Raegan stared down and away as he said, "She can. It's just that when one becomes that far gone from what they used to be, it is even more difficult to find their way back."

Silence fell over us like a cape as I considered everything I'd been told. My tongue ran along the surface of the inside of my cheek as I thought about what to say next. I still had so many corners to peek into.

I peered into Raegan's icy eyes as I dared to ask, "Why hasn't anyone killed Nisroc yet?"

He raised his brows. "For years, he wasn't a threat. After he threw down his curses, Kage stole something from him; unfortunately, it was returned. As soon as he got his mojo back, he went right back to forming his cult following, be it fellow guardians or humans. Most of the humans he plucked from covens. He offers them a show of cosmic magic, and they flock to him like a savior." He moved his weight from one foot to the other. "I say all this, Tess, to let you know, we *do* want him dead. But here's the hitch: the only way to kill a guardian is to access the same amount of magic harnessed in our swords, or a magic that is even more powerful. As I've said, we come from some of the most magnetic energy in the universe. There are very few entities who share the same amount of energy, save for the gods. No guardian, siren or not, wants to bloody their sword with Nisroc's blood; they do not want their swords to look like his." He gestured to Kage's blade.

I frowned. "What's so bad about what Kage has become?"

Raegan's chest inflated, then he slowly let the breath out through his nose. "Whether it is bad, is in the eye of the beholder."

"And what exactly *is* he?" Would someone finally tell me already?

"Kage is his own entity. In my opinion, what he is will remain a mystery to everyone except for him, always. Some believe he is now the god of this world, but that is merely speculation. This, however, is truth: your grandfather left his post willingly and gave into the ultimate sacrifice known to our kind, because he was determined to understand that which most guardians don't stop to think about. We were created to serve, not to speculate about our own lives—yet we were given free will just as humans. We were given emotions and the ability to love. The shadows interested Kage; these dark spaces everyone was so governed to believe were evil. He saw a new dimension where creatures and people of all kinds could gather and heal in a new way." Raegan looked to his sword, as he did an image materialized inside. I gasped, causing the striking pair of bluish green eyes that had been looking out of the magical tool to fade, like a lake's ripple dwindling away.

"There are some that believe love doesn't exist in the shadows. That is false."

I blinked a few times, before I asked, "Who was she?"

"She used to be my partner. Not in love, but in work. Though I harbored feelings for her . . . she never saw me for more than what I was. Her heart belonged with someone else; but as luck would have it, that special someone never returned that sentiment. It was and is a circle of heartache. But to be clear, it began on the surface. The shadows weren't responsible for what has transpired, though they've come to offer quite the playing field."

I looked at his sword again, then back to him. The image of the woman's eyes was gone, but her energy seemed to still be lingering, especially over Raegan's soul-hungry heart. "You lied to me just now." His gaze sharpened. "You said you harbor*ed* feelings for her, as if it was in the past. But that wasn't true. You still love her."

He neither confirmed nor denied my observation. Instead, he held out a hand towards my cards. I'd been so engrossed in his story, I'd nearly forgotten about the reading. "You've felt with your hands the pieces of our broken hearts. You now understand *our* sacrifice. There is no extra offering needed here. The shadows have gotten what they've wanted. You may move on."

I couldn't help but scoff. "Why do you all do this?" I asked, holding out my hands as if asking for scraps.

"Do what?" he asked genuinely.

"Offer breadcrumbs when you've got more loaves to spare than you even know what to do with." I gestured to all the other swords hanging magically around us. "There is so much more you could tell me. I'm guessing each of these magical tools has their own story, or did, before they were hung up. Why don't you elaborate?"

Raegan remained stiff as a board. "It does not matter how

human you are; it takes very little humanity to reign over your immortal self—to veil your eyes. It's as if you are dehydrated, and, because of this humanity still living inside you, your body will regurgitate the information we give you if you drink too fast. Therefore, we must give it to you intravenously. The thirst doesn't leave you as quickly, but at some point, you will realize that you are no longer thirsty. That your body has what it needs to survive."

I just stared at him. "*Okay.*"

For the first time, the man before me broke just a little. His expression cracked and a grin slipped through.

"What's so funny?" I questioned.

"It's just that—" he actually laughed. Like out loud. With his soldier-esque posture, I hadn't pegged him for the kind of soul who was capable of that. "Well, it's you."

I shot him a pointed stare. "I'm sorry, but what about me is so funny?"

"It's not that *you're* funny. It's the situation." He seemed to be trying to cinch up his emotions. "I'm standing here with the teenage version of someone who is destined to become— well, I must not say too much."

I narrowed my eyes. "You're frustrating me."

"Yes." He grinned.

I started to let down my guard as I saw the personality behind the siren. "You know, whoever she was—" I gestured to his sword, to the eyes I'd seen swimming in their reflection just a bit ago. "She was stupid to let you get away. I mean, I don't know you, but I'm *guessing* you might be a good guy."

"You should never judge a book too quickly, for endings have a habit of making a quick turn in the other direction. But thank you."

Gawd, everybody here was so weird.

I began to veer towards my cards, but before I left there was something I needed to clear up. "What did you mean when you said there is no *extra* offering needed here? I don't recall giving up a thing."

Raegan laced his hands together behind his back as he lifted his chin. "It has been feeding from you this whole time."

"What has?"

"The Hall," he stated simply. Then he bobbed his head in a brief nod and started walking back the same way he'd entered. "Don't act surprised, Tess Moreau," he said over his shoulder. "You know as well as I do that you've figured that much out already."

He disappeared into the shadows and then the door opened and shut. He was gone.

It was just me, the swords, the cards, and the rest of The Hall to experience.

How could he assume that I'd already figured that out? I sat before the cards and thought about it. I mean, I guess *there was* something I'd been ignoring.

Growing up, I'd never paid it much attention—the spark that lived inside me. It was from this spark that my magic originated . . . Don't ask me how I knew, I just did. When I returned that bit of ash on Mr. Greene's shirt to a cigarette, or when I read the story of whatever ashes were set in front of me . . . or when I returned them into an enchanted oracle deck— the point being, whenever I did those things, that spark inside me grew like an ember in the wind. And when it did grow, it felt *good*. A slow burn; not just a shot of power, but a shot of *life*. It was this feeling that had started to grow as I proceeded through every cell, room, or shadow in this place.

As my hand drifted down to the next heavy card I needed to flip over, I stared out to the last spot where Raegan had been standing before he left. "The Hall is taking my humanity and causing my magic, my spark, to take over. That's it, right? I'm getting closer to who I'm supposed to be."

Of course, there was no answer. I was alone in The Three

of Swords. Still, I knew that if he was still in here, he would have nodded.

"All right," I whispered, my breath heavy. "Let's see what else we got."

And away into the night I went.

CHAPTER TWENTY-FOUR

The ghost of a star passing . . .

The eighth card was called Stardust. The card was blank *or* full, depending on how you looked at it. At first, I veered towards blank, but as my gaze rose to investigate the transformation between one room and the next, I saw what no illustration could translate.

There was no floor, yet I didn't fall, and I was able to walk around as though there was. My oracle spread remained intact and flat as if the cards were lying on the ground. When I rose to observe this new dimension, the darkness dissipated, and stars began to fill in all around me. It was the most beautiful thing I'd ever seen. So much so that I became lost in the grandness of it all and didn't see them as they began to walk into the room as if it were a stage—three entities made of light.

"I think she's enjoying the show," said a female voice, prompting me to let go of the hypnosis I'd fallen under.

I knew at once that these were guardians, or at least they had been at some point. They were much like ghosts; there was no direct color to them. Though, the longer I studied them, I might have argued that they were *every* color. All three were built like the sirens I'd seen—grandly—and each one carried something by their side. One of the males had a sword, like I'd just seen in The Three of Swords, the female had an orb, and the other male had a snake coiled around his forearm. The sword, the orb, and the snake all matched the color and texture of the guardians.

"She sees us now," said the woman.

"It is nice to formally meet you, Tess," said the male with the sword.

I couldn't be sure how I knew this—but I was positive as I stared at the three of them that I knew who these alien beings were.

"You're the guardians Kage murdered."

They all three lowered their heads in a reassuring bow.

"Sharper than most," said the man with the slithering snake bound to his arm; his voice was monotone and without emotion.

"Yes," echoed the woman. "Definitely a descendant of Kage."

"You say that without regret . . . almost like you admire my grandfather."

"It sometimes takes leaving one's body," started the man with the sword, "to see the universe as it truly is."

"Even guardians can be blind," added the woman. She wore a neutral smile as she turned from where she'd been facing me and held out a hand to the twinkling lights. "When a star dies it can create a black hole." She returned her attention to me and held up her orb. In it, a small movie played. "This was the star whose dust created our kind, along with many other species. Including humans. A black hole formed from its death and bits of its stardust were sucked into it. The black hole then separated and created worlds within worlds—portals and dimensions. Planets and beings. Magic and doubt."

I didn't blink as she spoke, as the movie played.

From the death of the star, beings arrived made of stardust. Elongated bodies with heads to match. They began to multiply and bear seeds. From the seeds grew different species, including but not limited to humans and guardians. Just like she'd said.

"Life made from death," the woman reiterated, piercing my eyes with her own. The movie faded away. "Pieces of stardust, mixed with bits of the dark matter created by the black hole, scattered like ashes . . . they fell around Earth, and many other planets. Some became dimensions, like what we have here in The Hall. Others, the pieces with more depth and intellect—" She froze, her gaze so locked onto mine that I felt paralyzed. "They became something else."

"Like what?" I whispered.

"The seeds from which gods and goddesses may grow," said the man with the snake on his arm.

My body became slightly boneless. "Why are you telling me this?"

The man with the sword replied, "It is part of the rehydration process."

"Okay . . ." That made sense now. "So once Kage killed all of you, you saw these truths?"

"No one is ever truly killed," stated the woman. "We are only separated from our bodies. Our energies are not meant to stay in one body indefinitely—even gods fade away at some point."

"Right." I closed my eyes firmly, took a breath, then reopened them. "So, you're not mad at my grandfather?"

"He followed his destiny," said the woman. "One cannot fault another for that."

"And this has always been our destiny," stated the man with the sword.

I found myself tracing my lips with the tip of my tongue as

I studied the three entities—their shiny bodies standing against the starry background like *they* were gods. And then I was struck with a thought, one that erased any suspicions I'd had about my necklace up until that point. "Is this where he's hidden them—the Stones of Gehenna?"

"No," the woman replied almost instantly. "This is an explanation for those who enter the Stardust dimension. Everyone else but you would see a recording of us."

"Okay. . ." *So maybe back to my original hypothesis.* "But, I mean—you're really here, right now. Right?"

"Yes," she affirmed. "When Kage impaled our hearts and we became stones, he did bring us into the dimension that would one day become the Hall of Shadows. In doing so, The Hall fed from our energy until it was able to manifest the same power on its own."

"So that's why hunters will always be searching a way into this place," I said in realization. "Regardless of whether the stones are in here or not."

"Truth," she said.

"So where are the stones now?"

The female's eyes danced as she replied, "They were removed from The Hall many years ago."

There it was.

When next I spoke it came out as a croak. "Everyone else who comes in here would see a recording because you can't appear unless—"

"We appear to the one who owns us," the woman clarified.

Heavy.

Finding Maggie had been no accident; neither had been going to that fair.

As the pieces began to fall into place, I shooed the dizziness of realization away by focusing over what each ghostly guardian held.

"Why does only one of you have an actual sword?" I asked.

As soon as I said it, the orb and the snake turned into swords.

My jaw unhinged and I almost laughed as I realized what I was looking at. "They can shapeshift."

"Truth," said one of the male guardians, his sword returning to a snake.

"They are our familiars," said the other man. As soon as he said it, I was reminded of my first encounter with Liz. Her familiar was a dragon. "Their original form is a sword," he said.

"We each carry what keeps us feeling secure," added the woman.

A shiver ran down my spine as the sword in the female's grip returned to an orb. "Does it work that way in and out of the shadows? I mean, can *all* guardians shift their swords like that?"

All three of them nodded.

"We walk amongst humans as if we are one with them. Often, you can find our kind with an animal, or a cane, or—"

"A crystal ball," I answered for the man with the sword.

"Correct," he replied.

The mechanisms in my brain were suddenly spinning a little too fast.

"She is wise," said the guardian with the snake.

"She will rise," said the woman.

"Truth," added the man with the sword.

A fire had been lit under my feet. Before these last two shadows, I'd been moving through these dimensions like a girl shopping for a prom dress I wasn't sure I needed. I was too young to attend the dance on my own and I hadn't been invited yet. But the smoke was beginning to clear. The future was getting refined. I was surer than anything that by the end of all this, I would have a date; it just wouldn't be in the form of a teenager, and it wouldn't be at the prom. My match was one that had been set up by the ghost of a passing star. Destiny. And it wasn't going to include dinner and a dance.

I guess that's why my grandfather or grandmother or whoever made sure I got this necklace. I was going to need all the help I could get.

"I have to go," I stated to the three guardians.

"Go in strength," said the woman.

"We will be with you," said the guardian with the sword.

"Summon your stardust," added the man with the snake.

I jerked my chin up and down then returned to my cards. Just before I reached down to them though, I looked back at the guardians. They were starting to fade. "Is this the only place you can show yourselves?"

"No," answered the woman. "We may appear any time to whoever has access to our magic."

My jewelry gained even more weight over my chest. And then they were gone. At least from sight.

I started to reach for the ninth card, but just as my hand lowered to grip it, my limb began to tremble. My gaze lifted and my attention peeked as the stars began to grow, like the light was bleeding into the darkness.

"What the—" I began, but the rest of the sentence was cut short as my feet were pulled out from under me and I was laid flat against the surface.

My throat locked up and my lungs began to pull at whatever had breached them. I reached for my throat, fighting against the burning in my heart. As the stars continued to shine brighter, a yellowish-white shimmer began to lift from my body. I froze. My struggle was put on hold. My eyes grew as the glitter that had lifted from my body began to mesh into the starlight until it all eventually became one glowing ball levitating about five feet over my stomach.

Play it cool. Let it happen, I thought. By now I understood,

I hadn't been brought here for torture; this was my family prepping me for what was to come.

I did my best to remain calm as I lived without air for what felt like an endless time. The ball of light twisted and churned above me, its color shifting from sparkling white to a dark and shimmering gray. Finally, the plug sealing my lungs from one of my most vital needs uncorked, and just as I'd done when I'd fallen from the lake, my mouth unhinged so I could receive as much air as it was possible to consume. As soon as breath found me, the shimmering gray cloud fell *into my body* with such force that my body crashed down to the ground and bounced back up before falling one final time.

I laid still for many moments after that. I didn't move, not an inch. I was as quiet as a corpse. Eventually, I decided it was over and very slowly rose to a sitting position. Once more I was floating in space; the stars had returned to how they'd looked when I'd first arrived.

But there was one thing that was very different. My life force was now in the hands of my magic. I was breathing . . . and my heart was dancing to the song my blood always played for it, but—I didn't know how to explain this. I knew if I wanted to, I could stop breathing and it wouldn't matter. Air was just air. It was the magic in my veins that was going to keep my heart beating from here on out. These acts of humanity . . . they were going to fade away from my body very soon.

I stood, my head lifted, and my shoulders rolled back. I was so much stronger than I'd been moments ago.

For the second time, I returned to my oracle spread. Before I reached for that ninth card, certain it was ready for me now, I placed my hand over the stones around my neck and whispered softly to them. "Thank you."

CHAPTER TWENTY-FIVE

The ninth card was called The Weapons Room. This place looked to belong to some secret sect of the military. I mean, literally, there were weapons for as far as the eye could see.

I stood apart from the steel table where my cards had turned up and continued to look around. Darkness swept over every inch of the cell that wasn't occupied by a bow and arrow, rifle, sword, knife—or whatever else some of these deadly contraptions claimed to be. Like the sword room, the only lights were those over the weapons, but there were so many of them that it was far from too dark to see. I'd wandered over to one of the shelves and was just about to wrap my hand around a spear with a leather grip when a familiar face began walking out from the shadows.

"Rachel?" I asked. I hadn't seen the waif since the beginning of this twisted carnival.

She inched closer to where I was posed before the spear; she looked so much different. It wasn't like she looked younger —she hadn't appeared all that old before. Just, you know, deadish. She was alive now. Her hair was thicker and shinier, her skin a light peach, her lips rosy, and when she was close enough, her breath was way less hideous. She'd even updated her wardrobe. Instead of the nasty orange fabric she'd been encased in when I met her, she was wearing a green boho dress with black flats.

I was just about to compliment her on the new outfit when she spoke. "Looks like you're good at names . . . among other things."

I grinned. "And you no longer stink."

She matched my expression. "Since I was the first to know that the doors were reopened, I didn't have to wait to get back to work. But never mind that. Looks like I found you just in time. Man, you don't waste a single second, do you?" She reached up and pulled my hand away from where it was lingering before the spear. "You have one choice here, and there are no trade ins. I encourage you to choose wisely."

My eyes flitted back and forth. "For what?"

"You may only choose one."

"You already said that." I observed, fixing my mouth into a straight line.

Before she could explain, we were interrupted by the sound of a door opening and shutting. A small set of footsteps signaled we'd been joined by a third party and soon enough we saw the face of the intruder.

"Annie?" I questioned, as the changeling appeared by our sides.

The little one didn't hesitate. "It began when a select few grew weary. Some from a life lived too long, others from apprehension. They removed themselves from reflection, but they can never escape the shadows. There is but one way out for them. Get close enough to smell them and it could be your last breath. There are no heartbeats. The clock ticks in the tower. You must stop time."

I lowered down so I could look into the child's eyes, but

she never gave me the chance to see into her soul. As soon as her message was laid out, she turned and made to leave. Probably returning to her forest home.

Once she was gone, I turned back to Rachel. "That was foreboding."

Rachel had clasped her hands together. "She must like you. She's never offered a hint like that before. Not to anyone." Then, holding out her hand to the shelves full of weapons, she said, "Take your time, Tess. Think over the changeling's words before you make your final choice."

My final choice . . .

"For what?"

Rachel grinned. "Wouldn't you like to know."

"You're not going to tell me anything more, are you?"

She shook her head slowly from side to side.

So, this was like a riddle that if I got wrong could end in death. Cool, I couldn't wait (*heavy* sarcasm). I tried to slow down the churning thoughts in my head for long enough to think over what I'd already been told. From what Annie had said, I was supposed to kill something, or multiple somethings. She'd said 'they.' She'd also hinted that it wouldn't be in my best interest to get too close.

I turned toward the nearest shelf, my gaze lingering between a machete and a wooden stake. What would Kage allow to be exterminated from his world? It would have to be something that wasn't adding any value.

They didn't have beating hearts.

There was only one thing I could think of.

"All right," I whispered, leaving Rachel's side and wandering through the aisles and endless shelves of weapons.

I lingered around a set of bows and arrows. Those could afford me to shoot at my targets from a distance, but the question remained: I didn't know how many of these things there were, or how many I would need to kill. There were only seven arrows in the pack. And I'd never shot one of those. What if I was a terrible shot?

My next thought was a gun or a rifle. There were plenty of those hanging around. I stared at a pretty black Glock for the better part of ten minutes, deciphering. But again, I'd never shot a gun. I didn't know how to load it, or if it came preloaded—or how many bullets there were. If any.

After a while I made my way back to the waif.

"I need more information."

She shook her head. "I'm not at liberty to expose any more truths. You got more than most. You'll have to remember to thank the child after you survive."

"Right," I muttered disgracefully as I returned to the game pieces. Then, more to myself than to her— "What the hell does a clock ticking in a tower have to do with anything? And how am I supposed to stop time?"

"Don't be so literal!" Rachel shouted to my back.

I halted in my steps and flipped around to face her. I thought about saying something but stopped. This was my journey, my shadow to pay. She'd already offered all she could.

I returned to the collection. As I perused weapon after weapon, I repeated Annie's riddle. "The clock ticks in the tower. You must stop time." I shuffled the brainteaser around in my head like tarot cards as I walked down yet another aisle. Before long, something snagged my attention.

I squared my shoulders before something that looked like a gun but wasn't.

I wasn't really into video games; still, it was coded in my rite of passage as a teen to at least experience role-playing now and again. I had a PlayStation and a few games I'd gotten from my grandma last Christmas. One of the games was about some fantasy world that I couldn't even remember the title of. I think I played it twice. It wasn't my thing, and Reanin should've known that. Or did she?

I narrowed my eyes to the white and black weapon. It was exactly like the one in my game. I released the hold my teeth had over my bottom lip and my chest lifted. "Was that a hint, Grandma? If not—well, it's all I've got to go on."

A minute later I walked back to where Rachel was waiting, the weapon in my arms.

She had the smallest and cleverest smirk on her face. "Interesting choice. May I ask why?"

"I'm going to burn the tower down."

Her eyebrows danced up and down and she nodded. A second later, I heard the familiar sound of a card turning over.

I spun around on my toes to find that the tenth card of my spread had moved of its own accord, crossing over The Weapons Room card, making a cross.

"Why the hell did it do that?" I whispered.

I clutched the weapon closer to my chest as the ground shifted under my feet, transforming into a piece of plywood; just large enough for me to stand on and move a few paces in each direction.

The room brightened, and my stomach sank as a new room materialized and the floor came into focus about fifty or sixty feet below where I floated on the plywood. An enormous stage appeared, making the one in The Pendulum room look like the size of an apartment kitchen. There were easily two thousand seats in this place, gathered on the floor and along three separate balconies. Everything was either ivory or the color of blood. And almost too far away to see, were my oracle cards. If I could pass safely through this dimension, they'd be waiting for me—all the way down by one of the exits.

I lifted my gaze to where Rachel was floating on her own piece of plywood, about fifteen feet away from mine.

"Welcome to The Opera House," she said.

And then the lights went out.

CHAPTER TWENTY-SIX

The lights returned, but only to a low dim. Rachel and I floated over the vast auditorium; every seat filled. I looked down into the endless rows; there were oceans of Victorian dresses, paired next to black suits—canes and top hats. One thing was for sure: we weren't in the 2020s anymore.

The symphony, tucked into their pit, was beginning to play; symbols crashed together creating an ominous ambience over an already haunting scene. Next, the players strutted onto the stage, and I knew immediately from their make-up and costumes that this was an old production of *Cleopatra*.

Rachel's plywood drifted over as though we were gliding across a lake on paddle boards. Without a hitch, she jumped from her board to mine, and not even slightly winded, she whispered to me, "It's a memory."

I looked at her, then lowered a brow. "Whose?"

"Reanin's." Her gaze shifted to the stage. "Got stuck in the walls; it plays every time someone new enters this place." She lowered onto the slab of wood and patted the space next to my foot. I didn't argue. I sat next to her and as soon I did the plank began sinking very slowly. As if she didn't notice the board moving, she added, "I think some parts of our lives are just so avant-garde, so precious, that they cannot be thrown out . . . even when we don't exist anymore."

I'd been staring at the performers as Rachel spoke—hypnotized by her words. But then the floating contraption began to turn in circles. When it stopped, the air completely left my lungs.

"Grandma," I whispered.

Reanin and John Wellington were seated side by side in the center of the second balcony. John was handsome but wore a firm and joyless expression. He and Reanin were both dressed extravagantly; Reanin in a purple corset dress with black stitching, and John wearing a cape over his suit, which was decorated with ivory silk lining.

"Man, they had good seats," Rachel observed.

That was the last thing on my mind as I cradled my chosen weapon against my chest and let my head fall to my shoulder. "She looks so sad."

Reanin's eyes were glued to the stage, but to any intelligent soul, the woman was nowhere near present. She was as beautiful as ever, but I could still see them, the dark circles under her eyes. There was no depth anywhere in her person . . . . what I was looking at was nothing more than a shell.

"She'd already given up," said Rachel, her voice distant. "This was the night she decided she *had* to do something so she could feel again."

My gaze reached for the waif's. "What did she do?"

"You'll find out very soon."

I didn't argue, and I didn't feel the same need as I had only a few shadows ago—the urgency to fill my curiosities right then and there. Ever since that gray cloud had fallen on me while in the Stardust room, my anxieties had dulled. All inquiries pertaining to this world and who I would one day become, just sort of washed away. I knew I would find out all these answers and more; if not today, then tomorrow. And if not tomorrow, then someday. I somehow understood that I had plenty of time to work things out.

Returning to the vision of who Reanin had once been, I asked Rachel, "Had she met Kage yet?"

"No," she answered. Then almost immediately raised her arm and pointed at a section just a few rows back. "But he'd met her."

I gasped when I saw the face of the man who had to be my grandfather. It was a face that I recognized . . . not because I'd met him yet, but because I'd recently communed with someone who shared many of his features. The resemblance caused me to grit my teeth and hold the flame thrower tighter to my chest.

Kage had pale skin, but everything about him was dark. It was like the shadows he'd already come to know and find fulfillment in danced around his flesh like lavender in a dense forest. People were seated around him—not a single chair left empty—but his presence, though surely solid, was haunting.

The last thing he was paying attention to was the opera. No, Kage had his attention placed wholly over that of Reanin Wellington.

"How?" I asked. It was all I could muster.

Luckily, Rachel knew what I meant. "Some have called it fate—like their souls were mates. That destiny pulled Kage towards Reanin, and Reanin towards him. Most of us believe that they met long before Reanin was even aware . . . in the shadows."

"Hang on. Reanin knew about The Hall while she was a dancer?"

"No, but that doesn't mean that a piece of her soul wasn't already breaking away and searching it out. It could've happened while she was asleep, or half awake. It's not unheard of."

I pressed my tongue against my bottom front teeth as I continued to watch Kage peer down at my grandmother. If someone had described to me the way he was looking at her, I would have imagined a predator. But I already knew that's not what he was; if anything, he was there to protect her . . . like the guardian he'd been once upon a time.

"He was watching over her," I realized.

"Yes." I saw Rachel nod out of the corner of my eye. "Protecting her from *him*."

I glanced at John before returning my attention to my grandma. After another pause—another moment of introspection—I asked, "Why was this moment so groundbreaking that it has to play over again and again for each new soul who enters this place?"

"I think," Rachel stated, "that it's because it was the first time Reanin realized the man who she'd been seeing now and again, creeping along the backside of her mirrors, was real. *This man,* who watched her dance, who stood on the other side of the reflection, who observed as she could no longer produce any more tears. And even though he stood in darkness, this man had the kindest eyes she'd ever seen. The most unusual eyes."

"My eyes."

"Yes."

We remained seated before John and Reanin for what felt like a long time. Eventually, the curtains fell and the opera house began to fill with light as hired hands walked around and lit all the candles inside the wall sconces. Intermission.

Reanin pulled at the fabric of her dress and began to stand, but John halted her by sliding a hand in front of her knees. She looked at him, and he gave a very curt shake of his head, before returning his gaze to the stage. Reanin very slowly relaxed back into her seat, but her spine remained rigid. Her emotions were palpable. She wasn't just vexed; she was a prisoner. The shackles were always there, even if no one could see them.

And then it happened, the moment Rachel must've been alluding to. When the break was over, and the musical vibrations began to fill in the spaces of the auditorium once more—the candles extinguished—Reanin very slowly and deliberately turned her head and set her eyes exactly in the spot that had been occupied by Kage just moments ago. I didn't recall seeing him leave . . . or simply fade away. But either way, he was no longer there. Still, the way my grandmother held her gaze over that empty seat made it clear as day—she'd known that the man she'd seen in the shadows had been there. Whether she'd been alerted by the hairs on her neck or sensed his existence in some other way, it didn't matter. The simple truth of it was that she had *known* he'd been there. As Rachel had already stated, that had been enough for her. Whatever she was destined for, it wasn't on the stage, and it wasn't on this side of the reflection.

I turned to mention my observation to Rachel, only to find that the waif was no longer there. Instead, she was back on her own floating platform. Her arms were crossed over her chest and there was a wicked smile planted securely over her now nearly perfect face.

I clambered up to stand, trying not to drop my weapon. "What's going on *now*?" I asked.

As she answered me, the memory began to fizzle. One by one, the people in the seats and on the stage—in the pit— began to fade away. Reanin and John were the last to go. As soon as they disappeared, our platforms began to move to the center of the opera house, levitating just a few feet below a giant glass chandelier.

"This," Rachel said, "is the fun part."

"Fun?" I repeated the word as an unsettled breath found its way to the top portion of my lungs. My head fell back in observation as scratching and scampering noises began to erupt from overhead, like raccoons trying to vie their way out of a locked attic. "Yeah, something tells me that's not the word I'd have chosen."

A loud inhuman screech sounded from the stage and I completely quit blinking as I stared at Rachel. The grin on her face hadn't yet left. If anything, it grew as she said, "They've been locked in here just as long as the rest of us. Their venom has to be super potent by now."

I glanced towards the stage. "Venom?"

Designs were embedded into the walls of the opera house, typical Victorian architecture, and as I continued to labor through my quickening heartbeats, a section of carved wood began to protrude from the wall, along with two of the sconces hanging under it. I gripped my weapon tighter as what *might have been an arm* slithered out from an opening.

"We don't have venom automatically," Rachel explained, "but once our hearts stop and we refuse to do what's needed to get them going again, well, let's just say it's interesting what the body does when it can't die."

More of the creature weaseled its way from the opening in the wall. I had yet to see a face, but there was definitely a shoulder making its way out. I'd already cracked the riddle—I knew what I was up against, but still, I had to ask, "These things are *waifs*?"

"Not all of them, but this all started with a pair of waifs who wanted to die. They figured if they just let it all go that their bodies would turn to stone or whatever. That's not what happened. The magic in their veins betrayed them—you see, we can't die. Nisroc made damn sure of that. Instead, if we discontinue our work, we become insane. Goners."

"Goners..."

"Yes. Goners who are either expired waifs or those who have been infected by the venom; either way, they are driven by a hunger for the flesh they no longer have. Their bite is fatal to any creature of any kind. The magic of a goner knows only destruction; it can infect anyone."

I pulled my gaze away from Rachel and back to where the creatures were about to erupt from the wall. "How many?" I asked, gravely.

"More than there should be," she answered simply.

"How am I supposed to kill them if they can't die?"

"Oh, they can expire; they just need a little help in that department."

The sconce that had been hanging on the wall by a thread, fell, and my body froze as sheetrock tore apart and goners erupted from it like spiders. Rachel's voice danced around my head as the opera house rapidly filled with flesh hungry creatures.

"All it takes is one bite. It is a plague on our shadows; there are now hundreds of them. We've been able to contain most of them to this one cell, but the infection takes time to eat away at the brain, and there *have* been escapes. Hunters roam the shadows at all times, keeping watch for those who might have been bitten and are trying to keep a low profile, or those who were sent here but somehow got out." Her gaze fell heavy over mine. "Twenty marks is the price to move on. Failing is not an option. Welcome to quarantine. Smell ya later."

And just like that, she was gone, leaving me to defend myself with a weapon I'd never used outside of a video game.

"Motherfu—" I started, but my curses were swept away as my vision settled over a gigantic goner, crouched against the wall like Spiderman. As I hesitated over my piece of floating plywood, a pair of tattered wings grew from its back and its head turned around in the most unnatural way, just as a pair of yellow eyes peered at me like it had just found the Hope

Diamond. "What the hell *is that?*" I said with a shudder. I couldn't tell if the thing whose mouth was now watering with venom had previously been fey or a guardian—either way I didn't care. There wasn't time for introspection. As that thing broke free from its spot on the wall and started flying towards my platform, I had just enough time to adjust my weapon, aim it at the goner's head, and fire.

I crammed my eyes shut and pulled the trigger; instantly I took the punch backwards from the force of the heat firing from the flamethrower into the gnarly beast. I could only imagine what its face looked like up close; luckily, I never had to find out.

The goner screeched like a wolf being strangled by barbed wire, and a smell grew from its destruction like a stew of swampy water filled with the rotting guts and feces of several animals. I fought the urge to get sick on the spot as I clenched my fists around my weapon. When I finally reopened my eyes, it was just in time to watch the winged creature erupt in red and black sparks, before eventually evaporating into nothing.

At first, I couldn't move, other than my chest filling and emptying faster than I could keep up with. There was no time to think about what had just happened, for seconds later goners began to crawl up along the rafters, some of them dropping to the floor as they attempted to aim for my platform. But the fall didn't stop them; their bones wouldn't break, even if all that was left of them was bones. Instead, the broken ones began to put themselves back together in a way that might have terrified the vilest humans on earth, and as soon as they were back in one piece, they simply returned to the path that would lead them towards the nearest flesh.

I slowed down my breathing, staring out into the spot where the flying goner had evaporated. "Throw the flames at their heads." I swallowed as I nodded. "That's how it's done. They are insane—the clock that ticks are their twisted thoughts. If I stop the ticking, I stop the time they are fixed at." A goner fell from the ceiling and caught the edge of my platform with hands that were halfway covered in gray flesh, and the rest only bone. "And when I stop time" –I aimed the flamethrower at the moving skull that was the goner's face— "they die." I pulled the trigger and this time I watched.

This goner didn't scream as the other had, instead he held on as long as he could—until his forearm joint separated, and his body fell. In the end, he turned to sparks and evaporated, just like the other one.

"Okay," I said, my heartbeat carrying my words. "That's two. Eighteen more to go."

When I looked up, the ceiling was crawling with goners. It very soon began to rain the rotting creatures as they each fell, and even with all their insanity, they aimed for my platform. It was pretty apparent, though, that someone had unprogrammed their intelligence. I quickly understood that it was dumb luck that the one who *had* fallen onto the wooden board had.

Another couple of them grew wings and flew at me separately. They each met their end in their own ways. I was beginning to see that if I couldn't get this platform to move, that I was going to be stuck in that spot for a long-ass time. This was going to take *for*ever. Not to mention that I had to access my oracle cards to even leave this place, and unless I was brave enough to jump—waning humanity or not—I was going to have to figure out how this thing moved.

Rachel had made it look easy. She floated around on hers as if it was gliding over a lake. I had to figure that I was perfectly capable of doing the same thing.

As the possibilities rolled around in my head, another goner landed on my platform—on its feet this time. There was no time to think, only time to move. As if I was one of the players in the game my grandma gave me, I aimed the flamethrower at the goner's head, shuffled my feet into combat stance, and blasted the creature to bits. A bit of the contagion that had been dripping from its purple lips fell to my feet in the process.

"Sick," I whispered, stomping on it as if it were a cigarette.

After that, three more landed on my platform. I took care of them in the same fashion, blasting them into oblivion. One after the other after the other. They were fizzling like bugs against a zapper, until . . .

A female goner who must've only been recently bit, shouted down to me as she fell from the ceiling. "Don't move! I've got this—I can make it!"

I didn't care if she was still lucid, or that she looked completely normal except for her eyes, they were golden like the rest of the goners. A sickly yellow, like the contagion was swirling around in their irises. Either way, there wasn't time to decide if I could trust her. There was only time to get out of the way before she managed to land next to me. Treating the platform like a snowboard or a skateboard, I simply hunkered down and shifted it to the side . . . and it worked.

My lips parted in awe as the she-goner screeched on her way down. She was definitely one of them, for the fall didn't kill her. It did, however, piss her off, which was evident by the middle finger she threw my way as she stood back up and glared at me. There was ooze sliding down the corner of her mouth as she yelled something up to me that I couldn't hear.

So now I knew there were some intelligent goners in The Opera House. Infected souls who hadn't yet completely turned. Great. Still, there was no time to spare. I redirected my gaze and, as I did, I planted my feet in yet another combat position. I loosened my grip over the flamethrower and concentrated on my next move. I closed my eyes just long enough to center myself; I imagined I was floating over the surface of a lake, that all I had to do was retain my balance as the board under my feet moved with the waves. And then, out of nowhere, the platform began to glide.

My eyes popped back open. "About time something went my way," I muttered, before spotting a way less intelligent group of goners stumbling over one another near the stage. They were trying to crawl up the curtains.

In one swift movement I used my hovercraft to pull up inches from them and pulled the trigger of the flamethrower; my upper lip curled in satisfaction as fireworks erupted. Seven of them exploded into sparks.

From there on out, it was so simple it was stupid. I moved around the room like a BMX legend, throwing flames and extinguishing curses. I didn't even realize I'd broken a sweat until Rachel reappeared, floating beside me on her own platform.

"Nice job," she said unenthusiastically. "But I said you only had to take out twenty."

I rested the weapon down by my side as I caught my breath. "I've lost count."

"You're at seventy-eight. It's not that we don't appreciate the extra clean-up, but we should probably leave a few behind for the other players to mangle. There's also the matter of you returning to your cards, and you don't want to run out of ammunition."

My lips formed into an 'oh.' I'd gotten so caught up in taking out the infection that I'd forgotten about that minuscule detail. "Shit."

Rachel smirked. "Be respectful enough to use the ticker you've got when you're around those with only festered brain cells remaining."

I deviated my jaw. "I hadn't thought about it that way," I started, but Rachel was already gone. *How was she doing that?*

I backed my platform back to where I'd started, at the center of the room, then took in my surroundings. There were still so many of them, but at least they weren't coming out of the hole in the wall via clumps anymore. Now they were jumping out one at a time. Seriously, how many of these things were there? I loosed a heavy breath and directed my gaze towards one of the exits—to where my cards were waiting.

"Dammit," I cursed. The female goner who'd yelled down to me earlier was planted right before my spread.

I didn't have a choice; I moved the platform down towards the cards, all the while holding my flamethrower. It was pointed at the back of the she-goner's head. I didn't say anything as I swooped down, near enough to the blood red carpet to rest a toe on the surface. At first, I wasn't sure if she knew I was there, but then she spoke.

"I helped her come up with this, you know."

Without easing up on the trigger, I frowned. "I'm sorry —what?"

She turned and looked at me. She was disgusting, but she still had her skin. If it wasn't for those eyes, I may have thought she was just a waif who had been neglecting its duties for far too long. "Reanin." My grandmother's name was heavy over her tongue. "She came back to the shadows after speaking with the gray witch." *Maggie.* "She said we had to make a new entrance and it couldn't be a reflection, that Nisroc would be looking for something like that. It had to be something physical. Something that could be disguised . . . something we could hide." She pulled out what at first looked like a small wooden stake, but I quickly realized what it really was, because I'd seen something like it before. In Maggie's hand. The goner raised her honey eyes to meet mine. "I was a witch before this happened."

I lowered my weapon by half an inch. "Do you mind if I ask how this *did* happen to you?"

A wheezing sound fell from her rotting lips as she nodded. "It was right before the doors unlocked. One of my friends, a waif, lost herself in the waiting game. She didn't know she was that close to the shift . . . all the waifs looked pretty bad. She changed while I was asleep, her bite woke me up." She turned her forearm around so I could see the chunk of flesh missing. Then she held up her wand. "It won't work for me anymore. I guess that means I'll be one of those things sooner than later."

I couldn't help but furrow my brow. "You *are* one of those things. You tried to eat me up there."

She rolled her eyes. "I wasn't trying to snag a bite. I was trying to land on your platform so we could talk."

"Oh . . ."

"Look, I was the one who said the new entrance should be made from oracle cards. Not just because it was convenient to make each card an entrance to a different door in the main hall, but because every witch knows that between the cards of every reading, there is a space where one might discover something that's been hidden."

My elbows relaxed and I lowered the weapon by another inch. "What are you trying to say?"

The woman looked back down at her wand, then, with a palpable heaviness, handed it to me. "Here. Take it."

I was already swinging my head from side to side. "No way, I can't do that. It's yours."

But I could already see that she wasn't about to take no for an answer. "See between the cards, Tess." She held the wand out yet again. "Even though no one believed that bastard Nisroc would ever get his hands on her, Reanin was way too smart to go out into that world without an insurance policy." A short breath seeped into my chest. "You'll need this. Show it to Kage—he'll know what to do." When I didn't accept it right away, she crammed her eyes shut and shook the wand out before me. "Take it. Very few of us knew about her heart. It was—it was safer that way."

"Her heart," I whispered.

She reopened her eyes. "Everyone of us is a part of this place. *We* are in the cards. I'm even more invested, which is maybe why I felt it the second Reanin's heart was pierced. I'd already been escorted into this hell hole by the time that happened; leave it to fate to decide that yours has been the first face I've seen clean of infection. I've had no one to explain this to."

I was still trying to make sense of it all, but the dots were definitely starting to connect. "The waifs have her heart . . . Does that mean something to you?"

The goner began to nod. "Yes. But without this" –she stared down at the wand— "the organ is useless."

My gaze began to flutter back and forth. "You mean, it was literal. Whoever these waifs are, they have my grandmother's *actual* heart?"

"Yes."

I lowered the weapon so it was down by my leg. "You mean to say that my grandmother isn't really gone?"

The woman looked at me with her wolfy eyes. "She doesn't have to be."

I continued to balance one foot on the floor and one on the platform as I reached out my hand. The she-goner gave the wand one last squeeze then passed it to me like a baton. The second it was against my skin, a breeze hugged my shoulders and the scent of pine needles and embers nearly overwhelmed me.

My jaw unhinged as I looked up at the woman. She was smiling, though I could sense sadness in her. "He's trying to tell you where he was born. They do that for their new owners."

"What? But I'm not a—"

"He's yours now. He will be until your end is near, and then it will be up to you to hand him off. Please treat him well."

Mine. *He* was mine? And he was gender specific—interesting. "How is this going to bring my grandmother back?"

"Kage will know what to do, as will the others in the company."

"The company . . ."

Before I was able to usurp any further information, my attention flared. I looked up. One by one, the goners who had been clustered by the stage, were falling from the curtains to the floor like monkeys. Some of them were shuffling, others walking, and some ran. Either way, I'd been spotted, and they were after me.

"Oh no," I muttered, readying to pocket the wand and readjust the flamethrower.

"Wait."

I looked at the she-goner.

"You might as well get acquainted now."

I reconfigured my eyebrows. "What?"

She gestured to the wand that was already halfway tucked into my front pocket. "Ask him to freeze them for you." When all I could manage was a confused look, she sighed. "Just do it. All you have to do is mean it. He's already yours; he's ready to take your commands."

Normally, I might have looked at her like she was crazy, but that was before I'd reincarnated a pile of ashes into a cursed deck of oracle cards. "Okay," I said, balancing the flamethrower over my shoulder as I pulled out the wand and did as she'd said to do. To my utmost surprise . . . it worked. Every single goner in the opera froze; it was like the video game had been put on pause.

"Well," I said as I lowered the weapon and the wand. "That's a fun trick."

"Unfortunately, it won't last. You should go—now."

"Right," I said, finally stepping away from the wooden

platform. It continued to hover in place. I felt kinda terrible just leaving the goner, but the truth was she could turn at any second. I was just about to say those things out loud, when she laid a hand over my arm.

"I need you to do me a favor."

My last breath lingered in my lungs. I should've known, everyone had a price in the shadows.

"I need you to use that one last time." Her gaze moved from mine to the flamethrower I'd been readying to set down. "This wasn't supposed to happen to me. I was supposed to take glory in watching what this place could become. But shit still happens, whether you're here or there. So . . ." She let her hand fall away from my arm and took a step back. "I'm asking the girl with eyes like he who once saved me from burning at a stake, to return those flames to my flesh before I actually become the monster people once thought I was."

My chest filled with a foreign rhythm. "You were going to be burned at a stake?"

She lengthened her spine. "The world I was born into wasn't ready for me. Kage was though. I was here long before your grandmother—before this place grew into what it's become. At least I got to see its potential."

A chord in my heart pinged. "I'm sorry this happened to you."

The woman batted her yellow eyes and lifted her chest, a raspy memory of a breath filling her dead lungs. "Me too."

"I wish you'd become ash. If that was the case, I'd bring you back."

As soon as I said it, her expression tightened. "What makes you say that?"

"Because that's what I do," I answered matter-of-factly. "But it doesn't matter. Nothing remains of a goner once you're set on fire—"

"No," she was shaking her head. "I'm *done*. That's why

they call us goners. What I meant was—can you really do that?"

I hesitated. "Yeah."

She moved in on me, readying to place her hand against my cheek, but she must've thought better of it. Staying close, but lowering her hand, she said, "A piece of the shadows brought back as creation . . . the wand and the chalice." I could barely make out her words as she added, "It finally makes sense."

"What finally makes sense?"

But just as the woman opened her mouth to respond, one of the goners who had been frozen over by the stage flinched —causing a prop to fall on its side. Both the expiring witch and I turned in its direction.

When she looked at me again, she did so with urgency. "You don't have much more time. You must go. But first . . ."

She just stood there, her arms opening as if she was expecting lightning to come down and strike her. I wanted to tell her that I couldn't do it, that I'd already fulfilled my quota and then some, but I knew keeping her alive was worse than ending her misery. So, I did the only thing I could do. I asked her her name.

Her shoulders lifted then fell. "Bea."

"Well, it was nice to meet you, Bea. Thanks for the wand." And then I aimed my weapon at her and returned the flames to the witch who had once escaped them.

As soon as it was over, I dropped the weapon and then my knees. And not a moment too soon. I didn't have to turn around to know that goners were coming back to life (or back to whatever). I could hear their sick attempts at breathing as they began to race towards me just as I reached down to turn over that tenth card.

"You've got to be kidding me," I said, as the title began to color in with who my next coffee date was going to be.

Who was I going to have to murder now?

But as my spread and I began to fade from The Opera House and float in the black sparkle that took us from one dimension to the other, the face of the card showed itself and before long a familiar voice cut through the transition.

"Hello, Tess. Told you we'd be seeing one another again."

CHAPTER TWENTY-SEVEN

"I knew it," I said, as I began to come up from my knees. I knew it the second I saw that fang in her mouth last we met. This woman with red hair and red eyes and—except her eyes weren't red anymore. They were blueish green. Either way, it wasn't a shock to find out that Cai was The Vampire.

"Caught sight of the twins, did ya?" she said with a wink.

"What happened to your eyes?" I questioned, taking a step further into what was obviously her . . . bedroom? Or maybe lair was more appropriate. There was a four-poster bed in the corner. The floor was covered in decorative rugs, and the main attraction, a large fireplace, took up almost an entire wall. Just to the side of the fire burning inside the stone opening were two red velvet chairs and, between them, a small black table with an old rotary phone on top.

Just before she responded, a tiger jumped up on her bed as if it were just an ordinary house cat. She grinned. "That's Sasha; she's only visiting." I had so many questions. She pointed to her eyes as she ran a long fingernail over the top of one of the red velvet chairs. "I hit up the surface for a little fuel and *grocery* shopping. As you might imagine, I've been getting rather hungry down here. I was able to supplement with a stash I'd kept handy and, when that ran out, I nibbled on some of the witches now and again. But still, I've never been one to enjoy a diet. I was glad to finally get full."

I swallowed hard. Deciding to skip over whether she was a killer or just a feeder, I gestured to the fireplace. "Nice place."

"Thanks."

"Is it just you here?"

"Yeah." Her poise shifted and she gestured to the chair opposing the one she was hanging onto. "Have a seat, Tess. It's been a while since I've been able to have a good girl chat."

I reluctantly did as she'd asked and sunk into the comfort of the velvet chair, the cozy fabric was warm from the fire. I wasn't afraid of her, but I couldn't shy away from the buzzing in my head. Yes, I'd just butchered countless zombies, I'd sang to a bar full of waifs and sirens—I'd just learned my grandmother might not be completely dead. But a vampire. I mean, dang.

"It's okay," Cai said, taking residence in the other chair. "I won't bite."

"I wasn't worried you would," I retorted a little too quickly.

Back in The Lake, she'd said her kind had a habit of imposing their empathy over others. What if she was controlling me?

As if reading my mind, she replied, "That majestic heart of yours is racing." I opened my mouth to argue, but decided it wasn't worth it. She fed upon blood—she could of course hear how quickly mine was spreading through my body. She lifted the receiver of the black and gold phone and dialed one. "Yes," she said. "Could I please have a raw steak, a glass of O negative, and—hang on—" She nodded my way. "Would you like anything? A drink? Maybe something strong."

The back of my throat was as dry as sand. But at this point, I needed something with more hair on it than soda. "Bourbon," I answered without a hitch.

Cai nodded appreciatively. "And a Reanin special."

When she was done, she returned the receiver to its cradle and folded her hands over her lap. Hardly a second later, a rapping erupted from behind a wall. I hadn't yet realized it, but there was no door to be found in this place. Cai hollered for them to come in and a bookcase swung open. A very beautiful young woman sauntered in with a tray. On it, a steak, a wine glass of blood, and a glass tumbler filled with amber liquid.

"Thanks," Cai said with a sharp nod as she took the wine glass and small square napkin. When the female turned to me, I did the same, bringing the napkin and drink straight to my lap. Then she neared the tiger named Sasha and placed a fine-looking dinner in front of the animal. The steak was gone before the shadow waitress left.

When the bookcase closed, and it was just the three of us again, I asked, "Was that another vampire?"

Cai took a long satisfying sip from her glass. She licked her lips as she brought it back down. "No. Vanessa is a waif. She's been to the surface as well, that's why she looks so refreshed. As far as I know, there is only one other vampire . . . but that will change."

I timidly brought the bourbon to my lips and took a small drink. I expected it to be harsh, but it went down smoothly. When I looked back at her, Cai was grinning.

"You're more like your grandmother than I could have ever expected."

"Thanks." We studied one another for another moment before I decided to rip off the band-aid. "So, what's all this about? This room is so much different than the other dimensions. What is there to learn here?"

She grinned; her teeth were so white. I expected them to be stained by the blood she fed on. "Meeting with me is all about self-discovery. Before one leaves, they must make a choice. But you're here for another reason."

"Oh? And what's that?"

"Two things: truth and foreshadowing."

I turned my cheek to her.

She took another sip from her blood before resting it over the napkin on the table. "The foreshadowing is something you will figure out on your own." She ignored my flustered expression as she continued. "As for the truth—well, Tess, I am the one who is responsible for your grandmother's death. And from what I've heard since the doors reopened, your mother's as well."

The witch's words from The Mirror danced through my head, *a traitor in the midst.*

My grip hardened over the glass in my hand. I took another drink, a healthy gulp this time.

"Don't try to bury them, Tess. Your emotions are welcome here."

With a stiff jaw, I simply said, "Keep talking."

Her giant black eyelashes fluttered. "Just so you know, no one knows that it was me, apart from Raegan and Kage. And Reanin."

"My grandmother knew you were the traitor?" The one responsible for giving Nisroc back his power.

"Yes. When I realized I'd been played, that *he* never loved me—" her words drifted, and my heart sank. Suddenly, I knew exactly where this was going. "He was just using me. My true home was in these shadows all along." She paired her gaze with mine. "I was the one who discovered them in the lake, who first heard them whisper; it was my soul who was drawn to this place. Kage only discovered the entrance after I showed him. He might have found it if I hadn't, but—who knows."

Her attention fell into the fireplace; I studied the way the reflection of the orange and red flames danced against her perfectly tinted skin. I should've been disgusted by her, angry. But I couldn't find it in myself to be that way. Not after I'd had my hand against her sword and experienced her heartbreak.

"It was always *him*, wasn't it? Nisroc. You loved him more than you loved yourself."

She didn't move an inch. Didn't blink. "I loved him from the moment Raegan and I were paired with the two brothers. That's how it works. Guardians work in pairs, all throughout training and celestial puberty—all our lives. When it's time for you and your partner to fulfill your guardianship roles, you're assigned a planet and region. If the area is large enough, then two sets of guardians are put together. This is how Raegan and I met Kage and Nisroc."

The pain and suffering I'd felt when Raegan placed my hand against Cai's sword rang through me all over again. It was unbearable.

"You loved Nisroc . . . and Raegan loved you." It was all there, the truth written in their swords.

The corners of her mouth crinkled as the air was filled with regret. "We never fall in love with the right one, am I correct?"

"I wouldn't know," I said softly.

She placed her blue green eyes over my color shifting irises. "You will."

I started to frown but quickly forced it away. I could've cared less about my future love life just then. Romance was about as foreign to me as a mother's love. Still, the face of a faery I'd just come to know flashed before me.

"She'll break your heart," Cai said with a sad grin.

I chose not to retort. Instead, I returned to the subject. "Raegan loved you. You loved Nisroc. And Kage—"

"Was always yearning for something else," she finished for me. "Kage has always been open whereas Nisroc has always been blinded by tunnel vision. Your grandfather was written into the shadows from the moment he was born." She pressed her lips together as if in thought. "We were never taught to believe any of us was ranked higher than the other, but even though guardians operate on a higher frequency than humans, it doesn't mean we are safe from iniquity. The yearning humanity experiences towards power and greed—it exists in guardians as well."

"Let me guess, our mutual *friend* was never all light."

"Not even close. But the way he held himself, like he was so sure of himself all the time—it worked. It *does* work. Nisroc has never had a problem growing followers. They've always listened blindly, like he was some sort of messiah." A tired breath fell from her lips, and she shook her head.

"Cai." Her eyes, like emeralds floating in the sea, moved in my direction. "What's your story?"

She didn't hesitate. "It began at the lake, the one that forced you to accept death. As I've said, I was the one who discovered the portal, the reflection inside the waves. The whispers coming from it. The music. But when I brought Kage to the water, I knew immediately that if any of us had been chosen to slip between this curtain and that one, it had been him."

"You heard music?"

"Yeah." Her coloring began to deepen. "It's different for everyone. I heard singing, Raegan heard the river, Kage heard creation, and Nisroc never heard a thing." Her attention balanced over my shoulders as she went on. "Look Tess, to understand what I'm about to tell you, I'll need to explain a few things about how the universe works."

I inched forward in my chair, still gripping the bourbon. "All right."

"Most planets are ruled by a certain species. There are several rulers out there, but to make things less complicated, let's just say that there truly is a dark and light at the top of all things. Some planets are seeded by malicious creatures while other systems are curated by only light. Earth is one of the few places where both sides of the coin exist." She took a minute to explore my reaction.

"I'm following," I said.

She nodded then took a quick sip from her blood. "I've already stated that guardians and humans are alike in that we are born into free will. I'd like to take that discussion one step further. You've learned that our souls are born of different star systems, correct?"

I nodded.

"Once we become souls, we go on to incarnate. Frequency and vibration lead us into our paths. For instance, those with higher vibrations may be assigned to guardian bodies, while those operating on lower frequencies may take, for instance, human bodies. Though, higher frequencies have been known to plant themselves into human shells."

"What about me? From what I can tell, I'm neither guardian nor human."

"Aha," she said, pointing a long red fingernail at my face. "You're catching on quickly." She bit her lip as she perused my reaction. "You are the latter, and you're not the only one of your kind. You're made from . . . *unique* materials. They define your specialty—although, it will be interesting to find out in a few short months if you will serve a dual purpose in this world."

I lowered my chin. "Huh?"

"You'll understand soon enough," she said with a smirk. "But for now, let's remain on topic." I agreed and she continued. "Part of our free will as both humans and guardians is that we can choose how much light and how much dark to bring with us into our incarnations. I'm saying all this to you because I need you to see what I saw, to understand why I did what I did.

"I used to think Nisroc shone so brightly because he took only light with him. I mean—he literally glows—"

"I know," I muttered.

She flinched. "I'm sorry?"

"Nothing." I shook my head.

She looked across the table at me with scrutiny, but if she was curious, she left it. "I was blinded by my feelings for Nisroc. I chose to believe that he had too much of a higher power in him to understand the other side of the light. But after so very long, I finally see it: anyone can wear a cross and say he works for a god who may or may not exist, but if he or she preaches hate of any kind, they are not coming from a place of light. No matter how brightly they shine.

"Nisroc didn't care that the shadows could give Kage something the sun never could; he regarded the whispers coming from the lake as evil without ever hearing them." She sat forward and planted her elbows over her knees. "Let's cut to the chase, now, shall we? Kage was the first in, you know all about that. Here's the part you don't know: Nisroc convinced me to follow his brother—to pretend like I wanted to be part of this world. From there, I was supposed to find a way to convince Kage to leave the shadows. To get him out in the open so he could attach a mark to his chest. Nisroc knew if Kage surfaced, *someone* would try to take him down. He was counting on it."

"He'd kill his own brother?"

"Correction. He would still kill his own brother. Not directly of course—he would never take that risk. But you better believe he wouldn't stand in the way of anyone else who was willing to take that gamble. You see, regardless of what Kage is now, he started out as a guardian. No one knows if his death would leave his killer cursed; furthermore, no one really knows whether he *can* be killed."

My gaze shifted to the side then back as I posed the question, "What do you think?"

"About whether or not he can be killed." I nodded. "I'm not sure. There's speculation that Kage and The Hall are connected. That if one goes down, so will the other. I know for sure that Nisroc believes that hypothesis to be true."

That son of a bitch had deceived us both, but he'd really done a number on her. "Did you know that from the very beginning he was after the stones Kage had won against those three guardians?"

Cai answered me very seriously. "Absolutely not. I hate to admit it, but I was so enthralled with him that I couldn't and wouldn't see reason. Not from anyone. I was his pet." She downed most of the contents of the wine glass then shifted her gaze to my lap. "I was the one who told him about the Stones of Gehenna. I never thought he'd take to them like he did. I thought he wanted them because he knew Kage was using them to grow The Hall, when what he really wanted was to get them into his possession so he could destroy his brother's world and then who knows what. He probably would have just used them to start his own kingdom."

Even if she hadn't told him, that dickhead was bound to find out about the stones; something as powerful as the Stones of Gehenna would most definitely be a 'trending' topic.

Right then, there was something else I wanted to clarify. "Kage used the stones to grow the Hall of Shadows?"

"Yes, of course. I mean, they aren't really needed anymore because we have so many residents, and I'm sure it'll just continue to grow from here on out—"

"*That* is the sort of magic the stones are capable of . . ."

She narrowed her gaze. "Oh Tess, the sort of magic found

in those things is limitless. It is why Kage was so careful with them."

Did she know? Did she know where they were now?

I felt incredibly exposed.

"If they are that powerful, then how could Kage just leave them on display in the sword room for so long? Couldn't anyone just walk up and take them?"

"They could," she replied. "But no one here would do that."

"You could have," I shot back. "You were Nisroc's pet. You said so yourself."

"And Kage knew it. He didn't leave the stones out to see if I'd bite. He did it as part of my shadow training. You see, he knew I would never take them because this place was where I truly belonged. He just needed me to realize that on my own. And he was right."

"So Kage . . . he knew what was going on?"

She batted her eyes. "Kage knows everything."

"Just like he knew when it was time to move the stones."

"The stones disappeared the same day Reanin left. No one knew, save for Kage, where they went. There were rumors circling around facial recognition, like only someone with the right eyes could unlock their hiding spot and retrieve them, but that was just speculation from the shadows." I could've sworn there was a smirk on her face.

She knew. She had to.

I knotted my fingers together over the bourbon tucked between my thighs, working out everything I'd been told. "So, you discovered the reflection in the lake that would serve as the entrance to what would become this place. From there, Kage fell in love with it and decided to take the plunge, angering a good portion of guardians. The Stones of Gehenna were created. You and Raegan followed Kage into this place, but *you* were still in contact with Nisroc." I flicked my tongue against my teeth a few times. "When did he turn you guys into sirens?"

"When I wasn't moving fast enough. As soon as he cursed us, Kage fought back. He hired someone to swipe his brother's sword."

Of course. "And without his sword, he was—"

"Weak. The gods created us knowing full well that we came with enough power to come in second only to our makers. The idea behind our swords, our familiars, was that if we got out of line, our sword could be confiscated, and we would be humbled. It is not an uncommon thing for a guardian to have his or her sword taken from them. Nisroc is not the only one of our kind to have lost his mind."

"Soooo, is it kind of like being put in jail?"

"Yes," she nodded.

"And that must mean that you were the one who paid his bail."

Again, she dipped her chin. "His army was thinning out after being stripped of his power. His rage surfaced, but I was still blind to his true colors. I was still so madly, deeply, in love with him. I came to him and pulled out my shadows. I told him I loved him and that I always had. That everything I'd ever done had been for him." Her attention fell between her legs. "I believed him when he said we could be together if I returned his sword, because that's what we do when we are obsessed with someone. We look past their greed, their neediness . . . their lies." She connected her striking gaze with mine. "I delivered his sword, and he rewarded me by stopping my heart. Vampirism is what happens when a siren refuses to feed for too long. The heart stops and instead of craving souls, it is blood that is needed."

The taste of bourbon was fresh over my tongue as I asked, "What was his driving force to do that to you?"

She sighed. "I don't know. To make a point, I suppose. To

show me instead of telling me that he and I would never be together. There was nothing left for me. And that's when I realized—Nisroc had never been my home. The shadows had been my home . . . and look what I'd done to them."

"You did it all for love," I whispered, as if it was a foreign thing.

She didn't comment. Instead, she continued. "It was all downhill from there. I had to tell Reanin, Kage, and Raegan. But Nisroc was cocky. Before he tweaked my curse, he was stupid enough to tell me what he'd been up to. He'd given me a detailed explanation of the vast number of hunters he'd created. That is why Reanin left the shadows. Nisroc had his strength returned and he was chomping at the bit to take down Kage, his world, and his mate."

As she talked, I'd been sorting everything out into piles, but something still wasn't adding up. "The Hall is full of security. I mean, one of the first encounters I had was with a witch who reminded me of a panther. Why did Kage send my grandma out into the world when they could have just held tight in here?"

Cai drained the rest of the blood and set down the wine glass. "Because." She licked her lips and centered her gaze just in front of me. "Kage is a master magician, but the real interior designer was always your grandmother. She didn't just hear music in the shadows; she heard instructions. When I returned to tell them what I'd done, Reanin looked at Kage and said, 'It is time.' You see, she'd already known everything that was going to happen. She said she knew Nisroc would have his sword returned to him, and that he would put his vengeance into action. The magic in the Hall of Shadows would never be completely safe from him, and if he got his hands on the Stones of Gehenna, it would be devastating. There was only one person who had the power to take him out, but as she said in her own words, that person wasn't available yet."

My voice was hoarse as I said, "Why?"

"She said, and I quote, *their soul is not yet their own.*"

I'd just taken the last sip of my bourbon and as she spoke, I held it in my mouth for longer than was necessary. When I finally let it slide down my throat, I asked, "What was that supposed to mean? Like they weren't born yet?" A chill ran down my spine.

Cai shrugged. "I don't know. That's how she left it. She said the doors had to be locked, and she wasn't about to get stuck in The Hall while she was carrying Kage's child."

I gulped. My mother was the reason she left. My horrible, terrible, good for absolutely nothing, mother.

"You were right when you said security is tight here, but it's never been off the table that someone at some point could figure out a way in. Nisroc had preached about the magic inside The Hall to far too many souls. *He* may have never been slated to enter, but it wasn't without question that he'd been training his followers to find a way in."

Silence filled in over the table between us, until she motioned to my tumbler. "Would you like another?"

"Uh—no," I replied, setting down the empty glass. "So . . . is that it, then? You just wanted to confess your screw ups to me."

She chuckled. "Was that not a heavy enough load for you?"

I grimaced. "Sorry. I'm just—it's a lot, you know." I found myself fingering the stones around my neck. Her gaze fell to them and her smile evened out.

"Yeah. I get it," she said.

After a somewhat uncomfortable moment of silence, I added, "So my grandma knew who was going to kill this bastard all along?"

"She didn't say she did," Cai clarified. "But I'm pretty sure that was the case."

"Right. Can I ask you one last thing?"

"Shoot."

"How does the magic work? You know, like with the Stones of Gehenna? How did Kage use them to fill this place with magic?"

She lifted her left shoulder up to meet her ear. "Only the stones know how they work. The stones and their owner."

"Right." It seemed it was the only word I could get to function.

"Got anything else, Tess?"

"I guess not." I wanted to know more about the stones, but evidently no one was going to fill me in on that. "Thanks for being honest. It means a lot." I started to get up, because it seemed we were done, but Cai stopped me.

"Not so fast." She had a dagger in her left hand that hadn't been there a second ago. "You should understand how this works by now. A sacrifice is needed."

My gaze danced over the sharp blade in the vampire's hand. "Uh—"

"Relax. I just need to get into your veins a little."

I hesitated before questioning, "Why not just use your fangs?"

Her smirk was going to be permanently etched into my mind if I ever got back to the surface. "Normally, there is a choice. Whoever enters my room must pay a fee. They may choose the dagger, or they have every right to let me drink directly from their veins. But my bite is fatal unless I offer some of my blood, and that *is* an option for them as well."

"So, they can turn into a vampire, or they can just donate a little blood for your dinner and move on." She nodded. "Why aren't you giving me the option?"

"It's complicated."

I relieved my chest of a heavy sigh. "Why? Can't witches be vampires?"

"Witches can. You're not a witch."

The tip of my tongue met with my top lip as I furrowed a brow. However, I knew it was pointless to ask if she knew what I was becoming. She wouldn't answer, even if she knew.

"Fine," I replied, holding out my hand for the dagger. As soon as it was in my possession, I moved so my wrist was hovering over Cai's empty wine glass. When I cut open my flesh, I didn't flinch. Not one bit. There was hardly any pain.

I filled the glass about halfway up; when I was done, the cut on my wrist healed in a matter of seconds.

"Cool," I observed.

"You're more *not* human than human now," Cai said, clearly amused by my reaction as she reached forward and took back her dagger. As I ran a finger over the healed skin, I saw her bring the glass up to her lips out of the corner of my eye. "Now that's good." When I locked eyes with her, she grinned. "Just kidding," she said, setting the glass back down. "That would've made most people queasy, but blood hasn't ever bothered you, has it?"

"Not really. Why didn't you drink it?"

"It'd likely be suicide. But don't worry, it'll be put to good use."

I squinted my eyes as I prepared to question her further, but then thought better of it. "Never mind, I don't want to know." I waved both hands in front of me as if I was crossing out the energy I'd just served up. "Can I go now?"

Cai held out a hand towards my cards. "Be my guest."

I heaved a sigh as I sauntered backwards to where my cards were waiting. I was just about to reach for the twelfth card— I'd come so far—when I turned back to face the vampire. "Have you spoken to him since he stabbed you in the back? Nisroc."

She scoffed. "No way. He told me if he ever saw me again, he would turn me to stone."

"Dick," I muttered.

"Yeah," she agreed, clasping her hand around my blood again and giving it a good swirl.

"Do you still love him?"

Even though I'd never experienced that kind of love, I knew it wasn't a stupid question.

Cai peered into the wine glass as if it was a crystal ball. "That's not an easy question to answer. I've had over forty years to hate him . . . and I do. But love is a lot like a bad spell. Even though the idea of him and I ever being an item is about as possible as undoing one of his curses, there are still beats of my heart that belong to him. And for that, I hate him even more."

Her green eyes locked into mine and I instantly felt in my own heart what she felt every day of her life. The small slice of humanity I had left spoke for me. "What can I do to make it better?"

Without pause, she answered, "Don't give him what he wants."

I nodded. No explanation necessary. I knew exactly what she meant.

"See you around," I said.

"You can bet on it."

And with that, my hand dove for the second to last card.

"Night Terrors and Roses," I said as roses filled in around the card over a black background.

I barely had time to adjust to my new environment that from first impressions, was nothing but a black canvas and what I thought was maybe a two-way mirror, when a voice, filled to the brim with shadows, spoke from the darkness.

"I've been waiting for you, Tess. I've been waiting a very long time."

I had only one thought.

Grandfather.

CHAPTER TWENTY-EIGHT

He was waiting for me, that much was obvious. Sitting on a wooden chair in the corner of a dark room. The only light offered was coming from the reflection of a two-way mirror. His long legs were crossed, and his pale hands were laced together over his knee. Just the sight of him took my breath away.

I didn't stand apart from the cards right away. I could hardly take my eyes off him. When I did stand, I glanced away long enough to catch sight of all the rose petals that had begun to scatter over the floor like spilt blood. The petals were falling from above, where there was no ceiling to be found. It was just an endless black hole.

And then he spoke.

"You've done very well. Reanin would be more than proud."

Anything I had to say was stuck in my throat. This was my grandfather. An ex-guardian who sunk his sword into three of his own kind so that he could fall into the depths of what most souls on the surface could, but never would, experience. Lucky for me, I didn't have to say anything. A vision was already unfolding in that two-way mirror, and my focus was quickly removed from the one individual I'd been seeking this whole time and exchanged for the one person I missed more than any forsaken breath of air.

Most people would have only seen an empty room. Four white walls, hardwood floor, natural light filtering in through three windows near the ceiling. But my attention fell at once to the ballet bar.

"This is where you met her."

I knew he was watching me as I stepped up to the portal. Without pause, I laid my palm against it. It rippled, but unlike the reflection in The Mirror, I knew this gate would open. Sure enough, as I pushed my hand forward, it slipped through to the other side. A small gasp escaped my lips, and I wavered for only the amount of time it would take a feather to fall from a nesting bird to the ground, before walking from darkness into light.

My boots thumped against the hardwood as I stalked around the room. When I looked to the mirror I'd just walked through, I didn't see myself. Then again, as I was about to find out, I was a ghost in my grandmother's memory. A truth that became clear the second Reanin appeared.

She wasn't dressed for her time. She wore a man's button up shirt, the bottom tied together around her middle, the sleeves rolled halfway up her long, thin arms. She had on black undergarments and, though her feet were bare, she danced around the room as though she wore ballet shoes. Every muscle in her body was on display; she was beautiful. Her dancing was also . . . beautiful. But as fluid as her movements were, so assuredly was the melancholy bleeding from her heart. It was one of those moments where I wished I *could* cry.

Her routine ended in fifth position—her feet turned out with the heel of one foot residing next to the toe of the other, one arm held towards the mirror, and the other raised in the air. Her gaze rested upon the hand reaching for the sky. And that's when I saw it. A line of blood falling from her hand down to her elbow.

My hands came up to cover my nose and mouth as my grandmother very slowly melted from her pose. Her feet began to meet the floor from where they'd been raising her calves, her arms floated down, her shoulders following; finally, she bent her knees and her body crumpled gracefully to the floor. It was there that she bowed her head over her crossed legs and unfolded her fingers from around her bloody palm like rose petals.

Inside her hand was a jagged piece of mirror. Without paying a lick of attention to the blood streaming from her palm, she picked up the sharp glass with her other hand, and in an almost hypnotic state, dug it into her wrist—dragging it lengthwise. Instantly, a ribbon of blood fell from her limb.

I fell to a crouch, about eight feet away from her. My jaw shook as Reanin's head began to fall, her shoulders following, until her whole body was lying sideways on the cold, bare floor. All I wanted was to go to her, to pull her back up and wrap up that wrist to keep her veins from emptying; but this was only a memory, and the show was far from over.

My grandmother was barely breathing when the large mirror I'd used to enter began to ripple. He appeared as if out of a waterfall—Kage. He walked towards her without even a hint of urgency; like he knew everything would be okay. He bent down and cupped her head in his arm.

She rolled her eyes up to meet his. "I knew you were real."

"If I had never known that death came before creation, I would have still known your heart beat to the sound of a dying star."

"I am so very alone in this world."

"No. *However,* I do know that, for you, it feels like you are." Reanin was growing closer to death with every last drop of blood that fell from her wrist. With Kage's lips only a couple inches from hers, he asked, "What is the worst thought you ever had before this day?"

Her eyes were growing heavy, but still she answered. "That no matter which life I live, it will not matter. No one here desires to hear what I have to say. No one ever will."

"Many humans live in a simulation. You are unhappy because you see past it." He kept Reanin's head balanced in his left hand as he reached for her bleeding wrist. "I can change things for you, Ms. Wellington, but it means sacrificing most of who you are."

"I don't even know who I am," she whispered.

Kage lifted his brows. "Oh, but you do. All those times you spent searching for me in the mirror, you were searching for *her* as well. I do believe you even found her a time or two; unfortunately, you've been trained to turn from her. I can show you how to accept her."

Reanin looked like she was about to fall permanently into sleep. "Who is she?"

"She is your terror of the night, your thorny rose. She is, my dearest Reanin, your shadow." He paused, and they stared into one another's eyes as though they were looking into other dimensions. "Will you come with me?" he asked, almost as if he was under *her* spell.

"What's your name?" she asked in lieu of an answer.

"Kage."

"Kage . . . The magician meets the star." Her words hung between the two of them like a spirit. "For so long I've heard the whispers . . . the chatter from muddy street puddles, from the mirrors in the tavern. It's even been scattered in the leaves of my tea." She ran her bloody fingers through his dark hair. "I see things from time to time. You've the dust of dying starlight in your eyes. Just as *she* will."

A lump began to form in the back of my throat.

Kage held her in his arms for a little longer, then just as it looked as if she might be getting ready to die, he whispered in her ear, "I will take that as a yes, my love. My queen."

He held out his own wrist over hers, which had fallen, limp, to the floor. Without the use of a blade, his skin parted and his veins opened as blood began to seep from his arm into Reanin's open wound. Within seconds, the blood that had fallen from her veins began to turn into rose petals, and her wound healed. Shortly after that, Kage's skin sutured itself back together.

Reanin's skin began to sparkle and glow, a halo of light encompassing her like a cocoon, until it finally dimmed back down to the same pearly white skin I'd learned to know and love as my grandmother's. My grandmother's favorite book was *The Last Unicorn*, and she'd literally become a mythical creature right in front of my eyes.

Before that moment, Reanin had had a reflection in the ballet room's mirror. But after Kage changed her, it disappeared. Leaving three souls in this space without a reflection.

Kage lifted my grandmother's body and walked back through the portal. The studio was left bare. There would be no body for John Wellington to find. No note. Only a shard of glass from a broken mirror along with a few scattered rose petals.

I made my way back through the rippling waves of the portal and faced Kage. He was standing there, waiting. In a calm voice, I asked, "What did you do to her?"

He tucked his hands into the pockets of his slick black pants. "She had lost too much blood, so I filled her veins back up."

"With *your* blood. What you did made her something else. A siren eventually."

"Yes."

"You saved her."

Kage smirked but said nothing. At least not right away. He seemed to be eating up every inch of me. "She knew you'd be born with my eyes." When I didn't react, he added, "You've given most of it away while you've been in here. Are you aware of that?"

"What are you referring to?"

"Your humanity."

"Oh, yeah. That." We could have been talking about a rip in my pants. "I think it's becoming more apparent."

And it was. I was less anxious, more unafraid—and my heart burned in a way that felt comfortable. The shadows that had hugged me from the moment I'd turned over that first oracle card had also started taking on another depth. The darkness shimmered. Whether it was magic or the dust from a dying star that glittered in every dimension of The Hall—I didn't know and I didn't care. All I knew was that I gravitated towards its beauty.

"Walk with me, Tess," Kage said as he pulled a hand from his pocket and waved me along.

This was the face of the man who I'd been seeking from the moment I'd heard Maggie say the word grandfather. I didn't think twice about the instruction. I fell in step with the tall, illustrious Kage.

As his shoes slapped against the black marble and my boots pounded, he noted, "You are very much like Reanin."

"How can you know that?" I questioned. "We've just met."

Out in the distance, bits of light began to come into focus.

"True, but I have been known to have very good observation skills."

I turned to find him grinning.

"That's fair," I replied quietly. Then with a little more

muscle, I said, "Am I allowed to ask what you are? No one will tell me."

He kept our pace lively, more and more of the bits of light appearing in the distance, like stars. The closer we got, though, the more I realized they weren't stars at all, but windows of pure white light. A system of breaks in the darkness, but with no particular pattern.

Kage spoke. "I didn't find the shadows, they found me. To be fair, they find everyone who is willing. The shimmer is found inside the echo for those who search for it. A mirror is only a replication until the image of the one who is staring into it asks for more."

It was then, as he spoke, that I began to understand that the breaks in the darkness were reflections, from mirrors mostly. However, some were in the shape of puddles, and some were just floating orbs.

As we drew closer to the endless highway of reflections, figures began to arise from the shadows as well. Waifs. Some were speaking into the light while others waited in the masses for their turn. I wasn't sure yet if I agreed with Maggie's assessment that the Hall of Shadows had turned corporate, but this *was* one hell of an operation.

"All of these reflections are portals," I observed.

"Yes," Kage answered simply. "Each comes with its own story." We'd come to a stopping point and, as we halted our steps, he turned to me. "Tess, you asked me what I am. This is my answer: what I did to enter these shadows wasn't a sacrifice, not to me. It was a necessary means to a new beginning." He turned and stared out into the endless lines of waifs. When next he spoke, the word bellowed through the interminable space. "OUT."

As if his voice had signaled a fire alarm, the waifs immediately stopped what they were doing and either jumped through the portals or fell away from them, scurrying off like mice. Within seconds, the chamber of reflections was emptied, and it was just me and my ex-guardian grandfather.

"You really have a hold over them, don't you?" I said in an airy tone. The thousands upon thousands of whispers that had filled this place had been shut out. It was suddenly so quiet that you could hear a pin drop.

Kage was still in performance mode; a smaller version of the grin he'd worn earlier was again on display. "I am no longer the guardian I used to be." The darkness we stood in began to gather around him, shimmering into physical matter. Within seconds, black feathers began to materialize until the largest set of wings I'd ever seen formed around my grandfather. They had to have spanned at least ten feet tall, and their width was equally impressive. "I don't know if there is a name for what I am now, Tess. All I can tell you is that *now* I am as much the shadows as they are me." He lifted his left hand and closed his eyes, then began to move like a man with music in his veins. "Anyone can feel it if they really try. The vibrations that dance in every particle of your body—that swim in the shadows of your heart." He'd started to tap his foot and was now directing his arm as if a symphony surrounded us. He was so animated that I *could* almost hear the music. And then his wings disappeared. And he stopped dancing. His hands filled his pockets. "Do you believe in the devil, granddaughter?"

My waning humanity reached up and pulled down a shade of uncertainty. "I—I don't know."

"It's what you think I am."

It wasn't a question.

"I've been told you're not."

"But still, it's what your thoughts circle back to again and again."

There was no denying it, and something told me I couldn't lie to him. "Yes sir."

He jerked his head to the side. "I am not sir. I am your

grandfather."

"Yes," I whispered, nodding too quickly.

"Come," he said, after what felt like a very awkward moment. He faced the infinite pattern of reflections glued to the darkness like postage stamps. "Look at them with me."

With an undecided look on my face, I asked, "Why are there so many?"

The glare from the lights danced over his phantom-like face as he said, "Everyone lives with shadows. It is the job of a waif to find them and bring them here, and it is in their contract to coerce the owners of these portals to listen to their inner selves. Whether those who own the other side of the reflection listen or not, depends solely on their motivation." He pivoted his stance and peered down at me. "Do you believe this operation to be a violation, Tess?"

My answer was stuck in my vocal cords; I wasn't sure. Was it a violation? That was an interesting way of wording it. It was also straightforward, in the same fashion Ethan had been teaching me to be while reading the tarot. In fact, the longer I stood there, the more I saw how connected it all was.

"All of these things you're learning," Ethan had said after only a couple of tarot card lessons, "it's not so you can pretend to know someone's future. This isn't fake—we are here to help. In order to do this, you must throw away all the crap that's been ingrained in you so far. Remove the blindfold. See past what the world only wants you to see. Don't look at this card and see a hanged man—" He'd literally held the card between his finger and thumb. "Tell me what the card is telling you. What do you *see*, Tess? What is the art portraying? And once you do see something, dig further. Because each card does have a voice, just like every soul who comes to sit across from you. It's just that you're trained not to believe it." He'd set down the card. "You create life from death. Sometimes the people who come in here just want to have their cards read because they think it's fun and exciting, and maybe even a little naughty. But most, Tess—most need your touch. Because the true zombies are the ones who walk around in the sun, completely unaware that they've been bitten."

Redirecting my gaze from my grandfather back to the infinite ocean of reflections, I said, "It's not a violation. These shadows belong to these people, and just because their owners may be ignorant of them, it doesn't mean they don't exist. All you're doing is giving them the attention they wouldn't receive in a world that doesn't welcome them. In a world where most of the inhabitants only know how to be awake when the moon goes down."

When I looked back up at Kage, he was smiling.

"I am very proud to be a part of you," was all he said.

"You aren't the devil," I said, an awakening brewing somewhere in my person. "You *are* as much of this place as it is of you. Whether that makes you the god of it, I don't know."

Kage remained rooted in his stance. "Yes," was all he said.

I knew just then that the realization I'd just muttered aloud was as much of an answer as I was ever going to get pertaining to who Kage was. My attention fell back on the reflections. "What happens now?"

Kage snapped his fingers and all the reflections tipped downwards, rain beginning to fall from them. In their likeness, storm clouds. Lightning clapped and thunder followed. I jumped, the bellowing of the storm raging in my belly.

"You've but one card left," he said. "In order to decipher its message, you must face what's left of your shadows."

"I figured," I replied easily, holding out my hand for the giant raindrops. As they sunk into my palm, my skin remained dry.

Kage turned and began walking back to where we'd initially traveled from. He gestured with a flick of his hand for me to follow. "This is you, Tess," he said, opening his arms as wide as they would go, just as lightning struck overhead. "For years, this was inside you, but now things have changed. You've learned while in The Hall to not only face death, but your fears as well. You care not what others think of you anymore, nor do you worry about your future. Correct me if I am wrong."

"Something tells me you're never wrong."

Again, with the smirk. "If your grandmother was here, I would imagine she would argue against that theory."

I bit down over my bottom lip as I touched the pocket where I'd stuck my new wand. Without digging it out, I asked, "Do you miss her?"

He reached an arm toward the portal we were nearing—Reanin's old dance studio. Except that now it reflected only the storm. "You can't create shadows like these. Not without pouring pieces of yourself into them. Reanin has always been here, just not in the way you're used to seeing her."

"The grandmother I knew was nothing like the woman I've met down here," I said softly.

I caught sight of him wrinkling his forehead. "I imagine the outside world was very difficult for her. She doesn't belong there."

I chewed on his words all the way back to where my cards were waiting. They were all face up now, save for one.

"How are you feeling, Tess?"

My nostrils flared as I inhaled deeply through my nose. It was purity that I welcomed around my ribcage. "Lighter."

My gums tightened and, for a second, I thought I felt pressure behind them, but it went away too soon to keep my attention.

Kage bowed his head, his eyelids following in the dance. He then reached a hand up by his heart. "You are trained, by the poets and dreamers, to listen to your heartbeat. I ask of you to find that rhythm, then search for what is directly below. It's in the silence, in the shadow of your heart, that you will find what you are looking for."

As he spoke, I unknowingly reached for my heart. The Hall of Shadows had already taken so much of my humanity. I hadn't tried to use it yet, but I could feel my magic rushing through my veins. Whatever I was—a guardian hybrid, some kind of demon, or fire-breathing dragon—if I wanted to let my freak flag fly and release my power, I knew I could figure out how to do it.

"My humanity is keeping me grounded, isn't it? As soon as I let that last little bit of it go, I will become what I truly am."

The corners of Kage's mouth crept up slowly. "I believe The Hall has spoken."

I bit the corner of my lip, peering at my grandfather for a little longer, studying the way the color in his irises shifted, just like mine. Finally, when I knew it was time, I pulled out the wand I'd received from Bea and offered it to him.

His expression dulled as he looked down at the tool. "What is this?"

"Bea gave him to me; she said you would know what to do with it." I was suddenly reminded of another witch's last words. "And the witch who helped my grandma create these cards—Maggie—she told me to tell you that the waifs have Reanin's heart." I paused. "Do you know what that means?"

Kage visually inspected the wand before reaching down and taking it gingerly from my hand. I expected him to experience what I had when I'd first held it, but Kage didn't flinch. The storm was still raging around our shoulders as he remained stiff as a board.

"It's a shame," he said after a short while. "Bea was a very valuable component of our world. Reanin will be saddened by her departure."

I lowered my left brow. "She *will* . . ."

"You said it yourself; the waifs have her heart. 'Tis the first step in a spell that will need finishing." His calico eyes moved to mine. "Or says the wind." And then he held the wand back out for me to take.

Before I took it, I deviated my chin to the side. "Bea said to give it to *you*—that you would know what to do with it."

"Yes. This is what it wants. He is yours after all."

I gathered both brows together. "I'm confused."

"The wand is yours; he will be until you pass on. That is how magic wands work."

It wasn't the first time I'd heard this, but still— "But I'm not a witch."

My grandfather licked his lips, which were cherry red, then smiled for what must have been the fourteenth time. "No Tess, you are much more than that." Placing his hands back in his pockets, he added, "Witches love wands, but that doesn't mean the other magic wielders cannot own them as well. He could've been mine if he wanted, but he doesn't want me. He wants you."

A dull pain began to radiate through my skull. "Hang on. Are you trying to tell me that it is up to me to finish the spell that will bring my grandmother back?" He made no move to answer. Still, I saw the truth everywhere I looked. As the pain in my forehead began to throb, I said more to myself than him, "How am I supposed to revive her if I don't even know how this thing works?"

"I dare to believe that you will figure it out," Kage said with a wink.

Nearby, the space lit up where we stood and I closed my palm around the wooden stick. "Right." My attention rose to meet the storm. It hadn't even begun to die out. "So, what am I supposed to do about this?"

"This," Kage echoed, holding out his hand to the rain.

The two of us still dry as a bone. "This is up to you. You cannot leave The Hall without a decision. And in case you're still at a loss, then listen here, because this is all you need to decide: would you rather walk with your storm, Tess? Or hide it away inside of yourself."

As I opened my mouth to retort, he immediately shook his head. "It is not something I need to know. That is a decision only you can make. You already know that at some point, what you truly are to become, will find a way to surface. But that is something that will take many years to happen. You have the luxury now to play the rest of the game as all the others who have graced the shadows. And, if you allow, all of the future participants."

I dug a finger into my temple and massaged it. "What do you mean by *if I allow*?"

He gestured towards the oracle cards. "History has shown that if the cards are ruined, then so are all the other entrances and exits. When you leave here, you may decide to choose only light. You may decide to end our world. Reversely, darkness is always there hungrily waiting for anyone to join its side. Very few think to find the shimmer that dwells between the two."

Those were such haunting words.

But so were these ones: *Choose the light.*

It seemed even when I was done with this spread, I wouldn't be finished. I had a decision to make, and it wasn't going to be easy. These shadows, they weren't exactly benevolent. I couldn't get The Forest out of my mind. The smudge that had been Annie's mother would remain as such, probably forever.

"It's darker in this place than it is light," I said, absentmindedly.

"Truth. We have made some connections with those who breed without light. But we keep a cautious eye on those particular residents."

"And the waifs have a hideous disposition," I added, as if going through a list of pros and cons.

"Again, I have no argument. There are those who were created before my brother twisted the agreement I'd made with them, and for that I have experienced regrets. But since then, hundreds of waifs have been made; all of them aware of the stipulations at hand. It is the same for the guardians who choose to free their wings and hang up their swords. You see, it is not a cursed life, but a chosen one. There will always be those who do not understand the calling. Who will proclaim our lifestyle as immoral, but we have come to terms with that. We would rather be locked in the shadows, our doors permanently closed, than live a life of ignorance. Therefore, we do not fear the choice you make once you open that final door. Or any others that come after you."

"And this final choice I make—will it affect who I become one day?"

"Most definitely. We all have our specialties. I daresay yours, granddaughter, is already running through your veins."

My chest rose as I tightened my lips together. "I understand." Finally, I knew, it was time to go. "It was nice to finally meet you. I'd shake your hand, but that just feels . . ."

"Weird." Again, he smirked.

"Yeah," I said, copying his expression.

As I began backing away towards the oracle spread, he stopped me just as I was about to bend down to touch that final card. "May I ask, Tess, what *are* you going to do about this?" He signaled to the storm.

Without thinking about it, I lifted my right hand and snapped my fingers. In a flash, the storm was gone.

"Why should I tell you?" I grinned. "I thought you knew everything."

"Yes," Kage said, just as my hand met the thirteenth card. "Reanin will be proud of you."

CHAPTER TWENTY-NINE

True to so many of the decks I'd laid my hands on in the short time I'd spent reading cards, this oracle deck contained a card with the title on it, the Hall of Shadows.

It didn't falsely advertise. It was, in fact, one of the longest halls I'd ever seen. At least from where I'd arrived, there was no end in sight. The walls, the floor, and the ceiling were all made from the same material. Black marble. To my left was a door with the roman numeral I. and the words The Library etched into it. I stood from my reading, every card now flipped over, and stood before the entrance to the first dimension I'd entered. My hand lingered before the doorknob . . . would it open if I tried? But before I even got the chance to find out, it swung open from the other side.

"Well look at you," Rachel said with a coy smile. "You did it."

My mind was literally vacant. I'd sacrificed, sang, swam, and murdered my way through thirteen different dimensions, and from the looks of things, I was only a long walk away from the exit at the end of the hall. At least I supposed there was an exit.

"How many others have there been?" I asked, my gaze uncentered.

"It's customary for anyone who desires to join our ranks to enter each room. However, you are the first to experience it *that* way." She gestured to the cards lying on the floor. "Most of us were only able to encounter the rooms one at a time, or as they were built. Sure wish I would've been able to live through them the way you just did." She hung a hand on her hip and examined me. "How do you feel?"

I should have been exhausted. But I wasn't.

"I'm not sure."

She smirked. "Wanna come in for a bit?" she asked, pulling her arm away from the door frame and backing up. I gave her an apprehensive look (because come on, I was still in this place, and nothing was what it seemed, especially invitations). "Don't worry," she said with a chuckle, "you're at the finish line. It's the same as the starting line. Kinda like an actual tarot reading, you know. You can come back to your initial question and revisit it after finding enlightenment. Plus, if you'd seen what was in here the first time, you wouldn't have understood it."

I stepped one foot onto the carpet. "And I won't have to run the race again?"

"Not unless you want to. Now that you've been through it all, you can come and go as you please. Enter through any door or window."

"Okay . . . fine." I walked all the way in and let the door shut. It was the same bookshelf I'd tried to escape from last time I was here.

"When you need to get back out, pull on this one." She pointed to a red book with some swirly gold detail. "It's the only spine in here without a title."

I nodded as my attention drifted to the other spines. There really weren't any titles, at least as far as I could see. They were all authors. Running a finger down the spine of a mint green edition of an Amber Sparks, (I'd never heard the name) I asked, "What are these?"

Rachel had moved to a table, a single book sitting before her. "Names."

"Names?" I repeated, looking from her back to the books.

Jared Spink, Harold Spinolli, Judy Spinolli, Kerry Spinolli . . . The names went on and on, and there were at least twenty or more Spinollis.

I turned and faced the waif. "These are people?"

"Yep," Rachel said as she flipped over the cover of the book she had in her possession.

"Is this every person who has ever lived on Earth?"

"Living, deceased, and not yet living. As soon as they sign that life contract, they're in our system. Whoa, you wet the bed until you were eight?"

I flinched, then almost immediately snapped back at her. "What are you doing?" I lunged for her table and plucked the book from her hands. Sure enough, the spine had my name on it. "This is personal information!" I griped. "Is this what you all do all day when you're not finding other people's shadows? You read about them?"

She shrugged. "Call it homework."

I shook the book in my hot little hand. "That is *so* not cool."

"It's our job," Rachel said matter-of-factly.

I sneered at her for a good thirty seconds, then began to flip through my book. It had a prologue and fifteen chapters; one for every year I'd been alive. As I returned to the beginning, I shot Rachel an aggrieved look, before reading the introduction.

Tess Moreau: From the star system Tessandra. NOT A SOUL SEED. Named by her grandmother.

"That's it?" I asked.

"What's that?" Rachel asked, her attention slipping away as though she was getting bored with me.

"My prologue is like three sentences. Is that normal?"

"Eh. Not usually, but then again, you're not really *normal.*"

I glared at her. "I'm aware." I turned the book around and pointed at the prologue. "What's a soul seed?"

The waif placed both palms over the reading table. "It's what most of us started as. We are bred, then sent out into the universe to deliver energy—both good and bad."

"Okay. But then if I'm not a star seed, then where did I come from? What's Tessandra?"

Rachel clicked her tongue. "Even if it was my job to tell you that—which it isn't—I wouldn't need to. You've been through twelve of your shadows and you are being prepped for your thirteenth right now. I think you know. I think you've known for a while."

My mouth, which I'd let fall open, closed. I shifted my focus back to the prologue, then without uttering a single word, began to skim over the pages of the rest of my book. It was literally an account of my life; from my first steps to the very second I discovered my magical abilities, to when I found out about the deaths of my grandmother and mother.

I glanced up at Rachel. "It's written in third person."

She nodded.

"Who's the author?"

"I'm not sure. The books just sort of appear and the pages are added as needed."

I flipped to the last page and watched as a few new sentences appeared.

As Tess stood in the library, a dimension inside of a

dimension—a design crafted by her grandfather—she began to awake on yet another level. She remembered her grandmother's constant evaluation of the world they lived in. How Reanin nearly always referred to it as a simulation, a veil to cover the eyes of the Earth's inhabitants. Yes, Reanin hid her life in the shadows from her granddaughter, but she couldn't resist molding Tess to fit the shape her granddaughter was destined to take one day.

I closed the book with one hand. "What am I supposed to do with this?"

"Nothing. It stays here."

"Then why has it been introduced to me?"

Rachel rolled her eyes. "That smidge of humanity crawling inside you is enough to stunt your progress. Don't you see? If you have any questions about who you are, about what to do going forward—" She pointed to the book. "You're holding the answers."

I stilled. How had I not put that together? Was my humanity seriously that much of a crutch?

Before I could say anything more, Rachel stood. "I'll leave you to it. When you're finished just leave the book on the table. I'll return it to the shelf later."

Suddenly I was struck with an obvious thought. "Are you, like, the librarian here?"

She grinned. "Yeah. It's what I did . . . before."

Curiosities began brewing in my mind. It was refreshing to have them for someone else for a change. "Alright—spill. I'd love to hear *your* story."

She just stood there, her shoulder sloping. "Okay, fine. The year was 1955. I was recruited by a waif who I'd only known as a regular at the library I worked at. I thought he had eyes for me." The way she said it, it was like she was embarrassed. "Then one day there was an extra book in his stack of returns. He laid his hand over the pile and told me he'd brought something for me to take a look at. He said he hoped I'd find it interesting.

"Before that day, I kept mostly to myself. I didn't fit in with society—I loved a good pant suit," she chuckled as her gaze rose to the ceiling. "Anyway, after he left, I sorted through the books and came across the one he meant for me to find. It had my name on it."

"He brought you your book?" I asked in disbelief.

"Yeah. They can leave the library as long as they are being checked out to their owners. It's a common way for waifs to reach out to possible participants."

I chewed over the word participants but said nothing.

"When I first held my book, it made me dizzy; to be honest, I took it home and buried it under a pile of dirty clothes. Eventually I moved it to my coffee table and spent hours staring at it. It was days before I resisted the fear in my heart." She ran a hand through her beautiful, honey hair. "I read the whole thing. I'd just turned twenty-five. I'd had a lot of thoughts growing up, so it was a bit of feat, you know, reading all of it. But I did. I gotta say though, if there is ever a way to face your shadows, it's to read about them from the point of view of someone else.

"As soon as I read the last line of my book, another appeared. It said, 'And then the man with the kind eyes and shaggy hair knocked on Rachel's door.' And sure enough, as soon as I read the line, there was a knock. I answered, and it's all fairly textbook from there—ignore the pun."

"So, I mean—that was it? You decided right then and there that you wanted to follow the waif into the shadows?"

She tossed her head from shoulder to shoulder. "Not directly. I thought it over for a week before accepting. Ya see, they needed a librarian, so they let me come into The Hall and have a look at everything before taking the plunge."

"They let you think about it—like it was just any other job?"

She raised her brows. "This isn't a prison. Everyone is given the opportunity to explore The Hall; it's up to them whether they want to transition or not." She held an arm out to the bookcase that served as the one way in and out. "Your humanity is out there waiting, Tess. You are the one who ultimately decides whether you take it or leave it."

I narrowed my eyes. "I didn't realize I could take it back. I thought it was a sacrifice."

"Believe it or not, doll, the Hall of Shadows was created to aid in soul development. Yes, a sacrifice is appreciated, but like a tip at the end of a meal it is up to our patrons to decide, once they are finished, how much gratuity to leave."

I fidgeted in my stance. "You're comparing someone's humanity to a tip?"

"Humanity, or in other cases, whatever grounds them to the planet. We see more than just humans in this place, after all."

"Riiighhht."

She snickered. "Most decide to leave at least twenty percent, while some empty their pockets. Others leave nothing at all. It's up to the participant to decide, and that is a decision that can only be made after facing their shadows."

"You make The Hall sound like a carnival."

"And to some it may only be that. A destination dared to be found by dimly lit rumors. And that's fine. We are here for everyone." She winked. "Okay Tess, now you know my story and how I got my mark—"

"Your mark?"

She paused. "Surely you've noticed them by now. We all have them."

I shook my head. "Have what?"

She turned around and lifted her hair out of the way. "The

sign of the waif. A little 'gift' from Kage's brother. That sleazeball sure does love his rune magic."

Electricity purred through every vessel in my body. To the untrained eye, the mark could've looked like a tattoo of a yin yang lightning bolt with a slanted cross in the middle. But it wasn't the mark itself that was causing a rift in my belly. It was something I'd seen before.

Rachel turned around. "What's wrong?"

"N—Nothing. I just—I guess I have noticed it."

She peered directly into my soul. "Groovy. I'll leave you to it, then. When you're done, just leave the same way you came in. I'm sure you'll know just what to do."

Groovy.

I waited until she was out of earshot to say anything back. "At least that makes one of us."

CHAPTER THIRTY

I pulled the book away from where I'd been clutching it to my chest. I had no desire to curl up with this one-of-a-kind copy of *Tess Moreau*. It's not that it wasn't appealing, but it just didn't make sense to waste the time on it. Sure, I could have scoured the thing—read through every chapter. If I read close enough and between the lines, I might even have discovered a few things. But what would be the point? My shadows had already surfaced. I was learning to walk alongside my storm.

A warm breath escaped my lips as I tossed the book onto the table before heading towards the hidden door that would take me into the Hall of Shadows.

"I don't need to read about myself," I said as I made my way towards that nameless book that served as the doorknob. "I know who I am. I know every lightning strike that has ever run through my body, every twister . . . every roll of thunder." But just as I was about to depart from the endless shelves of books, a thought occurred to me.

I glanced over my shoulder, pausing in hindsight. I already knew everything about myself, but there *was* someone who I'd always wanted to dissect. Someone who should've been the brightest star in my sky, and who I should've shone the brightest for as well. Someone who should've been but never was . . . someone who never could have been a star because she refused to shine.

My hand fell away from the handle it had been resting over, and like a first-time visitor to a museum, I moseyed over towards the place I'd been just seconds ago. I'd already found the S's, so I knew I had to backtrack a little. And that's exactly what I did. I brushed my fingertips along the spines of hundreds (thousands upon thousands) of personal accounts until I reached the M's.

Books were like air to me; before I discovered Hexed, I spent most of my time in used bookstores. I liked the quiet that could be found in such places, and the smell of dusty covers. Wandering through rows of alphabetized books, arranged by genre and author, relaxed me. The Library was easier to navigate since there was no genre to worry about, and the familiar routine of meandering through endless words was comforting. Even though my anxieties had dulled, I was thankful for the consolation.

I arrived at my destination, pricking the name on the spine with sharp eyes. "Hello, Mother." I pulled the spine decorated in gold letters. Janine Moreau-Wells. When I peeked into it, it cracked like a book that had never been opened.

A soft sigh escaped me. Fate was waiting on the other side of these shadows. I hadn't just been brought here to find out the truth about my family and my magic; this was training. I had a date with destiny, and unfortunately there wasn't time to have a seat and scratch out every last detail of my mother's twisted life with the tip of my fingernail. At least this book was a solo act; I'd seen plenty of versions that came in box sets. Part 1, 2, and 3. Thankful that all I had of my mother was a stand-alone, I flipped to the first page and began to speed read. My mother's prologue wasn't any longer than mine, but then again, my mother wasn't quite 'normal' either.

Janine Moreau-Wells: From the star system Malcutta. Draconian star seed. Mother named her. Twenty-third lifetime on Earth.

Draconian. Well, that explained some things. I'd never heard of Malcutta, but I had to assume it wasn't Disney World. I didn't linger over that bit for too long. I was still trying to patch together the concept that souls were *bred* and came from all different galaxies.

I flipped to the first chapter and set in. The thickness of the book indicated that there would be countless pages that I'd find useless, so I breezed through the paragraphs, searching for what could be informative. I was still able to catch an interesting tidbit now and again, and even more intriguing was that buried between the details of my mother's life, were excerpts from my grandmother's point of view. One such passage caught my eye; a description from my mother's sixth birthday.

Reanin had decided to take Janine out for her sixth birthday. As a mother, she'd been torn. She hated to keep her child locked up in their apartment, away from other children. What if the interaction could aid her in 'normal' development? It was a question that Reanin had asked herself on numerous occasions. But the other question she'd asked herself, more frequently, was what if the play date went terribly wrong? It would be more than just an angry parent she'd have to deal with if her child acted out—it would be a crime scene.

The decision had been made. They were going to the park. If Janine was a good girl as they'd spoken about, and if she could play on the swings and the merry go round and perhaps even interact nicely with the other children, then she could have her favorite treat. But it wasn't ice-cream and cake Janine desired for her special day. No, she craved something a little sweeter.

Something that made her mother cringe. But if the promise of such a thing could curb her child into assuming a positive behavior, then Reanin was willing to make the offer.

The park was a success. Reanin stayed very close, keeping a keen watch over her daughter. Since she'd been locked out of the Hall of Shadows and found herself with her current disposition—the one she'd handed down to Janine—she had learned how to usurp what she needed from those around her without them even knowing. Being what they were, sirens, they were able to charm nearly every soul they encountered. All Reanin had to do was coerce someone into a dark corner and take just enough to keep her eyes a deep blue. Once they began to turn red, her heart would eventually stop beating and she would crave something else. And once she gave in to that urge, it was all over. She would be something else completely. Luckily, it didn't seem that way for Janine. Reanin had already tested those waters—keeping her from the feed for long segments of time. And even though the little girl had become extremely volatile, she hadn't begun to grow fangs.

Two weeks was about the max Reanin could go without pressing her lips to another person and treating them like a human inhaler. Two weeks and the walls seemed to shrink, and she could hear blood rushing through a person's veins as if their hearts were made of savage beasts working against a clock. No, it did not take long for one curse to become another. Reanin was contented by the fact that, at least right now, Janine was safe from 'the change.'

Reanin had tried to explain the appropriate way to feed to her daughter, but Janine was so little. Even if her steel heart wasn't written on her size six sleeve, Reanin would still have to help her daughter meet her needs so that they could continue with their everyday lives. Surely it was the girl's age that explained her malicious behavior . . . that was what Reanin told herself in those early years. However, Reanin was somebody whose life's work pertained to facing one's shadows, therefore her days spent in denial were few and far between.

As previously stated, the park had been a success, mostly. Janine had made it through an entire hour with at least ten kids her age. From any other perspective the girl seemed quite ordinary. She laughed and played and even held hands with a slightly older girl, allowing her to drag her around to meet the others.

When the hour was up, she pranced over to where Reanin was waiting for her on the bench, her hands in the pockets of her little purple overalls. "Okay, I'm done."

Reanin didn't post a smile for her daughter and her good deeds. How could anyone smile with what they knew was coming?

"You did well, Janine."

Reanin's daughter wasn't smiling, so there was no expression to let fall when she pointed her eyes at her mother. "You promised."

Reanin continued to study her offspring. This soul—it didn't share her or her mate's origins; she was positive of that. Those ever-changing eyes she'd seen that would rescue her one day, they didn't belong to her daughter. "Isn't there somewhere else you would like to go?"

The girl stared bullets into Reanin. "It's my birthday."

Reanin had thought that she was through with internal struggles when she met Kage. She'd left the devil for the underworld.

In the end, she'd made a promise, and as much as it disgusted her, she needed to follow through. But as Janine walked up to the lady sitting across the playground, watching her little boy play on the slide while she held her newborn baby in her arms, Reanin knew this was a promise she should've broken. She held her breath as the lady smiled down at Janine and nodded, padding the bench, and inviting the little girl to have a seat. The woman very carefully placed the baby in Janine's arms, not aware of the greedy and hungry look on the girl's face. She was just as ignorant when Janine appeared to place her forehead against the baby's, when in fact she was sucking out part of its essence.

Janine only took a tiny bit, enough to put the baby to sleep. But Reanin knew that if she hadn't been there watching, her daughter would have taken every last bit out of that tiny little baby; that she would have sucked on the end of its soul like someone eating king crab.

A shiver ran down Reanin's spine as her daughter returned the sleeping baby to its mother and began to skip back to where her own sat waiting for her.

"See," she said, standing before her mother as if she'd just tidied up her room without being told to do so. "I can use control."

Reanin felt like she had shards of glass in her lungs as she inhaled a deep breath, taking her daughter's hand and leading her out of the park. "That you can," she answered.

Except the control wasn't necessarily a good thing. Yes, Janine had shown her mother what she was good at. Just like John, Janine was talented at putting on a good performance. She would inevitably run her life in this manner; putting on the preferred face that those around her sought to find. She would use it to gain desirable friendships, employment, and whatever else she was searching for. But not once would her daughter make a real connection. For Reanin had seen it that day, Janine was quite capable of doing whatever it took to get exactly what she wanted.

Reanin squeezed her daughter's hand a little too tight as they walked back home.

"Ouch!" Janine squealed. "Not so hard, Mommy."

"Sorry," Reanin said, without letting go of Janine's hand

and without looking down at her. "Just have to keep you on a tight leash, that's all."

And she knew right then and there that that's what she always would have to do. Not because she needed to keep the precious darling that she should love more than anything on this earth, including herself, safe—but because Janine was a predator. She always would be, and it was now Reanin's job and curse to keep others safe from her.

I looked up from the book. Dang, she was evil from the start.

With a delusional look painted over my face, I continued to skim the chapters. The more I read, the more apparent it became that my mother wasn't just hell bent on disobeying the way my grandmother had raised her, but that she was on a completely separate mission all together.

Most girls, by the age of thirteen, were discovering that their bodies did or didn't match what the media told them they should look like. Janine had overheard many of her female classmates speaking about their starvation diets or ridding their bodies of food to maintain a boyish figure. Janine could've cared less what she looked like, though she had what most of the girls were striving for. No curves—long legs and arms. She was built like a ballerina. Though, for reasons her mother never explained, Janine was banned from ever taking a single dance class.

Janine did go on to starve herself, but not in the usual way. She'd seen what could happen to her mother when Reanin tried to fight the curse she so hated. One time, it had gone so long that her mother grew fangs. And though Reanin would always inevitably find a soul and maintain her siren status, Janine longed to crave blood instead of souls.

Was it the movies she'd seen? The fictitious accounts of romanticized cannibalism? No one could be sure. One thing was definite however, like most psychopaths, Janine was a whore for power. That's what happens when someone has no feelings; they go to extremes searching for even the tiniest bit of emotion.

Janine was not fully aware of where her mother had come from or where her father currently was. The one thing she did know was that they had fled their home so that they could keep it from burning down, but still flames had found it. They had to wait until the one with the right eyes surfaced to get back to the place they came from, and Reanin had been very careful to never tell her daughter who she suspected that person would one day be.

"So, you wanted to be a vampire, mommy dearest," I mused, moving on from my mother's teenage years to when she first met my dad. I couldn't wait to read about *that*. I mean, unless I was mistaken, my father was anything but power hungry. Sure, he worked long hours, and was gone a lot, but when he had the chance, he was pretty laid back. He enjoyed a football game and a beer on Sundays just as much as other dads. It was true, the past few months he'd been wound so tight that I worried his head might spin off, but before my mom was killed, he'd been notorious for filling our house with composure. Then again, what did I know? For fifteen years I'd had no idea who the woman I called mom actually was. Regardless . . . *They found one another at The Laguna . . .*

It was a bar in the upper west side of NYC. It was summer. The sidewalks were hot enough to fry an egg, the air was muggy, and all the singles were out to get icy alcoholic beverages at their local watering hole. To Janine, it was a buffet.

Mattie was at the bar, dressed in khaki shorts and a pale pink shirt. All Janine had to do was walk up to be noticed, dressed in a mini skirt and blue tank top. She was never satisfied with just being average hot. She sipped on her margarita as she stared him in the eyes, then proceeded to lick the salt from her top lip. It was already written. He was hers and she was his. But what happened next wasn't what Janine Wells had in mind.

She took him to the back of the bar, near the exit. She knew The Laguna well and was familiar with the best feeding spots. He pulled her in against his body and she reciprocated, but just as she went in for a taste of his soul, she found herself unable to squeeze out a single drop.

She pulled her head back and gave him a discerning look, one of which he shared.

"Is that how you kiss?" he asked with a grin.

"Not usually," Janine answered.

It was the first and only time that she had ever been unable to feed from anyone. She found it bothersome and curious. Which is why she decided to stay in the man's arms for a little longer, and for the first time in her life, handed out her number before leaving the bar.

I scrunched my nose up as I lowered the book. Something wasn't right about that. What kind of person could be immune from a siren?

I bookmarked the spot with my hand as I perused the bookshelf for my father's name. But there was no Mattie or Matthew Moreau to be found.

"Interesting," I mused aloud.

There was really only one reasonable explanation, for everyone had a book here, regardless of *what* they were.

Matthew Moreau wasn't my father's real name.

"Great. What's *he* hiding?" No one in my life was who they said they were.

I'd come up against a roadblock but there wasn't time to do anything other than climb over it. My date with destiny was waiting. So instead of dwelling on my father, I returned to my mother's book and scoured it for the juiciest details. There were more than a few.

One thing that wasn't surprising was that my mother never loved my father. At first, she found him to be a challenge (other than disposing of all the bodies, life hadn't been much of a contest yet). And it wasn't like *that* was even that hard for her. She'd used her siren's charm to get close to the night manager at one of the local crematoriums. She flirted her way into disposing of more bodies than there was time to count. My mother had drained at least thirty people of their souls before she even turned nineteen. *And that was under my grandmother's watchful eye.* How many would there have been if Reanin hadn't been around?

My guts soured as I read about my mom trying to break into my dad's soul; she was denied access with every swipe of her siren's card. When he proposed, she saw it as a business opportunity. If she was with someone like him then my grandmother might stop lurking around every corner; and since he was in real estate as well, they could partner up and double their assets. Because apparently my mother wasn't just greedy for souls. She was just plain greedy. She wanted it all: fangs, fame, and fortune.

My hand was getting itchy from grasping my mother's book so tight. Habitually, I reached for the phone in my back pocket to check the time, only to remember that it didn't work. I needed to hurry up and get back to that hallway.

I released a ragged breath and turned to the last few pages. I could have read about my mother's twisted vampire aspirations all day, but what was most important was what happened at the end of her life. Nisroc was responsible for her and my grandmother's deaths—that much was obvious. But how did he find them? The goddess in The Pendulum had already alluded to the fact that it had been my mother's fault. *She'd gotten sloppy.* It was time to find out what that meant.

Janine Moreau-Wells died on her forty-second birthday. It was poetic, that the hand who took her life was the one hand she'd always thought could never hurt her. Then again, that was Janine's most detrimental downfall—she was arrogant to the bitter end.

It was a tradition for her mother and her to have a special birthday 'brunch.' Though over the years, Janine's tastes had evolved. She no longer cared how young or old the souls she drank from were; the truth was none of it excited her anymore. But it wasn't like any of that was going to matter for much longer.

Janine met her mother on the corner of the street that led to what had at one point been her favorite restaurant, The Hollow. They took Tess there quite often. Her daughter loved the elevated chicken and waffles, and Janine loved that it was run by witches—and not the fake kind. In a world full of mere humans trying their best to seek magic, there were a handful that could summon the elements freely. The Hollow was full of this sort. Their souls were just a little spicier.

"Hello, Mother. You're looking well," Janine said to Reanin as she stopped just short of where the woman was waiting for her.

"Happy birthday," Reanin returned.

The two then began to walk side by side towards The Hollow. "How is Tess?"

Janine replied as she would on any other day. "Fine. She's been associating with so-called pagans."

"I am aware."

"I've heard that sometimes magic displays itself on certain birthdays. Perhaps her petals will open when she's sixteen."

"She was born with her petals open," Reanin said nearly too softly to hear.

Janine snuck a look at her mother. Her hands were tucked into her coat pockets, and she'd made a fist around a golden pen given to her by the man she'd met last time she'd frequented The Hollow. It wasn't just run by witches, many of their patrons had magic in their veins as well.

"What do you mean by that?" Janine asked her mother.

"It doesn't matter," Reanin said, stepping into the alley just before the restaurant and taking several steps into it until she was hidden from the sun and from the people walking by.

Janine narrowed her eyes as she followed her mother to where she'd tucked herself in between the other side of a giant dumpster and the wall. "What are you doing?"

"Making it easier for you."

Janine closed in on Reanin, both now cloaked in darkness. She kept her hand wrapped around the pen in her pocket, and as she spoke her grip tightened. "I have no idea what you're talking about."

Reanin's eyes hardened, and the motherly role she'd learned to fake—for no one could be a mother to Janine—instantly faded away. "I realize I've never explained to you the depth of my character, but still, I am somewhat taken aback that you had the audacity to believe I wouldn't be able to feel what it is you carry."

Janine played dumb. She shook her head as she spoke. "I'm sorry, Mother, but I'm completely at a loss here. What are you accusing me of?"

"I'm not accusing you. I'm calling you out on it. You've brought me here to kill me." Reanin waited while Janine continued to plead ignorance, and when her daughter was done, she continued. "You can put it off for as long as you like, but I've been around enough swords to know when they are near." Janine's eyes grew for a second before she forced them to relax. "I would ask what he offered you, but that part is fairly obvious. You've always wanted the other curse. From the moment you saw me fight it, you wanted it."

Finally, Janine dropped the act. "How do you know it was a he?"

"It's always been a he, Janine. And I never told you it was he we were hiding from, because I never trusted you. I knew you would try to find him and make a deal. That's why I'm guessing he found you."

"You always said we were hiding from a man with wings. The man I made a deal with is a witch."

Reanin was not above rolling her eyes. "Dear child, you are so blind."

Janine stiffened at the insult, then pulled out the golden pen. As soon as it was by her side, it transformed into a large golden sword. It shone so bright that she knew she had to move fast; even as hidden as they were, the light shining off the weapon had to be seen from the sidewalk, if not space. "Are you even going to fight?"

Reanin didn't move a muscle. "What's the point? He found you which means he found me. My days are numbered either way."

Janine remained still, the sword in her hand, heavy. "If he's not who he told me he is, then who is he?"

There was a teaser of smugness in Reanin's eyes as she said, "He is someone who uses people. For instance, I would bet that he found a way to have you slice open my heart because he was too afraid to do it himself. I was once human, but I've become a siren. Only guardians have been known to become sirens. Therefore, he wouldn't know whether killing me would result in the dimming of his sword. He didn't want to take the chance, and he must have figured out that as long as it's not his hand holding his weapon during the act that the curse will not rain down over his shoulders." Reanin paused, observing the muddled expression coloring the face of her daughter. "It wasn't a witch who gave you that sword, Janine. It was your uncle. And if you think he will turn you into what you desire, then you've got another thing coming. Not that it'll make a difference, you've made up your mind."

Janine did nothing for a full minute. She didn't even breathe. Finally, she spoke the last words she ever would to the woman who had conceived of her in the shadows. "You never even told me my father's name. You didn't ever trust me enough to even know that much."

"You're right," Reanin said, before folding her hands

together in front of her stomach, almost as if she was finalizing her last pose.

Janine took the sword by both hands and in one swift move, impaled her mother's heart.

Reanin fell against the brick wall as her eyes shut peacefully. She didn't scream or whimper, her body simply slunk down to the ground as she died.

Janine felt a surge of power rush through her, similar to the first time she'd taken someone's entire soul and felt their life fill her as their body died in her arms. Now she would get what was coming to her, now she would be rewarded, and she didn't care if the man was her uncle. He'd shown her a vision of herself in the reflection of the sword. He'd shown her as a vampire.

Janine reached for the hilt of the sword so that she might retrieve it and return it to the man who was supposed to be waiting in The Hollow. He had told her that if she did what he asked her to, that the sword would return to a pen and if the pen wrote with Reanin's blood when she handed it back to him, then he would transform her into what she desired. But just as she was about to grasp it, the sword completely faded away.

"What the—" Janine started.

"She tried to warn you," said a familiar voice. "Nisroc was never going to turn you."

Janine flipped around on her toes. As soon as she saw his face, the color in her cheeks, which had been rosy from the kill, washed out. "What are you doing here?"

"My job."

The little light there had been went out, and the curtains over Janine Wells-Moreau's life fell.

The End

I looked up, book spines for days looking back at me. I was dizzy . . . nauseous. Nisroc didn't kill my grandmother (at least not directly). My mother did.

I guess it wasn't that hard to believe. None of our names had popped up that often in my mother's detailed account—not me, my grandmother, or my dad. If anything, we were props that sometimes got more in the way of her performance than anything. Janine's only focus in life had been herself, and she was so vain that she couldn't believe anyone would take her for a ride of their own.

Nisroc wasn't the only narcissist in this script. And speaking of—it was Nisroc who'd foiled my mother into killing her own, but it didn't seem like it was Nisroc who killed Janine. The book closed in my hand as I replayed the last few moments of my mother's life. It was the way she'd said those last words, "What are *you* doing here?" That's what had me thrown.

I tossed the book onto the nearest table and headed for the exit, all the while my thoughts were churning. My grandmother *let* my mother kill her because she knew it wouldn't matter; she already had an insurance policy set up. Whoever killed my mother stated that he was just doing his job. So, who did that person work for?

I had questions but the answers didn't live in the shadows, of that I was sure. I pulled on the book lever and the bookcase swung open. All I needed to do was get through this last dimension and I would be home. Or I'd be back . . . I was no longer sure where home was.

As I stared out into the shimmering darkness, I heard my grandmother's voice echoing in my head. "*She was born with her petals open.*" It was so obvious—she knew what I was the moment I was born. She knew about my magic the whole time, and that pointed to only one conclusion: she knew I was the key to reopening the Hall of Shadows. My whole life she was stalling because she didn't want my mother anywhere near the world she'd helped create. But that didn't erase the fact that Reanin was a mother, and no matter how evil Janine was, she couldn't find it within her heart to kill her own daughter. So, she waited . . . waited until the day came that Janine would go too far. She knew when that day came, that once the two of them were gone, I would follow the breadcrumbs she'd left behind; and with a little help from some very unique magic gifted to me from my grandfather, I would repair all the damage that had been done. That I would rescue the rest of the unicorns.

A shiver ran down my spine as I stepped into the hallway. "This one's for you, Grandma."

The door slammed shut behind me.

CHAPTER THIRTY-ONE

When I'd first turned over the last card, this dimension had been made of an endless black tunnel. The hall had been vacant.

This was no longer the case.

Now, for as far as the eye could see, there were silver holograms in the shape of yours truly, formed into a single file line. As I inspected the closest one, an eerie vibe washed over me. There was no face or any other distinguishing features; they were like cardboard cutouts, or the more I thought about it—shadows.

Rachel's speech echoed through my mind: The Hall didn't steal from the participants. This was it, my chance to take back some or all of what had been siphoned from me during my experience.

As I thought about this, I turned and looked for the cards I'd left behind when I met with Rachel in The Library. They weren't there. I peeked further into the corners, but there was absolutely nothing in this hallway but pieces of me. Perhaps that's what happened when someone was done playing—the cards disappeared. Whatever the case, I was anxious to get going and it seemed pretty clear that the cards were gone, so I started down the long corridor, passing my shadows as I went.

I assumed if I touched the holograms, they would sink back into my body, so I was careful to keep my arms tucked into my sides. Eventually, I began passing doors to the rooms I'd already had the pleasure of exploring. The Mirror, The Pendulum, The Forest (icy fingers tickled the back of my neck as I passed that one), The Lake, The Muse. When I came to The Three of Swords, I paused.

Now, so close to the end of my journey—or at least as I got ready for what came next—I couldn't help but feel like it was that card I pulled under Ethan's watchful eye that had started it all. I had to wonder which it was that the card had been communicating: the storm I'd discovered while in these shadows, or betrayal. Or was it both? I was still planted in place, rereading the words etched into the door, when it opened. Framed by the door was a beautiful young woman, dressed in a super classy black jumpsuit.

At first, I had no idea who she was, but after only a moment, I placed those haunting eyes. And then she spoke— "You are burdened by instinct." A formless shadow moved behind her. Bingo. The dots were connected.

"Annie?"

She didn't nod or shake her head. Instead, she answered in her own way. "A new perspective is advantageous."

I took in her innovative appearance. She had shifted into the mold of a girl about my age, if not maybe a hair older, and she was strikingly beautiful.

I hesitated before asking, "Why are you here?"

"To be led is instruction. To follow is to inquire. Somewhere in the middle is observation."

I let the fortunes soak in and translate in my mind. Then, tipping my head to the side, I asked, "Have you been following me?"

She opened the door as if she was holding it for the person behind her, and the smudge that was her mother slithered into the hall like a snake, before scampering off into the nearest hiding place. Once Lydia had passed through, Annie entered the hall and let the door close behind her. I couldn't help but stare longingly at the door as if I could see through it to what was stored inside.

The changeling spoke as if she could sense my motivation. "The hilt of another's steel is taboo to the touch. To venture forward, you must wield your own sword."

I began to shake my head. "How did you know that I was—"

"You are in search of a weapon."

"I—I don't have my own." And I wasn't about to meet my date with destiny unarmed.

Annie raised a finger and placed it against her temple. "Do not think with your eyes or your logic. Remember the stardust that created your heartbeats. Listen to its song."

Her expression soothed into an easy grin before she turned away from The Three of Swords and began moving in the direction of Stardust. I willingly followed, Lydia scampering back and forth just behind me.

Listen to its song . . . Both Cai and Kage had mentioned hearing music in the shadows. "But I haven't heard any music down here," I shouted to Annie's back. "Does that mean something?"

"One must only listen," her speech echoing up and down the hall like she'd just shouted into a large cave. She reached into my shadows as she strolled by like she was feeling through curtains. They moved like sheets in the wind as they were touched, but they didn't flutter away. When next she spoke, I knew she'd moved on from the music. "She disregards what she may have returned unto herself."

As we passed the eighth door, I hollered back, "I'm not

disregarding them; it's just that I don't want to be any more human."

She didn't miss a beat. "The burden of others is heavy. Time will be eternal. Hastiness cannot be undone." She flipped around on her tiptoes, walking backwards as she faced me. "It is the smallest bit of the human DNA that will ground her."

She turned back around, and I narrowed my eyes, trying to decode her message. As my thoughts churned, I mindlessly reached for my necklace. Immediately, I was struck with a super heavy vision and unwillingly came to a halt.

I'd already seen the storm that lived inside me; the storm composed of all these creepy shadows lined up like life-size paper dolls. But what I saw upon grasping those three stones was a hurricane. I had been removed from the hall and set directly into the storm. All the colors of the earth whirled around me as the wind shifted and circled around me as a cyclone.

You are the wind.

You are the fire.

You are the dirt.

You are the river running wild.

I remained in the center of the shifting wind as the three different voices continued to enter my mind.

You are the reflection most of them cannot understand. You will learn to be as fate intends. Listen to the changeling: your role will inevitably find you. You need not rush.

My voice came out as a howl, as I repeated the words into my mind. *Are you telling me to take back my humanity?*

No one can tell you what to take or leave. You worry about your strength—don't. You already have all you need to face thine enemy. Slip your hand into your pocket.

My hand slipped away from the necklace. Annie was facing me.

"Did they clarify things for you?" she asked like a receptionist ensuring the patient in the waiting room had been taken care of.

My eyes bulged, and not from the heavy clue I'd just been handed from the ghosts of three guardians. "Annie, you spoke. I mean, you know, like a normal person."

She didn't budge from her stance. "Did they?"

"Uh . . . yeah. I mean, I think so." My hand rested over my pocket—over my wand. My *magic* wand.

"Good," she replied, before swinging around and strolling forward.

I followed, as did Lydia, but neither of us spoke again for quite some time. I couldn't be sure what Annie was thinking, but my thoughts were occupied by what would be waiting for me once I left this place.

"Can I ask you something?" I asked as we passed The Opera House. There was mad scratching coming from the other side of the door as we skipped by. Annie didn't answer, which I took as an invitation. "Do you still belong to the fey?"

She didn't answer, not until we passed Night Terrors and Roses. "It is up to oneself to be as one desires. To exist at all is a choice."

Finally, I could see where my shadows either began or ended; just a few steps after that stood a door. It was just as black as everything else, but unlike all the other doors that were clearly labeled, this one was blank.

The exit, I thought.

Annie's blonde bob wrapped around her cheek as she spun around and faced me. "My home is in The Forest; it's where I feel comfortable. Where is your home, Tess?"

I studied her eyes. When I first met her, I thought they looked a little dazed; I even wondered if she was under some kind of spell. But now I understood—changeling or not, Annie was her own person. She was also part of the shadows.

Like so many who lived in The Hall, the shadows breathed for her just as she breathed for them.

I twisted my fingers together in front of my stomach. "I don't think I know just yet."

She took a couple steps towards me, then lifted my chin with a single finger. "This is truth."

Her touch felt like mine. Like she was reanimating the part of me that had died. Again, I had the urge to cry, but I'd been cursed to live a life without tears. "Yeah, I guess."

Her head fell to her shoulder. "The ocean doesn't have tears; this is why it rages."

A half smile formed over my face, and I had a feeling my eyes were shifting from green to blue. "This is truth."

She dropped her hand away from my chin and took a step back, then held out a hand to the blank door. "Are you ready?"

I contemplated my next motivation before turning to face the last shadow in the long line of silver paper dolls. I placed a hand over its shoulder, and as soon as I did, the hologram began to melt and flow through my fingers and into my soul. When it was done, I squared my shoulders with Annie once more. "I am now."

"Just the one?"

"That's all I need."

The right side of Annie's lips curled up into a half grin as she raised her chin. "Off you go, then, Tess of Tessandra. And please, take these."

I looked down and found that she had the full deck of cards in her palm. I wavered for only a second before accepting them. Once they were in my hand, it was like I was holding a book I'd just finished—one that had opened new neural pathways in my brain. I suppose, though, that it was exactly like that.

"Thank you," I said, tucking them into my other pocket.

"Of course," Annie said. I nodded in appreciation then

began to reach for the exit. But just as my hand was about to meet the doorknob, she added, "Proceed: wand, books, fey dates. Don't: look into the sun, reruns, forget about me."

I licked my lips as I laid a hand over her shoulder. "Never."

The shadows I'd left behind began to sink into the floor, becoming one with The Hall, and I reached for the knob and gave it a turn.

Darkness turned to light, at least on the surface. I was back in my grandmother's apartment, right where I was before I flipped over that first oracle card, and from the location of the sun I could tell that it was evening. Unless it was a different day, little to no time had passed on the surface since I'd been diving through my shadows.

No sooner was I out of my grandparents' world than I heard the voice of another distant relative. Not just any voice, but *the* voice. It was the very one I'd been expecting. The waifs that lived in this building wouldn't have stopped him from getting in here; they knew, as well as I did, that for the Hall of Shadows to have a chance at survival, this intervention was going to have to happen.

"Hello, Tess."

I reached into my right pocket as I faced him. With my wand in my hand, I said without an ounce of fear or regret, "Nice to formally meet you, *Nick*. Or should I say, Great Uncle Nisroc."

PART THREE

CHAPTER THIRTY-TWO

There was about twenty feet of plush white carpet standing between me and a murderer in guardian's clothing.

"Where's Lucille?" I asked, shoving my tongue into my back molar.

He grinned. "It's nice to see you again, too."

I waited for him to lunge at me, or use some sort of celestial magic, but he didn't move.

My expression dimmed. "How did you find my family?"

He showed his teeth as he consented to a full smile. "Your mother was so driven to become a nightmare that she grew careless."

"Yeah, I've sort of figured that part out."

"Witches are like hens—they chirp a lot. When more than three went missing from the same place, word spread quickly. In this case it spread as far out as San Francisco, which is where I was, scoping out the local covens in search of any new information. Your grandmother had enough magic to rule the world—she was very discreet when it came to her location. But even the strongest building will have an occasional crack in the foundation. That crack came in the form of a very special NYC restaurant."

I exhaled the name of the institution. Even if I hadn't just read about it in my mother's book, I would've known. My mom had taken me there whenever I asked to go out, and she had a habit of disappearing for multiple bathroom breaks during our rendezvous. I'd always thought she just had a weak bladder. I hadn't known that what she had come to feed upon wasn't on the menu.

"That head of yours is a lot fuller than it was when you came to get your fortune told," he said in a condescending voice.

"I didn't come to you—you sought me out."

"Actually, no. I didn't. That was simply divine intervention."

"There was nothing divine about it."

He continued to grin in a way that filled my guts with poison. "I didn't even know you existed. I followed Janine for ages, and never once was there anything in or around her person that suggested she had a family."

"Then where *did* she lead you?"

Smugness radiated from him like stink from a sewer. "She had an apartment on the other end of the city. It's where she dined if you get my drift." I did my best not to give him the satisfaction of anything other than a neutral expression. "I didn't even consider the idea that she lived somewhere else. At least while I was tracking her, she never went anywhere other than her apartment after work."

Yeah, it wasn't out of the norm for her to skip coming home for nights at a time. She claimed she slept at the office. "If you're trying to upset me, you're wasting your time. Janine was nothing more than a surrogate. She's not the one I'm pissed off about."

His arrogance was unrelenting. "I only trailed her for two days before she led me straight to the boss. At first, I thought Janine was just another siren—locked out from The Hall. But then I realized she wasn't just your average soul sucker, but Reanin's *daughter*."

"Yes, which made her your niece. I'm surprised that someone who claims to be so shiny, didn't have the slightest feeling one way or the other about that."

Finally, the smirk fell from his face. "The substance in your mother's veins and what runs through mine are two very different materials."

"Are you so sure about that?" I retorted with a sneer.

His face softened before he narrowed his eyes over mine. "Janine was nothing more than a pawn. Even you have to admit that the world is better off without her."

I refused to agree with him, even if that last part was true. When I said nothing, he continued. Cai was right, he really did like the sound of his own voice.

"I followed your mother to the park where she met your grandmother. As soon as I saw Reanin, I knew I had to strike quickly, but when I realized my brother's queen had turned into a siren, I understood the importance of proceeding with caution."

"Yeah, yeah, yeah—let's cut to the chase. Even though my grandmother didn't start out a guardian, she carried the fallen guardian's curse. You didn't want to risk impaling her heart and ending up with a dull sword, so you enlisted her daughter —my mother—to be your hitman."

"Your mother was so bored with her curse that she didn't so much as blink an eye when I offered to tweak her affliction in exchange for her services."

"It wasn't the first time you lied to someone to get what you wanted."

His mouth was unhinged as he readied to take back the

mic, but after I said that, he paused for a minute. "You've met Cai. Sad little creature, isn't she?"

I shook my head. "Not really. In fact, that's the opposite of how I would describe her."

He was visibly annoyed. "Do I even need to go on?"

For the love, anything to shut this guy up. I'd already read all about it. Janine had met with Nisroc, who had told her he was a witch who could evolve her curse into a pair of fangs. All she had to do was get rid of Reanin, which she was more than happy to do because she didn't have an emotional bone in her body.

"I think I can add it all up just fine on my own, thanks."

He didn't miss a beat. "When I asked her to kill your grandmother, she didn't flinch. All she did was ask how to do it." He retrieved a small golden pen from his pocket which almost immediately transformed into a crystal ball.

"I don't suppose Lucille can tell us who killed my mother. I know it wasn't you."

He gave me a speculative look. "Unfortunately, no."

"Do *you* know who it was then?"

"It doesn't matter who it was."

I pressed my lips together. He didn't know; he was far too cocky to keep a juicy tidbit like that to himself.

Inside my pocket, my fingers were still clasped around my wand. "Don't you think it's in your best interest to know who it was? I mean, whoever killed Janine could be after you as well."

He looked so sure of himself as he said, "That wouldn't make sense. I'm not the one being hunted—I'm the good guy."

"Actually," I said, tossing my head from side to side, "in this story, you aren't."

The words were barely out of my mouth when Lucille changed from an orb to a sword and a pair of gray and white wings began to span out from behind his back. I took out my wand as he began to take small, thoughtful steps in my direction. "You came to *me*, Tess. I went to that fair because I was searching for something else, and then there you were— with eyes unlike anyone else's I'd ever met, save for one. As soon as you gave me permission to peek into your head, I saw it all." He was close enough that all he had to do was lunge forward and take my heart with the sharp end of Lucille's blade . . . but I wasn't afraid. Not even a little. "I know what you are, where you come from, and that to keep you alive would be a betrayal to my station. Your heart on my sword will not curse me, for it is the darkness I have come to slay."

The amount of fuel he was pouring over his theatrics was a waste of his energy. I didn't care. I'd only heard one thing in that speech that interested me. "What were you looking for?"

He replied with a short and snippy, "What?"

"At the fair. You said you went there in search of something. I'm curious, what was it?"

"Now then, that's a rehearsed question if ever I've heard one. You know what I was out for. Looks like I'd been right to follow its scent." I didn't budge, not even when he used the tip of his sword to lift the necklace from over my chest. But as soon as Lucille touched the stones, the chain holding them together evaporated and the stones floated out between the two of us as if there was no such thing as gravity.

My eyes grew as black tourmaline, labradorite, and blue kyanite shrunk away into nothing and three bright red stones took their place. I knew just then, as soon as I saw them in their raw form, that it didn't matter who you were. *Anyone* who laid eyes on those stones had the capability of falling under their spell . . . their power. Not even I was immune but, unlike my great uncle, I was able to pull my gaze away from them long enough to notice that the ghosts of the three guardians had begun to materialize around me.

"Breathe Tess," said the woman.

I hadn't realized I'd stopped, but as soon as she said it, my chest rose and fell.

"He can't touch us," she affirmed. "We belong to you. The only way for him to take us is to kill you."

"Can he do that?" I asked. If Nisroc heard me, he didn't show it.

"You haven't let go of all your humanity," she said. "So yes, at this point, it is possible."

My breath had thickened but I made sure to inhale and exhale through my nose in steady beats. I'd come *way* too far to lose this battle now.

"So then," I said, a bit shakier than I'd intended to sound, "I guess I have no other choice but to let you help me."

My great uncle was still lost in the heartbeats that could be heard radiating from each ruby. The woman guardian closed her eyes in agreement and when she reopened them, she nodded down to my wand. "Give it a go."

Confusion ran circles around my busy thoughts, but I had a feeling that all I needed to do was believe. I raised the wand in my hand and watched in amazement as it turned into a sword, identical to Lucille.

"You're welcome," said the woman.

"Thanks," I whispered, so much in awe. This magic seriously was no joke.

"The time to strike is now," said the guardian with the snake wrapped around his forearm.

The glare coming from my new weapon was enough to shake Nisroc from his hypnosis. As he looked at my sword, he muttered breathlessly, "How did you do that?"

Was that apprehension?

I hinged slightly forward as I answered. "The wand was a gift from a witch I met in the shadows, and with my inherited magic, I can pretty much do whatever I want."

He was almost huffing as he intervened. "You shouldn't be able to hold a guardian's sword."

"Yes, you should. It's in your blood," the ghostly guardian with the sword said.

I moved to hold the sword with both hands—it was heavier than it looked. Thinking over the guardian's words, I said to Nisroc, "You forget, regardless of what I'm destined to become, I have celestial bones in my family tree. I am allowed a familiar."

He spit out his next words as he moved into a predator stance. "It's a pity that the two of you won't be able to get better acquainted then." And in one fell swoop he used his sword to shove the one in my hands to the ground. It turned back into a wand. He didn't waste time kicking it out of his way as he kept Lucille pointed at my chest.

My blood was pumping in my ears and my eyes moved to each of the guardians, who were still there, watching, but making no move to help.

"Looks like you're rather screwed, Tess," Nisroc seethed. His sword was literally an inch from sinking through my clothes and into my heart.

The ghosts moved so they surrounded us.

"How do you figure?" I asked, trying to stall.

"I can smell your humanity. Your heart is mine for the taking."

Even though the guardians were right there, their magic available to me—what was the point if I didn't know what to do with it? I crammed my eyes shut and tried to shut everything else out as I whispered, "What can I do? How do I navigate around this?"

I could almost see his frown as my great uncle spoke. "Who are you talking to?"

His voice was quickly drowned out as the ghosts began to chant.

You are the wind.
You are the fire.
You are the dirt.
You are the river running wild.
Never forget, child. You are the reflection. YOU are the
storm.

They repeated it three times. Every round became more like a song.

"And *you* are the music," I whispered to them.

It'd taken me leaving The Hall to hear it, but now that I could, I couldn't *un*hear it.

"The music is in you, Tess," spoke the woman. "To rise, all you must do is turn it up."

Just turn it up . . . she made it sound so easy. I mean, yeah, I'd learned how to manage my storm in the shadows, but I had yet to figure out how to deal with my powers. They'd been hibernating since the day I'd been born. But either way, there was a very sharp sword pointed at my chest and I didn't have a lot of time for training.

All this time, I'd had the magic around my neck. My grandfather had made sure it found me before I faced the enemy. He believed in me just like Reanin had.

I lifted my gaze to Nisroc. It was my turn to believe.

"I am the wind," I whispered.

He hissed over the howling currents. "You don't have a clue how to direct your storm."

"You don't know me," I answered darkly.

"It's all over your head."

I inhaled a thick breath through my nose.

"I have guidance," I muttered.

I am the ocean. As soon as I rehearsed the words at the forefront of my mind, imagery began to bleed into my thoughts. Waves sloshed up and down sandy shores. There was a rhythm.

I am the earth. I was digging the toes of my boots into the carpet like it was sand. And then the heat came.

I am the fire.

Flames licked at the blood pumping through my veins as I spoke. I stood taller and Nisroc steadied his gait, his wings standing almost straight up as he held strong to Lucille, who was still pointed at my chest. "You were never about the light; that's just a tired line from a script you wrote a long time ago. You've only had one goal since the moment you were born, and that has been to raise to the status of a god. You thought you could butcher your brother and take his stones—use them to take you to an artificial status. But guess what, even though they appeared in *his* sword, they were never his."

"That's complete nonsense," he spat out.

"Is it?" I questioned without missing a beat. The wind had spoken, and the fire had lit a fuse. I'd seen and heard the truth as if Kage had whispered it to me himself. As I walked forward, unafraid of Lucille's bite, Nisroc stumbled back an inch or two. "Kage moved them to keep them safe. He ensured that the only other person who could take care of them had to share his eyes. But even he knew no one could ever truly own them. No one can own someone else's magic." I took another step towards him, and he shrunk back another foot.

"I don't like all these accusations—"

"They're observations, *Uncle.*"

His face quickly turned cherry red. "Everything I've done is for the greater good of all things. I am a guardian! It's in my description. I'm meant to protect this world and its inhabitants. And to me, that means erasing the shadows and *anyone* affiliated with them."

I continued to move into him, backing him into a corner; as I did, sparks began to fly from my fingertips. It didn't faze me one bit; what concerned me was the hypocrisy being spilt all over my grandmother's beautiful carpet.

"You killed Maggie."

"I gave her a chance," he replied, his eyes narrowing until they became snake-like.

I sneered at him. "I wasn't aware 'giving someone a chance' included butchering them like a pig."

And then his walls came down.

"She was just another useless witch." Spit flew from his mouth as he centered in on me like a wicked goblin who'd come out to get a quick glance at the sun. "She *feared* you, you know. When I first knocked on her door, she let me in. Whatever the two of you had been discussing had shaken her to her core."

"She feared you, too."

He shook his head. "She knew what I was the second she laid eyes on me, and she knew *who* I was. Just as I knew that she was a very skilled magician. I was surprised at how easy it was to manipulate her into telling me everything. She fessed right up to her involvement with Reanin, and admitted she felt like it was karma punishing her when her wife fell under the spell of the magic The Hall was hiding in its walls."

"Juanita was after the Stones of Gehenna . . ."

"You're so blind," he said with manic eyes. "Who do you think was by my side, scripting those runes around her wife? I have extreme magical talent, but so did Maggie. She came from old magic. Even I couldn't have ever gotten her down on my own."

He wasn't lying, he was bragging, and it made me sick.

I'd heard enough. He was vile. "You're like a minister who preaches hate against 'the wrong kind of love,' and then can't keep his dick in his pants around his male bartender." As I spoke, my voice grew and so did my storm. My grandmother's apartment was suddenly filled with the wind that had been blowing around my heartbeats. The shelves shook, and books fell to the ground. A cyclone encased the two of us, and all I had to do was think about moving it to move it. "Who is to decide who has the right to stand in the sun and who should hide in the dark? Some of us feel more at home in the glitter that falls between day and night. The shadows never did anything to you, Nisroc." I shook my face in his direction and the cyclone dispersed, replaced by hail and sleet. "You felt threatened by the lake because you couldn't understand its reflection. You hated anyone who could hear the whispers because they made you feel unworthy. And then, you let hate and ignorance guide you until you got a whiff of something you decided might give you the power you've always wanted."

Even though my powers were shaking him, he held strong to his sword. "Look at what he's done to you! If you could just see yourself—"

"My gawd, Uncle, could you just *shut up*!" He grew quiet as my head fell back and my feet lifted from the ground. Every element was springing to life inside of every cell in my body. I still had a touch of humanity, so I knew this wasn't the moment I would fully rise—but that didn't mean I couldn't access a few of the powers that were coming my way. And that included the fancy pair of thick, feathery, jet-black wings that sprouted from my back side.

There was a curve to my lips when I next looked down at him from where I floated near the second story ceiling. My gaze turned to the mirror across from where I floated, and I saw that my eyes were ablaze with white fire. Stealing a word from Jamae's vocab yet again, I muttered a hearty, "Rad," before letting my attention fall back down to that piece of shit guardian.

"You seriously knew what I was and still thought you could take me on?"

He started to retort, but I cut him off.

"Huh uh," I said, shaking a finger down at him. "You were *so* wrong, and you messed with the wrong stardust."

I threw down my arms, and with it, enough lightning to set a rain forest on fire. I didn't let up for a whole minute—I didn't care what the rest of the building thought of the chaos (the residents were probably all waifs anyway). When I was positive that he'd had enough, I let my wings lower me to the ground, the electricity coming from my fingers, dulling.

There'd been so much excitement, I'd almost forgotten about the three ghosts lingering around the three red stones— the rubies still hanging in the air as if they'd been part of a beaded curtain. The guardians were staring at Nisroc, who was now crumpled on the floor like a smashed bug. He wasn't dead though; no, there was only one sure way to kill a guardian, and that came with a heavy curse.

As if reading my mind, the man with a snake as his familiar said, "Your title comes with certain privileges. Your sword will never dull—not until your death day."

I didn't reply, but I did proceed with a curt nod before nearing Nisroc's corner. My wings disappeared as I bent down and retrieved my wand. As soon as I picked it up, it lengthened back into a guardian's sword. A storm raged in its reflection.

With the help of his own tool, Nisroc hobbled up to his feet. "You shouldn't have that. The shadows in your blood make you unworthy."

Pulling out my best valley girl impression, I lowered my ear to my shoulder as I said, "Did I, like, ask for your opinion?"

His face pinched tighter together as I took slow, methodical steps in his direction. When I was close enough, I raised the tip of my sword to meet his heart. The lightning I'd thrown down upon him had left him weakened; the wall was the only thing holding him up.

"Any last words, dickhead?"

But just as he was about to retort, his attention was captured by something behind me. I turned just in time to find that the mirrors hanging on my grandmother's wall had started rippling. But they weren't mirrors. Not really. *They are all doors,* I realized. Doors that had been reopened. I turned back to make sure Nisroc wasn't using the distraction to weasel away, but all I saw was his eyes grow as his mouth unhinged.

"Cai," he said.

I flipped back around to find the vampire standing tall, *her sword* hanging by her side. When she spoke, she addressed me, not him. "Looking good, Boss." *Boss?* "But if you don't mind, I'm going to have to ask you to step aside. You see" –her gaze fell over Nisroc's shoulders— "this one's personal."

I didn't hesitate. I lowered my sword and did as she asked. "Be my guest."

My storm began to lift as Cai centered in on he who had wronged her, more than once. Her shadows curled around her shoulders like lace and smoke; they suited her.

Nisroc, the imbecile, still wore his ego like a badge of honor. The way he looked at Cai, it was as if he were watching an old friend take their final step towards the edge of the world. "What are you doing, Cai? This isn't you."

She raised her sword and slashed down through the air so quickly that I thought for sure she'd threatened the veil between this world and another. "You," she said, putting her face just an inch from his, "no longer get the stage."

Disregarding her warning, he said, "If you do this, there's no turning back. Killing me could end you."

"I'm already dead," she grinned.

His gaze roamed until he found something to connect to. "Your sword!" he exclaimed as if he'd just figured out the answer at trivia night. "If you were truly dead, your sword would be too."

She scoffed. "You stopped my heart from beating. I live from the life force of others now; if I stop feeding, I'll turn to stone, as will my sword. Even if I wanted to return to who I used to be—a guardian uncomfortable in my own skin—you've made it nearly impossible to do that. At this point my original wings might not even fit right if I did find them, so it just makes sense to get a new pair." She leaned on her sword like a cane. "Remind me, what was it you told me when I admitted I'd heard music coming from that lake *all* those years ago. When I discovered the first entrance into the Hall of Shadows." He opened his mouth, which had a slight quiver to it. But she silenced him before he could utter a single word. "Oh yes, that's right. You said to me that I must not love you as much as I believed I did. For what spawn of the underworld could possibly love? Oh! And then you went on to say that it was an insult to your *rank* that I should have the audacity to even tell you that I'd been fraternizing with the other side of the light." Her sarcasm faded and she looked like she could spit. "There is no hierarchy as far as guardians go. Like humans, we were created equal. I wish I hadn't been so smitten with you. It took me far too long to realize that you've forever been too in love with yourself to ever love anyone else."

"Cai," he said, shaking his head and pushing out a hand in surrender. "Think about what you're about to do. Look at Kage—there's no turning back. Put down your sword and step away. I will help lead you back to where your wings have been waiting." And then he smiled, in a way that soured my stomach enough that I doubled over. I couldn't believe what I was hearing and seeing. He actually thought he could convince Cai to believe him. Gross. "We will be together, Cai. The two of us. Forever."

I'd stopped breathing. I was just a quiet audience member at this point, and I knew better than to interfere; but in my head, I was screaming for her to whack him. Maybe I was inexperienced when it came to love, but I was a reader. I knew what it felt like. I was so worried that her emotional addiction to this piece of crap would, yet again, sway her from her path.

Would she stay strong, or would she take the heroin needle he was offering? The suspense was killing me.

Her head fell forward as if she could no longer take the strain of holding it up. I clenched my fist, ready to strike—his heart was going to stop beating one way or another. But just then the room was filled with a sinister chuckle and when she lifted her head back up, her eyes were as red as they'd been the first time I met her.

"What makes you think that I want to reverse who I am for even a second?" Nisroc's lips began to tremble as he tried to reply. "SHUT UP!" she bellowed. For sure, the whole building had heard that one. She moved in on him, her head tilting from side to side, and her fangs dropping down at least an inch. "I've had over forty years to think over what you did to me. How all you ever gave me were false promises. How even when I *knew* you were full of it, I somehow convinced myself that you weren't. Well guess what, honey, I'm not that scared little cherub anymore. That bright eyed princess who knew she had a dark side but was too afraid to look for it, she's grown strong. *My soul is my own now*, and my wings—I think they're ready for a revamp."

Her last words replayed several times in my head; things had taken a complete one-eighty.

"Cai—wait!" He pulled Lucille up into his hands. "Look inside. You'll see it—the two us!"

"Nisroc," Cai said in a tone that suggested she felt sorry for him. "I should have listened to you the first time we met. Do you remember what you said?"

His silence answered for him.

"Of course you don't." She shook her head. "I said you had the most beautiful eyes. And you said, and I quote, 'Never trust a pair of baby blues like these.'" Then, before he could appeal his case one last time, she pulled up her sword and rammed it into his heart. "Dick," was all she said, as she held onto the hilt of her sword.

I hadn't moved, breathed, or said a single thing. It wasn't my moment, and I knew that.

With a single grunt, Cai pulled her sword from Nisroc's stone cold heart, and as she did two things happened. First, he disappeared—like completely. So that was cool; it made for an easy clean up. Second, Cai held her sword up as if she'd just pulled it from a rock; as she did, it began to dull to the color of Kage's and wings began to spread out from behind her. The feathers melted together, transforming into scales . . . like a dragon. They looked strong enough to take her to the moon.

My jaw unhinged as I took it all in, as Cai, very slowly and with a grin she'd more than earned, held out her hands and observed as her sword turned into a bronze crown. She turned it around so I could see as she said, "I always imagined he'd give me a diamond, but this'll do."

Unaware where the description came from, I muttered as I stood back in awe, "The Blood Queen's Heartstone."

She grinned. "Coming from you, the title seems legit." She raised the crown and gazed up at it. "May it be just as sought after as the Stones of Gehenna."

I bit down over my lip before realizing— "You sacrificed any chance you had of returning to your old self."

Her eyes sparkled as she replied, "Pish posh. That girl is dead. And I'm finally happy." She placed the crown over her head then retrieved a vile of red liquid from inside her leather jacket. "Here ya go, you'll be needing this."

I caught the vile with both hands. It was so totally blood. "What is this?"

"It's yours. Use it to bring back Reanin. You'll need some pure vamp blood as well, but I'm not the only source."

I shot her a look of disbelief. "You know about the spell? The one that can bring her back?"

She shrugged a single shoulder. "Of course."

"So—but wait—aren't you going to come help, then? Where am I going to find another vampire?"

"Right in front of your nose is where. And I promise, you'll be fine without me. I'm starving and there's a few rotten witch cults that, thanks to the recently deceased, need to be taken care of. It's rumored he encouraged them to find a way to become waifs to gain entrance into The Hall. Might as well hit two birds with one stone." As I chewed over her words, her wings folded up behind her back. "Thanks for letting me finish him off—damn, that felt good. And hey, don't forget those." She gestured to the three stones still levitating in the air.

"Oh . . . right," I said, still a little dazed from—well—everything. I started to move towards them. The guardians were no longer in my sight, but that didn't mean they weren't with me still. "Hey—" I said to Cai as she headed for the mirrors. She glanced over her shoulder. "These witches who Nisroc turned . . . did any of them succeed at becoming waifs?"

She raised a brow. "That, I don't know. But there's only one way to find out." She winked. "Catch ya later, Tess."

She was already a quarter of the way into one of the mirrors by the time I muttered a good-bye.

After everything, I was all alone in Reanin's apartment, and it sure as hell felt that way. With a heavy sigh, I reached for the stones and started to give the one closest to me a tug—but it refused to move. I tried again but still couldn't get it to budge. The other two were just as stubborn. Finally, I held out my hands and looked around the room.

"Okay losers, what the hell?"

This time, only the female came to me. She appeared, and

as she did, her attention fell upon my sword. "We feel most comfortable in the hands of a familiar."

"Kay," I said, somewhat sarcastically. "You mean to say you would like to rest in the handle of my sword?"

When she did nothing more than continue to smile, I heaved a sigh and raised my sword up to meet the stones.

Again, nothing.

The woman's expression remained the same (as if she was in on a hidden joke), and the sword returned to a wand.

"What am I doing wrong?" I asked.

"He is *your* familiar now. He used to be called Orien, but when Bea turned him over to you, he lost his identity. He's been performing well, but it is difficult to function when you don't know who you are."

"*Okay*." As I stood there trying to figure out what that meant, it came to me. "He wants a name."

She nodded, and her ghostly eyes twinkled. That's when I knew.

"What was your name when you were a guardian?"

Her lips widened. "Adhara."

"Adhara," I repeated, admiring the way the name felt as it ran over my tongue. "It's perfect. I mean, it's a he, but—"

"I think he likes it," she said, gesturing to the object in my hand. He was glowing.

"I guess he does." When I looked back up, she was gone. However, I could still feel her warmth.

"Okay then," I said, pointing the tip of my new wand at the stones. "Do your thing, Adhara." And just like that, they sunk into the wand as if they were water being siphoned.

Just for grins and giggles, I shook out the wand until it became a sword. Sure enough, just like they'd been fitted into my grandfather's familiar, there they were—the three Stones of Gehenna.

"Cool," I whispered, before returning Adhara to a wand and sticking him into my front pocket.

I was just getting ready to leave when I checked my phone (which was working once more). I wasn't surprised to find that it was 5PM; the sun was more than setting, and if my calculations were correct, time hadn't existed in the shadows. I'd leapt in and leapt out around the same time, but I easily could have been down there for hours.

Just as I was about to exit my grandmother's apartment, my phone beeped.

"Dad?" I muttered, pulling up the text.

D: Hey Tess. Home early and got a pizza. You planning on returning anytime soon?

I froze. That was more than bizarre. He never texted before seven at night.

T: Yeah. Be home soon. Need anything else?

D: Just you.

A boulder materialized in my stomach. I *had* left The Hall with one looming discrepancy—my father. He didn't have a book, and if he did, it wasn't under Matthew Moreau. Who was he? *What* was he? And where did he fit in with all or any of this?

Whatever little bit of humanity I had was working on sprinkling a teensy bit of anxiety over my still beating organ. I knew, more than anything, that my night was far from over.

CHAPTER THIRTY-THREE

Ethan was waiting outside my front door when I arrived home. My first reaction was to come to a dead stop . . . which I did. I'd long since figured out *what* my supposed friends were, but I wasn't sure which side they clung to. As much as I didn't want to, I figured it would be in my best interest to see the glass as half empty. Sure, the Three of Swords had most likely been trying to communicate to me that I needed to release my storm, but the wise are always wary, and betrayal could still be lurking. Therefore, as I came out from the shadows, I didn't hesitate to do so with my wand in hand.

As soon as he saw me, his eyes lit up. "Hey! Lil Tess—there you are."

I scowled. "Don't call me that."

His expression melted; he knew I'd figured it out. "So, we don't gotta keep secrets from one another anymore, hey? We figured you'd catch on after you found those cards. You're a smart girl."

The wind I'd let fade away inside my grandmother's

apartment began to pick up again, but just around my shoulders. "I'm not a girl," I retorted. "Where's Jamae?"

His expression remained still. "Inside."

My eyes darted to the door as if I could see through it. There were only two possible scenarios that were playing out in there: one, that Jamae was pacing endlessly around my poor, ignorant father who was shackled to a chair. Or two, that they were simply awaiting my arrival—because my father wasn't who I thought he was either.

My attention snapped back to Ethan. "Show it to me."

When he didn't move, I forced a flash of white fire to roll over my eyes. "Your mark, Ethan. I know you have one. Show it to me."

He stalled only for a moment before nodding. He turned around and lifted his shaggy hair to reveal the 'tattoo' on the back of his neck. The same one Rachel and every other waif had; the same mark I'd seen scripted over Jamae's skin one time while she'd been absentmindedly pulling at her hair.

When he finally let his moody locks fall back in place and had turned back to face me, he asked, "Does that make you feel better?

"No."

He sighed. "Look Tess, I'm sorry we couldn't be straight with you, but—"

"You know what, you guys really suck at pretending to be something you're not. You let down your guard—you've been starting to stink."

He shuffled his feet around and his shoulder dipped as he gripped the handrail. "I thought you'd have put two and two together. We were working with Reanin—"

"How could that even be? You're part of Juanita's coven. I know all about how Nisroc was training witches to do anything to get into The Hall, even if it meant trading part of yourself for eternal magic. Juanita is—"

"Probably on the other side of Cai's boot by now," he said.

I tried to keep my posture firm because he could very well be lying. My dad could be in there, dead or worse, while Ethan gained my trust. That's all they had to do—get me inside. Sure, I was strong as an ox now, but they'd been using their magic longer and were prepared for anything.

On a whim, I shook out Adhara until he was a sword, proudly displaying the three red stones. "Your guardian leader is dead and if you want these stones, you'll have to pry them out of my cold, dead hands—and I can pretty much tell you that killing *me* is a near impossible thing." Mostly.

Ethan nipped at his bottom lip before responding. "Are you done?" My eyes grew sharp, but I said nothing. "Like I was saying, Jamae and I were chosen to escort Reanin to the surface. We were part of her guard, but also part of *the plan* if shit came at us. *Confronting Your Shadows* wasn't an accident —we made sure you found it. And we also ensured you met Maggie. The only reason we joined Juanita's coven was to keep an eye on her, because it was apparent from the beginning that she couldn't be trusted. Even her wife knew that. And as far as the duplicitous waifs Nisroc formed, they do exist and we are aware of them. They are being dealt with."

My tongue was stuck on my back molar. Sure, the story worked, but I was still on edge. There was a fifty-fifty chance that that's all it was—a story. However, just as I was about to step forward with my next argument, the front door swung open, and my father nodded down at me.

"Come in, Tess. You can trust him. He's with us."

My foot teetered between the next step down and where I was currently standing. "Dad? What are you—wait—what do you mean *he's with us?*"

"I mean he's on our side."

"See," Ethan said with a smirk. "Your grandmother

brought a *few* of us with her." His eyebrows danced as he added, "And not all of us were waifs."

I stared up at the man who I'd always called father. "Who *are* you?"

He waved me in. "Just come inside. We've got work to do."

CHAPTER THIRTY-FOUR

If this had been a play, the set would have been straight cr —eepy. And that's saying something, considering I'd literally just spent loads of time in an alternate reality where light was only welcome in tiny increments. My dad led me into the living room; it was the only room other than my parents' bedroom with a fireplace. I often used it to read.

The flames dancing under the mantle were the only light. The walls and carpet glowed an orangey red. Seated cross-legged in front of a stainless-steel bowl was Jamae. She lifted her gaze to meet mine as soon as I entered the room. She sounded apologetic as she said, "Hey Tess."

I didn't have the energy for any more reactions to anything. I'd just learned my father's real name was Matthew, but that he'd never had a surname. Not until he'd needed one to fit in on the surface. He'd been born a guardian, but they needed him to become something else because, even though Cai had claimed she was one hundred percent over Nisroc, the insurance policy Reanin had put in place required something more concrete. It was pretty ironic —my mother was so determined to become a vampire that she'd been completely blind to the fact that she'd married one.

This also shed light on the fact that neither of my parents had been human when I'd been conceived. What I'd learned while in The Hall was accurate. Any humanity I owned had been manifested by *me*.

Jamae was now staring at me with a dolly face. The white streak in her hair was gone.

"You're not falling apart any longer," I said dryly.

"No," was all she said.

It was clear by the hurt in her eyes that she sensed how stiffly I was holding onto my guard. I knew I shouldn't be mad —her and Ethan (and my father) had been working with my grandmother from the start. Ethan and Jamae had been sent out to spy on all the covens they could to see if any of them had been infiltrated, and my dad had been set up with my mom so he could keep an eye on her. Not to mention, Reanin had seen it; her daughter was supposed to have a daughter. That meant Janine needed a match, even if it was a front on both ends. But back to Jamae—even though I knew I shouldn't be holding her accountable, I couldn't help how I felt. I'd thought she was truly a friend. An older sister even.

"Tess—"

"No," I said, holding up a hand. "It's all good. Don't worry about it. You were just doing your job."

"I wasn't just—"

My dad walked up between us and, in the process, cut her off. As he stood in the fire's glow, I couldn't understand how I hadn't realized just how unhuman he'd been. He was giant as were the fangs he proudly displayed when he opened his mouth. "We don't have time for this." He held out his hand and I gingerly took it. He led me to the other side of where Jamae was sitting and pointed down. I did as requested and leaned down beside her. My breath got stuck in my lungs when I saw what was in the bowl: my grandmother's *beating* heart—swimming in a shallow pool of blood.

"So . . ." I started, my voice barely more than a whisper. "This was your part of the spell." I looked up at Jamae. "You and Ethan were the waifs assigned to heart duty."

She swallowed before answering. "Yeah."

It didn't take me long to figure out the other part. "And she was keeping you guys from rotting. You didn't start acting weird until after she died."

Ethan and my dad had joined us, taking seats on either side of the bowl.

Jamae wiped her dry nose with the back of her wrist. "The Hall of Shadows may have been closed but her building worked just fine as a hub. With her help, we were able to bring in new pledges. We filled those apartments with more waifs than there was room for. And to be fair, we wouldn't have started rotting right away after her death, but it took all the magic we had to keep her heart beating. It took a toll on us."

"Right." I had more to say, but I knew it wasn't the time. Instead, I addressed what I couldn't stop thinking about. "So, how is this going to go down?" I pulled out Adhara in his wand form. "Bea told me *this* was needed for the spell to work . . . She said something about a wand and chalice too, but—"

"Not even Bea knew what that meant when she first saw it," my dad explained. "We were all operating on the assumption that when the moment came, we would understand."

"That's risky AF," I muttered, looking down into the bowl.

"Yeah well," Ethan said, "the pieces came together pretty quickly when you confided to Jamae and me about your magic."

My eyes suddenly popped open. "Huh?"

"You can bring life back from death," said my dad, causing

me to give him my full attention. "Look Tess, your grandmother knew everything all the time. She knew when your mother met with Nisroc and when Janine had decided to kill her. We three" –he gestured to Jamae and Ethan— "were right behind them the day Janine killed Reanin."

I gasped, "*You* were the one who killed Mom."

"Yes. Something I maybe should have just done years ago, but I was following your grandmother's wishes. As intelligent as she was, Reanin held out hope until the very end that her daughter would change."

"That's because she was a good mother," I muttered.

"Janine was the one shadow Reanin couldn't deal with," Ethan said.

Nobody said anything, but we all knew he was right.

"Anyway," my father said, "I took care of Janine while Ethan and Jamae carefully got Reanin's heart, replacing it with another so there would be no suspicion."

I couldn't help but think, *where did they get the replacement heart*? I didn't want to know. I kept my thoughts to myself as my dad continued.

"So here we are, we now have everything we need to bring her back, all of her."

"Wait." There was something that needed to be addressed. "Grandma didn't want to become a vampire." It was written all over my mother's book.

"She won't be," my father said assuredly.

I started shaking my head. "But—"

He placed a hand over mine as he stared down at the wand fitted into it. "We will use my blood to get the heart beating on its own, apart from Jamae and Ethan's magic. From there, you will use the wand." I shot him a confused look, which he just shook away. "Don't look at it as a magical tool."

"Huh?"

"What else can you use that for?" Ethan asked in his best

teacher voice. When I didn't answer, he rephrased. "Think cult classic vamp movies."

I stared from the wand to the heart, then back to the wand again. "A stake."

My dad nodded. "The heart will be staked, ashes will remain, and your touch will bring her back."

"But what if it brings her back in vampire form? Technically that'll be what she was before she was killed for the second time."

"Hang on," Jamae said, cutting in before my dad started to answer me. "You guys left out a pretty important part." Giving me her undivided attention, she asked, "When your touch reincarnates a pile of ashes, what do they return to?"

I hesitated. "It—that depends." I thought back to the very first time I figured out what I could do. I'd held the ashes in my hand from our fireplace and began to hear a soft voice, and the longer it was against my skin, the louder its whispers got. I sifted through the images it sent me, from a seed to roots to a full-grown tree. Finally, together, we settled on where it would be happiest, and from the ashes grew a young sapling, ready to be planted in the ground. "I can choose for it to become anything, but more often than not I return the ashes to what they were when they were happiest."

Jamae let a soft grin fall into place. "There you go, then."

"Oh . . . okay," I said. Save for the logs breaking against one another in the fireplace, it was completely quiet. "Except, why didn't you all just burn the heart in the first place? Wouldn't that have been way less complicated?"

"It might've worked," said my father. "But when the spell was written we didn't know who or what would be involved. This was how it came to Bea."

"This is all new to you, Tess," said Ethan, "but as you'll come to know, once magic has been written, it is best to let it be."

Kay. That kinda made sense, but, "You all said there was a wand and *a chalice*. So far, I haven't heard mention of that last part."

Before anyone could answer, the fire rose in the stone hearth causing each of us to look that way. A second later, a strikingly handsome man dressed all in black stepped out from the flames, an actual *tiger* by his side. With little more than a nod hello, he stared down at me.

"Bea hadn't realized it was a vessel her vision was alluding to. You Tess, are the chalice."

CHAPTER THIRTY-FIVE

My magical heart skipped a beat.

I just stared at my grandfather . . . and his tiger. "Wh—What?"

Had I willingly just let a group of underworld junkies gain my trust and bring me indoors to a place where no one would hear me scream? If that was the case, then why had it all felt so very legit? I mean, my destiny felt so set in stone; I was to become the—

"Relax Granddaughter," Kage said with a smirk. The tiger sauntered over to a nearby rug; it groaned as it laid down. "Your body is the chalice. And I believe you've already made an offering from your veins."

My hand crept up and patted the vial resting in my front pocket. *Oh yeah.*

Kage winked and my chest slowly began to fall. I may have overreacted just a little.

"Please don't take offense," said my father. "Cai had to hold onto the sample just in case you chose the light."

I shook my head. "How was that ever even an option?"

"Free will," said Jamae with a shrug of her shoulder.

"Right," I muttered. As my breathing was returning to normal, Kage looked up at everyone seated around my grandmother's heart. "Well then," he said, backing up and taking a seat in one of the terribly uncomfortable decorative chairs that my mother picked out. He crossed one leg over the other as if he was simply waiting to get his name called in a doctor's office and laid a hand over his tiger's head. "Haven't we waited long enough? Begin."

Jamae loosed a heavy breath then held up her hands. "First we have to undo the magic Ethan and I have been using."

I followed the actions of Ethan and my dad as they began to reach for each other's hands. As soon as we were all connected, Ethan and Jamae began to chant. It was happening.

My grandmother's heart began to beat faster—so fast that the blood it was resting in began to splash, some of it landing on the carpet. It also began to rapidly shift from red to gray to brown, and even to green. It went on like that for long enough that my hands were getting sweaty from where they were intertwined with my father's and Ethan's. At some point, Jamae stopped chanting long enough to lay her eyes over my father's.

"Now," was all she said.

As soon as the word left her mouth, my father unclasped his hands from ours and in one motion, bit into his wrist and let his blood drape itself over the heart. It stopped beating as his blood met the organ. After about a pint of vamp blood had been distributed, my dad pulled his wrist away and licked at the wound. The fang marks healed instantly just as my wound had when I'd offered my blood to Cai in The Hall.

After all was said and done, they all looked at me.

"It's your turn," my dad said. "Time to kill the curse so she wakes without a thirst."

And this was my life now.

My mother couldn't have just been a nice person, my grandmother couldn't have just played puzzles with me, my dad couldn't have just shown me how to ride a bike, and I couldn't have friends my own age.

Without explaining myself, I whispered as I raised Adhara into the air, "But I wouldn't have had it any other way." I meant every word as I rammed my wand into my grandmother's heart, which had slowly started to beat again.

Immediately, it stopped. I could sense it; everyone in the room, except my grandfather, was sitting on pins and needles. This was new magic. No one had ever tried it.

And then the heart caught on fire.

No one moved. No one breathed—then again, no one really needed to, for no one was completely human. The heart continued to rage until it softly settled down into a decent size pile of ashes.

My father nudged me with his elbow. "Remove the wand, Tess."

I gulped. All the courage I'd brought back with me from the shadows seemed to have fled for the moment.

"It's okay," Kage said from where he was seated. I turned and gave him a fleeting look. "Go ahead."

With a stiff hand, I reached out and yanked it out from the pile.

"You know what to do," my dad whispered.

"Why the blood?" I asked softly, retrieving it from my pocket and holding it up to the fire light. "Why can't I just use my touch?"

Kage answered in a smooth voice. "To bring someone back requires *more*."

It was a simple answer, but effective.

I tucked Adhara back into my pocket then carefully uncorked the vial Cai had given me. Then, with one last swift inhale, I poured the contents over the ashes. As soon as every last drop was emptied, I felt myself being pulled backwards by my dad. His hands were so cold—how had I never realized that? I guess we see what we want to see. Believe what we want to believe. That is until we begin doing shadow work. Now all I could recognize was that my father was, and always had been for as long as I existed, a vampire.

It took a little bit for the gears to get moving, but once they did, they began to work at an incredible speed. Before long, we were watching the reanimation of Reanin on fast forward. First, the heart rose into the air, then the rib cage formed around the heart, then veins, arteries, muscles—it reminded me of an anatomy simulation on a computer. Finally, the face of the woman I never thought I'd be lucky enough to see again reappeared . . . except there was something different about her.

The heaviness I'd always noticed hanging around my grandmother's shoulders was gone. As I watched her come back into her own, I saw the woman Kage had brought back to life. She stood as if gravity didn't exist for her, and she sparkled like an ice sculpture planted under the sun. The room was dim, but anyone could see that Reanin had been stripped of the siren's curse and returned to the queen she'd once been.

Her eyes glistened as she stared across the room to Kage; she grinned like a schoolgirl. Next her head bowed in my direction.

"My darling, granddaughter," she said softly.

"Holy shit," I replied. It was literally all I could say.

"Now I've been rescued twice by those same eyes." She lowered herself down until she was eye level with me, then cupping my face with her hands, she said, "You never saw me fall, yet you were there to catch me. Now let us learn to fly together."

Heat escaped my lips as I exhaled the one thing I'd been

waiting to tell her. "I rescued them from the ocean—all the other magical creatures. You'll never feel alone again."

Her lips quivered. "You listened."

"Of course I did," I replied, the ocean raging from where it could not spring from my eyes.

She pulled away, and as she stood a pair of black wings, identical to her king's, sprouted from her back. As soon as they'd reached full extension, she held out her hand for Kage, which he gladly took. The tiger stood and joined them. Looking down my way once more, Reanin said, "It wasn't just our world you saved, Tess. It was yours. We may rule the shadows, but where they begin and end has always come from the same matter that makes up your heart and soul. You are the true mother; the fanged ones, your children."

She looked to my grandfather and the two of them shared an interesting look before Kage nodded. "Yes, my darling, I too believe it is time."

Kage looked me dead in the eyes. "We must depart." He raised a hand and held it out towards me. "Your storm has been released, granddaughter, and now the rest of you shall begin to unfold."

A shudder ran up from my lungs and got lodged in the back of my throat, but even if I could've found the exact right words to supply a witty retort—it wouldn't have mattered. The second Reanin had said fanged ones, my gums tingled. Shortly after Kage delivered his line, I doubled over. Pain seared through my jaw and a small earthquake rumbled through it until . . . No kidding.

I lifted a hand to my lips. "What the—"

My father reached for my shoulder. "It's okay, Tess. It's always been meant to be."

What? "I have—fangs," I all but whimpered. "Does this mean I'm a—"

But before I could get out the word, I looked up to find

that my dad and I were the only two left in the room. Sometime, between Kage speaking and my fangs dropping, the otherworlders and their tiger had departed for the shadows.

I held out an arm. "What? How could they all just leave like that?" I'd just gotten my grandma back—not to mention I was kind of like *going through something here.*

My mouth was still hanging open when I felt my father's touch against my back. "Don't worry. They'll return," he said.

I blinked, gazing around the suddenly empty room. Even the stainless-steel bowl was gone.

"What the hell, Dad! What's happening to me?"

He turned and placed both hands over my shoulders; my fangs were still so very *there.* "Rest your heart."

Was he completely cracked? "How exactly?"

"Turn off your emotions. It should be simple by now." I began to fidget, but he stopped me by gripping my shoulders harder. "Stop. Close your eyes." I did as I was told. "Return to the sparkle that exists in the shadows. Return to the darkness."

My chest fell. I returned to the moment I first noticed the sparkle that existed in The Hall . . . the way it made me feel. And then the fangs retracted.

I opened my eyes.

My father very slowly released his grip, letting his arms fall to his sides. "It is as simple as that. Like wings, your fangs will drop when needed. Over time you'll figure out how to pull them out whenever you want." He paused. "You are still numb. Recover your emotions."

I did as I was told. The fangs returned. My father cracked a Mattie smile.

I brought my hand up to cover my mouth. "I'm glad at least one of us thinks this is funny." He snickered then began sauntering over to a corner where he kept a decanter full of scotch. However, the amber liquid had taken on a darker color and a thicker consistency.

I slowly lowered my hand, talking around my new additions. "Why weren't we taken back into the shadows, too?"

He filled two glasses. "For now, we have work to do here." He pulled a glass away and handed it to me. I was slow to take it—there was no avoiding it. It was blood. "Unlike a vampire, you will not thirst. You will not be required to feed to live. But you will accept offerings and from them you will gain power and perspective."

"Uh . . . okay." Heavy much? "So, am I a vampire or not?"

"The vampires are your keep, the shadows, your castle."

Ye—ah.

"So then, you've always, like, known this?"

His answer lived in the way the corners of his lips curled up at the ends.

"You're acting like nothing extremely bizarre just happened. Like your daughter didn't just grow fangs."

He sipped from his glass before topping it off. "None of that is bizarre to me; acting like a human, however, has been a challenge." He lifted his glass up as he said the next part. "Here's to being ourselves from here on out."

I chewed over his words for a moment before returning to his previous statement. "What did you mean when you said we have work to do *here*?"

He motioned to the couch as he spoke. I followed his instruction, balancing the blood in my hands as I had a seat. "Reanin was busy while she was here. Her building is just one of many hubs that she started. We've got chapters in most of the big cities and a few in other countries. It's why I was so often absent—a truth I've always hated, especially considering how absent your other parent was. Anyway, now that your grandmother has returned to where she belongs, the growth that's accumulated on the surface will need looking after. You will be expected to help with that, but of course, school needs to come first."

I scratched my left ear, unsure if I'd heard him correctly. "Wait—you seriously want me to finish school?"

He widened his arms. "*This* is your school, Tess. This world—Earth—has everything to offer in the way of what you need to learn. You'll finish actual school, even if it's online, and you'll spend any free time you have observing human life. The good, the bad, and the gritty. If you can't understand or empathize with humanity—with the shadows they all live with—then you'll never be able to help them. And that, Tess, will be your greatest role."

"Kay . . ."

The fire crackled and I sorted through the numerous files accumulating in my head. After a few minutes had passed us, I turned to look at him. "So, you've like, been a vampire my whole life?"

"Yes," he answered just before he took another sip.

"Why have my fangs just come in now?"

"Kage already answered that for you. You've given away enough of your humanity that the transition period has already begun. You'll begin to notice subtle differences over the next couple of years, and then one day, you'll . . ."

"Rise," I answered.

He almost looked teary eyed. "Yes."

"And when that happens, where will I go?"

"Wherever you want. Don't worry, you've much training ahead of you, and many teachers. You won't enter your new role unprepared."

I thought of Melody and the goddess I'd met in The Pendulum. They'd both alluded to the fact that we would be seeing one another again. "My real school will be in the shadows," I added.

For once, my father and I were on the same page about my

education. "Yes, daughter, that is accurate." His next words came out as a scoff. "And please, try not to piss *that* faculty off."

I grinned like a little girl meeting her first pony. "I don't think it'll be a problem anymore."

The room grew quiet, except for the burning fire. After another minute, I brought the glass he'd given me up to my nose. I expected it to smell like metal, but it didn't. "It smells . . ."

"Good," he answered. "Go on, try it."

I raised it to my lips, then stalled like a kid forced to jump from the highest diving board for the first time. Finally, I crammed my eyes shut and took a huge gulp. When I reopened my eyes, I looked out to find that the colors in the room had deepened, as had the scent of burning logs.

"It'll heighten your senses," my dad explained. "What do you think?"

I licked the remaining blood from my lips. "It's . . . interesting."

He chuckled, then took the remaining blood from my hand, pouring the rest of its contents in with his. "Best to start with small bits at a time."

I didn't argue. But I *was* suddenly struck with a thought. "You must not be allergic to the sun."

He shook his head. "I prefer the dark, and the sun is brighter now as a vampire than it ever was as a guardian, but it doesn't burn me. However, there has yet to be a human made from our curse. I can't speak to what will happen to them."

I traced the armrest with my fingertip. "Can I create vampires with my bite?"

"Once you rise, you'll be able to do whatever you want."

"And every human who enters the Hall of Shadows now has the opportunity to meet Cai. They may choose to become a vampire if they wish. Do you think that's such a good thing?"

He lowered the glass into his lap and rested his chin in his hand. "You should know better than anyone now, it isn't the monsters who should be feared. It is those who refuse to acknowledge their darkness that should be approached with caution."

"True." I stared into the flames a little longer, then asked, "The oracle cards . . . They are mine now then, right? Until I pass them on."

"I do believe passing them on is part of the game. To let go of a whole world when you can forever hold that power tightly in your hands—that is legendary."

I pulled the cards out from where they'd been tucked into my pocket. "I will always have the world at my fingertips. I don't need to hoard another one."

"That's my girl," he said, causing me to look his way. "I knew from the moment I laid eyes on you what you were and how great you would become."

My face grew hot. "Did Mom?"

His expression began to smooth out. "The one good thing Janine did was you. I'm afraid that's where her good deeds began and ended."

"Right," I whispered as my gaze drifted back to the fire. "It must have been so hard for you . . . pretending to love her all those years."

"Hey," he said. I slowly returned to him. "I came to this world a guardian, and to be honest, I never had a problem accessing my shadows. I never needed the world Kage opened, but that didn't mean it didn't need me. I left behind my wings as a service, and I starved myself until these fangs grew in for the same reason. Your mother was nothing but a job I was given; she never meant anything to me—but you—" He sniffed, and I could've sworn I was going to see my father cry, but if he was going to, he held it back. "You offered me something that I never felt in all my years, and I assure you, I've lived through quite a few of those. You, Tess, are the reason I understand the meaning of love."

I inhaled a ragged breath, and as I did the ceiling began to leak. Rain fell upon us as if from an invisible cloud. I dropped my head back and frowned. As I tried to figure out what was happening, my father began to laugh.

"I guess that's what happens when someone like you really needs a good cry."

The cloud that had formed around my chest started to dissipate and soon after the rain ended, and the room became dry, I, too, started laughing.

"That could be a fun party trick," he said, swirling around what was left in his glass. "Speaking of parties and the kids that like to throw them, maybe you could work on making some of those things called friends."

I sighed. "Why's that so important to you?"

"Because. You have very little time left before you begin to transition. Unlike so many other entities that come here, you have an opportunity to live as a human and experience a youth. I don't want you to squander this opportunity. Embrace what is unique to you, Tess. Or at least try."

"I guess that's fair."

"Jamae left before she could say anything, but just so you know, she feels really bad that she had to lie to you. She and Ethan really do love you. The last thing she wants is to lose your friendship."

I ran my finger over the top card of the deck in my hands, then set them on the table next to me. "I understand. She was just doing her job."

"Yeah, but it wasn't in her job description to love you. That happened naturally."

I uncrossed and recrossed my ankles, suppressing and

surfacing my reactions at the same time. "I guess . . . I guess it would be counterproductive to argue. I don't want to return to that girl who didn't understand how to greet her shadows. That girl was completely lost and could only find joy in setting her chemistry partner's hair on fire."

It took about two seconds for my dad to explode. "Tess Moreau! You said you were framed."

I shrugged my shoulders as a coy smile snuck onto my face. "Actually, I never said I didn't do it. I just said those dick heads automatically thought it was me."

My dad leaned back and closed his eyes. "Teenagers."

"Don't worry, Pops," I said, slapping his knee before getting up. "We got this."

CHAPTER THIRTY-SIX

It was one of those spring days. The kind that retracts the scent of the leaves budding—that takes away any hint of warmth that's begun to settle in. It was the kind of day where the last wisps of winter budge their way back into line, refusing to bow at the end of their scene. Still, the air was fresh, even in the city, and I'd finished my course work for the week. I'd just helped Ethan and Jamae move the last of their boxes into my grandmother's apartment, because she'd said they should have it. Like the other buildings my father had helped her acquire with his real estate license (how handy was he?), her apartment building would now be a fully functional hub between the surface and The Hall; Reanin (with my permission of course) had gifted her heaven in the sky to the waifs who had taken her heart and kept it beating.

I hadn't seen much of my grandma since everything had changed. My dad had taken me back down to The Hall a couple times to check in. It was a little weird to use the mirror in the hallway of our home, but it was extremely convenient. The Hall looked a little different with Reanin back in place. She and my grandfather spent most of their time in Night Terrors and Roses. The dimension had been so big, I hadn't seen it all when I'd first experienced it. Turns out that was where their living quarters were located. They had a . . . lair. It was really the only way I knew how to describe it. Very similar to Cai's, but bigger. Like, way bigger, with multiple levels. And they had a pair of tigers who fashioned themselves into thrones when called to do so. Seriously, it was the greatest and most bizarre thing I'd ever seen. Even I had to admit, though, Reanin looked better than ever.

Now that everything and everyone was getting settled, I was treating myself to a little quiet time in the park. I'd situated myself on a bench. It was chilly but, since I'd given up much of my humanity, it didn't bother me anymore. I wasn't as human as I'd been a few months ago. I mean, the fangs dropping had been the biggest physical change, but the power that was beginning to fill in where anxiety used to live was also something to get used to.

I pulled the zipper of my coat down and let the wind find the exposed skin between my neck and upper chest. A couple of men sauntered by with a small poof of a dog; other than that, not a lot of people were out. The gray skies had NYC residents flocking back into their hideouts, munching on the last of their winter supplies before it was time to shed those extra pounds in the upcoming weeks.

A chilly wind brushed past my cheeks, and I relished the tiny fingers that drummed across my flesh as they scampered away. The breeze had a voice now; it, along with the water and the earth, were alive. I wasn't sure how I'd missed that before. I guess it was humanity getting in the way.

I had with me two sets of oracle cards. They were equally heavy in my coat pockets. For now, I decided to retrieve *Awaken the Goddess*. I opened the box and let the cards fall into my palm. My thoughts wandered as I stared mindlessly across the sidewalk, shuffling. When I was done, I flipped over the top card and looked down.

I wasn't surprised.

Almost immediately a small wind gust pushed up against me, but this time it was warm. It smelled of river water, cloves, and leaves that had been toasted by the sun.

I turned to my right, my cheeks immediately warming. "Hello, again."

My visitor smirked. "You rang?" She was dressed much differently than the last time we'd met. She was wearing a fitted suit and Manolo Blahnik heels.

I held up the card in my hand. "You keep popping up." She chuckled as I let the card fall back down into the deck. "I'm not sure what's up with the formal costume change, but either way, nice kicks," I said in appreciation. They were green satin with crystal enhancements at the toe. "$1295, am I right?"

She dipped her chin and raised her eyes to meet mine. "I wouldn't know. I'm not really in the habit of having to pay for what I want."

"Nice perk. Do I get to look forward to that one day?"

"Someday."

I looked out past the sidewalk in front of our bench and towards the trees that lined the other side of it. "I have to say, I like you better in a cloak."

"Yes, well, one of my witches works in the music industry. She called on me from her office to help with a *situation*. The men in her company weren't being very . . . chivalrous. Together, we concocted a little charmy charm." She laced her red manicured fingers together and placed them over her knee. "Let's just say that those sexist assholes won't be a problem anymore."

"Badass," I remarked.

She grinned. "Yes." She peered down at the card I'd pulled.

"So, what are you working on? Getting to know your future colleagues?"

I sorted through the cards. Before long the one I'd really been seeking reappeared. "I was curious."

"About what?"

"I was curious if this card was mine."

As I held up the card (the same one that had been ever so questionable a few months ago) it began to bleed with color. When the face of the goddess appeared, I gasped.

The goddess of the witches smiled. "I think you have your answer."

The shadows in my blood began to dance as the illustration grew more vibrant right before our eyes. The goddess was walking out from a gray cloud, she wore a cropped white T-shirt, frayed black jeans, and a red cloak. Her hair was anything but mousy—instead it was copper (like mine had started to turn). Her brilliant eyes looked into mine and two fangs fell from her lips.

"Now *that* is badass," chirped the goddess seated next to me.

"Whoa . . ." It was all I could muster.

After a moment or two had passed—when I could finally pull my gaze away from my future self—I looked to my mentor. "When did you, you know, realize what you were?"

"I was about your age." She paused "Perhaps it's puberty that shakes the truth out of us. Many of us arrive as you have, taking a human body. But unlike you, I hadn't been born into a circle of otherworlders. I found out the old-fashioned way; I was visited by another goddess who introduced herself as my advisor."

I thought back to what I'd read while in The Library. "We aren't star seeds. We are pieces of dying stars. *We* are rebirth. Once my humanity fizzles then—"

"Recreation will take place. You will be who you've always been destined to become."

I raised my chin as I said what I hadn't yet dared to say out loud. "Tessandra, the Goddess of the Shadows."

She opened her mouth and tapped her incisor. "Don't forget about the twins."

"Oh right." I paused, then grinned. "The Goddess of Blood and Shadows." As soon as I said it, the words bled under the illustration on the oracle card, just under the portrait of the goddess I was to become.

"Now that's a title."

"It sure is." My fangs fell, but only for a second. They retracted as I grinned.

"All right, you. You seem to be doing fine. I hear you've even got a new job."

"Yeah, I've been reading cards and ashes at Hexed." Jamae had finally caved. "The ashes thing has brought in a ton of new business. We're talking about opening a new location closer to their new place."

She raised her brows. "Wow, you shadow folk are really coming up in the world."

I chuckled. "We're trying."

"Alright then, it's time for me to get out of this costume and back into my cloak." She winked as she added, "I'll be seeing you around, Miss Tessandra. Training will begin in a few short weeks."

"I'll be looking forward to it," I started, but before I could even finish, she was gone.

I sighed, then looked around at the empty park. I set my gaze upon my very own goddess card for a few more minutes. I couldn't help but feel that this was what it was like for a published author to finally know what their book felt like in their hands. When I'd had enough (for the moment) I returned the deck to one pocket then proceeded to dig out from the other an entire world. I was busy debating how I should go about my next move, when someone else scooted into the empty seat beside me. When I looked over, my fangs fell back down, along with my jaw.

"Liz?"

I hadn't seen the faery since we met in The Forest. I hated to admit that, even through everything, I'd been searching for clues as to where I might find her. I'd even stood before the door to The Forest for so long last time we were in The Hall, that my dad had to drag me away. Even he'd said he didn't like that place.

"Sup bitches," she said, matching the expression on my face. "Wow, cool fangs." She hitched up her top lip and a pair of her own fell. "Now we can be twinsies!"

Disregarding her reveal, I leaned in and wrapped my arms around her, closing my eyes as she reciprocated. "What are you doing here?"

She pulled away but kept her arms around me. "Can't a girl just swing by for some trouble?" Her gaze fell to where my new car keys were dangling halfway out from my coat pocket.

I gave her a discerning look. "You caught wind about me riding around the city in my new wheels, didn't you?"

"Meh," she said with a single shoulder shrug. Letting her hands drift from my arms, she added, "I just remembered, that's all. I don't forget things about people I care about."

"Oh?" My everything was singing. My fangs retracted and so did hers.

She held my gaze for what might have been an uncomfortably long time if I hadn't been enjoying it so much. Next thing I knew, her hand was tangled up in mine.

"So, for reals, where can a baby goddess and a runaway fey princess go to have a good time in the city?"

I rolled my eyes. "You ran away again?"

"It ain't no thing. They won't even send out the search party for a day or two."

My head fell back as I muttered, "Oh my gawd. My first crush and it's probably highly illegal."

"It for sure is." When I looked back at her, she was grinning so wide that her faery sparkle had seeped out. She leaned in and whispered in my ear. "That's what makes it fun." And then, before she pulled away, she added, "P.S. I'm super stoked that you feel the same way as me."

My tongue danced over my top lip as she pulled away. "Fine. What do you wanna do?"

Keeping my hand in hers, she lifted her free arm and shouted, "We're in the city, bitches! And we're otherworlders. We can literally do whatever we want. Do you have the skinny on the best clubs?"

I chuckled. "Yeah, so, I really don't get out that much. I don't know where—"

"Oh my god," she smarted. "Those old waifs really are your only friends, aren't they?"

I lowered my chin but kept the smirk. "Maybe."

"Well shit," she said, standing up and pulling me with her. "I'm not going to be this young forever—let's go get into trouble. Piss off the old shadow keepers."

"Okay—but—what do you—"

"Seriously," she tapped her forehead to mine. A second later my keys were in her free hand. "Let me take the wheel. Once you rise, you're going to be bossy as shit."

"Oh? And you think you'll still be around when that happens?" I asked playfully.

She raised a brow. "I hope to be."

I was still smiling like a fool when she started pulling me away. I wasn't about to argue, but I still had one thing I needed to do.

"Hang on," I said, pulling free as she continued to skip down the sidewalk.

"Better hurry! I know you got wings now, but I guarantee I'm faster."

"I'll just be a second!" I called to her.

I opened the hand holding the oracle cards. Before today, I hadn't been able to let them go. Not because I didn't want to send them back into circulation, but because they'd literally changed my life.

As Jamae often said at the end of a spell, I whispered, "So mote it be." Then set them down on the bench.

And then I caught up with Liz and took her hand in mine. As we skipped along the sidewalk she leaned in and pressed her soft lips to my cheek. When she pulled away, she said, "As above, so below. I'm happy to be with you, Tess."

I looked into her purple eyes. "I'm happy to be with you too."

I *for sure* wasn't as asexual as I thought after all.

Ten minutes passed before someone else wandered up to the bench amid Central Park. Her name was Samantha Williams. She was a thirty-three-year-old woman who worked at a coffee shop. Samantha still craved the cigarettes she'd given up ten years ago and had a small drinking problem. She'd come to the park in search of fresh air because she couldn't afford the bottle of wine she so badly desired.

As soon as she sat, she caught sight of the cards. She'd been known to have eclectic tastes; she'd read some books on the occult but hadn't ever played around with tarot. Still, divination of any sort was somewhat appealing to anyone with a need to figure out if the life they're living is the one for them.

She leaned out from her perch, searching out both

directions to see if the owner of the cards was around. But it was cold and gray, and no one seemed to be out.

Samantha hesitated for only a moment or two before gingerly touching the top of the deserted deck. Nothing happened—no strike of lightning or devil man appearing out of thin air. With one look out into her surroundings, she pulled the mysterious deck of cards into her hands.

"Hall of Shadows," she repeated with a snicker. "Interesting."

Curious about the artwork, she flipped over the top card. But much to her surprise, before she was afforded a glance at the backside, the entire deck lifted from her hands and spread out over the sidewalk before her.

"What the—" she began, but her words escaped her. She couldn't stop looking at the top of that spread. It was like a clock, and the card that would be just to the right of twelve seemed to be calling her name. "What the hell?" she said, then reached down and flipped over that first card.

Immediately the trees across the sidewalk began to turn into shelves—all of them lined to the brim with decorative books. The sidewalk became carpet. And the skies, a dim light. Just bright enough to read.

A voice interrupted her racing thoughts. "Hello." She flinched and turned to find a woman sitting at a nearby table. Her eyes were soft and her hair a beautiful blonde honey. "Welcome to The Library."

Acknowledgments

Thank you to CJM for taking yet another chance on this new author. Jean Lowd, I'm not sure when you sleep but I'm very thankful for you! Also, thank you to my editor, Staci. You're a rockstar! Also, I'm so appreciative to all of my beta readers, for this and every project.

I must also thank all of the magical people in my life who, whether they realized it, helped me gain the courage to finally free myself from the broom closet I hid in for many years. It's taken me many more years to agree to pull out my shadows, but now that I have, I will never ever tuck them back in. I prefer to walk with my storm.

ABOUT THE AUTHOR

Mariah Stillbrook, originally from Iowa, lives in Colorado with her white german shepherd, husband, and little girl.

She graduated from the University of Colorado at Colorado Springs. She spends most of her days writing, reading, and enjoying the occasional hike.

In her late twenties she realized that her writing was missing something, magic. She now focuses her writing on urban fantasy and horror in both adult and young adult genres.

9 781956 183139